MW01688104

SOUL OF A HERO

TRUE HEROES EMBODY STRENGTH, PERSEVERANCE, PATIENCE AND LOVE. THESE ARE THEIR STORIES.

PJ FIALA   STACEY JOY NETZEL

DONNA MARIE ROGERS   RACHEL RIVERS

JESSICA LEMMON

RORY: FINDING HIS MATCH

PJ FIALA

Thanks for supporting our heroes!

PJ Fiala

USA TODAY BESTSELLING AUTHOR
PJ FIALA
BIG 3 SECURITY BOOK FOUR RORY
FINDING
HIS MATCH

1

Driving through the eastern side of town, dog-ass tired and ready for bed, Rory glanced over at the gas station parking lot as he neared the intersection. Suspicious of what looked like a drug deal going down, he quickly turned into the lot directing his headlights at two men exchanging a tiny bag for money.

Stopping, close to the men near the convenience store, Rory exited his vehicle and began walking toward them when they took off running in different directions. Choosing to follow the man who'd taken the money, he kept pace the best he could; but he was losing ground to the spry, lanky drug dealer, who was likely scared and surely not interested in spending the night in jail.

He was likely a low-level dealer, but with enough pressure sometimes these guys gave up a higher-up or two.

A gunshot rang out, then another. Diving behind a dumpster, which provided some cover, but likely not enough, he glanced around the side in the direction of the shots. His heartbeat quickened, but luckily his senses seemed to intensify as the adrenaline pumped through his body.

Seeing the flash of dark clothing duck behind the Longstone

Apartment building before him, he crouched low and squat-walked to the side of the building, then slowly moved in the direction of his perp. His gun was out and pointed before him, when his ears heard a slight crunching of feet on gravel. Slowly raising himself up, he pointed his gun toward the corner of the building and sent up a quick prayer to be spot-on today. No accidents.

A gunshot sounded, and a bullet hit the building about a foot above his head from the direction his perp had run. Quickly dropping to the ground, he slowly let out a breath, inhaled again and scrambled to the edge of the second apartment building, adjacent to Longstone, which he thought was the direction of the shot.

Standing quickly and twisting his body so he was leading with his right hand holding his gun, he moved around the building, the brick walls scratching his back as he hovered close.

Movement from the shadows just a couple of feet in front of him and a flash of metal aimed at his head had him leveling his gun back at this new target.

"DEA." She half-whispered, half-yelled. Her voice was tight, her emotions likely as high as his.

"Lynyrd Station PD." He responded. Then wondered where in the hell a DEA Special Agent had come from and why. Lynyrd Station PD didn't have the luxury of a DEA agent's help.

They stood for a few seconds, each assessing the other, guns leveled on the other, emotions still high.

She stepped into the sliver of light that shone from the overhead streetlights and he damned near dropped his weapon. Familiar eyes stared back at him, the hypnotic green he remembered from years ago. Before he'd left the Marines. Before he'd been married to Debra.

He watched those mesmerizing eyes change as she recognized him, then worried that the emotion he saw in them was more hatred than friendliness or happiness, his heart hammered once more in his chest.

"Beggs, what the fuck are you doing here?" he snapped.

"I'm chasing a lead, the same as you I suspect."

A bullet hit the corner of the building they now stood alongside of and pieces of brick rained down on him. His instinct to protect took over and he wrapped his arm around Beggs and shoved her against the wall, shielding her with his body.

He turned then to give chase, but Beggs shoved him out of the way. "Asshole."

Then she took off running to yet another apartment building across the alley, small expanse of lawn which served as the apartment complexes' green space and was surrounded by four three story apartment buildings, then she disappeared under the stairwell. Giving pursuit he followed in her wake, but was met with more shooting then nothing but silence. Hiding under a stairwell, trying to catch his breath, and forcing his brain to catch up with events, he slightly shook his head and listened. Nothing.

Venturing out from his hiding spot he looked around for Beggs, but didn't see the direction she'd gone or the perp they'd been following after the last shot. Ugly doubts crawled through his brain that he was ineffective at his job as he heaved himself off the wall he'd pressed himself against and quietly turned the corner, which led him back to the gas station where it'd all began this evening.

A cruiser had pulled up behind his car, and another was just now racing toward the station. Recognizing the officer interviewing two witnesses he walked toward them, all the while chastising himself for getting a tad out of shape and unable to chase a doper, even though he was only 42 now. The guys would likely have a bit of fun with him this week, but that he could take, he'd given his share over the years.

"Richards." One of the newly arrived officers, Anderson Tyler, walked toward him, his strides long and his gait determined.

"Ty, what do you have?"

"Calls coming into the station, gunshots hitting buildings, tenants in the apartments are scared and sick of the crime, the station is going nuts. Then someone calls in your plates and says they saw you running after someone. Needless to say, the Captain isn't happy; you went in without backup and we have more unhappy citizens. What do you have?"

He took a deep breath and looked into Ty's tired eyes. They'd all been putting in sixty to eighty hours a week recently and it was taking its toll on all of them.

"I came into the parking lot because I was pretty sure I saw a drug deal going down. Took off on foot to chase the dealer and ran into a DEA Special Agent. Anything at the station on that?"

The big man shook his head. He was easily six foot two or more, but his broad shoulders and massive arms made him appear larger than life.

"Nothing. Ask the Captain. " He pointed to the other officer, Jerry Robards, and said, "I'll go help Jerry interview witnesses. The Captain wants to see you."

"Yeah. I bet he does."

He let out a long breath and dragged his sorry, tired ass to his car. Captain Jason Peters was a great boss, low key, knowledgeable and easy to deal with. Unless he was pissed off. Then, he could chew on your ass for hours and not show signs of getting tired. Rory feared that's what was about to happen, and quite frankly, he was too fucking exhausted to have his ass chewed on. It was a recipe for disaster. And where in the fuck did Beggs go? That was something he'd not been able to wrap his mind around and he didn't know how to get in touch with her, either. But she'd said, DEA, so he would start with the Chicago DEA Division. Indiana was one of three states in that Division. To be here she likely was stationed at a DEA Office in one of them.

2

Fucking Rory Richards. Doesn't that just beat the shit out of a dead dog? Flipping irritating. Bastard never called her even though he'd promised he would. They'd dated for over two months then she was transferred to a different base in Arizona and he stayed in South Carolina. The first week, she thought he was just busy and so was she, going through the new paperwork and learning all the new faces and places. But then the second week rolled around and no call, then the third. She kept herself busy with duties on base and even went so far as to volunteer for a couple of extra duties to keep herself occupied. Then she realized he wasn't going to call, ever. Damned if she'd break down and call him, she had pride. Six months later she heard he'd married, and she went on a wild drunk with some battle-buddies, girlfriends she'd met on base and it took her a couple of days to actually sober out. Then, she put Rory Fucking Richards out of her mind and focused on her job.

And for all of that with Rory, she never thought to ask him where he was from and she never looked back to see where he ended up. Coming face-to-face with him last night was a shock to her system for sure. Though it was dark, he still had those same piercing blue eyes she remembered. That same dark hair and that presence. Oh, that's what rankled more than anything. Seeing him again stirred things in her.

Tossing her belongings into her overnight bag, she grabbed her shampoo and conditioner from the shower and threw them into the baggies she'd always packed them in, then into the bag with the rest of her stuff, she was ready. One more quick look around and she was satisfied she could go back home to Indianapolis and forget, once again, Rory Fucking Richards.

Hefting her overnight bag over her shoulder, she picked up the checkout notice that had been pushed under her door, then folded it neatly and tucked it in the side pouch of her bag to make sure she turned it into the Office for reimbursement when she got back. Opening the door, the cool, crisp fall air woke her up like nothing else could, except for that cup of coffee she was dying for. The diner connected to the motel she was staying at would no doubt have it; though it was likely not to the caliber she was used to, she'd take it. It always took two or three cups for her to get her bearings in the morning.

Walking down the sidewalk to the diner, she opened the door and was hit with the warmth of the room and the aroma of bacon and eggs. Her stomach rumbled, but she had no intention of staying any longer than she needed to. Her lead from her informant last night was nothing more than a setup and she was particularly pissed off that he'd double-crossed her. She'd deal with him when she got back, too.

"Can I help you?"

A pretty young waitress with bright, shiny eyes and long, blond hair, pulled back into a ponytail, asked her.

"Ah, yes, coffee. Black. In a to-go cup, please."

"You got it." The perky gal said as she immediately turned to begin filling up a paper cup.

Pulling a five dollar bill from her wallet inside her purse, she lay it on the counter and watched as the young lady continued to fill her cup, set the plastic white top on it and checked it to make sure it was secure. Turning toward her, she set her cup on the counter, smiled and asked, "Did you want anything to go with it? Our special this morning is a bagel, cream cheese and a side of bacon for $3.00.

"That sounds delicious, but I don't eat breakfast until around ten o'clock; I need my coffee first. Thank you though." She picked up her coffee, then said, "Keep the change." And headed toward the door.

Opening her car door and setting her cup in the console, she reached around the driver's seat, dropped her bag into the backseat, then settled in for her 170 mile trip back to Indy.

Starting her car and pulling out of her space, her phone rang, and she said, "Answer call."

A beep sounded. "Tucker," she answered.

"Al, I've got a job for you. The Lynyrd Station PD just asked for assistance from DEA. They're dealing with a mighty drug issue and since you're in town, I told them to expect you this morning. You'll be there until you can help them solve this problem. I think it mirrors our case in that the drugs filtering into Lynyrd Station are likely coming from that dealer and supplier you've been trying to nab."

" I know you're the Special Agent in Charge, Ben, but please, no. I don't want to be out of the Office again so soon."

"No one does, Al, but you're needed and you're there. This is what we do. Offices like ours even in a city the size of Indy don't just get to handle the inner-city cases like drug gangs. Al, you know all of us are tased to help rural areas that can't afford to handle these drug cases or don't have the people they need. Keep me updated."

Rubbing her forehead with her fingers, she stifled the litany of colorful words at the ready and remembered that this was her SAC she was talking to. Lifting her coffee from the center console she thought perhaps she needed to get caffeinated and soon. Drinking as much as she could due to the temperature of the coffee, she silently waited her boss out.

"Al, I know you're seething right now. I wouldn't ask if the Chicago Office didn't order it. And, since you'll be up for promotion next month, which will keep you home more, it's important that you do this. And, shut that drug operation down."

"Yeah. Got it." She'd better get that damned promotion this time. Last time they gave it to that whiner, Steiner. He was a pain in the ass for certain.

"Thanks, Al, be nice."

"Yeah."

She ended the call without another word, then took a couple of deep breaths, turned around in the parking lot, and headed back to Lynyrd Station and the police department, where she'd no doubt run into Rory again. Today was really beginning to blow.

3

Dragging his feet into the station, he hadn't even bothered to put his jacket on this morning, opting for carrying it in case he needed it. Lack of sleep and thoughts of Beggs filtered through his mind all night. He should have called her all those years ago when she'd left, it was a young dumb-ass thing to do. But he'd found out the day after she left that she could have stayed. All it would have taken was a word from her to her commanding officer. She chose to leave, which he took as wanting to get away from him. But he didn't want to settle down anyway and at the time and they were on opposite coasts. Long-distance didn't make sense then. He'd gone out three days in a row after she left to drink her away. One week turned into two and then he met Debra. At first, they were just having fun. She'd been like Beggs in that she gave him shit when he needed it and she was strong and confident. That was his kryptonite. Strong women when they needed to be, saucy in bed.

Flopping into his desk chair, he rested his elbows on the desk and swiped his fingers down his face.

"Long night?"

Removing his hands and looking at the man speaking, he sighed at Captain Jason Peters. "Yeah, Captain. A lot of them lately."

"Well, then I have good news. DEA is sending us some help. I guess some hotshot Special Agent from Indianapolis named Al Tucker. All I know is Tucker is good and we need the help."

Sitting back hard in his chair he looked his Captain in the eye. "I don't know if that's good news, Cap. I'm dog-ass tired, we all are, and training a new guy on our procedures and town sounds like a monumental task right now."

Captain nodded. "Maybe it'll only be a day or two, then Tucker should be up to speed. This is the first time we've worked with DEA, but they help police departments like ours all the time. The sooner we get these drugs off the street, the sooner we can stop burying our town's children. I've been to my share of funerals these days."

"Yeah." The feeling of defeat fell over him like a wet coat. More hours and now a "hotshot", which to his ears sounded like a cocky, self-centered bastard.

The Captain left his doorway and he shook his mouse to wake up his computer. Starting with the DEA Chicago Division database he wanted to satisfy himself that Beggs was far, far away hopefully in Chicago. He typed in her name Alice Beggs and half-assed chuckled. He'd only called her Alice once while they'd been together, always referring to her as either Beggs or Red.

He watched the little circle turn as it searched. Then, the chatter outside of his office stopped. Eerie silence fell as all eyes were trained toward the front door. Curiosity got the better of him. He stood and made his way to the door of his office and looked in the direction of all the other detectives.

There she was. Beggs. Her shiny red hair spilled over her shoulders in waves. The freckles that were abundant on her face seemed to stand out more just now, he'd always thought they were cute. Then, her intense green eyes looked up and focused on him. He felt it. The minute she realized he was watching her. Her eyes bore into his and the beginnings of a grin formed on his face, then her eyes narrowed and the look she leveled on him would have made a boner droop. She was not happy to see him.

It took his brain a few minutes to grasp the situation, and if he thought he could have run and hid in his office, he would have; but then she began moving toward him and his damned feet betrayed him and refused to move. He felt like a deer with his eyes caught in the headlights and his brain sent off warning signals that this was not going to be good. But, there he stood anyway.

She stopped just in front of him, her eyes no longer squinting but the stiffness in her face said she was not happy.

"Special Agent Al Tucker at your service." Her smooth sexy voice floated over him and his brain screamed, "NO!"

"Al? Tucker? You're Al Tucker?"

"Problem with that?"

"No. It's just I thought your name was Beggs."

She inhaled deeply, and let it out slowly. The fresh aroma of coffee swirled around, and he watched as she took a drink from the paper cup in her hand.

"My married name is Tucker. My first name, as you know, is Alice. I go by Al to my friends."

Swallowing the large lump in his throat, he heard snickering around him and knew he was going to have to answer a ton of questions this week.

Nodding once, he said, "Nice to see you again, Al."

"Alice."

"I thought you said Al..."

"I said my friends call me Al. You. Are. Not. My. Friend."

That earned her chuckles from the men sitting around observing this interaction and she bestowed a fantastic smile on them.

"Right. Well, please come into my office and we'll go over the information we have on file with this drug problem."

He stood back a step to let her pass, but she cocked her head and waited for him to move in front of her. Feeling sheepish and knowing the guys were all watching, he took her cue and preceded her into his office. Walking around the desk to sit in his chair, he waited for her to sit down as he pulled a couple of the files he'd been working on out of his desk drawer. Remembering his search, he quickly minimized his screen and was relieved to see her head had been down as she looked at the chairs.

Laying the files on the top of the desk he watched as she leaned forward, her long trench coat still cinched at her narrow waist, her body still slender, her long fingers still caught his attention as she opened the first file and began reading his reports.

"I'm sorry. I should have called. Or I shouldn't have promised to call, however you have decided to look at it."

Her eyes flicked to his and held. His stomach knotted but he waited for her.

"I guess it worked out for both of us the way it was supposed to. I heard you got married."

He squirmed in his chair a bit, then cleared his throat. "Yes. But I'm widowed now."

He saw an emotion flicker across her face, then she swallowed, her soft voice came back. "I'm sorry."

Nodding he ventured further. "How long have you been married?"

"Four years."

His eyes flicked to her ring finger. Not only was there not a ring there, there wasn't an indentation either. Curious.

"Tell me what we have going on here so I can go home."

4

Sitting in this small office, she could smell him. That same after shave, after all these damned years, she'd never forget it. They hadn't dated that long, just a couple of months, but he'd left a mark on her. More than just the hurt at how he'd just forgot about her. More than his scent. She sat here now, listening to his voice and her body responded. Her nipples puckered and when he glanced up to see if she was listening, he'd smiled a couple of times and dammit, that had an effect on her.

"Tell me what questions you have." She looked up to see him watching her.

Clearing her throat lightly, she flipped the file on top to another section. "So, if I'm clear on all of this, you've had two kids die in the past couple of weeks of overdoses and one of a gunshot which you believe to be part of a drug deal gone wrong. Then we have the events of last night. This is escalating."

"Yes. We had a crime family move into town last year and set up business, the Santarinos. Not only were they smuggling illegal weapons, they were art and jewel smugglers and thieves. We suspected they were involved with bringing in drugs, but we didn't confirm it until around the time the family's legitimate business was taken down and the brothers, Victor and Mangus, who ran the legitimate and illegal operations were dead. The family is gone now. Sofia Santarino, who lives in Italy, and is Mangus' widow. still owns the property in Lynyrd Station, where Limitless International, the legitimate business was located, before law enforcement shut it down. We thought we were done with the Santarinos, but now we've got this issue going on and I can't help but wonder if they had something in the works before they died. Someone is still bringing drugs into the area and distributing. We've been watching all known employees of their legitimate company, Limitless International, as well as all known cohorts of the Santarinos. So far we can't pin anything on them."

He flipped the page in the file and photographs, stacked neatly and clipped into the folder came into view. "This is Mangus Santarino and this is his brother, Victor."

He continued flipping pictures, his thick masculine hands mesmerized her. "This is Giovanni Santarino, their father. He's in his nineties now, living in Italy, not sure of his health. It's doubtful he has anything to do with the drugs here, though he could carry a grudge since both sons died in Lynyrd Station. But, we can't get any information on whether he's capable of running the family over there. And this is Francesca Santarino, daughter of Mangus. She's in federal prison."

He flipped to another photograph. "This is Chibs, he was one of the black-market gun distributors. He's incarcerated in federal prison now as well. And this is Xavier Creed, also a gunrunner, also in federal prison. The only local not in prison is Butch Ariens who owns a pawn shop, Black Gold Pawn, in town. He was the middleman exchanging money for art, jewels or drugs to work off a debt he owed the Santarinos. He left town and the shop is closed."

"Okay. So, of these men you have in your file, do any of them have family who would take up the job of running drugs?"

"We're checking into everyone, but we don't have the resources to watch all of them, hence here you are! And speaking of, how is it we weren't informed until this morning that you were coming and yet you happened to be here last night? And, why were you here last night?"

She sat back, her coffee cup now empty and she needed another one. The beginnings of a headache were starting as she sat here fighting her attraction to Rory and trying to process the info dump that she just went through. Trying to decide how much she should tell him, she felt exhausted already.

"I was here on a lead I got from an informant. I'm thinking he has more information than he let on and I believe it was a bit of a setup last night. I got an email this morning from another agent that while I was here chasing my target, which by the way, you screwed up for me, a major drug deal went down back home. Then, this morning as I was packing to leave, my SAC called to tell me you needed an agent and since I was already here, I'm now stuck here, literally."

"I didn't screw up your bust last night."

"Really?" She leaned forward and locked eyes with him. "What the fuck do you call tossing me against the building and blocking my view to his direction?"

"I didn't toss...."

The instant he faltered, she stood, "Where's the coffee here?"

He shook his head quickly as if to clear his thoughts, then stood and walked toward her. "I'll show you the coffee and introduce you to the guys."

He stopped just before her and held his hand out as if to tell her to go on ahead of him. She pulled her trench coat off and lay it in her vacant chair. She walked in front of him because she wasn't as pissed as she had been, and she rather liked keeping him off-kilter. One time she wouldn't precede him, another she would. She might as well have a little fun while she was here. Stepping out into the work area, she saw a couple of the guys stop and look up from their computers.

Rory stepped out from behind her and a couple of the men grinned shit-ass eating grins, which in her experience working mostly with men, told her they thought she chewed his ass out but good and they couldn't wait to get the rest of the story. That could be fun, too.

"Coffee's over here."

She followed him as he turned left and around a corner. There was a small galley kitchen with barely enough room for both of them, so she warned herself not to get too close, but the aroma of fresh coffee, even police station coffee, sent her thoughts racing to the need for another cup.

Rory walked to the coffee machine, and she watch the muscles in his broad shoulders move and bunch as he reached up into a cupboard to pull two clean coffee cups down. They were Styrofoam but still clean. He looked over his shoulder as he poured, "Still take yours black?"

Her heartbeat kicked up. "You remember how I take my coffee?"

He froze, the coffee pot mid-air before beginning to pour again. It was brief, but noticeable. "Yeah, I guess I do."

"What else do you remember?" Dumb, dumb, dumb. Why in the hell did her mouth say that?

He set the pot on the burner, reached into the cupboard for lids for each cup, snapped them on the cups, then turned to hand her a cup before answering. Her heartbeat kicked up ten beats per minute waiting for his answer. It seemed important for some reason. He looked her in the eyes, those light blue orbs she'd fallen for so flipping long ago, were still beautiful. Intelligent and captivating. The dark lashes that matched his dark hair were thick and full, giving his eyes the most envious frame. He waited a few beats before responding.

"I remember everything."

Angry with herself for loving that answer, she snapped, "Except to call."

She turned and stormed from the room and headed to the detectives who seemed interested in what was happening in the kitchen.

5

He'd been silently beating himself up about why he didn't stay in contact with her when she'd been transferred. Why he didn't try harder to have a long-distance relationship with her? Life may have been so different if he had. Of course, it would have, it would have been worlds apart from his lonely life here. But, just then, that snap of anger and sass that popped out of her mouth, reminded him of why, at least one reason why. When they were so much younger, he'd had this strange feeling that she'd run right over him. That all of his life he'd be cow-towing to her. She'd had a temper; it had come in spurts and dissipated almost as quickly as it had started And, as a young twenty-year-old, he wondered about marriage. But it seemed like there was so much life left to live single. Then he found out she could have stayed, and his hurt feelings and pride told him to move on. If she wanted to be with him, she would have tried to work it out. Note to self, steer clear of Alice Beggs Tucker, 'cause now, he found himself excited about her sass. He enjoyed her confidence.

Exiting the kitchen, his gut knotted when he entered the detective work area and there she was, her red hair shining in the sunlight from the window, shaking hands with each of the guys he worked with. By the looks of them she was enchanting each of them and for some reason that irritated the shit out of him.

"Well, it's very nice to meet you Detective Sam. I'm sure we'll be working together while I'm here." Her smoky voice flitted through the air and all the men seemed captivated by her.

"Nice meeting you to, Al." Samuel Bowers, looked up at him with the biggest fucking grin on his face and he knew what that was about. She'd told them all they could call her Al. But, he wasn't her friend. He'd see about that.

Taking a drink of his coffee, he walked past the group of them and snipped, "When you and your friends are finished wasting time, we need a task meeting to discuss what each of us knows about the murder last week and the other open cases of the past two months, where these drugs are coming from and the progress we've made. I'll be in the conference room."

Probably a bit childish. Probably a bit unprofessional. But he'd had three hours of sleep last night and not much more the previous couple of weeks and he wasn't in the mood. At all.

Turning the corner, he stopped in his office to grab his files, then exited and went to the conference room just two doors down.

Setting his files on the conference room table, he set his coffee down, pulled out the chair at the head of the table and sat down. Opening his files, he pretended to be reading but he was mentally chastising himself for letting his feelings get in the way of his work. He wasn't going to get involved with Beggs again anyway, besides, she's married, so it didn't matter if she thought he was her friend. His goal was the same today as yesterday, solve the murder and get the drugs off the street. If she could help with the drugs, perfect.

"Everything alright?"

He looked up to see Detective Callan Waters enter the room, his always perceptive gaze scrutinizing everything and right now he was looking closely at him.

"Yeah. A bit of a history in case you couldn't tell. Ended badly. This is going to be tough."

Cal pulled the chair next to him away from the table and sat down. He was a big brawny man and the ladies usually swooned when Cal walked in the room. More than once, he begrudgingly used Cal to get an uncooperative female suspect chatting. They loved his attention and he was fantastic at making them feel like he was on their side.

"Yeah, it's a tad noticeable."

Before he could say anything more, Sam Bowers, Anderson Tyler and Alice entered the room. Their chatter subsided and they quickly took their seats.

"Okay, let's start with the murder of Justin Tully. Ty, you were handling that case, fill us in."

Ty opened the file in front of him and just as Ty opened his mouth to start, Rory's phone rang. Reaching for it, Rory saw the readout said "Captain". Holding his finger up to let them know he had to take this, he tapped the answer icon on his phone.

"Captain, how can I help you?"

"Rory, we found a body behind building B at the apartment complex where you were chasing your perp last night. Bring a team with you, this is a bloody mess."

"For fuck's sake, what in the hell is going on here?" Remembering who he was speaking to, he continued. "We'll be right there."

Quickly standing, he said, "This has to wait, we have a dead body and it's a mess. Let's go, all hands-on deck."

Files closed and chairs rolled back as they all stood and headed to the door. He left before all of them eager to get to the scene and see what they were dealing with. Not really eager, it sounded a fright, but maybe this one would lead them to the information they needed to figure this shit out.

"Mind if I ride with you, Ace?"

He turned to see Alice staring at him her face serious, her posture straight and tall. She'd always been gorgeous, but just now, with dark-blue dress slacks and a nice white blouse, her red hair flowing over her shoulders, she was stunning. She scooped her trench coat from the chair in his office where she'd left it, he was irritated that she'd called him by the nickname she'd given him oh so many years ago.

"Sure." He walked past her and headed to the backdoor. She wore sensible shoes, but he could hear them behind him, not exactly trying to keep up, but in a hurry.

Pushing the backdoor open he didn't bother to hold it for her. He decided anger was a bit of what he needed at the moment to keep his mind on the task at hand.

As he neared his cool sleek black Charger, he smiled. He always did when he looked at this car. It had been his dream for a long time, and he loved every minute of owning it. Using the fob in his hand he tapped the unlock button and smiled again as the car lit up, taillights, dome light inside. She was a thing of beauty.

"Fantastic car, Rory. For some reason I pegged you as a truck kinda guy."

Opening his door, he sarcastically said, "That wouldn't be the first time you've pegged me wrong, Beggs."

6

The drive was quiet. Too quiet.

"Look, I'm sorry I hurt your feelings. But you hurt mine."

His head turned and she could see his jaw clench. Those piercing blue eyes landed on her and held, then he shook his head and looked at the road.

"And how's that?"

Taking in a deep breath, she swallowed. Knowing this conversation would come up, but not at all ready to hear that she'd been easily forgotten, she forged on.

"I was transferred to another base. You said you'd call and we'd stay in touch. You didn't. We didn't. Then, within six months you were married to someone else." She stared straight ahead, watching as the trees and shrubs breezed past the windows of the car. The sun was now high in the sky and the day seemed bright, though the air was chilly. It didn't seem possible that they were on their way to a gruesome murder scene.

"We were young."

"You still married someone else."

She watched his chest, which all these years later, was massively impressive. He'd continued to work out after getting out of the Marines. He'd always been impressive, but now, he was filled out and mature. He had a confidence about him he hadn't had back when they were stationed together.

"You could have stayed, Alice, but you didn't. I heard the position you took was volunteer, you could have refused."

"But then I'd be staying in a place, career wise, that didn't offer me the opportunities I got when I left."

His jaw clenched again but instead of answering, he turned into the apartment complex parking lot where they'd first seen each other last night. The place was teaming with police cruisers, an ambulance, the medical examiner's van and on-lookers standing behind the yellow police tape trying to see what was happening. A news truck was parked in the corner, the large antennas raised high and a reporter with long dark hair and a cute little cream-colored pea coat could be seen talking into the camera pointed in her direction.

Rory drove to a parking area blocked off for police personnel, a young officer guarding the area from unauthorized persons stepped aside when Rory pulled up, a smile on his face. He clearly admired the sleek black Charger as they rolled past him. Pulling in next to a cruiser, he put the car in Park, turned it off, and grabbed his keys from the ignition. Without another word, he opened his car door and exited the vehicle.

Taking in a deep, cleansing breath, one, because she didn't have the patience to deal with a surly co-worker and two, because once they got close to the body, there would be no clean breaths for a while.

Opening the car door and exiting, the doors locked, and she saw Rory pointing the key fob at the car, then turn and walked to an officer on the fringe of the roped off area.

Following Rory's path, she heard the officer as he pointed to an area behind him. "The Captain's between those two buildings. Medical Examiner is there, too."

Al moved on past them to the area the officer had mentioned, stealing herself for the scene. She hated looking at dead bodies. Sometimes it took a while to get the images out of her head and to erase the smells from her memories.

Refusing to wear high heels, even in dress clothes, she was once again grateful for what some would call sensible shoes, as she plodded across the uneven ground easily in her high-topped sneaker type shoes. Nearing the corner of the building the odor of death hit her before she saw anything, and she quickly pulled a scarf from her coat pocket to cover her nose and mouth should she begin to gag.

The scene that met her when she turned the corner was mostly the backs of a large man and a smaller man talking and pointing. As she stepped close to them, she finally made herself look at the ground. A male body lay on the ground, his face covered in blood, blank eyes staring up at the sky. One of his arms lay across his stomach, one lay out at a 45-degree angle. A red blob lay next to his face, in a pool of blood.

She heard Rory's steps quicken as she stared at the body on the ground, and then the steps of others as they neared. There was an area marked off for them where the forensic technicians had already collected evidence, documented the scene, and taken photographs. They now were photographing the area around them, taking notes, and continuing to gather evidence. No one was permitted on the part of the scene that had not been processed.

"Captain, this is Al Tucker." Rory introduced her. The taller of the two men turned to look at her, reached his hand out to shake hers, then motioned to the man alongside him.

"This is Medical Examiner Thomson."

The Medical Examiner nodded at her. "What do you have for us?", Alice asked.

"His throat was slit from jaw to jaw, and his tongue cut out."

She looked at the blob lying next to his face, then looked closer at the face staring up. The word snitch was carved into his forehead.

The Medical Examiner pointed to a forensic technician's

evidence tote where she could see evidence paraphernalia and plastic bags containing various evidence. "A wallet found on the victim identifies him as Sergio Mancuoso."

Her head snapped up as she stared at the Medical Examiner. But at that moment, her stomach quelled, and she stepped back in case she lost the coffee she'd consumed earlier. Rory followed her a few steps back.

"Do you know him?"

Breathing in slow and deep and letting her breath out slowly, she swallowed the moisture that had gathered in her mouth. Her heart hammered in her chest as her mind reeled with what this might mean. And the only thing that came to mind right now was that she might very well be in more danger than she's ever been at this juncture and she needed some time to think and call her SAC for his thoughts on the matter.

"Beggs? Do you know him?" Rory asked again.

She looked into his concerned face and, for the first time since last night, she was happy he was here.

"Yes."

7

"Who is he to you?"

"He's my informant. The instant I got to this spot last night, which is where he told me I'd find a major drug drop going down and possibly one of the organizers, 'The Big Guy' of this drug operation I've been trying to shut down, I was shot at. I thought he set me up because back home in Indianapolis there was a major bust last night. When I found out about it, I assumed he wanted me out of the area so I wouldn't break it up, and then have me killed because someone was waiting for me. But, he didn't set me up, he was found out."

"Are you in danger, Beggs?"

He watched her face and the myriad of emotions that flashed across it. The slight furrow between her brows told him she was worried.

"I don't know, but they may have gotten him to talk. It would explain why I was being shot at last night. I thought I'd gotten too close."

"Why were you here without backup?" He was bouncing between being pissed and being scared at her willingness to put herself in danger.

"I wanted to sneak up on the drug drop and record it so I had evidence. I wasn't going to bust anyone until I had recorded evidence and names. This case has been getting to me. I've spent countless hours researching, investigating, examining and I keep coming up with nothing. I realize I shouldn't have come alone, but my partner was working another angle at home.

"You still put yourself in dang..." Seeing her shut down, he stopped his forthcoming tirade and changed his tone of voice.

He took a deep breath and let it out slowly. "I think we need to get you to safety right now until we get the evidence back at the station and we know if your snitch gave the killers details about you. What did he know about you? How did he contact you?"

"He only knew my phone number and that I worked in Indianapolis."

"And that you were going to be here last night."

Her voice softened. "Yes."

"What did he call you?"

"Why does that matter?"

His gut twisted in several directions. The killing was getting more gruesome and now it felt very personal.

"I don't know."

"He called me sneakers."

Watching as she raised her pant leg, her sensible shoes were Rag & Bone Army high top sneakers. He had a pair of his own.

Inhaling deeply, he felt relief for some strange reason that he didn't call her Red. Which, considering what they were facing, was stupid.

He looked back at the Captain, who was now approaching them, the look of confusion clear on his face.

"Everything alright here?"

He looked at Beggs but it appeared she wasn't going to say anything, so he did. "That's Beggs' informant."

Captain Peters was a large man, 6 foot 3 and he was muscular. Built like a brick shithouse should have his name on it in the dictionary, 'cause he was a solid wall of strength, both physically and mentally. His jet-black hair and dark chocolate eyes, which normally were serious now looked worried.

"Are you in danger, Tucker?"

Beggs cleared her throat lightly, squared her shoulders and looked Captain Peters in the eyes, which wasn't that easy to do, she had to look up close to a foot.

"I don't know, sir."

The Captain stared at Beggs for a long time and to her credit, she never looked away.

"Richards, get Tucker back to the station and figure out where she's going to stay while she's here. The motel isn't safe enough."

"I can go back to Indy." She offered.

Captain shook his head. "Nope. We might be on to something. If they're here because you're here, we have them close. That's a far cry better than having them scatter. As long as they know you're still here, we have a better chance of catching these fuckers and that's what we're going to do. I'll call your SAC to see if he agrees with the plan."

The Captain started to walk away. "Richards, on second thought, your place is secured with the latest and greatest, isn't it? Take Tucker there."

What? No fucking way. This wasn't a good idea at all. "Captain, maybe we could..."

"Take her to your place and lockdown until we have this scene processed. I'll call you in a while."

Then his massive back was turned, and he walked back to the body and his crime scene investigators.

"He can't make me stay at your place. That is un-fucking-real. Besides, likely unethical. And to top it off, how fucking dare he. He'll call my SAC." Beggs seethed, though quietly. The Captain couldn't hear her and if he could, he didn't acknowledge it.

Taking a deep breath, more to fortify himself than anything else against her quick temper. " Beggs, let's get you out of sight for right now, then we can talk about what to do."

She faced him and crossed her arms in front of her. Totally protective move. He lowered his voice and tried again.

"Hey, I know you feel irritated with the way things have worked out today, but let's get out of sight and settled in, at least for tonight, and then we can talk. I'll talk about anything you want to talk about and if you need to scream and yell, you can scream and yell at me. But, right now, we don't know there isn't a sniper somewhere with his sights set on you."

She shook her beautiful head quickly as if she just realized she was in danger, then nodded her head and uncrossed her arms. At least for now, the temper had subsided. Now if she took him up on his offer to scream and yell, he'd have to deal with it, but at least he knew that would come out of frustration, and not so much about him. Maybe.

He turned and began walking to his car, turning only once to make sure she was following. After rounding the corner of the building at the apartment complex, he could see the crowd was still large and it made his stomach roll. Their perp could be in the crowd out there for all they knew. Or in one of the apartments above them. Everything was a crap shoot right now.

He heard a phone ring, it wasn't his ring tone, but he turned as he heard Beggs dig for her phone in her coat pocket.

"Tucker."

"Who is this?" she demanded.

He stopped to see she had stopped, her eyes looking all around. Seeing the absolute fear on her face, he walked back the few steps and took her free hand, grateful she didn't fight or argue. Pulling her along, he hurried his pace.

"Come out so I can see you or are you too cowardly?"

He squeezed her hand and looked back at her.

"Don't taunt him," he whispered.

She shushed him with a quick shake of her head as she listened to the person on the other end of the phone. He could only hear one side of the conversation, but what he surmised from that was that the killer could see them and that meant he needed to get

Beggs out of here and fast. He quickened his pace and continued to tug her along, though she slowed a couple of times.

"I'll find you. I will. I'll get you."

She practically hissed. "Oh, I won't kill you. I'd much rather watch them walk you into prison knowing what your life will be like in there. Death would be a blessing for you. I have no intention of blessing you."

8

She allowed herself to be pulled along but only because her mind was moving in a thousand different directions, not the least of which was that a murderer or murderers was watching. What that also meant was he or they knew for sure what she looked like, knew she was with Rory, and what he looked like. They were only minimally protected by the small police force in Lynyrd Station, but cops were killed all the time so it was possibly a false hope that they were safe anywhere.

Rory walked her to the passenger side of his car and opened the door for her, almost pushing her inside. The fact that he seemed scared began to freak her out, but she focused on her breathing, one minute at a time. Maybe after a good stiff drink, she could calm down and focus her thoughts on what she knew about this operation and her safety moving forward. She thought about the number of times her life had been in danger as a DEA Special Agent. She could handle this. She didn't want to stay at Rory's, not forever anyway.

He slid into the driver's seat and locked the doors. Immediately pulling his seatbelt on, he glanced over at her. "Buckle up, Red."

The inside of the car was warm and cozy, Rory's aftershave

filled the air, he called her by his old nickname for her and she suddenly felt better. Pulling her seatbelt on, he started the car, its low rumble, a sexy growl that gave her goosebumps, as he pulled from their parking space.

The young officer who'd let them pass by, stepped aside once again, that same grin as before, on his face.

"He has a crush on your car."

Rory glanced up at the young officer and nodded. "So do I."

He then left the parking lot, tapped the Bluetooth button on his dash, and upon doing so, the robotic female voice asked him what he wanted; he said, "Call Ford Montgomery."

"Calling Ford Montgomery on cell," came her reply.

The phone rang only twice before a deep, smoky male voice answered, "Yeah."

Rory chuckled before responding, "I have a situation."

"Yeah."

"Are you on a mission?"

"No. I'm in town."

"I have DEA Special Agent Alice Tucker in my car, and we've been ordered by the Captain to stay at my house. We're not sure if she's in danger, her informant was just found dead."

A long pause left her wondering if they'd been disconnected before Ford responded, "That's some situation."

"Right," Rory turned onto another road, leading them out of town, she tried running all of the scenarios through her head about what had happened last night, but wasn't totally successful. "My security system is in place and good, but I wonder if you can give it a once over, beef it up if need be?"

A baby cried in the background and Ford muttered something under his breath. "Yeah. I've got to help Megan get Shelby settled first; it's my turn to get her down for nap time, but I can be down in an hour."

Rory laughed, "You really are domesticated."

"Fuck you." Then the line went dead and Rory laughed again.

Turning into a cul-de-sac, she saw five larger homes each one spread out on close to two acres.

"This is beautiful."

Swinging the car into the driveway at one of the homes at the bottom of the cul-de-sac, the closest garage door of the three doors to the front door of the house began to open. The home was large; dark brown siding and stacked stone detailing at various places on the front of the home were stunning. The two-story home was tall and long and impressively sat perched on a hill. A true showpiece among the other homes.

"How does a cop afford this?" she murmured.

He didn't respond and she wondered if he'd turned dirty. Pulling the Charger into the garage, she noted that everything was neat and orderly. The walls were drywalled and painted white, the space organized with cabinets painted black along the back wall and nothing on the countertop except a picture of Rory's Charger and a Mopar sign.

"I have to tell you I'm impressed," she softly offered.

Turning off the ignition, he pulled the key out and opened his door. The look he landed on her was one of curiosity more than anything else. His words belied his look. "Glad you approve."

She exited the vehicle and followed him to a door which he unlocked. Stepping just inside the door he pushed a few buttons on a keypad, likely to turn off the alarm, paused for a moment, then a beep sounded, and he stood back and looked at her.

"Welcome to my home."

She stepped inside and the air felt warm and cozy, the faint aroma of citrus or something fresh filled the air. She followed Rory down the short hallway and to the right where they entered an impressive kitchen. Granite counters, oak cabinetry and tile floors looked out onto a large backyard. A small basket, filled with dog toys, lay on the floor next to the sliding glass doors leading to the backyard.

"You have a dog, Ace?"

His eyes landed on hers and held for a few moments as if he was trying to decide how to respond.

"I used to, but he died last year of cancer. I'd like another one, but trying to train a puppy with the hours I've been working would be next to impossible right now, so I'm waiting to see how things shake out."

"I'm sorry you lost your dog, that sucks."

She watched his chest as it expanded, filling his lungs with air. He was still an handsome man, though his build was more on the stocky side, the way he'd filled out over these past few years was sexy. His dark hair showed tiny threads of silver here and there, mostly at the temples and behind his ears. He'd be handsome gray, too. His light blue eyes still cast a spell on her, the blue so unusual and clear like no other color she'd ever seen before.

"Yeah, it sucks." He opened a cupboard above a short counter across from the island and hung his keys on a peg.

"Come on, I'll show you your room."

She followed him, wondering how she'd get her car here which held all of the clothes she'd brought along with her, which really wasn't that much because she'd only expected to stay a day or two. While she would never describe herself as the average woman, she was when it came to packing. You just never knew when you needed to dress for a dinner or a change of clothes in her case in the event she got filthy giving chase.

Rory walked through the open concept living room and turned left to ascend a large staircase. She silently followed him, wondering once again how he could afford this home. Cops usually lived modestly.

At the top of the steps, she looked out the large bank of windows onto the backyard and was enamored with the view, the decor, the entire home.

"Okay, take your pick of bedrooms, you have two to choose from and the bathroom is in the middle here. The entire upstairs is yours while you're here. I'll go down and call the station to have someone bring your car around and then I'll make us some lunch. Feel free to wash up. If you need clean clothes until yours get here, I can pull a t-shirt and some sweats from my room if you like."

She cleared her throat. "No, that's okay, I'll just wash my face and hands until my clothes get here." She looked into each of the rooms and chose the larger of the two. "How do you know my clothes are in my car?"

He chuckled. "Angel from the motel cafe dates Jason Robard's brother. You met Jason this morning, he's one of the police officers. He texted me a while ago and said you'd checked out of the motel. Not many secrets in town except who the drug supplier is."

Nodding she looked at his face, noticing his posture was stiff, his demeanor while not unfriendly, not totally open either. She had herself to blame for that, she'd started this morning off rather harshly.

"That's why I like living in a big city."

"Hmm, well, I like knowing who my neighbors are. When I walk into the Copper Cup, I like knowing more than half of the customers in there. I like having my friends close, because honestly, this town is small enough that it's impossible to be all that far, even across town."

He nodded then turned and walked down the steps, his pace a bit quicker than it had been bringing her up. As hurt as she'd been when he didn't call her, she admitted, at least to herself, that things do work out the way they are supposed to; and at that time in her life, she wanted to experience the military and learn all she could learn. She had had thoughts of joining the DEA. Which had meant college and eventually moving anywhere she wanted. That was a curious thing to think about now, after all those years of being pissed at him.

She heard Rory's phone ring downstairs and stepped to the edge of the top step.

"Captain, what do you have?"

9

Pulling items from his refrigerator, he berated himself for not going to the grocery store. Not that he'd had the chance lately, but still, even on the way home one night he could have made the effort. Remembering that Odie, a friend from high school, had started his own delivery business, he snagged his phone off the counter. Looking up the webpage on the internet Odie Eats, he tapped the contact us icon and held his phone to his ear.

"Odie Eats, you've got Odie here."

Chuckling, he said, "Odie, it's Rory Richards, how on earth are you?"

"Rory, my man, I'm fantastic. Business is booming. Who knew there were so many people who didn't want to go out and get things?"

"Well, that's why I'm calling. I haven't had a spare minute in weeks, and I need groceries. How does this work?"

"Check out my website. Click on the store, then the items you want. Pay with your credit card or a payment app, then I'll get a notification. Currently you're looking at about forty-five minutes."

"Perfect. I'm on it. See you then and congratulations on the new business, looks like a winner."

Odie's chuckling could be heard as he ended the call and he couldn't help but smile. Tapping on Odie's website, he found the local grocery store and ordered a variety of items he could use to make a few meals. Next order of business was to get Red's car here. Sending out a text to Jerry, he asked him to swing by and grab her keys, then go back to the station to get her car. If he was out on patrol, that wouldn't be an issue. Someone could follow him and take him back after.

"What's going on?"

Red stood before him, still in her slacks and blouse, but she looked refreshed somehow. He remembered her from the military, she was Army, he was Marine, but they were on base together in Iraq and he noticed her right away. That red hair, her confidence, her ability to adapt to whatever situation they were in. They'd draw fire, have to hunker down and fire back, chase the enemy away and as soon as the mission was over, there'd be a grin on her lips and she'd get to work on cleaning up whatever had to be cleaned up. She never complained. She never shrunk back. She never quit. When they got back to the states, they were stationed together for six months. It took him four months to ask her out on an actual date - they went bowling at the arcade on base. But they laughed and gave each other shit all night. It was exhilarating. She was exhilarating. So different from the other women he'd known but that's also what scared the shit out of him. When she got her orders to ship out to Arizona, she squared her shoulders and left without whining, at least that's what it looked like.

He'd said they'd stay in touch. He told her he'd call, but he didn't. Was it a mistake? Probably the biggest of his life. And to see now that it affected her stymied him to no end. He thought she just left as quickly as she'd come without looking back. Blow him over with a light breeze.

"Ace?"

Pulling himself from his musings, he cleared his throat, "The

Captain said we're to stay here and he spoke to your SAC who's agreed to the plan. He'll send backup if the Captain thinks we need it. The Captain will have everything uploaded into the system soon. Then, we're to look at the video from the convenience mart and the apartment complex and see if you see anyone who looks familiar, suspicious or both. We'll also be able to go over the evidence, though there's very little of it from what he's told me. Tomorrow, we're to call in first thing and see what he wants us to do."

Crossing her arms in front of her, she quipped, "I don't like being locked up like I'm fragile."

"Red, no one thinks you're fragile. He just wants to see if the person who called you makes any kind of move."

His phone chimed that someone breached the security at the end of the street. He walked to the laundry room, which was located next to the garage entry door, and his phone buzzed. Looking out the window he saw Ford's truck pulling up the drive.

Stepping back out to the kitchen, he caught Red's attention. "Ford's here to shore up my security system."

Walking to the garage entry door he tapped on the opener on the wall and opened the garage door for Ford, who climbed from his truck looking a little worse for wear and walked toward him.

"Tough mission?"

"You could say that."

"Come on in and try not to talk our ears off while you're here," he grinned when he said it and got a grunt in response.

Walking into the kitchen, Ford behind him, he watched Red look up from her phone, a hint of a smile on her face, then her eyes rounded when she saw Ford. Ford was what his wife, Debra, had called dark and broody.

"Red, this is Ford Montgomery. Ford, Alice Tucker, DEA."

"Nice to meet you, Alice."

She nodded, smiled and replied, "Nice meeting you."

Rory's phone chimed again, "Ford, I think you remember where everything is. Holler if you need anything in the meantime. Jerry's here to get Red's keys."

She nodded and walked to the staircase and he couldn't not watch her walk away. She had what you'd call a "yoga ass". Perfectly shaped and firm from exercise, likely yoga, but could be anything.

Ford chuckled then turned and walked to the office, which was just off the kitchen and facing the front yard. Scowling slightly, he turned and walked to the garage to wave Jerry in.

Waiting at the entry door for Jerry, he noted the officer exiting his cruiser, and walking toward him with a bit of a stoop. He was dragging, too.

"She's getting her keys, come on in," he called to Jerry, who merely nodded and followed him inside.

Red came down the stairs, keys jingling in her hand and bestowed a glorious smile on Jerry, who then stood taller and graced her with a large smile of his own. To say it didn't irk him would be a lie. It did. A lot.

"Thank you for handling this, Jerry, I appreciate it."

"You got it." Jerry nodded. He half-saluted, turned and walked out the door. Fucker.

Red's phone chimed and he watched her facial expressions as she read the message in her text. Her nose scrunched then relaxed before she tapped a few times, then held the phone to her ear. A moment later she said, "Who died?"

10

"It appears they're targeting not only my informant, but his family as well. His brother was found dead about an hour ago. No word on whether he was informing for anyone else, but they're checking." She calmly stated.

"Is that your District?"

She watched Rory's face; he would make a great poker player.

"Yes. He was found in the back-parking lot of a pizzeria in Indianapolis."

"Did you know the brother?"

She briefly bit her bottom lip, then shook her head, "No."

His chest expanded then released as his eyes locked on hers. Ford walked out of the office, looked at Rory and said, "You should call Jared."

He turned then and opened a door next to the office door and descended the basement steps without another word.

Turning her head to watch Rory's reaction as he turned to open the fridge.

"You want a beer?"

"Yes."

Pulling two beers from the fridge he set them on the countertop, twisted the tops off with his hands, which she still admired. His hands were strong, his fingers graceful in a manly way. She'd always enjoyed watching him on his computer or cleaning his gun in service. Sure, strong, flexible, he was coordinated in ways she felt clumsy.

Curiosity was killing her. "Whose Jared?"

He picked up a bottle of beer in each hand, handed her one of them, then tapped his bottle to hers.

"A friend."

She took a long drink and tried not to think about how she'd like to down the whole bottle. She'd never had a drinking problem, but once in a great while, she liked getting lost in absolutely nothing. Having a few drinks and not having to think about death, drugs, destruction, not always in that order.

"Why would you call this friend?"

"Red, how about we sit in the living room and chill? I've got groceries on the way. Jerry will have your car and suitcase here soon. Ford is making sure security is good and we can't go anywhere for a while, so can we just sit?"

She lifted a shoulder in a shrug, turned and walked the few steps into the open concept living room. Sitting on the sofa, which was across the room from the large wall of windows, she allowed her eyes to look out onto the landscape of the backyard. A tall wrought iron fence could be seen across the yard, though it was camouflaged with trees and shrubs in most places.

"How far does the fence go?"

Rory had followed her into the room, sat in the large brown leather recliner and lifted the footrest.

"Around the six houses on this street."

"I didn't see gates when we drove in."

"No gates. We each have security and when the plane is broken at the street entrance, we each get a notification. At first, I wasn't a fan because who wants their neighbors knowing when you come and go? But, over time I've come to like it, we all do, and we watch who's on our street. Plus, times are logged and cars coming and going are recorded so we know when there are deliveries, etc. In other words, we don't have porch pirates."

Taking another long pull from her beer bottle she let that all sink in. Rory did the same.

"Why would you call Jared?"

Rory rubbed his forehead with his fingers, then ran his fingers through his thick dark hair and to his nape. She envied those fingers right now. She loved his hair. How it felt between her fingers, how it smelled, how it looked.

"Jared has special skills on the computer and can find things out our systems can't. Let's just say he colors outside of the lines; we have to stay firmly within ours."

The sound of a metal box closing could be heard and soon after, Ford's footsteps on the stairs echoed. At the top of the steps, Ford looked into the living room at Rory, his eyes flicked to hers, then her beer bottle. A slight grin formed on his face and he didn't look so broody. Actually, he was rather handsome in a dark sort of way.

His voice was deep, and he spoke with a slow deliberate intention.

"You need an upgrade and I've saved the files from the front gates, then cleaned the cache. I can upgrade remotely, which I'll do as soon as I get home. It won't affect anything, and I'll call you after the upgrade is finished so you can reboot the system. Otherwise, all of your security points are operating,"

Rory stood and shook Ford's hand. "Thanks man. How's life these days?"

"Good, great actually. The job is good. Megan is fantastic and Shelby is growing and happy. What more could a man want?"

Rory's smile was outstanding. It hit her hard as she remembered when he used to smile at her like that. She'd sought it out it was so fantastic, and now, it was like a punch in the gut how much she'd missed it. Dammit, why did she have to be thrown together with him after all these years and all those tears getting over him? She'd been doing fine. She'd moved on. Excelled even.

His dark handsome head turned toward her, his smile still in place when he said, "Ford has a gorgeous wife and the most beautiful little girl you've ever seen."

And there was Ford's smile again. He reached for his back pocket and pulled out his phone. As if magnetized she stood and walked toward them just as he turned his phone, the picture of a beautiful auburn-haired woman with the prettiest green eyes she'd ever seen holding a dark-haired little girl about ten months old. Megan and Shelby.

"You have a beautiful family, Ford. You're luckier than most I'd say." She meant what she said, but somewhere deep inside it hurt. A child was something she'd always wanted but had never gotten around to having. Life just didn't seem to be lining things up for her to have the sought-after family unit.

"Thank you. I think I'm incredibly blessed. Which also means, I'm anxious to get back home." He looked again at Rory, "You good here?"

"Yeah." Rory's voice sounded a bit sad, and she couldn't help but wonder if he'd ever wanted a family himself.

Rory's phone chimed and she now recognized that as a signal that someone had turned onto the street. Ford turned but said, "Nice to meet you, Alice."

"Nice meeting you too, Ford."

Rory's phone buzzed this time and she recognized that someone had now pulled into the driveway.

Rory and Ford walked to the garage entrance and she sat on the sofa, suddenly feeling depleted and sad. "Well fuck me, this day continues to deteriorate with every minute." She muttered to herself.

11

He watched as Jerry rolled to a stop in front of the far garage door and another car, likely Red's pulled in right behind him. Walking to the garage door panel next to his entry door, he tapped the button for the middle door and ushered the man driving the second car inside. He'd keep Red's car in the garage for protection. Dax climbed out of his cruiser and walked to him. The officer in Red's car exited and walked to him, keys in hand.

Reaching out to hand him Red's keys, he nodded, "Officer Paul Delhurst."

"You're the new guy I've been hearing about."

"Yes, sir. I've actually been on staff for six months now, but since I'm the last hire, I'm the new guy until someone else comes on board."

Jerry stepped up to them, "He's largely working pms, but we're all now usually working doubles."

"Welcome aboard Officer, I'm sorry I haven't met you before now."

"Thank you, sir."

Jerry tapped Paul on the arm, "Let's get cooking, we've got stuff to do before end of shift. Take care, Rory."

"Thanks for the help guys. Keep your heads down and stay safe."

The two officers climbed in Jerry's cruiser and Rory tapped the buttons to close both garage doors. Entering the house, he locked the entry door then sighed. Maybe he'd even get a nap in since they had to be locked down.

Red met him in the hallway to the garage.

"I'd like to get my overnight bag out of my car."

Holding up her keys, he allowed his fingers to graze hers as they exchanged them. He saw that it affected her, her pupils dilated, and she swallowed. When she walked past him, she brushed against him and his brain couldn't get past the fact that she'd done that on purpose. There was plenty of room here, and now his cock was thickening, and his heartbeat raced and her scent still hung in the air, and he needed another beer.

Walking to the refrigerator he pulled a bottle from the shelf, turned and saw her empty bottle on the counter and pulled out another one for Red. Setting them both on the counter, he twisted the caps off, slid open the garbage bins, tossed the tops in the garbage and the empty bottles in the back bin. Slowly closing the door, he inhaled a deep breath and closed his eyes trying to remember Debra. All that came to his mind was shiny red hair and crisp green eyes. His heart raced. How could that be? How could he not be able to picture Debra?

"Thanks for taking care of getting my car and my things here, Ace."

Red turned the corner, her overnight bag in her hand. She froze as she looked at him, her head cocked to the right, her brows furrowed.

"Are you alright?"

Sliding a beer bottle across the counter toward her, he nodded once.

"Yeah, Red, I'm fine."

Picking up his bottle he took a long pull of his beer, then walked toward the living room when his phone chimed again.

Stopping halfway there, he turned and said, "Groceries."

He kept walking through the living room and to the front door, looking first out the side windows before opening the door to see Odie walking up the sidewalk with four grocery bags in his arms.

"Odie, thank you so much."

He met him halfway, snagging two bags and walking back to the house. Odie followed him to the kitchen, and he noticed Red was nowhere in sight. Likely upstairs freshening up. That conjured all sorts of naughty thoughts in his mind and his body responded. Shit.

"Thanks for your business, Rory, and thanks for the tip. I'd stay and visit but I've got four more deliveries before I head back for more."

He reached out his hand and Rory shook it, firmly, as he'd always had, rather sad that he couldn't visit with Odie after all this time, but happy that he had some time to himself to straighten out his thoughts about Red. Closing the door behind Odie, he twisted the deadbolt and reset the alarm. Then he heard the shower running upstairs and muttered under his breath as he walked back to the kitchen. His phone buzzed in his pocket, and he read a text from Ford, short and to the point.

"Reboot."

Changing his direction, he walked to the office and woke up his laptop. Before rebooting, he opened his photos, searching for older photos of when Debra was alive. Finding an album labeled, Santa Fe he clicked it open to see pictures of their vacation to Santa Fe some ten or more years ago. There she was, her face shiny and bright, a big sombrero on her head, but her smile lit up the whole picture. He stared at her face, guilt crawling up his body because he'd failed to recall her in his mind earlier, his eyes watered slightly, and the shower shut off upstairs.

Shaking the melancholy from his head, he closed the photo album, then rebooted his computer. Time to get back to work; he had a lunch to make, and then they had work to do pouring over the crime scene videos and evidence. No rest for the weary, or was that wicked? Either seemed to work at this juncture.

Unpacking the groceries, he decided on making grilled double ham and cheese sandwiches and a salad. It was one of his favorite lunches.

Gathering the items he needed, he pulled a frying pan from the bottom cabinet and set it on the stove. Pulling a loaf of bread from a grocery bag, he set it on the counter next to the stove, then pulled out the other groceries and finished putting them away. A blow-dryer sounded upstairs and he shook his head to keep thoughts of naked Red out of it.

Slicing the cheddar cheese into medium slices, he lay a piece of cheese on a slice of buttered bread, then stacked the ham on the cheese, then added another slice of cheese, topping it off with a slice of buttered bread. Laying it in the frying pan, he turned the heat down low and put the lid on the pan. Beginning on the second sandwich he heard Red's light footsteps descend the steps and his heartbeat kicked up. He was acting the fool today with all of these ridiculous feelings for a woman he'd left behind years ago. Must be time to get laid again, but that would have to wait until Red was gone.

"It smells fantastic in here."

"Double ham and cheese sandwiches. There's more beer in the fridge if you need one and lunch will be ready in about fifteen minutes."

Walking to the stove he glanced at Red who stood at the counter, a pair of loose-fitting comfortable pants on, like pajamas and a soft looking flowing gray t-shirt. The bra she wore was definitely not padded and didn't need to be as she'd always been well enough endowed that she turned heads. But right now, her nipples strained through the flimsy material she wore, and it was fucking distracting. On top of that, she had a light gloss on her lips and her fresh clean scent wafted across the counter to him and his dick began noticing.

His eyes locked on hers and she smiled, a perfect, beguiling smile.

"Red?"

"What?"

Inhaling deeply, he let out a breath, gritted his teeth and lifted the lid on the pan. Pulling a spatula from the drawer he slid it under the sandwich, flipped it over and added the second sandwich to the pan.

He could sense her walking toward him. The tiny hairs stood on his arms, his lungs struggled to fill with air and his mind was going south faster than a freight train.

He turned when she leaned against the counter, her arms crossed just under her breasts, her left hip jutted out to touch the counter, oh he remembered those hips.

"You can't...what are you trying to do here?"

12

"While I was showering, I thought we might as well enjoy ourselves. And, as I remember, something we were very, very good at was enjoying ourselves."

"Aren't you married?"

"No."

"I thought you said you were married for four years."

"I was. I've now been divorced for more than ten years."

She'd missed him. She tried fighting it. Being angry with him earlier sure helped her not remember the things she loved about him, but then she got into the shower and realized a few things. He was going out of his way to make her comfortable. He was down here making them lunch. He was still so friggin' handsome. He still smelled fantastic and when she watched his hands earlier today, she missed them. On her. All over her.

Cooling the water down in the shower did nothing to change the direction of her thoughts and since they were here and both unattached, why didn't they just have some fun?

"Oh. Why didn't you say that?"

"I just did."

"You know what I mean."

"You didn't ask."

"Fuck." He muttered softly under his breath.

He moved away from her to the stove and pulled a delicious smelling sandwich out of the frying pan and lay it on a plate. Quickly flipping the other one, he set the lid back on the pan and cut the first sandwich in two. Walking toward her with the plate he set it in front of her, looked into her eyes like it was the first time. And she looked into his. They said so much about him. She could see who he was by looking deeply into his eyes, he wanted her. He was a man who lived an orderly life, by the looks of his house, which was spic and span. She could see him wrestling with what to do so she made the decision and lifted up on her toes and planted her lips against his.

Her tongue slipped out and slowly swiped along the seam of his lips, the taste of beer still on them. She palmed his face with her right hand, tilting his head slightly so their lips fit perfectly together. She felt his resolve, then she felt it explode as his strong arms wrapped around her body and pulled her tightly to the wall of chest she'd been admiring earlier today. She instantly wrapped her arms around his neck and lifted her legs to wrap them around his waist, which earned her a shove against the counter where she instantly felt his hardness push against her in the most delicious way. She groaned into his mouth and he reciprocated which made her nipples pebble so tightly they tingled.

He moved them down the counter, her ass against the edge, then he broke their kiss, leaned over and turned off the burner, moved the pan off the hot spot then his hand grabbed her ass, tightly, he squeezed hard and she moaned. He still liked it a bit rough. Perfect.

Kissing along his jaw to his ear, she latched on to his earlobe and nipped at it just hard enough to show him she still liked it that way, too. His large intake of breath excited her beyond reason and his second hand cupped her ass and both hands squeezed tightly.

"Give me what you've got, Ace."

"Fuck." He growled.

One of his hands reached up to the waistband of her lounge pants and pulled it down over her ass exposing her skin to the roughness of his hand. He grabbed her cheek with that hand as the other mimicked the motion, pulling her pants the remainder of the way down her ass. His eager fingers didn't stop long, and he reached around as far as he could and explored her naked flesh, moving roughly past her asshole and further up, almost but not quite where she wanted him to be. Arching her back to give him more access the tip of his finger slipped inside of her and she whimpered.

"More." She groaned into his ear.

Before her head could register what was happening, he set her feet on the ground, spun her around, grabbed her pants and tugged, then quickly undid his pants. Soon he pushed gently on her shoulders to bend her over the counter and the tip of his cock was at her entrance.

"You sure?"

"God, yes."

He thrust inside of her with a force that made her want more so that's what she asked for.

"More, Ace. Harder."

He obliged. Shoving himself into her again and again, with the strength she'd remembered, maybe more now that they were both grown. She shoved back as far as she could to take him all the way inside of her. She faintly realized she'd likely have bruises on her ribs, but she didn't give a shit as she held her right hand up to brace herself against the wall so she could feel him completely, he then pulled her back a bit and his delightful fingers found her clit and quickly circled, adding pressure after every couple of circles.

Her breathing increased and her vision, well that was gone. Her heartbeat raced, the feel of his cock sliding in her the best feeling in the world, the memories of the past now replaced with this one, which she would remember forever.

"My God, Ace. Shit." She panted.

He increased his speed, their pace rapid and wild and she loved it.

"Ohmigod. Ohmigod." Her orgasm hit like a flood wall and he pulled out and growled as she felt the warm sticky ropes of cum shoot onto her ass.

His breathing was ragged but he managed to huff out, "Fuck that's hot." And she knew he was watching himself cum on her. She lay her head on the cool granite of the countertop and allowed herself a moment to lock this memory away and catch her breath, in that order.

13

He finished cleaning himself up, changed his boxer briefs and his Khakis then walked out of his bedroom to the living room. Red was still upstairs, and his eyes floated to the second level where he could hear the water running. Taking in a deep breath his mind whirled at the speed at which things had happened today and he was trying to keep up. They'd always had amazing chemistry, even before he'd screwed up the nerve to ask her out.

Continuing to the kitchen, he slid the frying pan to the burner on the stove and turned the burner on to once again heat up their sandwiches. His thoughts floated to Red, back when they dated so darned many years ago, what was it 15 or more years? How was it she was as sexy as ever and felt better than he remembered? So much about her dug into him and he could feel her taking hold. He had to stop that. As soon as they stopped this drug operation, they'd be once again facing her leaving and either not seeing each other again or a long-distance relationship. History had a way of repeating itself.

Letting out a long breath as warm hands circled his waist from behind and slid sensuously up his abdomen. Her breasts pressed against his back, then her head lay against the back of his shoulder where she sighed.

"That felt amazing, Ace."

Slowly he turned in her arms, moving them away from the stove. Her head then rested against his shoulder and he lay his head on top of hers as he encircled her in his arms.

"You felt amazing, Red."

Her phone rang out the song Close to My Enemies. Her head popped off his chest, her brows furrowed.

"That's Sergio's ringtone."

"So, someone has his phone. But when they called you earlier today, didn't they used a different phone?"

"Yes."

"Hmm, let's be smart about this and find out what game they're playing."

She snagged her phone from the counter where she'd left it, looked at the readout, turned the phone to him and he saw the name Twitch. She mouthed Sergio and he nodded.

Taking a deep breath, she tapped the green answer icon and quickly tapped the speaker icon.

"Who am I speaking with?"

"Well now, Hightop, who do you think it is?"

"I'm not in the mood to play games. What do you want?"

Her green eyes narrowed, and her lips tightened. Scared or mad she could look fierce. Her quick temper rose but he knew it would dissipate just as fast.

Laughter from the other end of the phone could be heard. Quickly pulling his phone from his back pocket, he tapped the record icon and lay his phone on the counter. Red's eyes met his and held.

"I just wanted to see how you were doing since you saw what a great job I did on Sergio or what is it you called him? Twitch?"

"If you don't have anything productive to say, I'm ending this call right now."

More laughter and his temper started to rise. This asshole wanted to play cat and mouse with her.

"I simply wanted to offer you an invitation."

"An invitation to what?"

"I thought you and me should have a sit down. Since I know you were paying Twitch, I thought maybe you'd like to pay me something to go away."

"Huh, you think the Indiana State Police will pay you to go away from Indiana? Then what, you'll set up shop in a different state? Or come back in a few years and do it again?"

"Look, Hightop, I think we can make a great deal here. You get what you want, we move our operation out of the state, and I get paid to move said operation. It seems like we both win."

He shook his head no. She was not going to meet with this asshole. She would not make a deal with them. They didn't buy off criminals to make their problems go away, they put them in jail where they ceased all drug operations.

She looked away from him and his heart began a rapid cadence.

"Where do you propose this meeting take place?"

No. No. No.

He wrapped his hand around her right upper arm to get her attention, but she shrugged him away.

"Glad to see you might be interested. I'll call you in one hour to discuss this further."

The line went dead and she grabbed her phone and ended the call. He stopped the recording on his phone, both angry and bewildered at the lengths she would go to get this operation off the streets.

"Red, you cannot be thinking about meeting with him? It'll be a set up and you could end up dead."

"I'm going to explore all of my options, Ace. I've been working on this case for more than two years. I'm getting close. Last night told me that. This morning confirmed it. They know I'm getting close too or they wouldn't have gone to such lengths. And to offer to move out for money, that's a new one. They must be getting nervous."

She tapped a few times on her phone then held it to her ear. "Plus, I'm up for promotion next month, I want it."

She tapped her phone a couple of times put it to her ear then waited, "Ben, they've made contact and want to meet to discuss me paying them off to move from Indiana."

His guts twisted; she could not be considering this.

Moving back to the stove and flipping the sandwiches into the hot frying pan he braced himself for the inevitable. Then it dawned on him, this is what bothered him about her all those years ago. Her confidence scared the shit out of him because it was easy to be too confident. Being too confident got people killed.

His eyes glazed as he watched the cheese on their sandwiches begin to drip down the bread and onto the hot pan, then bubble and brown. Flipping each sandwich over, the aroma of his favorite sandwich wafted in the puffs of steam that rose from the pan. His stomach growled then tightened as he heard Red end her call with, "I'll wait for your call."

14

She was close, so close. Once she finally brought down this drug syndicate, she'd get that promotion. Then could have her pick of other jobs either within the DEA or FBI where she'd be an FBI Special Agent until the age of 57. She could really set down some roots. That's all she really wanted. All her years in the service she'd moved from base to base. Then she left the Army and went to college so she could join the DEA. After her training in the DEA, she was transferred as Special Agent to a few different Divisions over the years. Once she'd gotten her position in the Chicago IL DEA Division and was assigned to the Indianapolis District Office, she thought she'd finally have a place to call home base. But in the three years she'd been in Indy, she'd been on one assignment or another either with her District's teams or on her own helping law enforcement agencies more than she'd been at the District Office. She knew this would be her life when she joined the DEA, but she was growing tired of it all.

Looking around here at Rory's home she felt cheated of this. A home. A dog. Maybe a couple of babies. She was still young enough to have them, though at 37, she was nearing the end of her career fighting drug cartels, suppliers, syndicates. DEA Special Agents couldn't be older than 37, so it was earn this promotion for the job she wanted or be transferred to some other location and feel like a newbie again and be located who knew where. And time for bearing children was ticking away.

"Red?"

Glancing up at Rory, he held two plates with the most delicious looking sandwiches on them. He nodded to the table and she tried to smile, but her brain was already working on possible scenarios.

Sitting at the table, in front of one of the sandwiches, Rory walked to the refrigerator and pulled two more beers from the bottom shelf. Twisting the tops on each of them, he tossed the caps in the garbage, then came and sat at a right angle to her. Handing her a bottle he nodded, but he didn't smile, and her stomach tightened. He was mad.

"Smells good, Ace. I didn't know you cooked."

"I love cooking. I haven't had the time to cook lately, and this is nothing compared to some of the meals I've learned to make, but it's pretty fucking good."

She picked up one half of the sandwich and bit into it. She hadn't had breakfast and the morning had been a bit of a blur, but her stomach appreciated her eating now and it was fantastic.

"Omigod." She tried talking with her mouth full of sandwich and choose to wait until she finished so she didn't make a pig of herself.

Swallowing and taking a swig of beer, she continued, "Ace, this is wonderful."

"Thanks." He bit into his sandwich and looked out the sliding doors on to the backyard.

Taking his lead, she quietly ate her sandwich trying to puzzle out what she had that was getting her near enough to scare this operation out in the open.

"Do you want to talk about it?"

She looked into his eyes and realized he was allowing her to piece things together out loud.

"I do." She finished half of her sandwich, then took another drink of beer.

"Twitch has been informing for me for about five years. At first it was petty stuff. Then it became bigger stuff. His reasons were his own, but what I deduced was that his nephew got hooked pretty bad on drugs and OD'd. It made him realize what he'd been doing, and he started turning on the people who supplied him. We brought down a couple of low-level pushers. A few street thugs and dealers and an enforcer for one of the suppliers. Then, something changed, I don't know what. Twitch started telling me about "The Big Guy". He'd disappear for a while and then come back with information. I asked him once if he was going in deeper to get me information and he only said, "Worth it.""

Wiping her fingers on the white paper napkin alongside her plate, she changed her position on her chair, folding her left leg under her right and twisting slightly to face him.

"Then, last week he told me about the deal going down last night. I think what you saw was simply a low-level street dealer who'd just gotten a large load to distribute. I do think it's happening in one of those apartments next to the convenience store where you had parked. It's too much of a coincidence that I'd be told to go to the apartment complex to see the big drop and then that Twitch would be found dead outside of the Longstone Apartment building only for "The Big Guy" or whoever to see us leave this morning. So, I'm thinking there's a vantage point in one of those upper apartments that they use probably in Longstone given its location. They must be able to see a point of interest or have some reason that they've chosen that place. And, it seems unlikely that a high-level trafficker would hole up in a shitty apartment building unless it is very profitable. So, it appears that's the place I've been looking for."

Rory twisted to face her head on and leaned forward on the table. "Why here? What is it about Lynyrd Station? They could blend in easier in a larger city."

"Right, but what do you have here that is more attractive than blending in?"

"Off the top of my head, I'm thinking a supply system. After

Limitless was taken down by the cops and Victor Santarino was killed, Mangus went into hiding, but continued the family's illegal activities. Mangus was moving and smuggling some things, including arms and jewels, underground through tunnels near his hideout at the bottom of Ryker Mountain. Mangus' minions dug tunnels through the mountain so they could move without being seen. There was always a suspicion that the Santarinos were moving drugs as well as arms and jewels."

"Okay, who has access to those tunnels now?"

"There was a huge shootout that brought down Mangus and his gang. It's a result of the shootout mostly that the family and former minions, whose pictures I showed you, are dead or in prison. Dodge Sager, who's a friend of Ford and me, took Mangus down. I'll have to check but once all the law enforcement agencies were finished with their investigations, since the property on Ryker Mountain is owned by the Santarinos or one of their companies and the family must still have access to it. But, any of them that were in the United States are either dead or in prison."

Leaning back, she pushed her hands through her hair and into a ponytail at her crown. Rory's eyes floated to her arms, then down to her chest, then back up to her eyes. It made her feel sexy. Alive. Wanted. Gawd she'd missed feeling like that. She'd folded herself up into her career these past few years and just made work her life. Had she been stupid all these years? When she looked at how Rory had made a home and tried living a normal life, she realized how she'd fallen so short at making any kind of life for herself.

"We should check with Immigration and Homeland Security to see if they have travel records of any members of the Santarino family. You should check with DEA since we know that some of their activity internationally was drug trafficking."

He pulled his phone from his pants pocket and tapped a couple of times.

"Captain, can we have someone check with Immigration and Homeland Security to see if the Santarinos or anyone associated with them traveled to the US in the past year?"

15

Beautiful. Smart. Sexy. Badass. All rolled up in a creamy-skinned, redhead who made his heart race. Why did life have to keep putting them in proximity with each other only to pull them apart? His life was here. This was his home. His parents were here. Debra was buried here. His siblings were here. Most of all, he loved it here. He had a gorgeous home, friends, a fantastic job. He had it all. Except her.

Picking up their empty dishes he loaded them in the dishwasher, wiped down the counter, walked to the laundry room and tossed the dishrag in the washer, then came back to the kitchen. Red had gotten up and walked to the living room. Her silhouette shown in the large floor to ceiling windows looking out on to the backyard, the light created shadows. The shadow of her form wholly appealing. Inhaling deeply, he walked into the living room as his phone rang.

"Richards." He snapped, surprised at his own terseness.

"None of the Santarinos are here in the States. The daughter, Francesca is out of prison and back in Italy. Rumor has it she's learning the ropes from grandpa, but that's none of our business now; Italian authorities need to deal with their own shit."

"Thanks, Captain. Who is controlling Mangus' hideout on Ryker Mountain and any other buildings and land here in the States that the Santarinos or their companies own? The building Limitless is in, the home on the mountain Victor used and especially all those tunnels they dug "

He could hear his Captain clicking on his keyboard, while his own eyes were glued to Red. She turned to stare at him, just as eager for information as he was.

"The Limitless International building and land is for sale, sitting empty now and listed with a realtor in town, Van Steel Realty. It's been empty since authorities shut the place down."

He sat in his recliner, elbows on his knees. "Does anyone go in periodically and check to make sure no one is using the place for illegal operations?"

He heard his Captain take a deep breath. "We don't have authority. We could see if the realtor minded letting us in, but she doesn't have to."

Red nodded her head and he agreed with her. "I think it's worth a shot, Captain. Maybe that's something Tucker and I could do. I know Margery Van Steel from my shooting pool days. Maybe she'd do me a solid."

"I don't see that that could do any harm. But, try not to get in trouble. I'll send Officer Delhurst to back you up in case there's trouble. Let me know when you've made contact and keep me posted on what you find. Also, evidence has been uploaded, so you two need to look it over and write up a report."

The line went dead before he could say anything more. They were short staffed at the department and having him and Red off the beat for a while sure didn't help. Maybe they'd get lucky and find something at Limitless.

"Evidence is uploaded, Red. I'll log you in on to my computer while I call Maggie, and see if we can get her to let us in Limitless."

"What if she doesn't let us in?"

He stood, suddenly weary beyond reason. "A rock through a window might be enough to let us go and check things out."

Her smile was brilliant. "I love the way you think, Ace. I had you pegged for straight-laced and buttoned-up. Glad to see I was wrong."

"The Santarinos brought a lot of shit to this town and we thought we were finished with them. So doing something outside the lines a bit isn't the worst thing to make sure they truly are shut down for business. Ford has it made with his company. They color outside the lines quite a bit. But they get shit done. But, of course, they're not cops like we are."

"You've mentioned this company before; I'm intrigued beyond reason."

Shaking his head he silently chastised himself. "I can't really discuss it, Red. If he wants to share it, that's his business."

"Fair enough." She shrugged her slender shoulders and walked toward his office. Her scent wafted to him as she passed and goose-bumps formed on his arms. He needed to put some distance between them and soon.

He let out a long breath and followed Red into the office. She stood staring at his computer, which was running a slide show of pictures, mostly of Debra and him in their better times. Some of him in the service. Some of his siblings Rochelle, Rourke and Rowan at Christmas. A picture of Debra laughing at him at his mom and dad's anniversary party slid onto the screen and Red's head cocked to the side.

"She looks happy."

"I suppose she was then." He moved to shake his mouse and stop the pictures. She reached out and took his hand before he could do that.

"Were you happy?"

She turned then so they were facing each other, and he saw seriousness in her eyes. He cleared his throat.

"I was at first."

"But not later?"

"No." His voice was quiet, as if saying it out loud made him a bad person.

Her hand cupped his cheek.

"Why?" Now her voice was quiet.

"Red, this is a heavy conversation..."

"Why?"

Inhaling deeply, he let it out slowly and tried to relax.

"At first she was a lot like you. Confident. Strong. Independent. Then she grew needy. She hated my job because it often kept me out late or had me up early. She liked consistency; I couldn't offer that. She grew more and more depressed. I grew more and more irritated, frustrated and pulled in multiple directions. On the day she was killed, we'd had a fight. Afterward, she still was very upset; she'd packed a bag for a few days and was going to stay with her parents for a while. We were never able to work it out because she was killed on her way to their place."

Her arms wrapped around his shoulders and pulled him to her body as she whispered. "Oh, Ace. I'm so sorry. That's a lot of guilt to hold on to."

Wrapping his arms around her waist, he pulled her close and enjoyed the way her body curved into his. When he held her like this, it felt like they were made for each other. Just like this. Working together. Making love. Talking. Understanding.

As if she read his thoughts, she said, "Not everyone understands people like us."

16

He hugged her tightly, his arms strong and solid around her and she never felt more secure. When his head dipped down to rest against hers, so they were temple to temple, the roughness of his whiskers against her cheek sent shivers the length of her body. The gruffness in his voice when he whispered in her ear, "Not many do, but I know you do." Well, that sent a riot of emotions running through her body and mind.

She closed her eyes against the moisture forming in them. The harsh reality was that they once again lived in different places and had careers to tend to. Careers that they'd both worked their entire lives to earn and they were more than a hundred miles apart on the map.

He kissed her temple then and bent over his computer, shaking the mouse to stop the photographs from scrolling past, and quickly logged on to the police database so she could look at evidence. He then sat in a chair across the room, his relaxed posture belying his emotions because she'd felt the slight tremors that ran through his body just now. She felt them, too.

Out of the corner of her eye she watched him pull his cell phone from his pocket, and scroll through what she assumed were phone numbers, then tapped on one and sat back in the chair, crossing his left ankle over his right knee.

"Maggie, it's Rory, how are you?"

He smiled at what this Maggie said in his ear and she pushed down that little green monster that threatened to rise up.

"No, not interested in selling, I just got things the way I like them, think I'll enjoy it for a while."

His chuckle was deep in his chest and genuine, she must be a friend, but hopefully not a former lover.

"No, I understand you're selling the Limitless International building and properties. I wondered if it would be possible to go in and take a look around?"

Scrolling quickly past the pictures of Twitch's carved up face and hunk of tongue lying alongside his body, she'd leave that for the forensic lab, she was mostly interested in anything that led them to one of the apartments.

"How much?" He whistled. "That's rather steep for a tainted building and land."

Dropping his crossed leg, he leaned forward, placed his elbows on his knees, his eyes cast down to the hardwood floor between his feet.

"Okay, what do you need. I can get the pre-approval this afternoon."

Appearing at the opposite side of the desk, he leaned forward and grabbed a pen laying alongside the computer she worked on. Pulling a post-it note from a wire holder on the desktop, he wrote a string of numbers, then an email address.

"Okay, I'll be in touch in a bit. Take care."

Ending his call, he began dialing another number and she continued to read the evidence with halfhearted interest.

"Captain, I need to get a bank pre-approval for the purchase of the Limitless real estate before we can get in. Put it in Alice Thomas' name."

Her eyes looked across the desktop where his impressive package or at least the zipper of his Khakis was facing her. Frustrated with herself for the thoughts she was thinking and maybe more importantly, the one's she wasn't, she reminded herself she was a grown-ass woman and not a teenager. But, he did have a nice package. One of the best.

"Four million dollars."

She could hear the Captain's voice on the other end of the phone, and he sounded rather stressed. I suppose putting the department on the line for four million dollars was a bit of a stressor, but for some reason, it made her smile.

"I'll wait to hear from you."

He tapped his phone then set it on the desk. "Do you have anything of interest yet?"

Oops, she'd better start paying attention. "Not yet."

Pulling her head together she dove into the evidence file and began reading the police report, the evidence database, the forensic report, and the Medical Examiner's report. Once she'd finished with that police report, she came across the police reports from last night and looked those over checking the witness statements for similarities. There were four in total, from different residents of the apartment complex. They read the same, shots fired, yelling, drug deals going down in the common area between the buildings, needles, lighters, light bulbs found lying around all the time. The complaints went on and on.

Rory left the room and came back in a few minutes later, set a laptop on the desk, then pulled the chair up to the other side. Opening the top, he began typing then finally said to her, "I'm in the evidence database. What have you found so far?"

"How many computers do you have here?"

His eyes landed on hers, a slight amount of humor in them, "Why does it matter?"

Shaking her head, she honestly didn't know why. "This house is much more expensive than most cops can afford. You have fantastic furniture. Not one but two computers, one a laptop, state of the art security. What gives, Ace?"

Inhaling deeply, he leaned forward slightly, his voice lowered and took on a gruffness usually only heard when he made love to her.

"You think I'm dirty, Red?"

"No, you've always been too honest for that. But, how can you make it like this?"

It became more important than she cared to admit, and not because of the money, but because of the mystery of the money. If that made sense.

"Red, I don't like talking about this stuff, but so I can ease your beautiful mind, I happen to have a fair amount of money. My grandparents made a good living, very good. Entrepreneurial his whole life, my grandfather started several businesses in his days. When they died, my siblings and I inherited. When Debra died, I inherited again. She was from an incredibly wealthy family, not that it mattered because we never asked for a dime from either side of our families. But, I had to lose people in order to become a wealthy man. I try hard not to flaunt it, but the work I do, we do, requires a lot of mental fortitude. When I come home, I want my sanctuary. A place I can unwind, settle in and utilize to equalize my stressors. So, I spent a fair amount of money on this house and setting it up to suit me. And, my car, I spent money on her."

Leaning back in her chair she assessed his eyes, his features, and concluded that he wasn't lying.

"Usually rich boys don't join the military and serve, how many tours, three? How did your family feel about that?"

His right shoulder raised and lowered. "They weren't thrilled with my choice, but they respected it. What they're not happy about now is my job. But, we just agree to disagree on that."

Nodding she saw him in a new light. He wasn't spoiled and living on the family trust fund, he was admirable in a whole new way to her. As if that was possible.

His phone rang and he tapped the speaker icon. "Captain, what do you have?"

17

He hated talking about his money. Either people wanted something from you afterward or they treated you differently. Most of his coworkers didn't even know how much money he had. Of course, they knew his grandparents were wealthy, after all it was a small town. But they naturally assumed his parents inherited that money. He'd heard a couple of cops gossiping once about him and he'd shut that down right away.

Now he stood in his kitchen waiting for Red to grab her shoes so they could go over to the Limitless building. He felt restless and a little bit relieved. Which was a surprise to him to feel relieved that Red knew about his money. That was new.

The sound of her running down the steps, a new vigor in them now that they'd been sprung from house arrest. It was horrible feeling trapped. It was also nearing 6:00 p.m. and would be dark soon, not that they were actually looking at the building to purchase, but he wanted Maggie to think so.

"All set, Ace. I feel like I'm being released from prison." Her smile was infectious.

"Me, too." He started for the garage as soon as she'd reached him, and he had to stop himself from reaching out and grabbing her hand. Giving his head a slight shake, he opened the door to the garage and stepped back to allow her to precede him. She did with a smile on her face and damn if it didn't make him feel good.

She climbed into the passenger side of his car and he jumped in the driver's side, tapped the button to open the garage door and started her up. The roar of the V-8 engine always gave him a thrill and he couldn't help the smile that appeared on his face.

"Sexy sound." Red whispered.

He simply nodded his agreement.

"Okay, so Maggie is a friend from back when I shot pool for the Copper Cup. She used to tend bar there until her real estate business took off. She's smart, savvy, and very good at reading people. We need to go in as if we're purchasing for your family. She doesn't know you; she doesn't know your family. So, let's say you're a friend from the service here scoping out the building and I came along with you for fun."

"You think she'll buy that?"

"I don't know. But, what she needs to do is relay that information to whoever in the Santarino family has hired her. As to what she really believes, I highly doubt she'll relay any thoughts to them. She just wants to make a commission."

"Okay. That's plausible."

"And, Officer Delhurst will meet us there as a precaution."

"What are you telling Maggie about that?"

He chuckled. "He's your security detail."

She laughed and it was amazing. He glanced over to see her smiling face and it was like the sun shone right into the car. Stunning.

She was quiet for a while and it was pleasant riding and not feeling tension.

"Is Maggie an old girlfriend?"

"Nope."

"Friend with benefits?"

"Nope."

Glancing over at her he saw a slight smile on her face, and he couldn't help the grin on his.

"Were you jealous?"

"Nope."

They both laughed.

"She had a baby around seven months ago. The father is rather mysterious. No one's seen him and rumor has it he's some wealthy businessman from out of town."

"Rumors, sometimes they have a ring of truth to them."

Pulling into the Limitless parking lot, Delhurst's cruiser was already there but he wasn't inside. Red noticed it too as he could see her scanning the outside of the building looking for him. Maggie's car wasn't in the lot yet, so he must have been walking around alone.

Stopping in front of the main door, he put the Charger in Park and undid his seat belt. Delhurst appeared around the East corner of the building to their left and they both relaxed.

"Ready?" he asked, knowing full well she was.

"Let's do this."

Her phone rang then, and she pulled it from the pocket of her jacket, looked at the readout and said, “It’s the number from this morning.”

“Go ahead and answer it.”

“What?” She answered and he at once admired her spunk and worried she was too brash. He also had to remind himself that she’d been doing this for years and she had her methods.

“I’ve thought about it; but I’m not interested in working on your behalf to ask the State of Indiana to pay you to do anything. You’re a criminal and neither Indiana nor the USA negotiates with criminals.”

She pulled her phone from her ear and tapped the speaker icon.

“Well you paid Twitch to snitch for you.”

“You don’t know anything about what I did and didn’t do with Twitch.”

“I think you need to mind your manners, Hightop. I believe I’m calling the shots here. I can easily cut your tongue out and carve up your face just like Twitch, so watch yourself.”

The line went dead and he saw Red take a deep breath. “He’s scared about something.”

She opened her door and hopped out ready to get to work. He shook his head, unsure of his feelings about her being threatened and her casual attitude concerning it. But, then he remembered, this was the Red he’d known except now she also was an experienced DEA Special Agent. She loved the action.

Delhurst stopped on the sidewalk in front of the door, waiting for them to reach him.

"Checking the perimeter, Delhurst?"

Nodding, he replied. "Yes, sir. Just in case there was anything going on."

"See anything?"

"No, sir."

A car pulling into the lot had them all turning to see a gleaming white Cadillac Escalade stopping alongside Rory's car. Maggie popped out of her car, a huge smile on her face, her dark hair shining in the waning streams of sunlight, her over-sized sunglasses reflecting the rays off the little rhinestones on the bows.

Maggie walked to him; her slender form tightly encased in a black pencil skirt with a white blouse tucked into it. A large gold chain hung around her neck and a substantial diamond bracelet glittered on her wrist. She screamed expensive.

"Rory, so good to hear from you and now see you. I got the pre-approval for Ms. Thomas a while ago, so we're all set."

She hugged him and he hugged her back, though not like he'd hugged Red earlier and it sure didn't feel as warm and inviting as Red's hug had felt. Weird.

"Maggie, I'd like you to meet Alice Thomas. She's a friend from the military and her family is interested in moving one of their businesses to Lynyrd Station. I'm along for the ride."

Maggie held out her hand and Red promptly grasped it and

shook. By the ever-so-slight grimace on Maggie's face, he believed Red probably made sure the handshake was firm. Showing her dominance at the beginning, that was so Red.

"Okay, well let's start inside. I see you brought police protection."

He responded first. "Yes, Alice's father is rather protective and he's heard about some of our issues here lately; it almost caused him to reconsider this place. But the Mayor has been trying to get someone in this building for a while and talked him into giving us a chance in Lynyrd Station."

"I'm so glad he rethought pulling out. We all know you are working feverishly to stop the recent flood of crime . It's only a matter of time and it'll be gone."

Using her phone to unlock the lockbox that held the key, Maggie inserted it into the deadbolt on the door; she opened it wide allowing them to precede her then quickly turned on the lights.

The air was surprisingly fresh for an empty, locked up building and he knew Red was thinking the same thing. Her red hair gleamed in the overhead lights, but her eyes were taking in everything. He saw her nose flare and twitch slightly as she was sniffing the air trying to puzzle out a few things that already didn't add up.

"Would you like to see the upstairs first or the main level?" Maggie asked.

Red smiled at her before responding, "I'd like to see the upstairs first if you don't mind."

"Certainly." Maggie walked to the left of the doorway that lead to a staircase. They each walked up quietly, he following Red and Delhurst behind him.

On the second floor Maggie switched the lights on and the pristinely polished dark wood floors gleamed under the lights. Walking to the end of the long hallway, Maggie opened the door, reached in and flipped the switch but stood outside of the office.

"This was the President's office. As you'll see it's beautifully appointed."

The white carpeting muffled the sounds of their footsteps and in its place made a swishing sound as they each entered the room. The mahogany desk was clear except for a telephone, a desk lamp, and a small wooden holder for pens. Everything was neat and tidy and while you could imagine someone loving to have this office, he knew the dirty secrets it held and to him, there was no appeal at all.

A small conference table stood to the right, and a credenza behind the desk held a neatly stacked pile of folders, which seemed out of place in the room.

Officer Delhurst walked to the stack of folders and glanced down but then turned to face them. Red looked around then stepped out of the room, and he and Delhurst followed.

They did the same type of perusal of the other offices on the second floor and he recognized Skye's office from Lincoln's description of it. He could picture her in this room, it wasn't nearly as pretentious as the others, which was Skye Winters. She was gorgeous and would make many models feel lacking, but she wasn't pretentious in the slightest.

Entering the break room, they had seen enough, and descended the stairs to the main level. Since this was the area that was largely an art gallery when the Santarinos were alive, there was a vast open space, gleaming floors and five-star bathrooms but little else.

"Okay, what do you think so far?" Maggie asked.

"It's impressive, but I would like to see the loading docks and shipping areas," Red responded.

Maggie's smile faltered which was unusual, of course a buyer would want to see the whole building. But, she caught herself and turned to lead them to the back of the main gallery area and through a door. A short hallway led them to another door which opened to a metal staircase leading down to the shipping area.

Red's back straightened and she stepped down from the bottom step and her eyes scanned the entire area. Delhurst was alert as well, walking slowly around the perimeter of the room. At one point he bent over and picked something up and dropped it in a nearby garbage can and then kept on moving. Looking at each of the dock doors, Red surveyed the area and he rather enjoyed watching her work.

She turned to Maggie and said, "If my father would like to come and take a look at it, will you be available later this week?"

"Of course." Maggie's smile returned and she promptly pulled a spec sheet and a business card from the folio she carried and handed the information to Red. "I'll email you the other specs I have on the building just let me know if you're interested. My email is on the card and, of course, Rory knows how to reach me as well."

Red smiled, but it didn't reach her eyes. "Yes, of course, Rory knows how to reach you."

18

Rory's door chimed as he got in his car and waited as she hesitated and glanced around as if surveying the area. What she was really doing was watching Maggie out of the corner of her eye. The look Maggie leveled on Delhurst sent a chill through her, something was up. She climbed into the passenger seat, buckled her seat belt, and asked, "How well do you know her? And, no I'm not jealous, but there's something off about her and I can't put my finger on it."

He started the car and put it in reverse, easing out of the parking space before Maggie. "I don't know her all that well, I suppose. As I told you, she was a bartender while I shot pool and I knew she was also working real estate. She's called me a few times over the past couple of years to see if I was interested in selling my house, but nothing more than that. And, I mentioned her baby daddy is a mystery as well."

"Do you know anyone who knows her better?"

He navigated the car out of the parking lot, his eyes scanning the darkening road in the diminishing sunlight.

"I can make some inquiries. What specifically are you looking for, personal information or business as in her real estate sales history?"

"Personal."

He wasn't looking at this like an outsider and that had been his mistake all along; he knew these people too well and trusted them, at least as much as a cop can. In that way, she had the advantage.

"Let me think on who I can call."

She nodded. "What about this Jared that Ford mentioned."

"Red, you want to color outside the lines?"

"Sometimes we have to be inventive. Is it really coloring outside the lines to gather information? I just want something that can lead me in a legal direction to search. Is she selling so much real estate that she can afford the Cadillac, diamond bracelet, thick gold chain and have her nails and hair done regularly?"

"But, if we do have to go to court or prove our trail is legit, we have to account for how we got the intel."

"May. It sounds like you don't want me digging into your 'friend's' life. Care to share?" The edge to her voice took on a different tone and she reminded herself not to let this get personal. Sure, Maggie was gorgeous and everything she wasn't. Sophisticated. Womanly. A smart dresser.

His voice broke into her self-defeating thoughts. "Nope."

He tapped the call icon on his dash and the robotic voice activated, "Please say a command."

"Call Jared Timms."

"Calling Jared Timms."

Jared's phone ringing sounded on the speaker system in the car.

"Yeah."

Rory chuckled, "Hey Jared, it's Rory."

"Dude, I know who it is. What can I do for you?"

"What can you find out about Margery Van Steel? Mostly personal. She has a mysterious baby daddy, and she's driving a brand-new Cadillac Escalade and dripping in jewelry. Is she selling that much real estate or is baby daddy funding her expensive lifestyle?"

"Okay, you know this costs, right?"

"Yep, no worries there."

Jared chuckled on the other end of the phone. "I know, man."

The call ended and the car was silent for a while.

"I take it he knows about your money."

Rory inhaled deeply and let it out slowly. "Red, there's very little Jared doesn't know."

Rory pulled his car into the garage and shut it off.

"I know we had a late lunch, but I'm getting a bit hungry, how about pizza and a couple of beers?"

She sighed, "That sounds fantastic."

It did. For all of Maggie's polish and poise she highly doubted the woman would drink beer and eat pizza. And again, what was it that bugged her so about Maggie? Seriously she needed to get her out of her head.

She followed Rory to the door and when he opened the door then stood back to let her go in before him, she got goosebumps on her arms. It was thrilling to have a man be solicitous to her. She'd played the tough cookie for all of her life and usually men just treated her like one of the guys, which generally, she liked. But, with Rory, she didn't want to be a guy; she was a woman and damn it all anyway, she was majorly attracted to Rory Richards. Even if her heart would be broken in a few days. Again. Likely forever.

She walked into the kitchen and stopped at the counter as his strong arms wrapped around her from behind.

His deep voice, took on a slight gruffness as he whispered in her ear, "I enjoy watching you work, Red. You're an impressive woman. Beautiful. Strong. Smart. The whole package."

Her nipples pebbled and a warm sensation ran through her body and landed between her legs. The warmth of his body against her back brought back a flood of memories of their afternoon sexcapades and she wanted to feel like that again. Wanted in such a powerful way, he didn't even hesitate to take her.

She pushed her ass back into the hardness she felt burgeoning behind his zipper and was met with his right hand sliding down her body to hold her hip as he pushed harder into her rear end.

"Red." His voice was barely above a whisper and sounded as if he was struggling to keep himself in check. The thought of his losing control with her sent another flood of emotions running through her body. She pushed back again only to have his arms wrap tighter around her body, holding her captive against him. His lips found her ear and his tongue dipped inside just a bit then his teeth nipped the outer edges.

"You want it again Red 'cause I sure do."

"Yes." She could barely get the word out her breathing was so stilted.

He released her and spun her around, his lips capturing hers firmly, before softening and caressing her lips in such a provocative way. Soft, wet lips danced with hers, coaxing her to give him more and more of her. His tongue slid into her mouth, touching each surface, mating with her tongue, his hardness pushing against her hitting that spot that was likely to drive her wild if he kept it up.

"This time, I intend to watch you."

Gawd. Right now she couldn't even form words.

He lifted her and her legs immediately wrapped around his hips as he carried her to the bedroom. Periodically he nipped at her throat, her jaw and her earlobe, just enough to feel but not to cause pain and she wanted more.

He lay her on the bed, his voice now gruff and rugged, just as she liked it. "Take your clothes off while I watch you. On the bed. I want to see you wiggle around."

The dimness of the light in this room lent itself to romance. Small shafts of light filtered in from the living room and a small night light on the wall added a yellowish hue to the room. She could see his features as she unbuttoned her blouse, slowly and he pulled his shirt over his head in a millisecond and let it drop to the floor.

Wriggling out of her blouse, he smiled and undid the button and zipper of his pants, pushing them down his sexy, firm hips and stepping out of them, his eyes never left her body. She arched her back to unfasten her bra and he smiled, though it was Cheshire cat like, he was a man whose prey was performing for him. As soon as her bra loosened, she pulled it off and let it lay on the bed, her hands immediately began unbuttoning her slacks and she wasn't sure who was more eager, him or her.

His briefs came off and he stood before her like a stone god, his muscles still perfectly formed, though he was a fuller version of the boy she knew in years past, he was now incredibly sexy and so sure of himself. He excited her. His full thick cock stood at the ready and she couldn't wait for him to enter her because she remembered the feeling of him filling her and it was simply perfection.

Wiggling out of her pants she quickly tucked her thumbs into the waistband of her panties and pushed them down her legs, now almost panting with excitement.

"Spread your legs, Red, show me."

She did as he asked and was greeted with a sexy smile.

"Simply perfection." He husked out and then his fingers toyed with her curls, at first lightly brushing them, which caused her to squirm, then firmer as he parted her folds, dipped his forefinger inside of her and spread her juices along the outside and around her clit. She couldn't stop the moan that escaped her throat and his grin told her he liked that. Dipping his finger in again he slid in and out a few times, each time going in deeper and pulling out only slightly.

His wet fingers toyed with her clit, adding pressure as she squirmed, "Show me your boiling point, Red."

She moved her hips so his fingers found that perfect spot and he began manipulating her clit in earnest, sending her spiraling out of control and finally crying out her orgasm.

Before her eyes opened, he climbed over her, both of his legs between hers. "That was fantastic. You should see your face when you cum, Red, it's stunning."

He positioned his cock at her entrance while looking into her eyes. Her legs raised to wrap around his waist and he grinned. "Now, I'm going to watch you again while I cum."

He pushed inside of her and the feeling was glorious. She felt full and the sensations as his cock filled and pulled out and filled her again sending shivers down her arms and legs. They were a perfect match size wise and after a few thrusts he ground himself against her swollen clit and her eyes rolled back it felt so fantastic.

He chuckled and she opened her eyes to see he was still watching her, and his pace increased. His thrusts grew firmer, and if possible, he went in deeper. His left arm moved down to under her right leg, lifting her slightly and she felt him seat himself fully inside of her and she moaned. She thought he said "yes" but she couldn't be sure where his voice began and hers did. They were in unison, both of them breathing heavily, both of them working to give the other pleasure while achieving it for themselves, too.

"I'm close, Red, come on."

His thrusts now showed his eagerness to climax and she moved her hips so he hit her clit in the perfect way. It only took a few thrusts and her head flew back as she moaned her climax and he thrust once more and let his release flow. A few small thrusts later they were both spent, and their heavy breathing lulled her to a blissful sleep.

19

Sliding the pizza he'd just made into the oven, he set the timer then pulled two beers from the refrigerator. He'd done it, he'd lost his heart to Red again. This time it would likely hurt more when she left. He heard his shower shut off and knew she'd be out soon, just in time to eat, then they'd likely just chill. They still had some evidence to look over and hopefully they'd call it an early night. The brief nap they'd taken a while ago would only last for so long.

His phone rang and he pulled it from his pocket.

Glancing briefly at the read out, he answered, "Hey Jared, what have you found?"

Red walked out of the bedroom, her long red hair damp from the shower but she looked fresh faced and happy. Relaxed and satisfied. Damn, he loved that look on her.

"So, for some reason Maggie's kid's birth records are sealed. Why does someone do that? My thinking is baby daddy is married."

"That's what I figured with all the secrecy."

"Yeah, so anyway, I'll keep digging, I've got a couple other ideas, just giving you an update."

"Thanks, Jared." The line was already dead before he got the words out of his mouth.

Red came into the kitchen, a soft smile on her face and he handed her one of the beers he'd just opened. Her warm fresh smelling body pressed against his and her lips landed on his in a soft wet kiss. When she pulled away his lips tingled.

"So, no news?"

"Naw, just that the baby's birth records are sealed, but he's still working on it."

He turned and saw that he hadn't wiped the light dusting of flour from making the pizza crust off the counter and grabbed the dish cloth off the sink. Wiping a swath through the flour, he pulled open the door that held the waste basket and swept the flour into the basket.

Alice exclaimed, "That's it. That's what's been bugging me."

A quick glance saw her staring at the counter. He stopped wiping and waited for her to continue.

"It's been bugging me since we were at the Limitless building. Now I know what it is. By two of the dock doors the dust on the floor had been disturbed. Like the loading docks are still being used. Did you notice that?"

"No, I didn't notice that, I was looking around for crates with drugs in them."

"Well they aren't going to leave that laying around, and since you called Maggie earlier to inquire, there was time for anything to be moved, except a stack of folders in the big office upstairs and whatever it was that Delhurst picked up and tossed in the garbage can. Everything else was pristine. Too pristine for an empty building."

He watched her mind working and it was a marvel. "Don't you think they'd keep it clean for showings?"

Her nose scrunched a bit before she replied. "Maybe, but the loading docks are just that. Industrial and I've been in a ton of buildings, Ace, they're usually not so clean."

"Okay. I'm following."

"So, Maggie calls whoever from the Santarino family hired her and says, 'We have a showing today, and the party is pre-approved.' Then, whoever is still using the building runs over quickly and removes anything they don't want the party to see. Could we be lucky enough to have cameras in the area?"

"I can check but Limitless is out there by itself and we can't record private property without permission."

"How about truck rental places or a warehouse where large trucks are stored. Something that could move large quantities."

"How large do you think these shipments are?"

"Usually it's not the drugs they need all the space for. Drugs are shipped inside coffee cans and other aromatic substances to throw off the drug sniffing dogs. They are often transported with other products to mask their detection They're also packaged smaller and placed into boxes and crates here and there. I made a big bust a couple of years ago and the drugs were wrapped up tight, stuffed into balloons, tied, and then tucked in olive jars."

"Let me make a couple of calls." He was still holding his phone from Jared's call, so he tapped the Captain's name and waited. Alice walked into the living room and stared blankly out the window, but he knew her mind was working.

"Captain, do we have cameras anywhere near the Limitless building?"

"The closest place we have is the convenience store a half mile down the road."

"Can you have someone check it for any large trucks coming or going around the Limitless building this afternoon after you got me the bank pre-approval so I could go in as a potential buyer?"

"I'll have Callan check it out and give you a call."

"Thanks, Captain."

He ended the call and walked to the office to check on trucking companies in the area. He could hear Red's footsteps going upstairs and he chuckled to himself, she was restless.

His internet browser began populating the area trucking companies, most of which weren't actual trucking companies at all, but had used the keywords in their ads to manipulate searches. As he scrolled through, one larger company jumped out at him as he remembered they'd had financial issues last year, and he wondered if they were still in business. Rush Trucking was located on the outer edge of town on the way to Indianapolis. It wouldn't surprise him if they resorted to hauling illegal substances to save their company and because of their location, no eyebrows would be raised as they headed in that direction out of town. But, they'd be running to Indy and likely other stops in between. Which reminded him to ask Red if there were towns between Lynyrd Station and Indianapolis that were also experiencing a surge of drug activity.

Her footsteps sounding on the stairs as she ran down them, as if she were in a hurry. Her head popped around the door and she said, "I've got to go back, Ace. You don't have to come if you don't want to, but I have to go."

"Wait, Red. It's dangerous and you'd be breaking and entering."

"Maybe, but I have a sneaking suspicion about something, and I just have to check it out."

He stood and walked to her, his hands landed on her shoulders, "Don't jeopardize the investigation, Red."

"I won't. I've done this before. I'll go in and satisfy my hunch, then sneak out and figure out a way to get back in there with a warrant. And, if there are people around and I see something, maybe I'll get lucky."

"Not if you're trespassing."

"Then, as you said before, a broken window just may get us what we need to go in and thoroughly search."

"I'll tell you what, if there's a trucking company they're using, we'll find a way to stop and search one of the trucks once they leave the property."

She kissed him quickly as she laughed. "Now you're talking big guy!"

He followed her from the office and grinned at the excitement in her voice. Turning the oven off and grabbing his keys from the cupboard, he followed her out to the garage and hopped in the car. They were officially investigating and no doubt breaking and entering, but it was the closest he'd felt to a solution to this catastrophic drug problem since it had started again shortly after the Santarinos were killed. And, as he backed his car from the garage the weirdest thought crossed his mind. Red had always been like this, eager and ready to go into a mission. She had confidence in herself that he hadn't had in himself back then. Did this mean he'd grown up?

20

Rory was quiet as they drove, which was fine, she needed the time to prepare herself. Times like this were when her confidence could easily turn into bravado and she could get herself killed. Of course, that would be bad, but what would be worse was to get Rory killed and have to live with it. He wasn't used to this stuff like she was. Indy and her territory were so much larger than Lynyrd Station, not that he wasn't used to making big moves. His training in the Marines had taught him well, and some of the missions they'd gone on during their time in the service reminded her of how strong and true he was. But, they were different when it came to things like this. She wanted to blast in and take names, he wanted to think things through and go by the book. Hopefully they could meet somewhere in the middle. Normally, her fellow DEA agents managed to restrain her gang-buster approach.

Turning down the road that led them to Limitless, she said, "Is there a back way in?"

His head twisted from side to side, then responded. "I can do better than a back way in."

Easing his car down the road he turned on to a lane, which was obscured by brush, over-grown trees and shrubs. He drove slowly a few feet in, then switched his headlights off. The moon was high in the sky which offered them some light, but she struggled to see any sort of driveway or path.

"How do you know where you're going?"

He chuckled, "I used to bring girls back here to park when I was much younger. Years ago, this was the farmland my great-grandparents owned. As generations passed, the land was sold off and no one takes care of it anymore."

She didn't like hearing that he'd brought girls back here to make out with, but of course it was likely that he'd had plenty of them in his day. She still thought he was the most handsome man she'd ever met.

He stopped the car, turned off the ignition, and they sat in silence for a few moments. Soon her eyes adjusted, and she could see through a copse of trees some lights higher in the sky.

"That's the Limitless building and the lights are lighting the parking lot. But, we can make our way on foot to the other side of the building by the loading docks without being seen, hopefully."

"Okay."

As her eyes adapted and the light breeze moved some of the leaves and branches here and there, she could see a bit more of the parking lot and agreed that walking across it would certainly call attention.

"Red, hang tight for a minute."

He reached up to the over-head light and popped the cover from it. Unscrewing the lightbulb inside, he set it in the cup holder, the cover next to it.

"When you get out of the car, the only thing that will illuminate it is the dash lights for a minute, don't slam your door but close it quickly."

"Here, let's do this."

She shrugged out of her jacket and pushed it onto the dash, covering the lights.

She could see his smile in the darkness of the car, his teeth glistened in the moonlight. He leaned forward and kissed her quickly, then opened his car door and hopped out, quickly pushing it to latch. Following suit, she mimicked his movements.

Walking to the front of the car as soon as she reached Rory, he took her hand and led her through the tall weeds easily and quietly, or as quietly as they could with their feet crunching on the downed brush and branches.

As they turned a corner, she could see the Limitless building come into view, her eyes scanning the area to see if anyone was guarding the perimeter of the building. Looking along the top of the building she didn't see any cameras which was a good sign because they wouldn't want evidence of their illegal activities for others to see. One thing she felt confident about, there was illegal activity going on there, she could feel it. All her years in the DEA told her that.

Nearing the edge of the wooded area they had walked through, Rory crouched down to look the area over. She did the same and surveyed the area around the loading docks. It didn't appear that anything looked any differently than it had earlier today, but she just had to go in. She stood and began making her way toward the back of the building. There weren't as many lights in the back of the building as in front, but there were two shining in the back. Deciding she could stay between them to get to a door just under the closest light to them, she moved that way. She could hear Rory's steps behind her, so she kept going forward. Just before she stepped out of the tall grass concealing their position, Rory tugged at her hand.

Leaning in he whispered, "What's your plan?"

"I'm going inside." From her back pocket she pulled out a lock picking tool she'd used dozens of times. "Then, I'm first going upstairs to see what that stack of files was on the credenza; after that I'm going down to the loading docks to see what I can find down there. The fact that Delhurst picked up a piece of something and threw it away when everything else was spotless tells me someone was a little sloppy."

"You think Delhurst is dirty?"

"I don't know, what do you think?"

He shrugged and shook his head. "I don't know that much about him."

She heard him inhale. "Red, you go upstairs, I'll check out the loading dock. If we split up the work, we won't have to be in there as long, the less time the better."

"Okay." Unable to resist the rush she felt just working with him, she stood up on her toes and kissed his lips, brushing her breasts against his chest which earned her a tight squeeze from him and hard nipples for her. Ending their kiss, she turned and quickly made her way to the building, Rory close behind her.

21

Trying not to be impressed he watched as Red made quick work of the lock, then slipped inside the door. He locked it behind them and watched as she made her way to the staircase that would take her up two floors. She didn't look back and part of him felt sadness that her instincts and training took over and he was in second place once again. That is if he'd ever been in first place with her at all.

Pulling his phone out, he switched on the flashlight and began walking to the loading docks to see the dust disturbance Red mentioned earlier. Shining his light on the floor to see what she meant, it did appear as if something had been dragged or pushed to the dock, then slid off into a truck or something else. Not seeing any equipment in the area, no forklifts or pallet jacks, if something was going on here, it was all done by hand.

The second dock door looked the same as the first, a fine line where the dust had been wiped away from the doorway on both sides of the door. He continued walking the perimeter of the room, his footsteps sounded incredibly loud in the vastness of the empty space, the sound bouncing off one cement wall after another magnifying with each bounce. A metal door hidden behind the staircase caught his attention and he remembered seeing it earlier, but for some reason they never went inside. Making his way across the vacant room he stopped just before the door and listened for any sounds coming from behind door number one. Testing to see if the door was locked, he smiled when the knob turned, and he quietly pulled the door open.

Inside, he stood in a windowless room, and he tested to see if the light switch worked. A harsh, bright florescent light came to life, flickering at first, then dimly staying on. As his eyes adjusted the light slowly became brighter and he looked around to see what this room was.

A metal desk sat against the far wall with an old battered chair pushed in under it, the dark green vinyl ripped at both edges where the chair had been pushed against the desk over the years. Assuming it squeaked, he decided to leave the chair alone and opened the desk drawers on either side; he hoped they didn't make any sound, but also knew that was likely wishful thinking.

The top right drawer only lightly rubbed against its tracking and was empty, so was the second, and finally the bottom the same as the other two. Moving to the left side, he pulled the drawer open slowly to reveal an empty envelope, three pencils and a smattering of paperclips strewn about. The second drawer held a ruler and an eraser. The bottom drawer was empty. Taking a deep breath and looking around some more, he found a four-drawer file cabinet in the corner with a coffee maker on top of it. Walking to the cabinet he pulled the first drawer out and the coffee maker wiggled a bit. What was strange was an inch of coffee still sitting in the pot, swirled around. Holding his phone light up to the pot what he noticed was a puzzle. The coffee didn't have a fine coat of mold or film on it which meant it had been made fairly recently. He pulled the pot off the burner and sniffed. It smelled relatively fresh.

Looking around he saw a wastebasket in the corner. Replacing the coffee pot, he wandered over to the wastebasket and saw two coffee cups and a napkin laying in the bottom.

Pulling the first cup from the can, he looked inside and saw only coffee stains, no moisture in the bottom. He'd have to be a forensic expert to know drying times based on room temperature, etcetera, so he dropped the cup into the can and pulled the second cup out. A small amount of moisture sat at the bottom of the cup, but the interesting thing was this one had lipstick on the edge. A woman. And, since the cup still had coffee in the bottom it had been used somewhat recently.

Hearing a noise from what sounded like the first floor, he dropped the cup in the trash can and crept to the door. Listening intently, he could hear his own heartbeat and hoped beyond all reason that what he heard was Red making her way down to him so they could get the hell out of here. He wanted this drug ring sitting behind bars, but he sure didn't want to be sitting behind bars with them. A cop in jail never lasted very long. Not that breaking and entering could get him thrown in jail, but no sense in pushing their luck.

Not hearing any more sounds, he turned off the light, exited the office, closed the door and decided to finish his search of the perimeter of this room before going in search of Red to get home. He listened again wondering what he'd heard upstairs and felt uneasy that Red wasn't on her way down here. Deciding to screw it and go upstairs, the garbage can that Delhurst had tossed something into earlier caught his attention and he walked as quietly as he could to the can, shining his light inside. There were some miscellaneous pieces of paper, mostly brown packing material, a newspaper and something white and shiny.

Reaching inside for the white object, he strained to grasp it at the bottom of the can; he stretched himself out fully, his fingers finally able to grip it. Pulling it from the can, he shined his light on the object and his heart hammered in his chest as realization of what he held flooded his mind. This was big.

22

This building was eerie in the deep, dark, dead of night, or more accurately after ten at night with no lights on and when you weren't supposed to be inside. But, she just had to follow this hunch. The staircase was dark and echoed with each footstep, but she continued upstairs keeping her eyes and ears alert and her focus on getting at those files.

At the top of the stairs, she heard a sound and hesitated. Trying hard to keep her breathing even and steady; she listened for any sounds except that of her own heartbeat. The constant hum of a motor reached her ears and she realized the sound she'd heard before was the refrigerator kicking on. Then she wondered why they'd keep a running refrigerator in an abandoned building.

Easing down the hallway to the room that was the kitchen or break room, she edged her way to the refrigerator, using only the light from her phone to find her way. Knowing full well once the door opened the room would be flooded with light, but then reminding herself that there weren't any windows in this room, she quickly pulled it open to find a couple of food containers on the top shelf and six yogurt containers in the door. Peaking at the food containers she popped the top off one of them and was surprised to see it wasn't old and moldy but looked rather fresh.

Closing the door and glancing around the room once again, she made her way into the hallway and down to the Presidential office to look at those files. Each doorway she passed gave her pause and yet, she knew no one was here other than Rory, so whatever she was worried about was purely her imagination.

Reaching the door to the big office, she slid inside and shone her light on the credenza across the room. Nothing. Those files were gone. Padding across the plush carpeting, she began opening and closing drawers looking for those missing files but each one was empty. Turning to the desk she began checking the drawers and when each of those was empty, she searched the file cabinet on the far wall. It had only been three hours or so since they'd been in here, so either Maggie moved the files or someone else had been inside while she was. Hopefully they weren't still here. That thought sent chills running down her spine.

Eager to get down to Rory but also wanting to make the most of this B&E, she decided to investigate the other offices along the hallway to see if the files were still in this building.

Hearing a sound from below, she pressed her back against the wall next to the door and took in a deep, slow breath, then let it out slowly to keep herself in check. A few moments passed and no other sounds could be heard, and she convinced herself it was either a furnace or some other system still running within the building. After all, the refrigerator was still on.

Easing out to the hallway she began moving slowly to the staircase, suddenly more eager to leave than to prove a hunch right.

"What are you doing here?"

She turned at the male voice, which sounded familiar, but she couldn't see the person it came from.

"Who's there?"

Her phone held up, she tried to keep her hand from shaking when the man stepped into the light revealing himself.

"Officer Delhurst, what are you doing here?"

"I believe I just asked you the same question."

"Oh, I thought I saw someone in here and came in to investigate."

"Really?" His voice deepened and the look he gave her was anything but friendly. "How did you get in?"

"The door down in the dock area was open."

He took a step toward her and she instinctively backed up. The grin that creased his face reminded her of the cartoon Grinch whose grin slowly spread across his face and looked purely evil.

"What are you doing here, Officer?"

"I got a call that someone was lurking about in here, lights flashing, etc. So, I came in to check it out."

"Oh."

"Did you find anyone in here?"

"No."

"I wonder why you wouldn't call the station and let them know you were coming in?"

"I happened to be in the area and just thought a quick investigation would be prudent. After all, I know you all are working so much overtime and if it was nothing, I wouldn't want to pull anyone off their assignment for a false alarm."

Her heart beat so hard in her chest it was downright painful and she realized how foolish this likely was. Rory was right; sometimes she was simply too impulsive.

Light footsteps could be heard from the staircase, much too light to be Rory's. Delhurst's eyes never left hers, which scared the shit out of her because he wasn't alone. Hopefully one of Rory's friends from the station came along and would be friendlier.

The door from the stairs opened and she stepped aside so her back wasn't to Delhurst, who stood stock still and never took his eyes from her, to see none other but Maggie standing in the doorway.

Looking her up and down, the perusal gave her the creeps and it was then that her brain registered that this was very serious. As in, possibly lose her job, or worse, deadly serious. Every horrible story she'd ever heard from the various DEA agents she'd worked with flooded through her mind and finally ended with where in the hell was Rory? But, if he was still here, he'd surely hear something and come looking for her.

"So, decided to come back and take a look around on your own, Special Agent Alice Tucker, DEA?" Maggie sneered.

Deciding sarcastic would not go well right now, she opted for nothing at all.

"What did she say, Paul?"

"Saw someone was in here."

"Hmm." Maggie walked toward her, still wearing the pencil skirt and heels from earlier today, still dripping in diamonds, still reeking of money.

"What are you really doing here? And, don't lie."

Moving her body as if she were talking with her hands, she tried making her way to the stairs, but Delhurst pulled his gun, "Not another step."

Maggie chuckled and it was sad or maybe pained in some way. "Take her downstairs, the truck is here, she can be discarded just like they did with my man. Toss her in a box and ship her out with the goods. Dump her somewhere where she won't be found for a long time."

Her mind screamed to keep up, but she struggled with it. Her man? Her baby daddy? Discarded?

"Let's go, Special Agent." The sarcasm couldn't have been thicker.

Delhurst used his gun to point to the stairs as she tried running all the odds through her brain. Run, no, he was taller and likely faster than she. Try and trip him? Could work but then again if not it would be worse. Go along and see if something better came to mind? That's what she had for now and that Rory would intervene and help her along the way. Hopefully, they hadn't found Rory yet. Where was he anyway?

23

Hiding in the back of the shipping area, Rory watched as the truck pulled up and three men jumped out. Cases of product were hauled out by hand and stacked in three separate areas. The workers seemed to know what each area meant, but he was still puzzling it all together. Once the truck was unloaded, the boxes and crates were opened, and the product unpacked. Coffee cans were pulled from the cartons, another worker opened the cans and pulled packages from inside. They were then sorted and repackaged in smaller boxes with false bottoms and sorted according to zip code based on the zip codes written on the side of each box. No one talked and everyone did what they were supposed to without a word.

He heard footsteps on the metal stairs and peered around the office he'd recently vacated only to see Red coming down the steps, with Delhurst behind her, a gun in her back. Not long after, he saw Maggie coming down behind Delhurst. That's when things clicked for him. Delhurst hid the files from them and threw the cocaine away. He surely knew what it was, but didn't want Red or him to see it and acted as if it was nothing. Slowly drawing his gun from his back holster, he calculated who he'd have to shoot first, Delhurst or Maggie or the workers if each was armed and how long it would take him to pull off enough shots to get each of them and not get Red caught in the cross fire. Or get killed himself.

Deciding he had the advantage while they were on the steps, he saw Red turn his way and slightly nod, she was ready and would hit the floor before anyone else could draw and shoot. He aimed for Delhurst and got him in the ribs, knowing instantly he'd punctured his lung at the way he buckled. Red jumped the final two steps down and rolled out of the way, then pulled her gun from her ankle holster. Maggie turned toward him, her eyes evil glints of steel as she followed Delhurst down the steps and he pulled his second gun from his ankle, this one not police issue, and aimed it at her. Before he could get off a second shot, Red shot Maggie in the stomach and then one of the workers who'd pulled a gun. He took care of the other two by simply pointing his gun at them.

"Lay down, on the ground, hands on the back of your heads." He yelled and they quickly dropped to the ground.

Walking to Delhurst, he heard the wheezing and saw the bubbles of blood on his side, but the man's eyes locked on his and he mouthed, "Sorry."

Maggie tried to crawl toward the gun Delhurst had dropped but Red ran to it and kicked it out of the way. Quickly pulling Delhurst's cuffs, she secured Maggie's hands behind her back. Red then pulled her cell phone from her pocket and called it in.

Keeping his gun trained on the two workers, he waited until officers arrived at the scene, at which point he was relieved from keeping them in his sights. As soon as his Captain arrived, he and Red were each taken to separate areas of the building and questioned, he by his Captain.

"What went down here Richards?"

"I won't lie Captain, and if you have to relieve me of my duties, then do what you have to do, but we came in here tonight because we knew something wasn't right about what we saw today and Red had a strong hunch that something was going down. I went along with it because she's smart and good and her senses on things have always been spot on."

"So, you were here illegally, and yet, it worked out, but we have an officer involved shooting, two of them, one a DEA Special Agent; we've got some issues to work through, but, on the good side, I do believe you've cracked this drug ring."

"Red did, Captain."

"Okay, Richards. Get back to the station. Go straight to the station, Tucker can ride with Waters. Don't talk to each other until we're finished with the questioning. Got it?"

"Yes, sir."

Officer Jason Robards came to the scene and gave him a ride to his car. Since they were all shaken at having a dirty cop in their midst very little conversation was going on other than what was necessary. He couldn't stop shaking, likely from the adrenaline and the fact that he saw Red with a gun at her back and the look of pure terror on her face. He'd never get that sight out of his mind and he never wanted to see it again.

Walking into the station, he felt bone tired and figured that Maggie was behind this whole mess. Talk about someone you'd never think would be involved with something like this and what about her kid?

He sat in his office, his mind still not able to process all that had transpired; and he hoped he'd find out the whole story so he could settle back into his life as usual.

He heard commotion and saw Red walking into the station with Waters and Bowers with her. Red seemed shocked and he wanted nothing more than to pull her into his arms and hold her. But, they were likely to be here for a long time yet. He took a deep breath and resigned himself to sitting in until the Captain got back and both of their interrogations were finished. Then, he'd hold her all night long. At least for as long as he had, 'cause now that this was likely wrapped up, she'd be heading back to Indianapolis and that promotion she was counting on. It's what she'd worked her whole life for and that was hard to walk away from, and he'd never ask her, just like before.

24

She was so warm and she felt like she had a weight on her, her limbs felt heavy, but so did her eyes. So heavy. Rory's deep, even breathing behind her warmed her neck and she sighed. Nestling her head deeper into her pillow his arms pulled her closer into his body. That's why she was warm, his arms anchored her to him, and it felt so good.

Prying an eye open she saw the sun shining brightly outside, dust particles billowing in the stream of light from the window. She'd discharged her weapon last night, something she hadn't done in a while. She hoped she never had to do it again. That was if she wasn't charged with wrongdoing. Maggie had still been alive when she and Rory came home last night; if she died during the night, she could very well be charged with some lower degree of murder. She had a solid argument of self-defense, or at least in the defense of another, because when she saw Maggie begin to point her gun at Rory, she didn't even wait to see what was going to happen, she just acted. That was her job to protect the cops. Aside from that, she'd never be able to forgive herself if Rory had been injured or killed. It was entirely her responsibility he had been there at all. Knowing she'd been right did little to ease her guilt. Hopefully time would be on her side.

Soft lips kissed the back of her neck before his soothing, deep voice whispered, "Did you sleep good?"

"Yes, better than I have in a long time."

"Mmm. Me, too."

His phone rang and with a groan he rolled over to swipe it off the bedside table.

"Yeah."

She listened to his side of the phone conversation knowing it was likely a summons to come into the station. Dreading that it may be someone calling to say that Maggie had died.

"Yeah."

He tapped his phone ending his call then dropped his arm and his phone to the bed.

"We've got to go in for more questioning."

"Okay. I'll get some coffee going. I can't do anything before coffee."

He chuckled and rolled off the bed. "I'll jump in the shower then start breakfast."

She sat up, realized she was naked, saw his shirt laying on the floor next to the bed and tried to remember how they ended their night here, but she couldn't quite remember it. Clearly exhaustion had set in.

Snagging his shirt from the floor she slipped it over her head and walked out to the kitchen. The first thing she noticed was the aroma of freshly brewed coffee and she smiled. Ahh, what a great thing to wake up to. Then she noticed two cups sitting next to the coffee pot. Pouring coffee into the cups she shook her head when one cup of coffee turned a nice caramelly color. He'd already put creamer in it. He must have done all of this last night after she dropped into bed. What a sweetheart. She would miss him terribly.

That thought had her heart dropping into her stomach; she didn't want to go through that again. What she realized was that she loved him, probably never really stopped loving him and dammit why couldn't they make this work?

She sat at the table looking out over the green backyard and the gorgeous flowers outside and thought how ideal this place seemed. What would she do if she lost her job? Did she want this promotion so bad she'd give up a chance at being with Rory? Maybe a baby or two? A house and a dog? She'd identified herself with that job for so long she didn't really know who Alice Tucker was without DEA after her name. What would she do for money? What did she want to do? All she'd ever known was the military and then the DEA chasing major drug traffickers. She'd likely never be able to do anything that wasn't police work. Working retail was definitely out of the question. Working as a waitress, nope. In an office, oh hell no.

"What are you doing?"

"Wondering what on earth I'll do with myself if I lose my job."

He nodded his head and grabbed his coffee from the counter, taking a seat at the table. His fresh scent smelled better than her coffee and that was saying something before she'd even finished her first cup.

"Well for what it's worth, and I have no idea what will happen, but you could always pick up where Big3 left off."

"What's Big3?"

"Ford, Lincoln and Dodge were Big3 Security before they joined GHOST. So, from what I understand there's still some private investigation work out there available. But, I sure hope it doesn't come to that."

Nodding she whispered, "Me, too."

"Get a move on, Red, the Captain just said he wants us at the station ASAP. Let's try and stay on his good side while he's deciding what to do with us. Yeah?"

"Yeah."

She stood and took her cup with her back to the bedroom, picked up her clothing laying around the floor, then headed upstairs where her overnight bag still sat with her toothbrush and makeup waiting for her.

Once they knew what would happen with them, she'd talk to Rory, but she sure hoped he'd bring it up first. Now to shower off yesterday and get ready for today, come what may.

25

Sitting in his office searching through his computer, Rory's mind raced with possibilities. He'd come in to find out that Delhurst had died during the night, and the Captain had confirmed he'd been dirty the whole time he was here. He was actually planted in the Police Department by none other than the Santarino family. Would they ever be finished with that no-good family?

Callan Waters entered his office. The giant blocked all the sunlight from the outer room, his shoulders barely fit through his door the brute was so built. But he was a good cop and a good friend.

"Richards, Margery Van Steel is still alive; Bowers just got back from interviewing her. He's in with the Captain who wants to see you."

"Where's Red, I thought she was with the Captain?"

"She's pouring herself another cup of coffee."

He shook his head remembering she didn't function well before at least two cups. Her meeting with the Captain must have been tough. He stood and walked to the door just as Red was walking toward him with two cups of coffee. She handed him a cup and whispered, "I'll wait in here for you."

He nodded then made his way to the Captain's office.

Knocking once on the door, the Captain looked up from a report and waved him in. Bowers sat in one of the empty chairs across from the Captain's desk, and Rory took the empty seat next to him.

"Richards, Bowers is here to fill us in on the interview he had with Van Steel.

"Yes, sir."

He twisted in his chair and looked at Bowers.

"As you know there's been a lot of speculation about Van Steel's baby daddy. Turns out, he's none other than Mangus Santarino. Giovanni Santarino set her and the baby up in a lavish lifestyle, but the tradeoff was that she has to help run the drugs through the Limitless building until Giovanni decides it is time to move operations. Giovanni was getting close to ending this operation here, which was why earlier Al was called and asked to a meeting, to discuss payment. He thought if he could get some money from the station or the State or the Federal Government, he'd take it. He was so angry that both of his sons were killed here, he wanted to twist the knife a bit before moving on. Never intending to get caught, of course.

"Who called Red?"

"Delhurst. He lives in one of those Longstone apartments and was watching everything unfold after Sergio Mancuoso was murdered."

"Who killed Sergio?"

"Delhurst."

"Why? Did he know Sergio was working with Red?"

"Yes. They were going to kill Red too if she got in the way. Last night could have gone much differently. Apparently they were going to call her to come and meet at Limitless later anyway, after they had their shipment sorted and loaded."

"So, Giovanni is still running the family in Lynyrd Station? Is he about finished with all his dirty tactics?"

"Time will tell. The baby will likely stay here with Margery's mother and there could be some ploys on the family's part to try to get custody of whoever has a Santarino baby, but we'll be watching. Also, he's supposedly teaching Mangus' daughter, Francesca the family business and she's about twenty, so we'll definitely work with Homeland Security to keep her out of the country and, hopefully, anyone loyal to the family. "

"Thanks Bowers, Captain. What happens with Red and I now?"

"There'll be an internal investigation and pending that, you're both on desk duty. Tucker can go back to her District Office, but she'll have to come back for hearings. The District Attorney also will investigate to see if any charges will be brought against either of you."

His stomach dropped at the thought of Red leaving and he knew they'd have to talk. He nodded and stood then bowed his head once more and made his way back to his office, dread weighing heavy in his chest.

Red sat at his desk, her feet propped up on a drawer, her eyes looking around the room at the photographs he had hanging on the walls.

"You look comfortable there."

She smiled, "I suppose I am."

He closed the office door, and sat in a chair across from his desk. "Red, what do you want to do? I mean between you and I?"

Her red hair shined under the light from the fixture above, her eyes still held the tiredness they'd had before, but she was still such a beautiful woman.

"What do you want, Ace?"

Swallowing he took a deep breath, "Take a look at my computer."

Her brows furrowed as she stared at him, then she glanced at his computer. She shook his mouse to wake it up and looked at his screen. The furrow between her brows deepened for a moment as she scrolled down the list of houses on his monitor.

"I don't understand, what are you looking at houses for? I thought you loved your house."

"I do, but the biggest problem with my house is that it isn't where you are. So, if you want us to give this relationship a try, I want to do it right this time and I thought I could buy a house in Indy to be with you."

She stared deeply into his eyes, hers a bright green, a color he wanted to stare into for the rest of his life. He saw her swallow, her eyes glistened as moisture gathered, then she took a deep breath and said, "I was just thinking I could get used to living here in Lynyrd Station. This is my last year as a Special Agent, at 37 we have to transfer. Maybe instead of a transfer, I could move here. I think there's a new opening here. And if it's too hard to work together, maybe I'll take over Big3. Depending on what happens with the investigation."

He watched her, she never wavered. "You sure?"

"Yep. You?"

"Yep."

He pulled a quarter from his pocket."What do you say, heads we stay here, tails we move to Indy?"

She laughed, her head back, her hair moving about like a cloud around her. "Yeah, but make sure it's heads, Ace."

ABOUT PJ FIALA

Thank you for reading! I hope you enjoyed ***Rory: Finding His Fire*** and any reviews for it, or the whole anthology would be greatly appreciated.

If you'd like to check out the rest of the **Big 3 Security** series, you can find links to all books and retailers here: https://www.pjfiala.com/books/

Hearing from readers is why I do this, so let's connect, and feel free to pop in and say "Hi!" at any time!

Website - Hearing from readers is the best, so let's connect, and feel free to pop in and say "Hi!" at any time!

https://www.pjfiala.com/

Join PJ's Newsletter - new releases, fun stuff, exclusive excerpts and special sales

Thank you for reading.
~ PJ Fiala ~

Writing has been a desire my whole life. Once I found the courage to write, life changed for me in the most profound way. Bringing stories to readers that I'd enjoy reading and creating characters that are flawed, but lovable is such a joy.

When not writing, I'm with my family doing something fun. My husband, Gene, and I are bikers and enjoy riding to new locations, meeting new people and generally enjoying this fabulous country we live in.

I come from a family of veterans. My grandfather, father, brother, two sons, and one daughter-in-law are all veterans. Needless to say, I am proud to be an American and proud of the service my amazing family has given.

DON'T DARE A DIAMOND

STACEY JOY NETZEL

Never Stop dreaming!

Stacey Joy Netzel

MUST
LOVE
DIAMONDS
Don't
Dare
a
diamond
NEW YORK TIMES BESTSELLING AUTHOR
STACEY JOY
NETZEL

CHAPTER 1

July
Lakewood, CO

Raine Diamond wasn't used to being ignored. She was the baby of her family, *and* the only girl out of five kids. She'd graduated valedictorian of her class. She was a world-class show jumper, having already won a gold medal in the Youth Olympic Games at eighteen, with aspirations of making the U.S. Olympic team in the near future. Possibly even next year. Her grandfather was a real estate mogul, her parents ran a multi-billion dollar investment firm, and one uncle was a senator, the other head of a jewelry empire.

She was a *Diamond*.

And what was he? A stable boy.

Well...man. A man who made her pulse race like never before—and that scared the crap out of her.

She fidgeted with seam on the back pocket of her jeans as she stood in her uncle's kitchen with her cousin Shelby, her brother Axel, and Reyes Torrez.

She didn't usually act like an entitled little rich bitch, but for some reason, Reyes triggered the need to prove she was worth looking at. By him. But while her heart went completely haywire at the sight of his thick-lashed green eyes and tousled, sun-kissed, caramel-colored hair, he gave her a cool, heat-inducing once-over, met her gaze long enough for her to offer a nervous smile, and then dismissed her without a second glance.

As he easily joked and laughed with her cousin and brother, she battled a foreign insecurity that left her confused and annoyed. Then he left without so much as a, *"Nice to meet you."*

Who was *he* to act as if she didn't even exist?

If he'd been into Shelby, she'd have understood. Heck, even if he had a girlfriend, he could've simply been pleasantly polite. That's what people did when they met someone new. But the way he'd openly ignored her had been an outright snub. The more she thought about it, the more offended she became.

She stewed all through brunch, only briefly distracted when her cousin Merit dropped a bombshell on the whole family that he and his girlfriend, Mae, were having a baby. Apparently, the girlfriend part had been news, too?

Uncle Mark didn't take it well, and after a dramatic argument, Merit stormed out, Mae followed, then Aunt Janine. After the meal came to an awkward end, her brothers and cousins and their significant others cleared the table and did dishes before settling back around the patio. While they discussed the drama and caught up, she couldn't stop glaring across the lawn toward the stables.

After a few minutes, she got up and wandered inside the house. They were staying one more night, so she'd have plenty of time for visiting, but right now she was restless. Bored with the conversation around the table—and irritated by repeated flashes of Reyes' rude snub.

If only she hadn't sent Diamond Fire home to Texas with their trainer. After they'd won their event yesterday, he'd more than earned a few days rest at home, but now she couldn't go down to the stables with the excuse of checking on her champion baby.

Seeing her mom and Aunt Janine coming down the stairs, Raine seized on a different idea. "Aunt Jan, would it be possible for me to borrow one of your horses for an hour or so?" She rarely went a day without riding, but she couldn't remember the last time she'd been on the back of a horse just for fun.

"Of course." Her aunt gave her a distracted smile, clearly still focused on the earlier brunch drama. "Just ask Estefan or Reyes who could use some exercise."

Her pulse skipped at the mention of the second name. "Thank you."

She hurried upstairs to change and tucked her black V-neck T-shirt into tan breeches before pulling on black, knee-high, leather riding boots. She felt a little bad not asking Shelby to go with her, but her cousin knew her too well and would see right through this move.

When she reached the stables a few minutes later, she had a hard time catching her breath, and it had nothing to do with her speed walk down the curvy driveway. As she approached the open doors, her heart lodged in her throat, and a mass of anxiety writhed in her stomach. She desperately wanted to see him, yet also hoped he was nowhere around, because really, what was she going to say?

Notice me.

Yeah, that wouldn't sound pathetic and self-centered at all.

She stepped inside the barn and scanned for Reyes, only to find the place deserted. Initial relief was quickly replaced by disappointment, until she realized just because she didn't see him didn't mean he wasn't around. Shelby had said he lived in an apartment above the barn.

Squaring her shoulders, she held her chin high as she ventured farther inside. Like at home, the aisles were immaculate, and a deep inhale filled her lungs with the beloved scents of horse, hay, and leather. Heads turned her way, delicate ears swiveling and perking up as pairs of curious brown eyes watched her approach.

She stopped in front of a stall halfway down the aisle and studied the bay thoroughbred inside. The gelding's shiny coat was a rich red, complimented by a silky, jet-black forelock, mane, and tail. He was a big boy like Fire, his withers the same height as her five feet, two inches, putting him at almost sixteen hands tall.

He turned his head with a soft whicker, and she stepped back when he moved forward to extend his head over the stall door. She let him sniff her hand, then stroked his neck as he lipped at her palm.

"Hello, gorgeous." While rubbing his forehead and laying her cheek against his velvety soft black muzzle, she glanced at the engraved name plate on his stall door.

RazMaTaz.

"Tell me big guy, do they call you Raz, or Taz?" she mused out loud.

"That's Taz."

Her breath caught as she whirled around to see an older gentleman step through a door off to her right. He carried an English saddle over one arm, and a bridle in the other hand.

"Raine?"

"That's me," she confirmed with a smile.

"Hi. I'm Estefan. Janine called and said you were looking for a mount."

Earlier, she'd heard Shelby tell Merit's girlfriend Estefan was Reyes' father, and she vaguely remembered him from years ago. She could also see the resemblance to his son in his olive-toned features and brown eyes from their Spanish heritage. The elder Torrez had a mustache peppered with gray in comparison to his son's neatly trimmed goatee.

"Can I ride him?" she asked hopefully as she stroked the bay's nose. Forget going for a trail ride, she'd love to see what the horse could do on a course.

"Taz is my son's horse," he advised with a hint of apology in his tone. "No one rides him but Reyes."

She blinked in surprise to learn he had his own horse here.

None of their employees kept their horses at the Diamond stables in Texas. Not to mention, the gelding looked to be easily worth twenty grand. Maybe more.

"I'll be saddling Stimpy for you. He could use some exercise."

Stimpy?

Did he not know what she did for a living? She smoothed out her wrinkled nose as she turned, anticipating an old, gentle gelding for beginners.

Estefan slid the stall door open, giving Raine a good look at a regal chestnut with a mass of wavy, reddish-brown mane. Smaller than Taz, the more delicate build and refined features pointed toward Arabian, and she grinned with anticipation. Okay, she could definitely live with Stimpy—which upon a closer look at his name-plate, looked to be short for Rumplestiltskin.

"Your aunt assures me you can handle some fire?"

"Of course." She gave Taz a final, longing stroke along his muzzle before crossing the aisle. "I've been riding my Trakhener, Diamond Fire, since I was seventeen, and I can assure you, he lives up to his name."

He nodded, clearly well-versed with the athletic attributes of her jumper's breed.

"Is it okay for me to take Stimpy out on the trails? Just for an hour or so."

"You remember them?" he asked with an arch of his brows.

"I do. I know it's been a while," she said with a shrug, "but as long as they haven't changed..."

"No, no changes," he assured her. "Warm him up in the arena, get a feel for how he handles, and you should be good."

He wasn't telling her anything she didn't know, but she nodded anyway. "Thanks."

Used to taking care of her own mounts, she stepped forward to saddle the gelding, but Estefan would hear nothing of it. Minutes later, he gave her a leg up and a few tips on the Arabian's personality, then left them with, "Enjoy your ride."

~

She didn't remember him.

Reyes knew the moment Raine Diamond gave him that warm, interested smile up at the main house, she didn't remember treating him like a smear of manure on the heels of her polished English riding boots during a summer visit ten years ago. His sixteen year old ego had taken a hit, but the memory of two fifteen year old girls drooling over his older brother wasn't what rekindled his resentment after all this time.

It was the fact she hadn't even seen him back then. Dev had been twenty at the time, home on military leave, enjoying his R&R at the pool while hanging out with Loyal and Asher. Reyes had been invisible down in the stables, mucking stalls, sweeping aisles, stacking hay. Fine, he had a job to do. But when he'd finished his shift and joined the rest of 'em, the pretty, brunette Diamond cousin hadn't given him the time of day as she pranced around in her little red bikini.

To her, he'd just been a stable boy. The hired help who'd been shoveling manure while she and Bells went for a joy ride earlier that morning. Of all the years he'd grown up hanging with the Diamond kids, even knowing the gulf of privilege that separated their families, he'd never once felt less than any one of them—until that day.

That feeling came roaring back again today. Didn't matter that he'd caught a flare of interest in the now twenty-five year old's hazel eyes, it was the knowing she didn't recall snubbing him that hit the hardest. To her, he hadn't even been worth remembering.

The irony of that pissing him off was a real kick in the ass. These days, he *wanted* to fade into the background. Since getting out of the Army almost a year ago and coming home, he made sure his usual happy-go-lucky smile and carefree attitude kept everyone from seeing all the shit he kept bottled up inside.

The only one who suspected was Dev, but ninety-nine percent of the time he was training or on a mission, so other than the occasional email or text, he left him alone. The horses were his mental therapy, and with the stables relatively quiet now that the senator and Janine spent a lot of time in Washington, he'd been virtually invisible and glad for it.

One look at Raine up at the main house had set his nerve endings buzzing with energy. His grip tightened on the windowsill of his above-the-stables apartment window as he watched her out in the arena astride Stimpy. Her slim form moved as one with the horse, her long hair streaming out behind her as she cantered him in figure eights with a firm hold on the reins.

The chestnut Arabian could be a headstrong sonofabitch, but right now, he moved willingly under her guidance, his lead switches smooth as butter. Reyes couldn't help but be impressed by her skill and grace in the saddle, though it wasn't surprising given he'd heard Shelby bragging she was in the running for a spot on the US Equestrian Team.

When she exited the arena for the riding trails surrounding the estate, he headed down to the stables. His gut clenched as his mind screamed to turn around and go back. It reminded him of being on patrol. Trouble was brewing, and he was heading right for it. But he could no more have kept himself from descending the stairs than he could've disobeyed an order from his commanding officer.

The certainty of that left him itchy and restless, and he needed to do something with his hands. In Afghanistan, he used to clean his rifle, and then clean it again. Now, he'd have to make do with saddles. It was almost as good.

In the tack room, he grabbed a cloth and some leather cleaner.

His dad walked by, then back-tracked. Reyes looked up when he stopped in the doorway. "You headed out?"

"Not quite. I'm waiting for Janine's niece to get back from her ride."

"Is Mom done with everything up at the house?" They always rode together when his mom worked on Sundays.

His dad shrugged. "She'll keep herself busy until I can leave."

"You can go if you want. I'll take care of things here."

"Got nothing better to do on your day off?"

Reyes lifted a shoulder as he avoided his dad's direct gaze. "I'm heading out later, so just killing some time for now."

"Hmm." He watched him quietly for a moment.

His pulse thudded hard as he waited for his dad to call him out on the lie.

Instead he gave a shrug. "All right then, suit yourself. Thanks."

It didn't suit him one damn bit, yet there he sat, scrubbing the already shining leather until the light sound of boot heels beat out a rapid rhythm on the cement twenty minutes later. He went on full alert as the steps came to an abrupt halt outside the tack room door.

"Oh. Um…is Estefan here?"

Reyes took his time looking up, partly to make her wait, partly to get his pulse to settle down. But one look at Raine's windblown hair and those bright hazel eyes, and there was no reprieve in sight. "He went home. Why?"

"I was hoping to get some jumps set up."

"Sure." He gestured to the left with the oil cloth in his hand. "Out the main doors, you'll find a large storage room on the left. Jumps are in there. Help yourself."

She blinked at him, her expression astonished. "Help myself?"

"Just make sure you keep them under half a meter. Stimpy doesn't have nearly the same level of training as your jumpers."

One hand propped on her hip, and her brow arched imperiously as her cheeks flushed with color. "You do work here, don't you?"

"I do."

Her gaze narrowed, and he deliberately returned to polishing.

"And you aren't going to at least come help me?"

"I'm busy."

After a long moment, she pivoted on her heel and disappeared toward the storage room. Reyes rested his fist on the saddle with a heavy sigh, waiting for the sound of the wooden rails as she dragged them out to the arena. When all he heard was silence, he conceded maybe he didn't have to be such an asshole because his pansy-ass ego was still bruised from ten years ago. Maybe he should go help—

The clip-clop of horseshoes rang out on the cement.

His brow dipped as he rose and walked to the doorway in time to see Raine leading Stimpy to the cross ties by his assigned stall. She didn't deign to look in his direction as they passed the tack room.

Leaning a shoulder against the doorjamb, he asked, "Change your mind about the jumping?"

"Shelby texted me to meet her at the pool."

Her snooty tone grated across his nerves while his fingers clenched the cloth in his hand at the memory of that little red bikini all those years ago. A mental head-shake banished the image as she secured the gelding in the cross ties. Then she gave him a rub on the nose and flipped her hair over her shoulder while turning to walk toward the main house.

Reyes couldn't help but drop his gaze down to the sway of her ass in those tan, skin-tight pants. He swallowed hard against a rising tide of awareness.

"Tell your dad thank you for the ride," she tossed over her shoulder while bending to fish her phone from the front thigh pocket of her breeches.

Reyes tilted his head slightly to watch the stretch of material—until he suddenly straightened from the wall with a jerk of indignation. "Whoa—hold on. Where the hell do you think you're going?"

"To the pool, of course."

"Not before you take care of Stimpy."

"I do believe that's what *you're* paid to do. I'm going to go have a swim."

It was, and it wasn't, but he wasn't about to get into semantics with an uppity little princess like her. "*You're* going to get your ass back here and take care of this horse. Now."

That halted her steps and brought her back around. She lifted her chin, somehow looking down her nose at him from twenty feet away. "You can't talk to me like that. I'll have you fired."

He snorted. "Good luck with that. In the meantime, the rule is, you ride in this stable, you take care of your horse. You may not remember everything about this place, but I know damn well you remember that."

"What does that mean?"

Annoyed with himself for revealing his resentment, he abruptly turned and went back into the tack room.

"I'll have you fired."

The echo of her threat had him clenching his jaw, but he forced himself to take a seat behind the saddle he'd been cleaning and focus on the rhythmic motions of his hand to soothe his pissed-off energy.

While his anger eased, a strange crackle and buzz woke up every cell of his body. The level shot up a notch when, five minutes later, she stomped into the room to deposit Stimpy's saddle and bridle on an empty rack and hook without so much as a glance in his direction. Then she went straight to the bins on the other side of the room, selected the brushes she needed to rub the horse down, and stomped back out again.

See? He shot a narrow-eyed look at the empty doorway. She hadn't forgotten where the brushes were located, and after today, he'd bet a hundred bucks she'd remember him the next time they met.

It could be a year, or another ten, but she'd definitely remember him.

CHAPTER 2

May - 10 months later
Dallas, TX

Raine leaned forward slightly in the saddle, heels down as she counted Diamond Fire's strides on their approach to the next jump, a vertical with two rails, one-point-two-five meters high. They could do this jump in their sleep—except her shoulders tensed and body stiffened as the nightmare of their fall during the final event of last season flashed in her mind with sickening clarity.

Fire tossed his head and stumbled a step. When he regained his footing, she wheeled him to the left, and they galloped past the jump with her heart lodged in her throat.

"It's okay," Charlie's voice rang out over the arena, the trainer's encouraging claps echoing up to the steel rafters. "Take him around and try it again. You'll get it on this round."

Nausea threatened to send up her breakfast from two hours

ago. Anxiety spiked, and she cantered Fire past the next jump, too. "Stop pushing so hard. I told you he's not ready yet."

"It's been four and a half months, Raine."

"Four and a half months and he's still stumbling on an easy jump."

"He did okay when Jess rode him while your shoulder healed."

"So it's all my fault?" She pointed her baby toward a pathetically low, single vertical. On his way over, one nick of his back foot bounced the rail from the cups. "How about that? Was that my fault, too?"

"He can sense your anxiety. He—"

"*I'm* fine," she hollered from the far end of the arena.

"—knows you don't trust him."

"He doesn't trust *me,*" she shot back.

Frustrated tears burned her eyes as she reined Fire to a stop in front of their trainer. Ever since the accident, nothing had been the same between her and her horse. Their perfect partnership had crashed into the dirt right alongside them that day at the end of December. Eight years down the drain. And now Charlie kept throwing it in her face—just like her dad.

"You gotta get this jump back if you're going to compete at your previous level," Charlie said, his tone firm, yet sympathetic. "You were almost disqualified last week."

Her stomach roiled. "You're not telling me anything I don't already know. And I certainly don't need to hear it every damn day."

A tiny voice whispered she wasn't so sure she wanted to keep competing, but she didn't dare listen. She hated the sliver of doubt that kept surfacing at the worst times. Jumping was her life. It had been since her first show when she was nine. If she wasn't riding, she didn't know who she was, or what the hell else she'd do.

She gripped the reins tighter to keep her hands from shaking. Fire danced backward until she relaxed her hold.

Charlie heaved a resigned sigh and gave a slight shake of his head. "Cool him down and then do your workout. We'll give it another go tomorrow."

Raine swung Fire around and posted as he trotted one circuit of the ring, then slowed him to a walk for a couple more rounds. Finally, she dismounted and led him from the arena into the attached stable while unstrapping her helmet. After removing his saddle and bridle, she gave him a thorough rub down before gathering the tack to put away.

"You're not pushing her hard enough."

The sound of her father's angry voice pulled her up short two steps from the tack room door.

"*She* complains I'm pushing her too hard," Charlie argued.

"She walks all over you, and we both know it. If she doesn't get back to competition level, she won't have time to qualify."

Raine grit her teeth, so sick of the two of them getting on her case about the Olympics. What did they want her to do, force Fire over the jumps? He'd really hate her then.

"I keep telling her that."

"And then you let her off the hook and cut practice short."

"I'm doing my best."

"Which isn't good enough. She needs better. Different." Frustration dripped from her dad's voice. "I'm sending her and Diamond Fire up to my brother's in Denver for the next month."

What?

Raine stiffened. That was news to her.

"Am I being fired?" Charlie asked.

"Of course not. You'll stay here to work with the alternates while they head up north. A change of scenery will do them both some good, and my brother has a trainer who's worked wonders with a couple of rescue horses."

Indignation spurred her around the corner to confront her dad. "Fire isn't some broken down rescue horse."

He didn't seem the least bit concerned she'd been eavesdropping. "No, but he does need some work. You both do."

"Which we can do here." She hugged the saddle tighter against her churning stomach. "I'm not going to Uncle Mark's."

He crossed his arms over his chest, dark eyebrows rising toward dark hair just beginning to gray at the temples. "Yes, you are."

"I'll miss two events."

"After where you finished last week, that's the least of our worries."

"Dad."

"Raine, it's not up for discussion."

It took everything she had to not stamp her foot like when she was five and didn't get her way. "Fire and I will be fine. We *are* getting there. We just need more time."

He shook his head. "You don't have time. If you have any hope of making the Olympic team, you have to get back to where you were."

Those damn tears threatened again as she choked out, "We will."

Her dad put his hands on her shoulders, the weight of them as heavy as his voice. "Honey, you've talked about going for gold since you were ten. I told you I'd help you get there, and that's exactly what I'm doing." He pulled her in for a quick hug. With her tucked in under his chin, he dropped a kiss on the top of her head before setting her back with a firm grip. "You leave tomorrow. Pack for a month."

She sputtered furiously as he strode away, even though she knew from that tone, nothing she said would change his mind. She should've known he wouldn't let her stonewall Charlie forever.

The trainer gave her a helpless shrug before following her father. She growled under her breath as they disappeared.

Alone in the tack room, Raine sank down onto a bench seat, saddle hugged tight to her stomach.

Shit. She was going back to Denver.

It wasn't just that she'd have to work with a new trainer she didn't know, but she'd have to face that arrogant jerk at the stable again. She wished she didn't remember his name. Or the color of his eyes, the way his shirt had molded his broad shoulders, or how her pulse had tripped each time they came face to face.

But she did remember Reyes Torrez. All too well.

He'd featured in numerous girlish fantasies since she was fifteen. She could hope he'd been fired for some other jackass thing he'd done since she'd seen him last summer, but given the long friendship between his family and Uncle Mark's, that was nothing more than a pipe dream.

CHAPTER 3

Reyes was bent over checking Morning Glory's horseshoes when the sound of approaching footsteps had him glancing under his arm. He released the mare's foot and straightened to face the senator—also his boss. "Afternoon, Mark. I thought you and Janine were heading back to Washington today."

"We're on our way out, but I needed to come ask a personal favor before I left."

"Sure. Name it." He glanced past his shoulder to see their town car waiting beyond the open doors, their driver and bodyguard leaning against the front passenger door.

"First of all, I'm going to hold you to that," the senator said with a grin. "Second, in the future, you might want to hear the favor before you agree to it."

Reyes returned his smile. "That's an ominous warning coming from a politician."

Mark chuckled. "So true. Anyway, do you remember my niece who visited last year? She came down here for a ride?"

Now his smile faltered. *Raine Diamond.* A dark-haired beauty impossible to forget—even though he'd tried over the past ten months.

Following her progress on the jumping circuit is not *trying.*

Whatever.

"I remember her," he confirmed cautiously.

"She took a bad spill at the end of last season and got banged up pretty bad."

Yeah, he'd read about her fall and resulting shoulder surgery. And while she should've had plenty of time to heal, she and her champion Trakehner had faulted to the bottom of the board at the first two competitions of the season.

Despite their adversarial encounter last summer, he had sympathy for her—in a general sense, nothing more.

"Sorry to hear that," he murmured.

Mark gave a solemn nod. "She's recovered physically, but she's been having some issues with her horse ever since. My brother called yesterday and asked if you'd be willing to work with them."

His pulse skipped at the request, and he had to fight to keep his expression neutral. "I work with horses, not people."

"They're a package deal."

"Then I'm not your guy."

"I told Matt what you've done with Janine's rescue horses, and he seems to think you'd be perfect."

He frowned in confusion. "Based solely on your word?"

"Well, he is my brother." A small smile curved his boss' lips. "And he also overheard you stand up to Raine last summer."

Oh, shit, seriously? Heat flashed through him at the thought of her father overhearing that exchange. He'd been blunt and rude—on purpose. Knowing Mark knew about their encounter heaped on yet another level of discomfort. "In that case, I'd think I'm the last person he'd want working with his daughter."

The senator shrugged. "My niece is used to getting her way, and it's not working with her current trainer."

"Shocker," he muttered before he could help himself.

"Considering she was nearly disqualified last week, and they're running out of time to make sure she can qualify for the Olympic team, Matt's desperate."

Her dad was desperate? Not her? Great. And if he didn't produce results, what then?

Didn't matter. He didn't do package deals, and he wasn't going to Texas.

His parents had left for a month-long European tour and cruise five days ago. Which moved him up from assistant stable manager to manager—because he was currently the *only* stable employee on the payroll. "Mark, I'm sorry, but you know I can't leave right now with Dad and Mom gone."

"That's why she's coming here."

Well, shit. "When?"

The senator glanced at his watch before digging into his pocket to pull out a set of keys and a slip of paper. "She'll be here about six."

"*Tonight?*"

"Like I said, they're running out of time." He held out the items in his hand, his smile somewhat apologetic. "Call Matt for the details, and give these keys to Raine, please. Janine made up the guest house, stocked the fridge, and left her Benz in the garage down there for her to use."

Reyes hesitated before releasing a sigh of resignation. "I don't even have the option to say no, do I?"

"I did tell you I was going to hold you to your initial acceptance."

He gave a grim smile and took the paper and keys from the older man's hand. "Lesson learned."

Mark clapped him on the back before heading out. "Thanks, Rey. You got one month to fix what you can. Don't let me down."

Just a personal favor, hey? No pressure.

Sonofabitch.

He watched the senator stride out of sight while fisting the keys in his hand. So much for the trail ride he'd planned on Taz. Now he had three hours to prepare for Her Royal Highness.

Scowling at the number on the paper, he reached for his phone.

Reyes' pulse sped up when the luxury transport trailer pulled in two hours and forty-seven minutes later. *Nothing but the best for a Diamond.* With one shoulder braced against one of the massive vertical support beams that bracketed the barn doorway, he shoved his hands in his front pockets.

He didn't miss the glance Raine shot in his direction as she climbed down from the front passenger seat, but she went straight to the back, followed by a guy he assumed was a groom. The driver got out and busied himself unloading five large suitcases from the cargo compartment. When he dragged out a couple of tack trunks, a dozen bales of hay and three sacks of grain, Reyes stepped forward. He wasn't about to play bellhop for Princess Raine, but helping with the horse's necessities fit his job description.

He transferred the trunks to the empty stall next to the one he'd prepared for her gelding, then made his way around to the back of the trailer. The doors were open, ramp down, but Raine and her horse were still inside. While she murmured in a low voice and tugged on the lead rope, he took a moment to appreciate the view. After skimming his gaze over her slim figure in a white T-shirt, skinny jeans cuffed above the ankle, and white canvas tennis shoes, he forced his attention to her horse.

Diamond Fire. Though he'd seen the gelding in videos of her events online, the sleek, black-bay Trakehner was even more impressive in person. He knew the jumper sported three white socks under his leg wraps, and had a distinctive flame-shaped marking under his ebony forelock. Standing about sixteen hands high, the top of Raine's head barely reached his withers. A tall horse for a petite woman, yet in every video he'd watched, they made a perfect pair.

"You two coming out, or what?" Reyes asked.

Raine started at the sound of his voice, but didn't look his way. "When we're ready," she advised in a cool tone.

It didn't appear they were doing more than just standing there. Another minute passed and he gave voice to his mounting impatience. "Maybe you don't have anything better to do, but I'm already two hours past quitting time."

"Then go," she snapped. "I didn't ask you to stay."

"No, but your uncle did. What's the hold up?"

She huffed out a sigh, shoulders drooping slightly. "He's being stubborn."

He frowned. "Is this normal for him?"

A shake of her head sent a ripple through her dark hair. "No. But then again, there's not much that's been normal lately."

The frustration in her voice sparked sympathy. He knew how it felt to miss normal, though his experience stemmed from an entirely different situation, and things had begun to improve this past year.

Marginally.

Setting that aside, he stepped up onto the ramp. "May I?"

She twisted around to glare at him, as if offended he dared to ask. Then she rolled her eyes and moved back while extending one hand with the lead rope in silent invitation. Clearly, she didn't expect him to succeed where she'd failed.

Or maybe, she *was* as desperate as her father.

Reyes entered the trailer, murmuring softly, keeping his gaze locked on Diamond Fire while taking the rope and easing closer to approach the horse from the side so he wouldn't startle him. Conscious of Raine watching with her arms crossed, he reached a hand to stroke the gelding's neck, then held his palm out for him to smell.

"Hey, boy, how's it going? I bet you're tired after the trip here, so how about we get you out of this box? The sun's still shining, and there's a nice, cool breeze outside."

He kept his voice low and smooth. The horse's ears flicked back and forth, then stayed forward as he arched his neck and turned to bump his forehead against Reyes' chest. When he leaned his weight into him, Reyes took a step back. The gelding turned to follow.

"There you go. Good boy." He gave a gentle pull on the lead and led him toward the ramp. "Come on. We've got a clean stall all set for you, big guy."

Raine muttered, "Traitor," under her breath as they passed. At the bottom of the ramp, she stepped forward and took the lead rope from his hands. "I'm going to walk him around to stretch his legs."

He lifted his palms and stepped away—but not before he caught a whiff of something light and flowery. The enticing scent amped up his pulse all over again. "I'll meet you inside when you're ready."

As she led her horse away, the groom and driver were already closing up the trailer to leave. Reyes stood by the barn as they drove away, leaving Raine's pile of luggage and horse feed stacked by the front doors. Looked like he'd be playing bellhop after all. He gave a low growl, then set to work transferring the hay and grain into the same stall as her trunks.

Nearly fifteen minutes later, the clip-clop of hooves drew him out of the office next to the stable's tack room. He made his way down the aisle to show Raine the stall he'd prepared for Diamond Fire, and the one next to it where he'd stored all the tack and feed.

"How's he doing?"

"He's fine," she said shortly. "I don't know what got into him. He's never done that before."

Reyes didn't know what to say to make her feel better about the horse's refusal to obey. It wasn't like the two of them weren't used to travelling and being in new places on a regular basis, so he couldn't blame it on that. He also didn't quite know why he wanted to ease her distress, so he kept silent as she put the gelding in the stall and checked everything over.

When he noticed her intense scrutiny of every nook and cranny, a spark of defensive annoyance surged forward. "Everything up to your standards, your Highness?"

The sarcasm earned him a sideways glare. “It’s fine,” she said. “You can go now.”

Oh, how badly he wanted to be an asshole after such a haughty dismissal. Instead, he gave her a smile that he hoped irked the shit out of her. “Come on now, I know you don’t *really* want me to leave.”

A flash of alarm lit her hazel eyes a second before she scoffed and arched her brows. “Wanna bet?”

“Wanna carry all that luggage to the guest house by yourself?”

Her gaze cut to the door where the transport driver had left her things in a jumbled pile. She clenched her jaw a second before her shoulders slumped. “No.”

“I’ll give you five minutes to finish up, and then I’ll drive you up to the guest house.”

“I’m not quite ready to leave Fire yet. Just leave everything at the door, and I’ll walk over when I’m finished.”

He had to give her credit for that one—not for ordering him around like her own personal servant, but for taking care of her horse. She looked exhausted after the trip from Texas, and if he was honest, he’d totally expected her to bail on the animal.

“Suit yourself,” he said as he pulled out the keys the senator had given him. “These are for the house. Janine filled the fridge and left her car in the garage for you to use, so you should be all set.”

“Thanks.” Her tone was grudging as she accepted the keys. Then she looked around as if searching for someone. After a long moment, she asked, “Did my uncle say anything to your dad about what’s going on? No one’s bothered to inform me who I’m supposed to be working with, or when we’re supposed to meet. I expected him—or her—to be here tonight.”

Reyes blinked. She didn’t know *he* was her new trainer for the next month?

No, of course not. After all, he was nothing more than a stable boy. It wouldn’t even cross her mind that he might be more than just the guy who shoveled shit for the senator.

This was going to be interesting.

CHAPTER 4

With her running shoes pounding the pavement, Raine made the final turn off the road, back into her aunt and uncle's driveway a little after seven a.m. the next morning. She didn't usually work out until after jump practice, but cooped up in the transport truck for twelve hours yesterday left her restless and full of pent-up energy.

It was cooler up here in Colorado than Texas, and the Rocky Mountains made a beautiful backdrop in the bright sunlight. If only the gorgeous scenery made a difference. Usually, a run helped her relax and decompress, but this morning, thoughts of Reyes Torrez dominated every step of the way.

She shot a glance toward the barn. Last night, his vehicle had been parked outside the doors again when she left Fire, and when she glanced back, she'd noticed lights on in the apartment above the stables. With her aunt and uncle back in Washington, she'd been mildly relieved she wasn't alone at the estate, yet also disturbed to realize the man taking up so much of her mind space lived so close by.

Yesterday, she'd hated admitting to him she didn't know what the hell was going on. She hated even more the smug little grin that had tugged at the corners of his mouth, as if knowing something she didn't was highly amusing. She hated most that when she'd fallen into bed, she'd dreamed about both smacking the smile off his face *and* kissing it off.

It made no sense that she was attracted to a man so wholly infuriating. She'd erroneously figured sleep would give her a reprieve from thinking about him.

"My dad's gone for the next three weeks," Reyes had informed her last night. *"Which means I'm in charge. Your trainer will be here at eight a.m. sharp. Don't be late."*

Even though she had plenty of time, she increased her stride past the stables, headed toward the guest house to take a shower and grab a quick breakfast.

"I'm in charge."

His firm tone when he said those words made her hate that fact as much as everything else. If his, *"Don't be late,"* were any indication, the jerk would probably be a major pain in her ass on purpose. He was already halfway there after getting Fire to follow him out of the trailer like he was the Pied Piper.

Reyes had stalked away last night before she could ask any more questions. Like, *who exactly is this magical, secret trainer my dad thinks will fix everything?*

Why are you such a jerk?

Do you have a girlfriend?

Nope, skip that last one. She didn't need to know, because it didn't matter one bit. She was here for work, not to be distracted by the sexy stable guy. If only Dad had given her the details of this month-long exile instead of making himself scarce so she couldn't hound him about it. And with Mom in Vancouver on a business trip, she'd been no help.

Raine hurried through her shower, ate a quick bowl of oatmeal, and then braided her long, damp hair so it would stay out of her way during the training session. Dressed in a long sleeved T-shirt, breeches, and riding boots, she entered the barn at quarter to eight to the sounds of hooves rustling in the stalls as horses munched their morning hay.

The comfort of a horse barn had always been her sanctuary—until it wasn't.

Reyes stepped out of a stall on the far side of the aisle from Fire, making her heart rate speed up. Geez, was he the only one who worked here? She realized with his father gone, and only eight stalls occupied, the answer was likely yes.

He paused when he saw her, his expression slightly surprised as he glanced at his watch, but then his jaw set, and he continued forward.

She gave him a tight smile and reached for the stall latch as he walked past. When her conscience got the better of her, she spoke over her shoulder while sliding the door open. "Thank you for taking my things to the house last night."

"All part of the job," he quipped.

His dry tone drew her head around, but he'd already disappeared into the office. So much for trying to be civil. She huffed out a breath and tried to put him out of her mind while getting Fire tacked up for work. Thankfully, he seemed closer to his regular self, nudging her shoulder as she tightened the saddle cinch. She took a moment to hug his head to her chest, placed a kiss on his forehead, and said a small prayer today went well.

Well would mean a decent trainer, successful jumps, and Reyes too busy to be anywhere around as a distraction.

After strapping her helmet on, she led Fire from the barn a couple minutes before eight. A glance around revealed no vehicle other than the hunk of junk Reyes had driven last night, and nobody waiting for her in the arena. Maybe her trainer should've received the, *"Don't be late,"* warning, too.

No big deal. She and Fire would start warm-up until he arrived. She led the gelding toward the mounting block.

"I'll give you a leg up."

Reyes' too-close voice made her jerk around with a gasp. How the heck had she not heard him walk up behind her? Only, he really was too close, and she ended up bumping face-first into his chest.

Damn, he smelled good. Like hay, and the outdoors, and an underlying hint of fresh citrus swirled in with all kinds of male goodness.

"Sorry." His hands grasped her shoulders to set her back a step.

She flicked her gaze up and just as quickly dropped it again while turning back to Fire. "I had it, but, yeah, whatever." His chest brushed against her shoulder as he bent to offer his interlocked hands for her boot. Two seconds later, she was in the saddle and looking down at him as she gathered the reins with shaky hands. "Thanks."

"Yep." He patted Fire's neck and headed for the arena.

Raine blew out a silent sigh, her stomach tightening at the thought of him watching them practice. Then she got a good look at the arena and her annoyance spiked as she squeezed her knees to signal Fire forward. All the rails were on the ground. Not a single jump was set up with even an inch of air between the rail and the dirt.

"What is this?" she demanded once she'd ridden through the open gate.

"Back to basics," Reyes replied.

"This is ridiculous. I'm not some ten-year-old beginner." She twisted in her seat to glare at him as he joined her inside the arena. Then she swept her furious gaze toward the barn, and the driveway beyond. "And why is it *I'm* not supposed to be late but this guy—or woman?—isn't even here yet?"

"Who says he isn't here yet?"

The fake innocent tone of his voice instantly stiffened her spine. The tension in her body sent Fire dancing sideways, and she spun him in a circle to settle him down before finally looking at Reyes. Amusement in his sunlit green gaze made her stomach drop out from under her.

"*You?*"

He offered a slight smile. "Me."

"Why didn't you just say so last night?"

"And miss this fun?"

She suppressed the urge to scream, but still tossed out, "Asshole," before urging Fire into a trot around the outdoor arena. She needed a few rounds to cool off. Reyes didn't say a word as she passed the first time. Nor the second.

Smart man.

By the time he'd climbed the fence on her third round and perched on the top rail to watch, she'd managed to get her frustration under control.

"Run the course," he instructed as she and Fire approached. "Mix it up, but take it easy. I want to get a feel for your rhythm."

"Our rhythm is fine," she retorted.

Still, she grit her teeth and did as he said. Three times through, during which he stayed silent. Her annoyance flared yet again. It was one thing to let her cool off, and Lord knew she didn't want to talk to the guy, but if he was supposed to be training her, he was going to have to say something at some point.

Finally, she rode over to the fence and planted Fire directly in front of him. "What exactly are your qualifications?"

He sat balanced on the top rail, hands braced on either side of him, the sun adding blond highlights to his brown hair. "I did some jumping back in high school."

When he didn't add more, she tilted her head in disbelief. "Are you serious right now?"

He smiled while sitting up straight. "I did jump some in high school, though nowhere near your level. However, I have been training horses with my dad since I was fourteen. I took a six year break while in the military, but after coming home almost two years ago, I've been working solo."

Raine snorted. "With what, the few horses my aunt keeps here now?"

"You do know Janine rescues horses, right? Most of them off-the-track-thoroughbreds?"

"Of course." Her dad wrote a check every year to contribute to his sister-in-law's non-profit.

"Well, then you should know, she doesn't keep them all. We celebrated a hundred and fifty rehomed last month."

She had not known *that,* but she should've.

"When they leave here, they've been transitioned into new careers in jumping, hunting, dressage, trail riding, pleasure driving—whatever we discover best suits them."

Still aggravated over the whole situation, she snipped, "So what...are you supposed to be a horse whisperer or something?"

He dropped his gaze as he lifted a shoulder. "The horses respond to me. Always have."

"And how many riders have you worked with?"

"You would be the first."

"Perfect." Her dad was putting her Olympic hopes in the hands of a guy with no professional experience at all. "How could this go wrong?"

He lifted his gaze once more. "I saw the tapes of your last two events. Whatever you were doing back home wasn't working. If you ask me, you've got nothing to lose."

"Well, I didn't ask you, did I?"

"Technically, you did."

"That was a rhetorical question. You do know what rhetorical means, don't you?"

He smirked at her sarcasm before jumping down from the fence to stride toward one of the jumps. She watched as he put the rails in the cups and then moved on to the next one.

Good. About damn time they got down to real work.

When the last rail was in place, he raised a hand over his head and swiveled his wrist in a circle to indicate she should get started. Despite wanting the real jumps, her nerves tingled to life as she urged Fire forward. Once around the arena to loosen him up, because her tension from the exchange with Reyes was making him antsy.

Way number one it would go wrong—the guy annoyed the hell

out of her and made her nervous. Which made her horse nervous. Not a good combination.

Stop thinking about him.

Focus on Fire. Focus on the jumps.

Imagine walking into the Olympic stadium with the U.S. Equestrian Team, the American flag rippling above your head.

Her dad had painted that picture with her so often over the years, the image sprang to life with ease.

Another half-round at an easy canter settled her and Fire into the familiar rhythm that had gotten them to the top, so she reined him onto the course. Over the next hour, Reyes directed them through a multitude of combinations. Other than the called out instructions, he simply watched. His intense scrutiny was really starting to mess with her head, especially when for the third time in a row, Fire refused an easy one meter vertical.

"You're breaking the rhythm," Reyes called out, shaking his head.

"*He* won't go over the jump."

"Because you're telling him not to."

"I am not."

"You're easing up on approach, sending mixed signals, and it's throwing him off. He doesn't know what you want him to do."

Just like Charlie, he was blaming her for Fire's refusal. Her jaw ached from the force of her clenched teeth. How did no one understand what the fall had done to him? He was afraid. It was going to take time for him to get over it and get his confidence back. She knew her horse better than they did, damn it.

"He needs a break," she announced. And so did she.

Before Reyes could disagree with her, she swung her leg over and dismounted. She didn't get more than two strides toward the gate when he moved into their path.

He held out his hand, palm up. "Give me the reins."

"I can take care of him myself."

"That's a given. But first I want to try something."

She wanted to tell him to go to hell, but after a long moment, she slapped the reins into his palm. He draped them back over Fire's neck while moving to the opposite side to lower the right stirrup. Grudgingly, she lowered the one on her side, too.

When he joined her on the left side, she wordlessly bent to offer her interlocked hands and boosted him up into the saddle. His western boots and jeans looked completely out of place with her English saddle, but his form was flawless as he nudged Fire into a trot, and then a canter. He made a circuit of the arena, to get a feel for the horse beneath him, she assumed, then took him over a couple of the jumps Fire had completed for her with ease.

Next, he pointed him toward the vertical Fire had refused three times in a row, and Raine's entire body went rigid. Her breath shortened as her pulse beat faster.

Fire sailed right over without a second of hesitation.

A flash of relief was replaced by fury. She clenched her fists at her sides as Reyes rode up and dismounted. Because she totally expected a smug smile, his solemn expression left her confused.

"And what do you think that proved?" she accused. "That you're better than me?"

"No. That you're the one who's afraid, not your horse."

Her stomach lurched as if she'd just done a loop-de-loop on a roller coaster immediately after lunch. She wanted to grab the reins from his hand and run, but she forced herself to face him squarely. "I am not afraid."

"There's no shame in it, Raine. That was a tough wreck by anyone's standards."

"How would you know?"

"I saw the tape."

Of course he had. Seemed he'd seen all kinds of tape lately. Her gut clenched at the thought of him watching her fail.

"It's going to take some working through," he added. "Especially if you haven't even admitted it to yourself yet."

"There's nothing to admit," she bit out. "We're fine."

"Come on now. You don't believe that any more than I do."

The surprising gentleness in his tone made her eyes sting, and she snatched the reins to lead Fire back to the barn.

"I didn't say we were done."

She ignored him and kept walking while reaching up to yank at the strap of her helmet. After pulling it off, she transferred it to her left hand with the reins so she could swat away the stray strands of hair tickling her cheeks.

"Hey."

All the gentle was gone from his voice. And the command that had taken its place pissed her off enough to yell over her shoulder, "*I* say we're done. In fact, I'm done with *all of this*." She reached back to wave her arm in a huge circle to indicate the entire arena behind her as she continued toward the barn. "I'm calling my dad, and I'm going home."

"Wow. You gave it what? Two hours?"

"That's all it took to see you don't have a clue what you're doing."

"So, you're not only afraid of the jumps, you're afraid of me, too."

His voice came from right behind her, and she flinched before whirling around. "I'm not afraid of you. I just can't stand you."

Liar.

He crossed his arms. "Whatever you gotta tell yourself."

She practically growled as she leaned forward. "I *don't* like you. Sorry if it hurts your fragile little ego, but you were a jerk last summer, and you've been a jerk since I got here last night. The truth is, it's taking everything I have not to smack you right now."

His eyebrows shot up as he gave a short laugh of disbelief. "Really?"

"Yes, *really*."

"Well, by all means then, go ahead." He bent closer, his green eyes locked with hers as he murmured softly, "I dare you."

She narrowed her gaze at the cocky taunt. After a few seconds, his lips twitched into a smirk and she lost it.

CHAPTER 5

Reyes heard the *crack* as pain exploded in his cheek. His head snapped to the side, and he froze for a stunned moment. Slowly, he turned his head back. Raine's cheeks were beet red—likely matching his left one.

"I can't believe you just did that."

Her chin lifted defensively as she took a wary step back. "You told me to."

"Yeah, but I didn't think you'd *actually* do it."

"Well, word to the wise—don't dare a Diamond, 'cuz we don't back down." With that parting shot, she pivoted and resumed her trek to the barn.

He raised his hand to his throbbing cheek as he followed at a distance. Hell, she was a lot stronger than she looked. Then again, he shouldn't be surprised when she spent her days in a saddle controlling a twelve-hundred pound beast. He'd underestimated her for sure—yet another lesson learned at the hand of a Diamond in less than two days.

However, he had his answer, didn't he? Yes, she was afraid, but she wasn't willing to give up without a fight. Now all she needed to do was come to that realization by herself.

Reyes went to the office to do paperwork while Raine took care of her horse. A half an hour later, he heard her boots a moment before her slim form shadowed the doorway. He glanced up from an email on the computer from Janine about Morning Glory's adoption.

"I'm not leaving," Raine stated.

Strong and smart.

He gave her a mocking smile. "Daddy said you can't come home?"

Her jaw clenched, and her hands fisted at her sides. Man, it was so easy to push her buttons. He couldn't help but wonder how responsive she'd be if he pushed other buttons. More enjoyable buttons.

His blood warmed, and he had to swallow hard against a wave of want.

"I didn't call my dad."

He'd already figured that. Her father had been very adamant on the phone yesterday, and if she had called him, Reyes was pretty sure she wouldn't be all blustery and challenging right now. She'd decided to prove to herself—and him—she wasn't afraid of anything. He'd like to say *good*, but first he needed her to face what had happened. Only when she admitted her fear could she confront it and *then* prove she could get past it.

In the meantime, a few more buttons couldn't hurt. "I'm proud of you, Princess. That's a big step all by yourself."

Her nose scrunched up in a scowl. If she knew how cute she looked, she'd be even more pissed than she was right now.

Defiance glittered in her eyes as she crossed her arms. "I'm only staying to watch you fail."

"Then we're both agreed." He leaned forward, bracing his forearms on the desk. "We'll be doing things my way."

"Whatever." She started to turn away, then paused to look back. "Dad must be paying you a lot to make this all worth it."

Reyes drew back the slightest bit, surprised not only by her words, but the offense they sparked. "He's not paying me a dime."

Her gaze narrowed, and she hesitated a beat. "He can afford it, you know."

"You can all afford it," he tossed back. "You're Diamonds."

She gave him a sugar-sweet smile. "You should've negotiated."

"Your uncle asked me to help. It never even crossed my mind to ask for anything above my regular wages."

"Hmm. Note to self. Save words to the wise for someone who's actually wise."

She was gone before he could tell her not everything was about money. Granted, he hadn't taken this assignment willingly, but even if he had, he wouldn't have expected to get paid more for doing something Mark and Janine already generously compensated him for. And if he was being honest, he wanted to help her get her confidence back so she could once more be the winner he'd seen in earlier tapes.

He glanced out the window to see Raine crossing the wide expanse of lawn to the guest house. He'd intended to schedule an afternoon session, but he didn't have her phone number—a fact he'd need to rectify—and he wasn't about to go chasing after her. Since it was only the first day, he decided tomorrow would be soon enough to set a firm schedule.

Returning his attention to the computer, he sent a message to Janine agreeing Moring Glory was ready to graduate, and yes, the Hamiltons would be a great fit for the mare. Then he confirmed a Friday morning showing with the couple who'd already adopted two horses from them. Counting today, he had three days to get in a little extra work with her.

But in the meantime, he was going to take his unexpected afternoon off and get out for a ride. Yesterday's schedule had been thrown off after he'd been ambushed by Mark, and Taz was as anxious for some exercise as he was for some solitude on the trails.

Though, come to think of it, the heaviness that usually settled in his chest after a few days of being restrained to the barn was absent. In fact, there was an energy invigorating his blood that had him looking forward to tomorrow morning when he should be dreading dealing with the headstrong brunette. But Raine provided a challenge—one he hadn't realized he'd even wanted until she announced she was staying.

"I'm only staying to watch you fail."

He was pretty sure she'd said that just to be contrary. It would make no sense for her to sabotage him on purpose, because if he failed, she failed. And he'd stake his job on that being the last thing she wanted.

For the rest of the morning and an hour after lunch, he took care of miscellaneous chores until it was time for a ride. In the middle of saddling his thoroughbred, his older brother strode into the barn. "Hey, Rey. You heading out or finishing up?"

He glanced at Dev over the saddle. "Heading out. Want to come?"

"Hell yeah. Who you got for me?"

"Morning Glory or Stimpy. Both could use the exercise."

"No offense to Morning Glory, but Stimpy's my guy."

Dev headed to the tack room for a saddle and bridle, and Reyes noted his limp was almost undetectable today. It became more pronounced in damp weather, but even so, his brother had progressed in all areas since January. Thanks to time and therapy—and Shelby.

It had seemed strange at first, Dev with the youngest of the Diamonds, but she'd been a key part of bringing him back to the man he used to be. Of making him realize he still had a whole hell of a lot to offer the world outside of the military. Their whole family had loved her before, but now, they'd be forever grateful.

"Shelby working at the clinic?" he asked as they rode out side by side a few minutes later.

"She's at the guest house visiting her cousin, so I decided to tag along."

"Ah. Should've guessed that."

Dev shot him a sideways look that held a combination wince and grin. "I hear you're her new trainer."

He laughed as he worked at containing Taz's energy beneath

him. "If that came from Raine, I imagine you heard quite the earful."

"She's not a fan," his brother confirmed with a chuckle. "Shelby sang your praises, but Raine was having none of that."

Reyes shrugged. "My job is to get her back to competition level in her jumping, not gain a groupie."

"A groupie?" Dev scoffed. "You fancy yourself a rock star?"

"I was sticking with the 'fan' analogy, that's all." He made the turn for the trail leading into the forest, and his brother reined Stimpy to follow.

"Shelby was telling me on the drive over about Raine's accident last year."

"Yeah." He slowed Taz until they were riding side by side again. "As far as I know, she hasn't been over the jump they wrecked on since then. She insists they're fine, but I saw it this morning—she's scared spitless when they head for that jump."

"And you're going to fix it?"

"I'm going to try."

"I wasn't aware you were working with horses *and* riders now."

"I'm doing a favor for Mark."

After a moment of silence, his brother glanced over. "You know what it sounds like?"

His solemn, sympathetic tone had Reyes nodding. Neither one of them needed to say post traumatic stress out loud. They both dealt with their own demons enough to recognize someone else's.

"Has she talked to a professional yet?"

"I didn't ask, but I doubt it." She couldn't even admit her fear, so yeah, he highly doubted she'd gone to therapy for it.

"And how about you?"

"I'm good." He felt his brother's intense gaze and shot him a quick glance while insisting, "Really, I've been feeling much better."

"I didn't ask if you were good, I asked if you've talked to anyone yet."

"I'm talking to you." At his brother's rough sigh, he met his gaze. "Listen, man, I'm living my therapy. Working with the horses.

Finding them homes with Janine. Riding out here in the woods. It's been helping more than you know."

"You still sleeping with the lights on?"

Reyes tensed, and Taz gave a little lurch forward. He tightened his grip on the reins and brought the thoroughbred back to a walk.

"I'll take that as a *yes,*" Dev said dryly.

He shrugged, but remained silent. Talking to his brother helped sometimes, and other times, not so much. It left him feeling like a fraud. So what if he had trouble sleeping if it was completely dark? Big whoop if he spent a buck or two more in electricity each month. It wasn't like he'd nearly lost his leg like Dev, or lost his life like Cory Neider the day the bomb had exploded.

The little flicker of resentment that accompanied those thoughts was immediately squashed. While he knew PTSD didn't have to be extreme to be legitimate, and everyone's threshold was different, he also wasn't going to wallow in self-pity when his physical issues had resolved themselves, and his only visible reminder was a thin white scar mostly hidden by the goatee he kept neatly trimmed. He hadn't been left with years of recovery and endless hours of physical therapy like so many others.

At times he almost wished he had been.

Almost.

Dev reined Stimpy closer, gaining his attention. "So, what's your plan with Raine?"

He never thought he'd see the day, but Reyes welcomed the return subject of his new challenge so he could focus on the therapy of the ride.

To answer his brother's question, he said, "First I've got to get her to talk. Then I'm going to get her over that jump."

CHAPTER 6

"It's still a little unreal to see you and Dev together." Raine handed Shelby a bottle of iced tea as they stepped out onto the guest house patio. "I'm really happy for you."

"Thanks." She twisted the cap off her drink. "Sometimes I still can't believe it myself."

"Well, you guys seem great together."

"We are. Don't get me wrong, it was bumpy at first, but now things are really good."

Shelby's soft smile was so sappy, Raine's chest thumped with envy. She smiled as her cousin kicked off her sandals and sat on the edge of the pool. Having changed into a lycra sport tank and yoga capris for her workout, she dropped down beside her, facing the mountains as they swished their feet in the warm water.

"Remember that summer we were fifteen, and we spent the day at the pool with everyone up by the main house when he was home on leave? We were a couple of giggling idiots."

Shelby laughed. "Oh my God, I know. But then again, who could blame us? The Torrez brothers were as hot then as they are now."

Ignoring the plural, she sighed dramatically. "No more drooling over Dev for me."

Shelby leaned to nudge her with her shoulder. "You don't fool me, Cuz."

"What?"

"Don't what me. You played it cool, but we both know you were teasing the shit out of Reyes back then."

Yeah, she'd gone in and out of the house for more lemonade than she could possibly drink. And each time, she made sure her path inside was right past his chair, or wherever he was in the pool. She'd been loud and outgoing while playing volleyball and chicken with her cousins, but the problem was, no matter how much attention she tried to draw to herself, he'd openly ignored her. Same as last July.

"I didn't even talk to him," she protested.

"But you made sure he couldn't take his eyes off you."

She rolled her eyes, though her pulse skipped at that revelation. She hadn't known he'd noticed her. "Reyes has always had a chip on his shoulder with me. Last summer we ran into each other at the stables, and he was a jerk. He's still a jerk."

Except for the luggage.

She shoved aside the flicker of guilt for purposely overlooking that when she called him a jerk to his face earlier. Why should she feel bad when she'd tried to thank him, only to have him brush her gratitude aside with his flippant comeback about it being part of his job? It so wasn't.

Shelby frowned beside her. "That's so weird. And so unlike Reyes."

"Lucky me," she quipped before changing the subject. "How's everything going now that your clinic is open?"

"Good. You should come check it out while you're here."

"I'd love to. Do you all still do brunch even when Uncle Mark and Aunt Janine are in Washington? Because I'm having dinner with Grandpa and Grandma tonight, but I want to see everyone—especially the babies."

"They're the best," Shelby gushed with a huge grin. "I *love* being an aunt."

"I bet. None of my brothers are even close to getting married," she pouted.

"I'll share, and yes, we still do brunch. Wait until you see the babies. Maverick has caught up on everything after being nearly two months early, and Ava is so precious."

Maverick was Merit and Mae's little boy, born last November. Ava belonged to Asher and Honor, and had been born in January.

She wasn't sure she could wait four more days until Sunday. "What about Celia and Robert? Any talk from them about kids?"

"They're trying, but no luck yet." She made a sad face. "I pray it happens soon for them, though, because I know Loyal and Rox are already trying."

She wasn't surprised. They'd been talking about kids at their wedding back in February.

"Does it give you the bug?" Raine teased.

Shelby's grin answered before her words. "A little, but we'd like some time to ourselves after the wedding. Especially after how crazy everything was this past spring."

Crazy was an understatement to describe what Bells and Dev had gone through with her psycho stalker. She reached out to squeeze her cousin's hand. "I'm so glad you're okay after all of that."

"Thanks. I was lucky to have Dev—even though I didn't want him as a bodyguard at first."

"Good thing he was."

"Believe me, I know." She fiddled with her bottle cap before offering a sideways smile. "And on that note...I want to say, make sure you give Reyes a chance, okay?"

Her pulse skipped, because her first thought after their talk of marriage and babies was, *give him a chance with what?* But there was only one thing her cousin was talking about. "Dad didn't give me much of a choice. And unfortunately, he's right. I'm getting nowhere with Charlie right now."

"Reyes is really good with horses, Raine. And when I say really good, I mean crazy amazing."

"Yeah, but no experience training riders at all." Resentment bled into her voice. She couldn't believe her dad would put her future in his hands.

"Maybe he'll be just what you and Fire need," Shelby said.

Raine gave her cousin a brief smile. "I guess we'll see, won't we?"

But she didn't *need* anything, least all him.

~

The next morning, Raine kept her gaze trained straight ahead as she passed the stable office on her way to Fire's stall.

"Hey—hold up. Can you come in here for a minute?"

Reyes' loud voice made her pulse skip a few beats before taking off like a thoroughbred from the starting gate. Having already been fighting a bit of irritating breathlessness from the thought of seeing him again, she halted, closed her eyes to suck in a fortifying breath, then blew it back out again before backtracking.

One look at the man and any calming effects flew out the barn doors. Yesterday, he'd worn a thin button up over his T-shirt, with the sleeves rolled up, tanned forearms on full display. Today was already warmer than yesterday, and she got the full treat of not only sexy, muscled forearms, but biceps stretching the short sleeves of a dark green T-shirt.

She dragged her gaze up from his drool-worthy arms. Damn it all. With his golden-tipped, caramely hair and those long, dark lashes, he was way too attractive for her peace of mind.

When she realized he was giving her a once-over, her pulse stumbled again, and her nipples instantly tightened. She crossed her arms to hide the reaction. His lashes lifted at the movement, and heat infused her cheeks as their gazes connected.

"What?" she asked, the word coming out clipped and defensive.

He gestured to a straight-back chair in front of the desk. "I set up a schedule for your training. I figured we should both know what's going on."

He set up the schedule, because *he* figured. She dropped down onto the seat, arms still crossed. "Yeah. *We* both should."

He flicked his gaze up to hers as he handed a sheet of paper across the desk. Raine snatched it from him and scanned the agenda line by line. He should've *figured* she should get a say in her own schedule.

A flick of her wrist sent the paper sliding back across the desk. "This isn't going to work."

His gaze narrowed as he leaned forward on his forearms. She glanced down, then forced her attention back to his face.

"What's wrong with it?" he asked.

"For starters, you didn't even bother to ask me what might work for me."

"I told you yesterday, we're doing this my way."

"It's *my* career," she snapped.

"And it's *my* job to get you back where you need to be," he countered. "Except it's only *part* of my job."

She had to consciously unclench her jaw, though she didn't speak. After a long moment, he sat back, the leather office chair creaking with his movements.

"What's wrong with the schedule?" he repeated, his tone unexpectedly softer.

"The only time you've left for my workouts is in the middle of the day, and it's not even enough time."

"You're worried about working out?" he asked with a frown.

"Yes." She drew the word out on purpose. "If you had bothered to ask, or you know, ever worked with a professional rider, you'd know strength training and cardio is just as important as the riding."

His frown deepened as he reached for the schedule. "You can't fit it in before or after?"

"If I do my usual three hours in the morning, I'll have to be up at four-thirty. If I do it after, my day won't end until after seven o'clock. It's a part of my job, and it needs to be part of my schedule, not something I fit in after hours."

"Fine. I'll move the afternoon riding session back an hour and a half and you can fit it in either before or after lunch."

"I ride in the mornings and workout in the afternoon. Then I only have to shower once."

Shower? Did she really have to say the word *shower* to him? In the next moment, she imagined him standing in a cloud of steam, biceps bulging on his raised arms as hot water chased suds down the length of his long, lean body. Her cheeks burned at the alarmingly vivid image just as his gaze flicked up to hers.

Oh my God, imagine if he could read my mind!

He cleared his throat and returned his attention to the paper. "I have a specific reason for morning and afternoon sessions," he stated, his voice slightly rough.

"And as I just told you, I have a specific reason for getting all the riding done in the morning."

His mouth pressed into a grim line before he set the paper down and linked his fingers together over the top of it. "Then let's compromise."

"There's nothing to compromise."

"Sure there is. We'll do my schedule Monday, Wednesday, and Friday, and yours on Tuesday, Thursday, and Saturday."

Though she knew it was childish, the thought of giving in irked her to no end. Back home, Charlie never had a problem following the schedule she set up. Same with every other trainer she'd had, because they worked for her, not the other way around.

Reyes blew out a breath that sounded as frustrated as she felt. "We've got twenty-nine days to go here, Raine. It'll go a lot faster if we work together."

The words were an unexpected slap in the face. He was already counting down the days.

She couldn't blame him. She wanted time to pass faster, too. Yet, hearing him voice the desire outright made her chest tighten with resentment and another emotion she refused to acknowledge.

"Unless your plan is to purposely sabotage this whole thing," he added. "Seeing as you only stayed to watch me fail."

She rolled her eyes. "I didn't really mean that."

"Good. Because that would be really stupid on your part."

Completely annoyed at the inference, she shoved to her feet and reached for the paper and pen near his forearm. Her fingers brushed against his warm skin for a brief second, and she jerked back from the contact at the same time he moved his arm. Ignoring the electric tingles spreading through her body, she leaned over to write down her version of the schedule for her set days.

"There. All set." She slapped the pen down and straightened. "And today is Thursday, just so you know."

"I'm well aware of what day it is."

"Good. Then I'll meet you in the arena in fifteen."

She turned to leave, quick strides carrying her to the door.

"Raine."

His tone was firm, yet it also held an unexpected plea that had her pausing in the doorway.

"I was a squad leader in the Army. My orders were followed without question. That's how we got things done."

"Yeah, well, I am not one of your soldiers," she snipped.

"No, you most definitely are not," he muttered.

A quick twist caught him jerking his gaze up from her ass. She was surprised by a slight tinge of pink in his cheeks as he straightened in the chair.

"Anyway," he said quickly. "I apologize for not talking to you about the schedule first. It won't happen again."

She nodded and left, because she didn't know what to say when he went and said something nice. After telling her yesterday they'd be doing things his way, the apology was right up there with the luggage.

CHAPTER 7

Reyes crossed the lawn toward the guest house later that night. He'd debated this move for most of the afternoon, but thinking back over Raine's morning riding session, he knew he needed to get through to her sooner than later.

Halfway through the session, he'd put her on Taz. Or tried to. She'd gotten pissed off and left early—because she knew if she got up on his horse and still didn't make it over the jump, he'd know for sure it was her who kept refusing, not Diamond Fire. He already knew for sure, and none of her blustery, logical excuses changed his mind.

Coming up on the side of the house, he angled toward the front until a splash from the back patio made him pause. Doing his best to block the memory of a little red bikini, he switched direction. Landscape lighting lit the way around back, where the in-ground pool glowed an inviting Caribbean blue in the dark night.

Clad in a black one-piece, Raine's slim form cut sinuously through the water, her movements sure and swift as she swam from one end of the pool to the other. He watched for a moment, wondering if a nighttime swim was part of her daily workout, or if she was driven by something else. A need to be completely exhausted just so she could catch a few hours of sleep before the dreams woke her up?

Stop projecting.

He moved to the edge of the pool, lining up with her before taking a knee to swish his hand in the water to get her attention.

Her fingers brushed against his when she reached for the wall. She jerked to the side and shoved away, the move sending a wave rolling across the pool. Surfacing with a sputter, she ripped off her swim goggles and glared up at him.

"Damn it, Reyes, you scared the hell out of me!"

He pushed back into a squat. "I wasn't sure how long it would take for you to realize I was here, and I didn't want to be all creepy by just standing and watching."

"Yeah, well, you failed."

When he grinned at her disgruntled tone, her glare intensified.

She swiped a hand across her face, brushing aside the wet strands of hair that had escaped her long braid. "What do you want?"

"To talk."

She huffed and rolled her eyes. "If this is about earlier, I'll make up the time tomorrow."

"It's not about earlier."

"Then what could you possibly want to talk about?"

"Your accident."

Her head jerked up. Panic flashed a second before her expression shuttered, and she averted her gaze with a shake of her head. "Nope."

"I'm not leaving until we talk, Raine."

"Gonna be a long night for you then."

Before he could say anything more, she put the goggles back on and swirled around to resume swimming. Reyes blew out a loud sigh as he rose. Raine reached the far end, executed a rapid turn underwater, and swam back toward him. At his end of the pool, she flipped and started another lap without slowing down.

The way she attacked the water confirmed she was doing her

damnedest to out swim her demons. Problem was, his mind was starting to wander off task. Instead of considering how to get her to open up, he was thinking about his hands gliding over her pale skin instead of the water.

Or better yet, his lips.

You're here to train her, not maul her.

Right. Stay on task.

Except she was right. If he waited for her to give in, he'd probably end up sleeping out here in one of the deck chairs.

Fuck that.

Reaching up behind his head, he grabbed a fistful of T-shirt to drag it over his head. He bent to pull off one boot, then the other, then stripped off his jeans and socks. When he was down to his boxer briefs, he dove into the water and swam after her. The temperature was warm enough to not be a shock, but cool enough to be refreshing.

Raine did that underwater somersault turn, saw him, and jackknifed to the surface. He rose up a few feet from her. She'd pulled off the goggles again and was already yelling.

"—kidding me right now? What the hell?"

He treaded water while reaching up to rake his dripping hair off his forehead. "I told you we need to talk, and I don't have all night to wait you out."

"That's your problem, not mine."

Her words were full of bravado, but her expression had a frantic edge as she moved to swim away.

Reyes lunged to catch her arm. Combined momentum made their bodies collide under the water. Shock widened her eyes, and a gasp parted her lips as a molten wave of awareness flooded his veins. Heart thudding hard, he released her and eased back a couple feet. She was already feeling threatened, last thing he wanted was for her to be afraid of him physically.

But she remained facing him instead of rushing to get away again. A glimpse of her pink tongue swiping across her glistening lips had him biting back a low groan.

Raising his gaze to the spiked lashes framing her luminous hazel eyes, he forced his brain to stop thinking with his dick. "Do you even want to compete anymore?"

Surprise flashed across her face a second before her forehead furrowed, and she looked away. "Of course I do. I just don't understand why you want to make me talk about what happened. I've been trying to forget it."

"*That's* why. You need to face it, not forget it." When she gave a wild shake of her head, he leaned to the side and scissored his legs to move back into her line of vision. "Trust me. I know what I'm talking about."

"You saw the tape, but you weren't there."

"I'm talking in general. We all have our demons to fight."

Her angry gaze speared into his. "Yeah? And what's your demon?"

"I don't like the dark." The words slipped out without thought, and his breath seized in his throat as she gaped at him in surprise.

What the fuck? Where had that come from?

"Why don't you like the dark?"

His heart beat thunderously loud in his ears. "This isn't about me."

She tilted her head. "Not so fun when the tables are turned, is it?"

Definitely not. Time to turn them back. "You said Diamonds don't back down. It's time to face this head on."

Annoyance narrowed her gaze. "Is that supposed to be a dare or something?"

He arched his brows and shrugged. "If that's what it takes."

She gave a slow shake of her head, then twisted around to swim toward the deepest, darkest corner of the pool. Her movements were slow and measured instead of a frantic escape. Reyes followed, keeping a good two feet between them when she folded her arms on the edge and stared into the privacy hedges along the back side of the patio.

After a moment of silence, she said softly, "How about we compromise?"

Her soft, almost empathetic tone made his gut clench with foreboding. He hadn't turned the tables far enough. Resting one arm on the brick rim, he warily studied her shadowed profile. "There's nothing to compromise."

She turned her head to meet his gaze. "Tell me why you don't like the dark, and I'll tell you about the accident."

Fuck.

He'd given her a hand grenade, and she'd just pulled the pin.

CHAPTER 8

Raine saw the hunted look in Reyes' eyes and knew exactly how he felt. What she hadn't expected though, was the guilt that squeezed her chest when she watched his silent struggle with her negotiation.

It was only fair, and yet she had to bite her tongue to keep from telling him to forget it. She also had to lock each hand around the opposite wrist to keep from turning to him, from reaching out to touch his arm, his chest, or from wrapping her arms around his neck as she plastered her mouth and body to his. Bet he'd forget about talking then.

But as much as she wanted that, she also didn't. Because while the man could rile her up like no one else, little glimpses of decency, kindness, and compassion beneath his rough exterior had her dying to learn more about *that* guy.

Like why *he* was afraid of the dark.

He hadn't quite admitted that, but she could read between the lines. Same as he could apparently read between all of hers.

So she waited, her gaze memorizing the details of his face as he wrestled with his demons. Prominent eyebrows, high cheekbones, somewhat square jaw. She'd never been attracted to a guy with facial hair before, but his was neatly trimmed and a hell of a lot sexier than she ever would've expected.

Her attention snagged on a thin, pale scar along the edge of his whiskers on the right side of his chin. Illuminated by the underwater pool lights, it stood out in stark contrast to the darker tone of his skin.

That right there. She wanted to know how he got it, and when?

Did he have more scars? Where?

She wanted to draw along the white line with her fingertip. Lean forward and trace it with the tip of her tongue.

A wave of heat relaxed her grip on her arms. She started to turn the rest of her body toward him, until his lashes rose, and the torment in his darkened gaze froze her on the spot.

"Three years ago, I was blind for five days."

Of all the things he could've said, she never would've guessed something like that.

Three years ago...he'd been in the military then, hadn't he?

"It was one hundred percent. No shadows. Nothing."

Raine swallowed past a sudden lump in her throat and whispered, "What happened?"

"Bomb."

She waited for more, but he shook his head, his jaw set.

Raine sighed softly. Even without knowing details, she couldn't imagine how terrifying it must've been to be blinded and believe you'd never see again. And though it appeared his vision had recovered, after something like that, she could totally understand why he wouldn't like the dark.

Guilt crowded in again, and she reached out to cover his hand with hers. "I'm sorry."

His gaze shifted from hers to their hands. Self-conscious, she started to pull back, but he twisted his wrist and caught her fingers. "You have nothing to be sorry for—but it *is* your turn."

Her heart lurched in her chest both from the warmth of his touch and the insistence in his gruff voice. Her experience paled by comparison.

"My fall over a horse jump doesn't really seem like a big deal now, does it?"

"Don't do that."

He shook his head, his fingers squeezing hers, the pressure almost painful before he relaxed his hold.

"Never minimize what happened to you. It doesn't have to compare to what anyone else has gone through. Someone else's experience does not make the trauma you experienced any less worthy of serious attention."

The lump in her throat doubled in size, and she blinked against the painful sting of tears. She hadn't ever really thought of her accident as trauma. Pulling her hand free from his, she turned back to the hedges, wishing she could hide deep in the shadows of their branches. He didn't like the dark. She welcomed the cover it provided.

"The whole thing is still so vivid in my mind," she whispered. "Just thinking about it puts me right back in the moment."

Water lapped against her back when he moved closer. Close enough for her shoulder to brush against his chest, her hip against his thigh. The contact was like an anchor she didn't even know she needed.

"Fire was on point that day. He sailed over every jump without a single fault. We were well under the course time limit, and when we made the final turn, there were only three jumps left." She closed her eyes, and the image was *right there.*

With a quick shake of her head, she opened her eyes again.

But the jump remained.

"The way they were set up, I misjudged the height on the vertical, which was stupid, because I *knew* the height from the walk-through. But the visual between the rails threw me off and I timed it wrong. Fire tried to refuse at the last second, and I wouldn't let him, so he tried to clear it but got tangled in the rails—"

"Breathe," Reyes murmured next to her ear.

She sucked in a gasping breath and realized her whole body was shaking.

Against him.

When had he moved that close? When had he put his arm around her? And damn it, she was crying.

"Now let it back out."

He meant the breath, not her tears. She did as instructed while his hand rubbed up and down the arm not pressed against his chest.

"Take another."

The soothing tone of his voice calmed her enough to think past the panic. Except when her words replayed in her head, a sob escaped her tight lungs. "Oh my God—it was my fault."

"It's no one's fault."

She shook her head while insisting, "It was mine. *I* messed up. Fire could've broken a leg—or both. I could've killed him."

"Is that why you're afraid of the jump?"

Raine gave a jerky nod without even thinking. "He trusted me. I forced him to jump, and he trusted me, and I could've killed him."

"He still trusts you."

"He shouldn't."

When Reyes pulled her closer, she didn't resist. Not only did she not resist, she turned to wrap both arms around his neck and held on for dear life while he held them afloat with his one-handed grip on the edge. The pool was heated, but it was the warmth from his body that battled the chill of her memories as his lips brushed against her temple.

"He trusts you because you're his partner," he murmured. "You have to learn to trust yourself again. And to trust him."

That lump materialized in her throat once more. "I-I don't know if I can."

"That's why you're here," he said. "We're gonna figure this out, Raine. I promise."

She wished his words offered comfort, but she worried what they were going to figure out was equally as frightening as the jump. She went back to the question he'd asked earlier. Did she want to compete anymore? Was she willing to risk so much for her dream of Olympic gold?

Was it *her* dream?

That question jolted hard, but another press of Reyes' lips suddenly shifted her awareness.

Or maybe she was desperate for a diversion, mentally running from the uncertainty of her future.

Whatever the reason, she became conscious of every inch where their bodies touched. He held onto the side of the pool with one hand, his arm wrapped around her waist and hers around his neck. There wasn't an inch to separate them, from their hips to where her breasts pressed against his bare chest.

She stilled, a hairsbreadth away from burying her face in the crook of his neck to drown herself in his arousing scent. When her brain registered his growing erection against her stomach, her pulse went all haywire. Molten heat flooded her veins before pooling into a yearning throb deep inside. Her nipples tightened, and her legs grew heavy from the wave of desire.

His breathing had become as shallow as hers. "Raine."

There was the tiniest note of regret in his voice. Or maybe a warning?

She ignored both. With her heart thumping like mad, she loosened her hold around his neck and flattened one palm against the side of his head to turn his face to hers. He didn't resist, but when her mouth found his, he tensed for a heart-stopping second.

With the proof of his desire against her belly, she licked at the seam of his lips, demanding his participation. From one breath to the next, his arm tightened around her ribs, and he slanted his mouth over hers to take control of the kiss with a toe-curling growl. His tongue dueled with hers, each stroke setting off a pulse deep in her core.

God, how many times had she thought of a moment like this over the past ten months—and even a few times before that? Reality was *so* much better than her imagination.

Swept up in the moment, she raised one leg to hook over his hip and ground herself against his hardness. Reyes sucked in a breath and muttered something against her lips, but dove right back in when she lifted her other leg and wrapped them both around his waist. How easy it would be to slip off her one-piece and his briefs and forget everything for a while.

Hopefully a long while.

The thought curved her lips under his, until his hand closed over her breast. Her breath hitched when he rubbed a thumb over her hard nipple, then she gasped when he pinched. She arched into his palm before maneuvering to drag one strap of her suit off her shoulder, then the other.

His gaze dropped as she peeled her suit down to her waist while lifting up so her breasts were out of the water for him to see and touch. The move earned her another low groan, but the unmistakable tone of regret in the rumbling sound sparked a flutter of panic in her chest.

"Fuck," he muttered while closing his eyes.

Yep. There it was again.

Her stomach sank, and she lowered herself back down until the water lapped at her chin. Still, her legs were locked around his waist. His erection still pressed against her core.

Dread chipped at her confidence as she asked, "What?"

He winced, his eyes still closed. "I can't."

She frowned in confusion, especially given his obvious arousal —until the word *bomb* echoed in her mind. Oh, God, now she felt bad. "Reyes…I…I'm sorry."

His eyes popped open, and his forehead furrowed. "Don't apologize. It's my fault, not yours. I shouldn't have taken advantage."

Wait—*what?*

Confusion kept her from resisting as he pulled her suit back up to cover her chest, then gently unlocked her legs, and guided her hand to hang on to the edge of the pool instead of his shoulder.

As he pushed away from the edge to put distance between them, she said, "I'm confused. You said you can't."

"I work for your uncle."

What? "What does that have to do with what happened to you?"

The lines in his forehead cut deeper. "What do you mean, what happened to me?"

She bit the corner of her lip, not wanting to say it, but forcing it out anyway. Gently. Softly. Her voice full of sympathetic understanding. "The bomb?"

"The bomb? What does that—" His eyes went wide and shocked horror flashed across his face. "Oh, God, that is *not* what I meant when I said I can't."

"What did you mean then?"

"Your uncle pays my salary."

It took a moment, but finally she made the connection. And was immediately pissed off. "So?"

"He asked me to help you, not sleep with you."

"Aren't you allowed to do what you want in your free time?"

His expression darkened. "That's not the point."

"Well, it's not like you're getting paid extra for me."

"Yet, he'd still probably fire me if he found out about this."

She narrowed her gaze before shoving away from the wall, saying over her shoulder, "Believe me, *I* won't be telling anyone."

He swam after her as she headed for the shallow end. "You're seriously mad right now?"

More like mortified.

"Gimmie a break here." He followed her up the steps. "I'm trying to do the right thing."

"The right thing would've been to not make me think you wanted this in the first place."

"I do want this, but you have to understand, I—"

"I understand perfectly." She grabbed her towel to wrap it around herself sarong style. Trying to salvage a smidgeon of her dignity, she half-turned toward him but didn't look at his face as she said stiffly, "I'm sorry I put you in a bad position. It won't happen again."

She spun for the patio doors, but didn't even make it one step before he gripped her arm and swung her back to face him. With her head tipped back to see his face, her breath caught when she saw the turmoil in his darkened green eyes.

"I want you, Raine. More than I've ever wanted anyone before." His lashes lowered, hiding all that heart-wrenching emotion. "But I *need* this job. *Because* of what happened, I need to be here, doing what I do."

His voice turned to pure gravel at the end, and her chest squeezed so tight she could barely breathe. She wanted to reach out and hug him, but he was still in only his wet, skin-tight boxer briefs, leaving nothing much to the imagination. Not to mention, if she pressed up against his bare chest again, there was no telling what she might do.

It took major effort to step back from temptation. His fingers skimmed down the back of her arm, past her elbow, and along the underside of her wrist before he finally dropped his arm to his side. As if he knew he had to let her go, but didn't want to.

She hugged her arms across her chest while suppressing a shiver. "I guess I'll see you in the morning then."

He gave a tight nod. "I have an adoption appointment for Morning Glory at eight, so you don't have to be down to the barn until nine."

"Nine it is." This time he didn't stop her when she went inside.

Raine locked up, took a shower, and went to bed. She turned off the bedroom television at midnight. When she got sick of staring at the ceiling round about two a.m., she went to the kitchen for a glass of water. As the cool liquid slid down her throat, her gaze was drawn across the sprawling lawn, toward the stables. The windows of the upstairs apartment were lit up as if it were evening instead of middle of the night.

Did Reyes leave the lights on to ward off the dark, or was he wide awake like her, wishing for what could have been?

CHAPTER 9

Reyes greeted Bob and Nancy Hamilton outside precisely at eight the next morning before accompanying them into the barn. They would be the perfect distraction to keep his mind off facing Raine at nine.

His step faltered when he saw her standing outside Morning Glory's stall.

He'd barely slept after walking away from her last night. All he could think about when he closed his eyes was the feel of her lips beneath his, the seductive slide of her tongue, the weight of her breast in his palm, and the erotic sight of her tight nipples as the water lapped at her bare chest. Taking the edge off in the shower hadn't been nearly satisfying enough and only lasted for so long.

Even now, the quick, hesitant smile she shot him before introducing herself to the Hamiltons had his dick taking notice.

It was going to be a long day.

Damn—try a long three and a half weeks!

"I saw what happened at the end of the season," Nancy said, having recognized Raine's name from the jumping circuit. "That was a tough break. How is everything going?"

Raine grimaced. "A little more down than up, but we're working hard to get back to where we were. Reyes is working with us for the next few weeks."

The openness of her reply surprised him. That was a step up from her usual, *"We're fine."*

"You're in good hands," Bob assured her before turning to Reyes. "We couldn't be happier with Ivy Rose and Dozer."

He seized the opportunity to shift focus. "Then you're going to be thrilled with Morning Glory. She reminded me of Dozer from the moment she arrived."

"Janice has told me all about her," Nancy said. "I've been looking forward to meeting her."

"Please, go ahead." He gestured toward the stall. "You know the drill by now, and if you have any questions, just ask."

The two of them moved ahead, and Raine sidled up beside him to ask in a low voice, "What's the drill?"

Acutely aware she was close enough for him to smell her fresh, flowery body wash, he kept his gaze focused on the mare. "They'll get her tacked up and head out to the arena for a bit before taking her out on the trails to see how she handles everything. If all goes well, we'll sign the papers, and she'll be off to her new home."

"How long have you been working with her?"

"About three months."

"And you've done this with over a hundred and fifty horses?"

The awe in her voice made his chest swell with pride. "I haven't worked with *all* of them, but I've had my fair share."

"Don't you get attached to the ones you work with?"

Unfortunately, yeah. And he was discovering it wasn't limited to the horses. He clenched his jaw against that fact, then forced himself to reply. "It helps knowing they're going to a good home."

And that he helped them get there, which was exactly what he needed to do with Raine. Help her, and send her on her way.

Without touching her again.

Her fingers grazed his bicep, and he flinched.

When he shifted away while glancing down at her, she tilted her head with a frown. "Is everything okay?"

"Yep," he said shortly.

"I was curious about how the adoptions worked, that's why I came in early. But if it's a problem, I can come back at nine."

It wasn't her fault he couldn't think straight for wanting to take her upstairs, strip her bare, and bury himself deep inside her. Well, it was, but it wasn't.

"Don't be ridiculous," he bit out more harshly than he'd intended. "It's fine."

"Good." She crossed her arms, twisting on her heel to stare right at him. "And since I'm here, is there anything I can do to help?"

Yeah, you can— "Muck the stalls."

Her eyebrows rose. "What?"

The affronted tone gave him the courage to finally look her in the eye. If he got her good and pissed her off, maybe she'd keep her distance. He'd put the horses out to pasture just before the Hamiltons arrived and planned to do chores between her morning and afternoon sessions, but this would work, too.

"You heard me. Unless you think you're too good to shovel shit?"

Her gaze narrowed. "I can muck a stall, Reyes."

"Good. Then do it." He abruptly turned and strode toward the office before he gave in to the insane urge to pull her into his arms and kiss her breathless at eight a.m. in the morning.

An hour later, Morning Glory was in the trailer and on the way to her new home, and all the stalls in the barn were filled with fresh, fluffy pine shavings. Raine had worked without complaint doing *his* work, which left him feeling like an ass. In trying to do the right thing out of respect for his boss—and her—he was unfairly taking out his frustrations on her.

Only now he had her good and annoyed with him, and she didn't bother to hide it as they made their way out to the arena for their morning training session.

He hoped their talk last night helped breakthrough the mental barrier she had over that one vertical jump, and watched carefully for any signs of distress as she and Diamond Fire warmed up.

Everything seemed okay, until he walked her through the new course he'd set up earlier that morning. Accusation and anxiety filled her silence when her glare told him she recognized he'd replicated the course from the day of their wreck back in December.

He signaled for her to run it through. As they started, he could see horse and rider were equally edgy, only he wasn't so sure if Fire was picking up her anxiety, or remembering the fall himself. When they approached the final turn, the gelding took the bit and blew right past the vertical. Raine brought him back under control at the far side of the arena. She twirled him around in a few tight, fast circles, her displeasure with her mount abundantly clear.

Fire was breathing fast when she urged him into a canter once around the arena, then turned him back onto the course. Reyes fisted his hands at the obvious discourse between the two. They were fighting each other instead of working together as a team. Raine didn't trust herself, and Fire was losing his trust in her. Anything else today would do more damage than good.

"That's enough," he called out before they reached the final turn. He had to figure out a new tactic before their bond was permanently broken. "We're done for now."

She reined up in surprise, her long braid flipping over her shoulder as her head whipped toward him. "What?"

"Take the rest of the day off," he said.

"I don't understand."

He waved his arm toward the guest house. "Go workout, swim, relax, whatever you want to do. But we're done riding for today."

When he headed back to the barn, she cantered Fire past and whirled him around to block Reyes' path. "Why?"

"Because I said so. We do this my way, remember?"

She glared at him for a long moment, her hazel eyes flashing fire.

"How can I forget?" She backed Fire three quick paces before spinning him toward the barn. "Apparently *everything* is your way."

Yeah, and sometimes his way sucked.

The thing was, when it came to the *everything* she referred to, not sleeping with her wasn't only about respecting his boss and friend. He'd realized half-way through the night that was really nothing more than a lucky excuse he was holding onto for self-preservation.

He'd felt a pull toward her from the first moment he'd set eyes on her years ago, and each time they met, it only grew stronger. Casual hook-ups had never appealed to him, and if he let himself get too close to her, what the hell was he going to do when she went home to Texas?

Because there was no question she would be going home in three weeks.

He went into the office to finish filing the paperwork for Morning Glory, all the while hyper-aware of the sound of Raine's movements out by the stalls. When it had been quiet for a while, and he had nothing else to keep himself busy, he broke down and called Jessica Wills over at Retired Racers. A bump of his elbow knocked over his bottled water just as she answered. He hit the speaker phone button and scrambled for some napkins.

"Good morning, Reyes," the older woman greeted as he wiped up his mess. "I wasn't expecting to hear from you guys until Estefan was back."

They hadn't brought in any more horses for training the past few weeks in anticipation of being shorthanded while his dad was gone. It was supposed to afford Reyes his own semi-vacation. Problem was, he had no desire for extra time on his hands today, or the next three weeks. While he did have the unexpected last minute addition of training Raine and Fire to fill some time, *she* was the exact reason he was desperate for the distraction of a much busier schedule.

"Morning Glory just left with the Hamiltons," he told Jessica. "I'm going to need something challenging to work with over here or I'll be bored out of my mind."

"Tell me why a nice guy like you doesn't have a girlfriend to keep him busy?"

"Horses like me better than women do."

"Quit yanking my chain, Rey," she admonished with a laugh. "We both know that's not true. You know, my cousin's daughter is still single. I'm happy to give you her number."

He made a face at the phone but forced a smile into his voice. "I appreciate the thought, Jess, but I'll be sticking with horses for now. Please tell me you can help me out on that front."

"Well, you know I've always got horses for ya'll. There's two here in particular I've been holding for you if you want to pop on over."

"Perfect. I'll bring the trailer."

Reyes hung up and tossed the soggy napkins in the garbage. Then he swiped his keys off the desk on his way out the door to hook up the horse trailer. His pulse jolted at the sight of Raine leaning against the wall outside the office door, and he jerked to a stop.

"Fire and I aren't challenging enough for you?" she accused.

Realizing she heard everything from the speaker phone, he shot back, "You hang around just to eavesdrop?"

Guilt flickered before she pushed away from the wall. "I wanted to talk to you."

"Well, that's a switch." He angled past her to head for his Jeep.

"Are you really that mad about what happened last night?" she asked from right behind him. "Because if that's the problem here this morning, I'll apologize. Again."

"I'm not mad at you."

"You're sure acting like it over one little kiss."

Geezus, that had been so much more than a *little* kiss. He opened his door, then thought better of it and slammed it shut again to face her. "I live in Colorado. You live in Texas."

"And?"

"I don't screw around just to screw around. Never have, never will."

"Neither do I." Her gaze met his for a moment, then faltered.

She stuffed her hands in her front pockets and turned to lean her butt against the front tire fender while hunching her shoulders. "So, I guess I do owe you another apology. I was scared. I *am* scared —about a lot of things. I was using you as a distraction to keep from facing some hard questions, and I'm sorry."

He should be offended by that, shouldn't he? No one liked to be used. He definitely should not be thinking about offering himself up as a willing distraction whenever she needed one. Hopefully often.

For the next three weeks, anyway.

He gave himself a hard mental shake and reached for his door once more. "Don't worry about it. Apology accepted."

She straightened from the side of his Jeep. "Are you going to get more rescue horses?"

Despite her already knowing that answer, he gave a curt, "Yeah."

"Can I come with you?"

"No."

"Please?"

Halfway onto the driver's seat, he paused with a frown. The less time they spent together the better. "Don't you have a three hour workout to get done?"

She gave him an innocent little smile. "My trainer gave me the rest of the day off."

Idiot.

"Then go shopping or something," he said impatiently. "Meet your friends for lunch."

"That's totally sexist. Besides, I hate shopping, and all my friends are in Texas, remember?"

Damn it all anyway. He scrambled to come up with a good suggestion. Anything to keep from being closed up in a vehicle with her. As if the overwhelming attraction wasn't bad enough, she wasn't quite the spoiled little rich girl he'd imagined, and he liked the woman he was getting to know. "Go visit your cousins then."

"They're all working. Besides, I want to see where you get the horses from and learn more about the whole process."

And he didn't want to bond with her over the rescue horses.

"Come on, Reyes," she pleaded, looking up at him through her lashes. "If *you're* bored, imagine how I feel, all by myself, all this way from home."

That last bit was laying it on a bit thick. She knew it. He knew it. And yet there he was, feeling the corner of his mouth tug upward before he could force it back into a forbidding line.

Raine's eyes lit up, and she hurried around to the passenger side of his Jeep.

Sonofabitch. "I did not say yes."

Undeterred by his stern voice, she flashed him a saucy grin as she opened the door. "Yes you did. But I promise, I'll keep my hands to myself."

"That's not what I'm worried about."

She muttered what sounded like, *"Maybe you should be,"* under her breath, but the slamming of the door drowned out the words, and he wasn't stupid enough to ask her to repeat them. He was already in enough trouble.

CHAPTER 10

Raine snuck a glance at Reyes' solemn profile as he made the turn out of the estate's gated driveway. He'd been grumpy all morning. His attitude had annoyed her at first, but while brushing Fire after their disastrous training session, her rational brain had finally managed to remind her he'd broken things off last night because he was a good guy. An honorable guy.

So, she switched her mood and found a little teasing had coaxed a peek at his reluctant humor. Very reluctant, and a very short peek. But still.

"I don't screw around."

She respected the hell out of that. Too many men in her circle at home and on the jumping circuit were only about screwing around. The guys at home were spoiled, rich playboys who used their money and status to get women into bed. Many on the circuit were mostly looking for a good time in the moment, because the time span between events made relationships difficult. On the flip side, others cheated on wives or girlfriends, because sometimes they were away from home for weeks at a time.

Either way, she'd learned early on it wasn't how she wanted to live her life. Last night with Reyes—acting on the siren call of their sizzling attraction—had been a first for her, and after realizing how her actions had come across, it was a last, too.

She couldn't shake how his voice sounded when he'd told her he needed this job. *Because* of what had happened to him. And she got to thinking that even though she was still insanely attracted to him, maybe they could be friends. A guy with his depth of integrity was someone she'd like to have as a friend. Plus, she had a feeling he could use one who understood he'd gone through some crappy shit, because she sure did.

Maybe he had one already. Heck, maybe he had a whole bunch already from the Army, but a person could never have enough friends, could they?

"Do horses really like you better than women?" she asked to break the silence.

He shot her a sideways glance before giving a slight shake of his head. "I distinctly recall your palm smacking my cheek only seconds after you telling me you didn't like me."

"I didn't know you yet," she said with an unapologetic shrug. "Besides, you dared me."

"Don't dare a Diamond," he mocked lightly. "I should've dared you to stay home."

"Why? Are you afraid if you spend time with me you'll like me?"

That got her another sharp glance from him, but he didn't answer as he rested his wrist over the top of the steering wheel and watched the road.

"I dare you to answer," she taunted. "*Truthfully.*"

"I'm not a Diamond."

"So you don't take dares?"

His lips curved into a smile. "I'm not ten years old anymore."

"My brothers still dare each other, and they're all older than me—*and* you're avoiding the question."

He shrugged.

She was trying to come up with something clever when his low voice reached across the cab.

"I already like you, Raine. That's the problem."

After a quick glance, she watched the passing scenery. "Does it have to be a problem? Because I like you, too, so why can't we at least be friends?"

"I don't usually want to kiss my friends. Do you?"

"No, but there's a first time for everything." She hoped the smile she shot his way did not reveal the nerves churning in her stomach. "We could give it a shot."

"Easier said than done."

"Come on. How hard can it be?"

The moment the question left her mouth, heat flashed through her from head to toe. He'd been *very* hard when she was plastered against his body in the pool. In the split second her gaze met his, she was certain he was remembering the exact same thing.

She bit her lip and turned her flaming face to the window. "Maybe you should just tell me about where we're going and the horse rescue."

After a moment of silence, he cleared his throat and told her all about Retired Racers, Jessica Wills, and the operation she'd been running for nearly ten years. Raine ignored a little spike of jealousy when she thought of the woman's offer of her cousin's daughter's phone number. He'd turned her down anyway, so there was nothing to be jealous of, right?

Right.

It turned out *"pop on over"* ended up being almost a forty minute drive before Reyes turned onto a pine tree-lined drive bordered by pastures with white fences, and more than two dozen grazing horses dotting the green land.

He parked in front of a huge hunter green stable with five roof dormers and white trim all around. By the time they got out of the Jeep, a tall, slim blond woman in a yellow T-shirt, jeans, and cowboy boots exited the open doors and approached with a wide smile. Reyes had said she was in her mid-fifties, but Raine wouldn't have guessed her to be a day over forty.

The woman gave him a hug and a kiss on the cheek before the two turned to her, and he made introductions.

Raine shook her hand as the woman eyed her with open curiosity. "Reyes told me all about Retired Racers on the way here. This place is very impressive."

"Thanks." Jessica twisted at the waist, her gaze sweeping toward the barn and back. "This is what my ex-husband gets for being a no-good, cheating sonofabitch."

Raine couldn't stop a high eyebrow arch, and the blond laughed.

"Jess has no filter," Reyes warned with a smile. "You get used to it."

"Too bad Thomas didn't." Jessica turned for the barn. "Oh well. His loss."

"Clearly," Raine murmured with a grin. She liked her—filter be damned.

On their way inside, the woman waved her hand in the general direction of the two of them. "What's going on here?" Her gaze settled on Reyes. "Is this English filly why you won't let me fix you up?"

English filly? Raine nearly choked on a surprised laugh, though she assumed her dark gray breeches and black riding boots had sparked the silly description.

"Raine and I are...friends."

Jessica laughed with clear disbelief. "Right. And I'm the bloody queen of England." Before either of them could reply, the blond stopped in front of a stall where a tall, black thoroughbred had its head extended over the door, curious brown eyes watching the three of them. "Anyway, this lady here is Willow Moonlight, and next to her is Saving Grace."

Raine grinned at the names. She absolutely loved the creativity involved in naming horses—especially thoroughbred race horses. Moving over to the bay mare's stall, she rubbed her forehead while Jessica went over what she knew of each horse's history.

Each had been with her for nearly two months to rest and de-stress after varying success at the track. Willow had been over-trained after her winning streak waned, and Saving Grace had needed a low-impact environment to recover from a gastric ulcer. Both situations were something Raine had heard of in her field as well, though careful monitoring ensured her horses never reached a level where drastic intervention was required.

Sometimes a horse needed to just be a horse instead of a high-performance athlete. Eat grass, doze in the sunshine, run through a green pasture. Some could go back, while most 'retired' to a new life, transitioning into lower-stress careers.

Listening to Reyes discuss possible paths for each thoroughbred gave her a new level of appreciation for his skill and knowledge. It was obvious he earned respect from everyone he worked with. Uncle Mark and Aunt Janine. The Hamiltons. Jessica.

Recognizing the depth of their confidence in him, she realized she'd been holding back during their training sessions. She hadn't trusted that he knew enough to truly be of any help to her and Fire. How could he when he had no experience with riders, and she hadn't actually witnessed proof of his results with horses?

But last night proved his instincts were dead on. In the dead of night, she accepted the fact she needed to face her fear of that one stupid jump. Things hadn't gone so well that morning, but it was time for her to confront what had happened head on, not forget it.

And if she was going to make forward progress, she needed to fully trust Reyes to do what was best for her and her horse. Because he'd also proved last night, and today, he had her best interests at heart—not his own.

CHAPTER 11

Reyes put the last of the horses out to pasture Saturday morning, and then found a western saddle similar to his to fit Diamond Fire. Taz was all ready to go, and he was tightening Fire's cinch when Raine arrived for her training session a few minutes later.

His pulse gave the usual excited skip as he swept his gaze over her standard uniform of T-shirt, breeches, boots, and braid. Then again, there was nothing standard about her ass in those breeches. They were killing him every single day—though, far be it for him to complain.

She, however, eyed the western saddle with a frown. "Why is he wearing that?"

"We're going for a trail ride."

Her gaze shifted from Fire to Taz and back. "What about training?"

He finished with the cinch and flipped the stirrup down from over the seat. "When's the last time you rode Fire for fun?"

She arched her brow. "He's not a pleasure horse."

"No, but he still needs to be a horse, doesn't he?" He saw understanding dawn in her expression just before she averted her gaze and moved toward the gelding's head to stroke her hand down his nose.

"Fire gets plenty of rest between events." Her voice had a defensive edge. "We take good care of our horses."

"I didn't mean to imply you don't, but after picking up Willow and Grace from Jessica's yesterday, I realized maybe Fire needs to de-stress like the thoroughbreds do. Maybe you both do." He leaned in to see her face over the saddle. "Did you take any time off after the accident?"

"Eight weeks after my shoulder surgery," she said.

"Besides that," he clarified. "Did you take any time to just ride him and relax? Maybe rebuild the bond the two of you have?"

Raine frowned, her gaze locked on Fire. "Once I could ride again, there wasn't any time," she said softly. "One of our junior riders kept him in jumping condition, and when the doctor cleared me, we went right back into practice to catch up for the beginning of the season."

Guilt darkened her hazel eyes to almost brown when she finally looked at him. He moved around to the front of her horse and handed her the reins with a smile. "Well, then today, we're just riding. I hope you like ham sandwiches, because I packed a lunch."

Surprise touched her features. "How long are we going to be gone?"

"'Til at least mid-afternoon."

"That long? Are there bathrooms along the way?"

He laughed at her pink cheeks and patted the leather bags secured to Taz's saddle. "I've got all the necessities right here."

Except condoms. He would be lying if he said the thought hadn't crossed his mind, but since they were doing the friendship thing in addition to training, he needed to provide obstacles to temptation wherever possible.

They led the horses from the barn, and he glanced over as the breeze blew a loose strand of hair across Raine's face. He tightened his hands on the reins, suppressing the urge to reach out and tuck it behind her ear. If he did that, he'd want to lean down and cover her mouth with his to see if there was any flavor to that gloss making her lips so shiny.

And on that note, he'd now be finding a log or a boulder to sit on while they ate their lunch and leave the picnic blanket packed deep in his saddle bag.

He'd chosen a longer trail that looped east onto public land bordering the Diamond estate before connecting with the trails on the west side of the property. As they rode past the huge main house, he noticed Raine's gaze sweeping over the estate. He knew her family had plenty of money like his employers, and wondered if their place in Texas was as grand.

"Does it make you miss home?" he asked.

She lifted a shoulder, her head still averted. "I travel enough I'm used to being away."

"That doesn't answer the question."

Now her gaze swung around to him. "I guess not really. It's a lot cooler up here, and I like that for training outside instead of always being in air conditioning. Plus, my family has spread out, much like everyone here has. My brothers all moved out years ago, and my parents both travel for work a lot, so it's hit and miss when we see each other. If I miss anything, it's all of them, not the house."

"You still live at home?"

A wry smile curved her lips. "It's where I train, so it's just easier."

"I live where I work, so I get it."

Her head swung back toward her uncle's one last time before they entered the woods. "I will say, though, I'm not used to it being so quiet around *here*. There was always a full house whenever I visited."

And these days, he was the one with the most permanent residence at the Diamond estate. "I'm not about to complain about the quiet," he said.

She tossed him a smile. "I suppose not. Though, with Shelby and Dev engaged, I bet it won't be long before you have a niece or nephew running around getting into trouble."

"They're talking about kids already?" The news shouldn't surprise him, but he hadn't thought about being an uncle anytime soon.

"Shelby said they want to be married for a little while first, but I'm sure with Merit and Asher already started, the rest will have kids sooner than later. I know Celia and Robert are trying, and probably Loyal and Roxanna, too."

The wistful note in her voice started his heart beating a little faster. "How about you?"

"Am I trying?" Her dark eyebrows arched over eyes sparkling with humor. "Um, probably best if I get myself a man first, don't you think?"

"Probably." He grinned even as his pulse skipped at the idea of offering himself for the position. "However, I meant in the future. Do you want kids someday?"

"Definitely." She tilted her head sideways, glancing at him from beneath her lashes. "You?"

"Yeah, I hope so." The smile she gave him did funny things to his stomach, and he quickly shifted the conversation. "How many brothers do you have?"

"There's five of us. Axel, the twins—Phoenix and Chance—and then Olix. I'm the only girl, and the youngest."

"Ahh. That explains so much," he teased.

"Shut up."

He laughed. "I'm the baby, too. I bet you got away with a lot of shit just like me."

"True—but it can suck, too. Especially for girls. I've got four brothers who are super overprotective, and my dad still thinks I'm his baby girl."

"You'll always be his baby girl."

Her nose scrunched up, and he laughed again. Riding like this always brought him peace, but today felt different. Lighter. Fun.

Man, when was the last time he'd truly had fun?

"What about you?"Raine asked. "I know Devante, and don't you have an older sister, too?"

"Solana. She's an FBI agent based in Washington state, though she's hoping for a transfer to the Colorado field office. We each left the moment we graduated high school, so if she comes back, it'll be nice to all be close again."

"That's cool. That she works for the FBI, I mean."

"It's her job," he said with a shrug.

Raine looked ahead, her expression suddenly pensive. "But it's a job that can make a difference. All I do is ride horses."

He blinked at the statement. "What's wrong with that? I pretty much do the same."

"You train them—there's a difference," she countered. "And you help re-home retired thoroughbreds. Shelby runs her clinic so low income families can have pets and not worry about the cost of caring for them. Loyal and Grayson run the veterans foundation, and Grayson also raises and trains service dogs. What good does me riding a horse over jumps do?"

There was an unexpected depth to her question that had him posing his own. "Would you rather be doing something else?"

"Maybe." As if realizing what she'd just admitted, she shot him a quick glance and a shrug. "I mean, I love what I do, but I guess I wonder sometimes."

"What else would you do?"

She grimaced as her shoulders shook with a visible shiver. "I have no idea."

"Maybe it's something you should think about."

She didn't reply, and they rode in silence until he noticed her rub her palm over her bare arm. He'd thrown a gray plaid button up over his T-shirt this morning, leaving it open and rolling up the sleeves. It kept him comfortable in the shade of the tall trees, but Raine's T-shirt didn't appear to be doing the job.

"You cold?" he asked.

She looked over in surprise and then dropped her hand back down to her leg. "I'll be fine once we're back in the sun. I'm usually warm when I'm jumping, but it's cooler here in the woods than I would've expected."

He should've thought of that and suggested she grab a sweatshirt. Shrugging out of his shirt, he rode closer to hand it over. "Here, put this on."

"What about you?"

"I was actually getting a little warm," he fibbed.

She hesitated one more moment before taking it to slide her arms into the sleeves. "Thanks."

It was huge on her, with the rolled sleeves nearly reaching her wrists. The unbuttoned sides fell down along her thighs in a way that had him imagining her in nothing but his shirt, her dark hair loose and wavy as it cascaded over her shoulders.

He let loose a groan under his breath. She shot him a questioning glance, and heat crept up his neck as he quickly urged Taz ahead of her horse. If he kept thinking along the lines of her in his shirt, in his bed—*don't go adding details*—the ride was going to get extremely uncomfortable very fast.

He scrambled for a distraction and went back to what they'd been talking about. "You know, who's to say you can't jump *and* do something more? As you pointed out, the re-homing isn't my whole job."

She and Fire drew even with him and Taz once more. "Can I help you with Saving Grace and Willow Midnight the next couple of weeks?" she asked.

More time together above and beyond the training? Absolutely not. "Sure."

"That would be great." Her hazel eyes lit with a sudden excitement. "If you show me what to do, I could start a program when I get home."

Home. In Texas.

The reminder hit like a kick to the gut.

But then again, that reminder was exactly what he needed. And often.

CHAPTER 12

Raine felt a little bad taking her scheduled day off on Sunday when it felt like she'd already taken Friday and Saturday off. But, seeing as those were both on her trainer's orders, she ignored the guilt and headed up to the main house for brunch.

The past few days put a spring in her step. Things had been good. Great even. First at the horse rescue on Friday, and then yesterday's ride had been amazing in a way she hadn't realized how much she and Fire needed. She was pretty sure her horse enjoyed the change of scenery as much as she did, and the company hadn't been too shabby, either.

She rolled her eyes at her understatement and lifted a hand to keep her loose hair from blowing into her face. Reyes had been nice, and fun, and surprisingly funny at times. They'd talked comfortably the whole time, and she didn't think he'd caught any of the countless instances she'd discretely lifted the collar of his shirt to inhale the tummy-flipping scent of him clinging to the material.

At least she sure hoped not, since she was the one who suggested they be friends. The very last thing she should've been doing as they ate lunch on a big fallen log was imagine sliding over to bury her nose in the crook of his neck—but dear, Lord, the man smelled so damn *good.*

Doing her best to put him out of her mind, she walked past all the vehicles in the drive and entered the house. A cacophony of voices led her to the kitchen. Of the dozen or so people gathered, her gaze landed on smack dab on Reyes holding Ava, Asher and Honor's little four month old.

Her heart lodged up in her throat at the sight of his uninhibited smile as the baby giggled while he ran her tiny little palm over the whiskers on his chin.

"Hey."

Raine jumped at the stage whisper in her ear, and twisted to see her cousin standing slightly behind her with a wide grin.

"I'm telling you," Shelby said in a soft sing-song voice, "there's something about those Torrez boys."

Yes, there definitely was. Looking back toward Reyes and the baby, she gave Bells a one-armed hug. "Only they're not boys anymore."

"Most definitely not," her cousin agreed with a happy grin.

A spark of envy burned in her chest. Not for her cousin's man, but because if she was being honest and said to hell with all the friendship stuff, she wanted what Shelby had.

With Reyes.

And yet, it wasn't going to happen. They lived in different states. Hell, they lived different lives.

Not that different.

Different enough though.

"You know, we've invited Reyes to brunch before. This is the first time he's come."

Her pulse skipped at her cousin's insinuation. She glanced at Shelby, then back to him. "We're becoming friends."

"Just friends?"

"There's no point in anything more." She didn't bother to hide the disappointment in her voice, and Shelby squeezed her shoulder in commiseration. "Neither of us is into casual flings, and other than this one month, our lives are hundreds of miles apart."

"Hmm. That's a shame. The miles apart that is—not the casual stuff."

You're telling me.

Someone called her name, and as she turned to look, Reyes' lashes lifted and their gazes connected. Her heart thumped hard. Seconds ticked by as the world shifted beneath her feet while undeniable yearning made it hard to swallow.

"A real shame," Shelby whispered before walking between them.

She blinked as the connection was broken, and then Merit stepped up to envelop her in a bear hug. Raine spent the next five minutes making her way around the island and table, giving hugs to everyone. Grandma and Grandpa, Asher and Honor, Devante, Celia and Robert, Merit, Mae, and Ian, and last but not least, Loyal and Roxanna.

Merit and Mae's little guy Maverick was firmly ensconced in Grandma Irene's arms, so she turned to Reyes, who still held Ava. "My turn."

He twisted away with a teasing smile. "I just got her."

"I haven't even met her."

"Fine, you win."

She leaned forward to take the baby, her pulse kicking up when his large hands brushed against hers in the exchange. She focused on Ava, teasing and tickling to make her smile and giggle. Asher and Honor watched from over by the island, but the two seemed content with having a break.

After a few minutes, the baby fussed and twisted in her arms, so she turned her around to face all the action. When Reyes held out a rattle, Ava seized it and shook her little fist with gusto. After the first smack to her face, Raine laughed before ducking backward to avoid a second. Reyes was quick to switch the rattle for a stuffed animal.

"Good call," she said with a smile of thanks. "I didn't know you were going to be here."

"Dev made me come."

His wry tone had her arching her brows.

He rolled his eyes the tiniest bit. "He thinks I need to socialize more."

Despite their acrimonious start earlier in the week—and last summer—anytime she'd seen him interact with other people, he seemed friendly and outgoing. But after their talk at the pool, she was pretty sure she could read between the lines. "Because of...?"

His eyes were a dark shade of green, solemn and shadowed. "Yeah." He shifted his gaze to the baby and reached out to let Ava wrap her tiny hand around his finger. "He's not wrong."

Sympathy pulsed with each heavy thump of her heart. Yet another reason they couldn't act on the chemistry between them—she wouldn't be the one to screw up a job that helped him deal with the horror he'd experienced in the military.

So...friends it would be.

She leaned the baby in to plant a slobbery kiss on his cheek as she said, "Then I'm glad you're here."

CHAPTER 13

Emotion swelled in Reyes' chest at Raine's soft statement. Other than his brother, she was the only one here who knew what he'd gone through. Well, he suspected Dev had told Shelby some, but he'd never talked to her about it himself.

Yesterday, he'd spent the entire day without any heavy moments cutting off his air until later in the evening when he laid in bed and tried to turn the light off. It took all of five seconds to flip it back on, but at least as he drifted off to a replay of the day spent with Raine, he'd gotten a restful night's sleep.

While he had told her his brother made him come today, knowing she was going to be there, he hadn't scrambled for an excuse when the invite was issued. And Dev was also right that he needed to stop isolating himself at the stables with the horses. Other than the Diamonds, he hadn't taken any time to reconnect with high school friends still in the area, and he only texted his Army buddies every so often.

Sitting at brunch with all of the new, happy families, watching how cute Maverick and Ava were as they interacted with everyone, he found himself yearning for more in his own life. And with that yearning, he couldn't help watching and listening to Raine across the table during brunch, and later, when everyone pitched in to clean up after the meal.

She was a vision with her loose hair falling in soft waves past her shoulders. A gauzy, mint shirt brought out the green in her hazel eyes, and a pair of white jean capris showed off her great ass and legs. Hell, even the gold sandals on her small feet were enough to make his pulse skip.

Stop looking.

Right. Like that was gonna happen.

He grabbed a towel to dry dishes as Asher washed and Merit rinsed, his gaze straying to Raine as often as possible without being too obvious. It was hard to recall back when he thought she was a spoiled little rich girl. Yeah, she'd had her moments, but he'd also seen her work hard both in the ring, and cleaning stalls. She was determined and dedicated, and he had no doubt she was going to ride Fire all the way to gold someday.

Which meant it would be stupid to imagine her in any way as part of his new-found desire for more in his life.

Dev carried the last of the dirty plates to set on the counter for Asher to wash, then grabbed a towel to help dry. "It would appear you and Raine called a truce," he observed in a low voice.

"For the most part."

"A truce?" Merit glanced over. "What were you two fighting about?"

Reyes grimaced. Talking about Raine in front of Merit and Asher—and damn it, here came Loyal—was not something he wanted to do. "Not fighting. More like not seeing eye to eye on her training. It's fine though. We're good."

"Well, I don't envy you. Raine can be stubborn as all hell." Merit handed him another dish as Loyal leaned his butt against the island. "When we were visiting them in Texas one summer, we were all playing hide and seek and ended up looking for her until after midnight."

"I remember that," Loyal groused.

"Did she get lost?" Reyes asked.

"No." Asher chuckled. "She just refused to come out until we found her."

"Even after we called out the game was over."

"I think she was six at the time," Loyal said. "*We* were all worried she was lost and afraid in the dark, but when she found out she was the last to be found, she declared victory."

"Uncle Matt always said she takes after her name." Asher and Merit exchanged a smile and they both said together, *"Can't stop rain."*

Reyes shifted his gaze to Raine just as her head whipped around.

"Oh my God—what are you guys talking about?" she hollered from the other side of the kitchen.

"Want to play hide and seek?" Merit teased.

She rolled her eyes, though a smile tugged at her lips. "Say what you want, I beat all of you guys *and* my brothers that night."

Loyal pushed away from the island and went to lift Maverick out of Robert's arms. "First and last time we ever played hide and seek with Raine. But we'll play with you some day, little man."

The baby grinned, drool wetting his chin as well as the hand stuffed in his mouth. He was six months old, but having been born seven weeks early, he and Ava were near the same size despite the two months difference between their birthdays.

"It's not my fault you guys were sore losers," Raine retorted.

Celia and Shelby jumped into the fray as the cousins continued to tease each other while Grandma Irene tossed in a story or two about Raine's dad and the senator. Reyes kept drying, smiling as he listened to them joke about her side of the family's ridiculous obsession with dares. It made him think of when she smacked him across the face last week.

"You know what you're doing?"

Reyes winced at his brother's voice. He didn't need to ask what Dev meant; he heard the real question in his tone.

"We're friends," he said, as much for his brother as himself.

"You don't look at her like a friend."

Yeah, Dev saw him watching her. Wanting her.

What he didn't know was how damn hard he was fighting to not fall for her.

CHAPTER 14

Reyes mentally psyched himself up for the Monday morning session with Raine while turning the horses out and cleaning stalls. Being friends with her, getting to know her and *really* liking who she was wasn't working for him.

Or, more accurately, it was working too well.

Yesterday, he'd left shortly after brunch and stayed away from the estate until evening chores. Today, his goal was to get her over the damn jump. The sooner she was over it and back to her regular training schedule, the sooner she could go home, and the less danger he would be in.

The light tick of boot heels on cement gave him a three second warning before she called out, "Good morning!"

Damn it, she was early. Though, to be fair, she'd been early every morning.

He glanced up as she came to a stop at the stall door, one hand hooked around the beam that rose to the rafters as she leaned into the opening, her braid dangling over her shoulder. He tried, but couldn't stop his gaze from taking in the snug fit of her white T-shirt, black breeches, and shiny black boots.

"Where'd you go yesterday?" she asked as he threw another scoop of dirty bedding into the wheel barrow.

"Out."

It came out harsher than he intended, and he saw surprise flicker in her expression before she lifted her chin slightly.

"Well, Fire and I went for another ride yesterday. Just the two of us, and it was nice."

"Good. Then you should be all ready to work today."

"I've been ready to work every day." Resentment edged her voice.

"And yet there you stand."

He expected her to whirl around and storm off. Instead, she straightened and pinned him with her gaze. "So, that's how you're going to play it? Like this weekend never happened?"

"Nothing did happen."

Except it had. They'd spent most of Friday and Saturday together, and Sunday brunch, all without a single note of animosity. Friendship had definitely been in the works.

"All right then," she said. "My mistake."

He had to turn away from the hurt in her eyes and was relieved when he heard her footsteps retreat. He finished cleaning the stall and met her out in the arena by eight a.m., where she and Fire were already warming up.

Keeping his tone businesslike, he called out instructions and suggestions on a few of their sloppier efforts. When she avoided the vertical jump on the first round, he let it pass. After the second pass, he huffed out a sigh under his breath.

"You can't keep avoiding the jump, Raine."

"I'm working up to it," she shot back with an icy glare.

"I thought you were a professional, but I could dare you if that helps."

"I don't need you to dare me."

The elevated tone of her voice revealed her anxiety. Reyes raked a hand through his hair as he moved closer, hand raised for her to stop. When she reined her horse to a halt, he stroked the gelding's neck while looking up at her.

"You know this is all in your head, right?" Anger flashed in her expression, and he reached his other hand to rest on her knee. "I'm not saying what you're feeling isn't valid, but physically, there's nothing keeping you from doing this."

"You think I don't know that? I hate this as much as everyone else." As soon as the words were out, she averted her gaze. Her fingers held the reins in a death grip, and her gelding sidled sideways a step before she halted him.

Reyes stayed with them. "Do you trust Fire?"

"Of course I do."

He shook his head at her automatic reply. "I'm not looking for the answer you think I want to hear. Think about it for a moment. Then tell me if you trust your horse."

Her gaze held his for a long moment before she leaned forward, almost hugging the gelding's neck as she rubbed her palm over his shiny coat. "Yes, I trust him."

"Then let *him* take you over the jump. Don't worry about counting strides or anything else. Close your eyes if you have to. Just give him the reins and let him take you over."

After a long moment, Raine sat up straight in the saddle. The breath she released was uneven, her gaze apprehensive, but she nodded. He gave her knee an encouraging squeeze a second before she pivoted Fire away. She cantered him around the arena once and then lined up with the jump.

"Don't think about it," Reyes whispered. *"Just ride."*

His pulse pounded hard with each stride Fire took toward the jump. Her posture was tense, but her rhythm with the horse was matched perfectly. The closer they got, the farther he leaned in, willing them to sail right over.

It's time.

Come on, Raine. You got this.

One stride before the vertical, she bent forward over Fire's neck

—and Reyes' gut clenched when he saw how far. *Too far*. Her gelding took the jump, but his front feet nicked the top rail, bouncing it from the cups holding it in place. As he came down on the other side with a hard stumble, Raine pitched forward way too far to keep her seat.

Sonofabitch!

Reyes took off at a dead run, heart jammed up into his throat when he saw her leave the saddle. He shouldn't have pushed her. If she got hurt because of him—

Fire came to a choppy halt with Raine bear-hugging his neck, her body dangling in front of him. Reyes reached them as she let go to put her feet on the ground. He gripped her shoulders to turn her toward him, his gaze searching for any injuries.

"You okay? Are you hurt?"

Despite her head shake, her eyes shimmered with tears. Her whole body shook as he pulled her into his arms. He hugged her tight in an attempt to ward off a huge wave of guilt. If her legs had gotten tangled up in Fire's—

"I'm okay." Raine's voice was muffled against his chest with her helmet tucked under his chin.

"I shouldn't have pushed so hard."

"It's okay." When he instinctively tightened his hold, she added, "Really. And we made it over, at least."

"Yeah, you did." Relief allowed a small smile. "I'm proud of you. Though, I would not recommend doing it *that way* in competition."

She gave his chest a little shove and snuck a hand up to wipe at her cheek. "Don't make fun of me."

"Never." He leaned back to assure her that's not what he intended. Seeing the tremulous smile on her lips, his breath caught. When her lashes rose and her still-teary gaze met his, all rational thought fled.

He lifted both hands to her face as he crushed his mouth down on hers.

All the emotions jumbled up inside him—relief she hadn't been hurt, days of wanting this, and more—it all took him from zero to sixty in seconds flat.

He angled his head to deepen the kiss, and Raine was right there with him. Her tongue met his stroke for stroke while her fingers fisted in his shirt, hanging on and pulling him closer at the same time.

A hint of mint teased his senses and had him searching for more. He swept his hands down her back, molding her to him, cupping her ass in those second-skin breeches. Her breathy little whimper penetrated the foggy haze of desire. The needy sound made his pulse surge in excitement while at the same time it gave him a cold dousing of reality.

Nothing had changed between them. If anything, now that she'd conquered the jump, she'd likely be leaving sooner.

Reyes forced himself to drag his mouth from hers. "I'm sorry," he breathed roughly. "I shouldn't have done that."

"No, we shouldn't have," she agreed.

He noticed her use of *we* took equal blame, and when her darkened gaze rose to his, it took everything he had not to claim her glistening, swollen lips with his once more.

The hands fisted in his shirt tightened for a moment, then flattened and pushed against his chest. Reminded he still held her tight against him, Reyes let go and stepped back so she was out of reach.

"I'm sorry."

"You said that already." Jaw tight, she reached for the reins. "Forget it."

Fat chance of that.

"I'm going to do flatwork for a bit and then maybe try the jump one more time."

He nodded, but she'd already turned back to her horse. He gave her a leg up into the saddle, then moved to the center of the arena to do the job Mark was paying him to do. Fortunately, she was focused on her job, because his thoughts were racing like mad.

Being friends wasn't working.

What had just happened wasn't going to work either.

So what the fuck did he do now?

CHAPTER 15

Raine sat on Asher's back patio sipping a glass of wine with Honor, Shelby, Mae, Celia, and Roxanna. Honor laughed at something Mae said, and Raine forced a smile to make it appear she'd been listening. Then she made herself pay attention. After brunch the first weekend, the girls had gotten together for drinks, and Shelby insisted they had to do it one last time before Raine went home to Texas in a week.

The guys were across the street at Mae and Merit's house with the three kids. All but Robert and the one she wanted—the one who'd kissed her senseless two weeks ago and avoided physical contact with her ever since.

Mae lifted the bottle of wine, offering refills. Raine shook her head, sticking to her one-drink limit so she could drop Celia off at her house on her way back to the guest house in Aunt Janine's car. Honor took a refill, because all she had to do was walk upstairs to bed, and Rox and Shelby finished off what was left in the bottle, since their designated drivers were across the street.

While their small patio fire flickered, lightening in the distance drew her attention to the storm clouds gathering over the mountains to the west. Each flash illuminated the jagged peaks of the

Rockies for a few seconds before they melded back into the dark sky. The storm mirrored her emotions lately. Bright flashes of hope quickly swallowed up by gloomy reality.

"We've got about an hour before that hits," Rox commented as the sky lit up again.

And it was already nine-thirty, Raine noted on her phone—in addition to the battery being low. "I should head out soon anyway. I'm not training tomorrow, but I still want to get down to the stables at a decent hour. I know I'm going to sound old, but usually I'm in bed before ten."

Honor snorted. "That's old? Between the bakery and Ava, Asher and I are eyeing the clock by eight every night. I might have two four a.m. bakers, but I still try to get there by six every morning."

"I always wake up when Robert goes for his run at five-thirty, so I just head into the office early," Celia said. "Even on a Sunday, he still gets up for his run."

Raine heard the hint of annoyance in her oldest cousin's tone just as Mae raised her hand.

"Five-thirty here, too, and to the construction site by seven now that Merit takes Ian to school."

"Ditto with the clinic," Shelby chimed in.

Raine gave a wry grin. "I guess seven a.m. is sleeping in then."

Roxanna raised her glass. "I'm with you, Raine. I don't open the shop until eight."

She clinked glasses in solidarity with the brunette, and then sat back for another sip of wine as the fire crackled in the center of their circle. The emotion swelling in her chest now had her speaking past a lump in her throat. "I have to thank you guys for these nights. I've really enjoyed being here these past three weeks and getting to know everyone. And I pray my brothers find wives even half as awesome as all of you."

"I'm going to miss you," Shelby said with a pout. "I can't believe you're leaving in a week."

Neither could she. Truthfully, she was torn over going home. She would've thought once she conquered the jump, things would go more smoothly. And while the jump had gotten easier, since that day—since that kiss in the arena—Reyes had retreated behind a brick wall as formidable as the mountains.

It annoyed the hell out of her he wouldn't even try to be friends. She was sad the month was almost over, and yet she couldn't wait until she didn't have to see him every single day while her heart longed for so much more.

Saying it over and over doesn't make it true.

Still, she needed to keep repeating it, in hopes it would help her to stop wishing for what she couldn't have.

"How's everything going with Reyes?" Roxanna asked.

Raine's stomach flipped, the psychic brunette's question too close to reading her mind. To admit things were strained would be an understatement, and invite questions she didn't want to answer. It would also invite confessions she was doing her best to avoid.

"It's fine. I'm sure he'll be glad to get back to his regular schedule."

Shelby leaned back in her chair and propped her feet on the brick edging along the fire pit. "Are you still helping him with the new thoroughbreds? What were their names again?"

"Saving Grace and Willow Moonlight. And yeah, that's been great."

Other than time with family, that had been the one bright spot over the past two weeks. Reyes may have been one hundred percent business-like in the process, but he'd gone over everything with her step by step, from picking the horses, assessing how to retrain them, the paperwork involved, and anything else she needed to know to get started.

Unfortunately, his knowledge and devotion had impressed her on a whole other level, making the distance between them hurt even more.

"I love the names they come up with for those horses," Mae said.

"Me, too," Raine agreed. "I'm definitely going to look into doing rescues when I get home."

First thing she planned to do was call Jessica at Retired Racers to see if she had any contacts in Texas, and if not, hopefully she could get a couple of horses from her.

It wasn't much longer before the approaching storm sent those of them who had to go home to their vehicles. A few minutes after she dropped Celia off at her house, Raine's phone sounded a severe weather alert. A tornado watch was in effect for the Greater Denver Metro area and surrounding suburbs until midnight.

By the time she turned into her uncle's winding driveway, the wind buffeting the car sent a small surge of apprehension along her spine. Things could get a little wild tonight.

She parked her aunt's car in the guest house garage, then tossed the keys and her purse on the island counter before plugging her nearly-dead phone into the charger. Thunder rolled overhead as she went to stand by the window to look out at the stables.

At nearly ten-thirty at night, the building was dark save for the lights shining from the second floor windows. The same lights that were on every night in Reyes' apartment. All night.

An ache throbbed in her chest, and she rubbed at the sensation. If he wasn't so determined to keep her at a distance, maybe she could've helped him like he'd helped her.

Vivid flashes of lightning revealed the trees swaying in the wind that had picked up even more in the past few minutes. Uneasiness had her heading back to her phone to check the local radar. The estate was right on the edge of a red cell, but any indication of possible tornados were north and east a good thirty miles. Still, future cast showed they weren't out of the woods yet.

A deafening boom shook the house and ground beneath her feet—and everything went dark.

Raine jerked so hard she fumbled her phone, barely rescuing it before it crashed to the floor. Heart lodged in her throat, she spun to face the pitch-black living room. That thunder had been so loud, she'd swear a bomb had gone off—

Bomb.

Reyes.

Her pulse revved like a freight train as she whirled to look out the window again. Reyes was over there in the dark.

Alone.

She yanked her phone from the charger and ran out the door and across the yard as huge drops of cold rain pelted down. By the time she reached the stables, her hair and shirt were drenched, but she only cared about making sure he was okay.

Slamming the barn door against the wind, she leaned against it, chest heaving as she sucked air into her tight lungs. "Reyes?"

A second louder call over the thunder received no response as the lightning filtered in through the windows with an eerie strobe effect. Using the flashlight on her phone, she hurried up the stairs to his apartment.

Though she gave a brisk knock, she didn't wait for an answer before turning the handle. The door swung open easily. "Reyes? Are you up here?"

"Raine?" The relief in his voice was edged with panic.

"Yeah, it's me." She shut the door behind her as she shined her light across the room.

He pushed to his feet from where he'd been sitting with his back pressed against the kitchen cabinets. His chest was bare, and black sweat pants hung low on his hips. His hair was a rumpled mess, as if he'd been sleeping—or run his hands through it over and over.

Recognizing the hunted air about him, like the night in the pool, she guessed the second. Her heart thudded with sympathy when she saw him grip the counter with white knuckles.

Definitely the second.

"The storm knocked the power out," she said, striving to keep her voice casual. "I wanted to check on the horses."

His head snapped up. "Shit. Are they okay?"

"I came up here first." When his gaze met hers, she offered a quick smile. "I was hoping you'd come with me. It's a little creepy down there in the dark."

His Adam's apple bobbed hard, but he nodded. "Yeah."

When his deep breath sounded choppy as all hell, she started across the room. "Do you have any regular flashlights, or a lantern or something? My phone battery is at like three percent."

He dropped his gaze to the countertop, his jaw clenched. He closed his eyes with a grimace, but then popped them open again as if he couldn't bear the darkness.

Raine was at his side by then, and he flinched when she reached out to firmly grasp his forearm. His gaze rose to hers, and her heart jolted at the dark torment in his eyes.

"Everything's fine," she said softly, the reassuring words tumbling out as she gave a light squeeze of her fingers. "The power's out, that's it."

His muscles flexed beneath her hand. "I panicked. I have a flashlight in the drawer next to the sink. And I have my phone..." He paused, a frown creasing his brow as he swept his gaze along the length of the island counter. "It's still in the bedroom on the nightstand. I panicked."

The second time he said those words there was a note of angry disgust in his voice.

"You're not alone." She set her phone on the counter, deliberately facing the flashlight down. Then she reached her free hand up to his face to cup the side of his jaw in the dark, grounding him with her touch. "Maybe it's time to face this, Reyes. When you have a friend to help you through it."

His hand rose up to cover hers, pressing her palm to the rough stubble alongside his goatee. "We're not friends," he said gruffly. Achingly.

"Yes, we are. We have been since that night in the pool. Now, let's get the flashlight out of the drawer and check the horses."

When she lowered her hand from his face, he surprised her by keeping hold of it. He didn't say a word as he threaded his fingers with hers, just held on tight, and she did the same.

Lifting her phone with her free hand, she aimed the light toward the drawer next to the sink. She noticed her battery was down to two percent as they moved together to dig out the flashlight. Once he clicked on the light, the beam glowed strong for a moment, then dimmed to half its strength.

When it flickered and dimmed more, Reyes shook it, cursing under his breath.

"Are there more batteries?"

He rummaged in the drawer. "No."

"Grab your phone, then. Mine's going to die any—" As if on cue, the screen went black.

"Mine's in the bedroom." He closed the drawer and turned, and she had to fight from leaning into him when the warmth of his bare chest brushed against her chilled arm.

All of a sudden he turned the weak flashlight beam on her. "You're all wet."

His surprise sparked a smile. "Yes. Because there's rain to go with that thunder and lightning outside." And now that her brain was focused on her wet clothes, the chill of them had her shoulders shaking with an involuntary shiver.

"You need a dry shirt." He glanced down at his chest. "I should grab one, too."

Don't mind if you don't.

She let her gaze trail down over his tight pectorals and the defined ridges of his abs with a faint trail of light brown hair that disappeared into the waistband of his sweats. He robbed her of the chance to truly admire when he pulled her with him toward the bedroom.

Their destination sped up her pulse, but he released her hand to retrieve his phone from the nightstand. Another curse grated past his lips. "Mine's almost dead, too. I forgot to plug it into the charger before bed."

"I'm sure the power will be back on soon."

Even in the shadows from the dim flashlight, she could see his tight jaw as he swiped a white T-shirt from a bench at the foot of the bed, and then went to the closet to pull out a light gray button up shirt similar to the one she'd borrowed that day they'd taken a trail ride. The one she had forgotten to return at the end of the day, and then 'accidentally' forgotten each day since.

"This okay?" he asked.

"It's fine." She'd have to roll up the sleeves a half-dozen times, and it would reach halfway to her knees, but it was dry. "Thanks."

She took the shirt and walked the few steps to his unmade bed to toss it on the edge before reaching for the hem of her wet top. As her fingers gripped the material, she thought of him behind her, and the bed in front of her, and the fact he'd been lying in those rumpled sheets not that long ago.

Her heart rate ticked along even faster.

The dim light from the flashlight suddenly went crazy, bobbing all around the room before leaving her in even deeper shadows. When she glanced over her shoulder, Reyes stood near the door, T-shirt on, his back to her, flashlight pointed at the ceiling.

Was it terrible that she was disappointed he wasn't going to watch? And yet, her heart gave a hard thump of appreciation at his gentlemanly respect. Yet another little thing she loved about him.

Love.

Hmm. Don't go there.

She quickly exchanged wet shirt for dry, and then buttoned all but the top two buttons and rolled up the sleeves. The hem reached to mid-thigh on her damp jeans. Her bra was also damp, but already she was warmer. While his back was turned, she lifted the collar for a discreet inhale of fresh linen fabric softener. His other shirt had had a faint underlying note of the same scent, and she bit back a soft sigh.

A loud overhead rumble reminded her of the real reason she was standing in his bedroom wearing his shirt. She scooped up her wet top and headed toward him. "All set. Let's go check the horses before the flashlight dies."

The light swung toward her, and she was thankful he kept it pointed down to keep from blinding her. He stilled for a long moment as he swept his gaze from the top of her wet head to the now soggy white canvas tennis shoes she'd worn over to Honor's.

He closed his eyes and tipped his head back, muttering as he turned to walk out of the bedroom.

Raine raised her eyebrows as she followed. She was pretty sure he'd said something about being *"totally fucked,"* though she wasn't so sure she wanted to ask him to clarify.

He slipped on a pair of tennis shoes at the door, and they went down the stairs. A few of the horses were restless, but it didn't appear that any were having major issues with anxiety from the storm. Raine slipped into her tack stall for a handful of treats before taking time to pet and murmur softly to each one that bothered to stick their head over the stall doors.

After giving Taz a treat, she waited inside Fire's stall while Reyes checked the doors on both ends of the barn were secure against the wind. By now, the thunder had moved off into the distance, and the lightning flashes were only occasional, but rain still thrummed hard and steady on the roof.

Reyes' curse from the far end of the barn drew her around, and she rose on her tiptoes to see over the stall wall. She noticed it was pitch black on his side of the barn at the same time he called out, "Flashlight's dead. My phone's dead, too."

Hearing the strain in his voice again, she hurried out of the stall and down the aisle. A weak flash of lightning revealed his outline at the far door. When she reached him, he fumbled for her hand and squeezed tight. She moved closer, pulling free to slip her arms around his waist. His whole body was stiff as a board, muscles tight as if he was doing everything he could not to panic.

"I'm right here, Reyes. I'm not going anywhere."

His arms closed tight around her as his chest heaved beneath her cheek. "I fucking hate this."

"I know. Believe me, I know."

"I know you do." After a long moment, he murmured, "Thank you."

His bent head put his gruff voice right next to her ear. She shivered as the husky sound set off flutters of awareness deep in her belly. A steadying breath only made it worse. The scent from his shirt was magnified times a hundred from the oh-so-warm flesh and blood man in her arms. Fresh linen combined with his musky scent was a dangerously tempting combination.

She nearly groaned in pent up frustration, then rolled her eyes in the darkness. Here he was dealing with his own PTSD, and she was getting all turned on by how damn good he smelled.

And felt.

Except some of the tension had left his body, and all of a sudden, she felt the warmth of his lips and breath on her neck. The past couple weeks of suppressed yearning flooded forward to intertwine with the more tender emotions for this wounded man taking over her heart.

She turned her head with a helpless murmur, seeking his mouth with hers.

CHAPTER 16

Reyes pulled back at the exact second Raine's lips met his. He almost gave in—God knew how badly he wanted to give in when he heard her second soft moan of protest—but it would be for all the wrong reasons. Or mostly the wrong reasons.

He didn't want her pity. Nor did he want to use her to deal with his fear even if his body was already half-hard in total approval of that plan. He couldn't let it matter that her voice and soft touch had a grounding effect that kept him from focusing on the dark. As long as she was with him, he could keep the panic at bay, and yet, he hated how weak that need made him feel. Even though she understood, he hated her seeing him shaking like a cowering dog.

He reluctantly felt for her hand, fitting her smaller palm against his. "Come on. I can take you back to the guest house."

"In this rain? Not a chance."

Her instant, firm refusal triggered a knee-weakening wave of relief.

"I'm waiting upstairs with you until the power comes back on," she stated. "Or the rain quits."

His chest tightened at the last bit she tacked on, and a knot formed in his stomach at the thought of her leaving before the power came back on. He didn't argue any further as he felt along the stalls to the stairs, because selfishly, he'd take whatever he could get.

In the apartment, he closed the door behind her before pausing a moment to picture the layout in his head. Dark or not, he needed to get some space between them. "You can have the bed. I'll take the couch."

When he led her toward the bedroom, she resisted. "I thought we could talk."

Keeping her moving, he countered, "It's late."

"I'm not tired."

Neither was he, but—

They'd reached the doorway, and he steered her into the room, but when he would've backed away, she grabbed both his hands and pulled him with her.

"Raine."

"We can't talk if you're out on the couch and I'm in here."

"Ever consider that's the point?" It was a half-hearted protest at best.

"No." She tugged him forward. "Come on, are you really going to leave me in here all alone?"

He should. He really, *really* should. Yet, his feet were still following her to the bed. "You don't have to do this," he said gruffly.

"Do what?"

"Babysit me. I can deal with this."

"I'm sure you can. But why do it alone when you don't have to?"

He shrugged, then remembered she couldn't see him any more than he could see her. It was crazy how truly dark everything was. Forget the bedside lamp he usually left on twenty-four seven, with the power out and the storm blocking any moonlight, not even a ghost of a glimmer shone through the windows. No power indicator lights blinked from any appliances to soften the inky blackness.

And then he realized a second later, even crazier still was how his back and forth kinda bickering with Raine shifted the focus from the black hole of his fear—even when they were beating around the bush about that exact subject.

"I want to be here with you, Reyes. We don't even have to—whoops—that's the bed." Her voice sounded a bit breathless. She pulled harder on his hands for a moment, and his body collided with hers. "We can just lay here if you don't want to talk."

A great offer, but if he lay with her without talking, he'd end up thinking of all the things he wanted to do with her.

Talking might be safer.

He disengaged their hands and stepped back, but didn't go any farther.

"*Or...*" she ventured, "you could tell me about what happened to you three years ago."

He'd rather think about all the things he wanted to do with her.

Rustling noises told him she was doing something, but he couldn't even see the shadows of her movement. His fingers clenched for a moment before he consciously relaxed them. Every last little atom of willpower he possessed wasn't going to get him back out to the couch, so he sidestepped around her to sit on the edge of the bed while toeing off his shoes. Then he swung his legs up onto the bed and scooted back against the headboard.

"I already told you what happened."

"I know, but—" The mattress dipped as she climbed up—right over him. "Oh. Sorry. I can't see anything."

He sucked in a breath when her hand brushed over his groin. He quickly reached to help her over to the other side of the bed and encountered a whole palmful of warm, bare thigh.

Holy shit—had she stripped down?

Heat seared through his veins as he jerked his arm away and grabbed the top of the headboard to keep from reaching for her again.

"What did you take off?" he asked before he could help himself.

"My jeans were wet."

Which meant she was in his bed in just his shirt. He leaned his head back against the headboard as the semi he'd been trying to will away swelled to full mast. Yeah, he was totally fucked.

She rustled around a bit more, adjusting the pillow by the sound of it. But then she scooted in close against his left side, and he stiffened when she tucked her shoulder under his arm, draped her arm across his stomach and pillowed her head on his chest. Her knee rested against his thigh—thank God, because if she'd draped it over him, he was pretty sure nothing could've stopped him from reaching down to haul her fully on top of him.

Reyes stared across the room in the dark, the headboard biting into his fingers as he gripped it tight while his pulse roared in his ears. Like earlier in the barn—and any other time he got too close—the airy, floral scent of her filled his senses and had him wanting to bury his face in her hair.

Working with her with the thoroughbreds the past couple of weeks had been pure torture. Self-inflicted torture as he came up with all sorts of reasons to keep her at the barn for hours past her training sessions. And even though he tried to keep it strictly business, watching her with the horses and how much she put into learning the process, he'd been helpless against the emotions he should be resisting at all costs.

Raine slid her hand up his chest to his face, her touch ghosting over his lips before shifting down just a bit. His pulse stumbled when she traced the line of his scar with her fingertip.

"Did this happen that day?"

He swallowed hard at the question and managed a slight nod and strangled sound of affirmation. She didn't press further, and after a long moment, he let out a pent up breath while lowering his arm to curve over her shoulder and arm. She snuggled closer, and his heart warmed, even as his gut tightened at the words rushing to the tip of his tongue.

"It was supposed to be a routine sweep of an isolated compound. Intel said the place had been deserted for weeks." He paused as vivid memories flashed in his head like snippets from a movie trailer. "I led the way in initially, but we spread out to check the rooms, and one of my guys hit a trip wire."

Her palm flattened against his jaw, warm and comforting. Reaching up with his free hand, he pulled hers back down to his chest and held tight.

"I have vague memories of screams and yelling and then nothing until I woke up on the plane to Landstuhl in Germany. I couldn't see a damn thing."

"I can't even imagine how terrifying that must've been."

He could only squeeze her hand in affirmation.

"What about your team?"

A lump formed in his throat from both her asking about the others, and what had happened. "Neider—the guy who tripped the wire—didn't make it."

Her palm pressed over his heart. "I'm so sorry."

Reyes tightened his arm on her shoulder for a brief moment in acknowledgment. "Hughes and Dice rode transport to Germany with me. They were both medically discharged because of their injuries."

"You weren't?"

He made a negative sound. "Once my vision came back, my injuries were all surface."

She shifted until he felt her rest her chin on the back of the hand she'd flattened against his chest. "Still, I don't think it's right they made you go back."

"I insisted on going back," he corrected.

"Why?"

He smiled slightly at the astonishment in her voice. "My team was still there. No way was I going to go home when I was still physically able to serve with them."

"And mentally?"

"Believe it or not, it was better there. After I came home is when things got worse."

"After you were away from your team?"

"Yeah."

A change in pressure on his chest told him she'd tilted her head. "Have you talked to anyone?"

"Dev. The horses. You."

The lamp on his nightstand clicked on.

Reyes blinked at the unexpected light and found himself staring right into Raine's hazel eyes. The hum of the refrigerator and other appliances seemed unusually loud in the suddenly awkward silence. He read sympathy in her eyes, not pity, and another raw, warm emotion that kick-started his pulse.

"Hi," she murmured softly.

His lips twitched. "Hi."

Her gaze dropped to his mouth, and in the space of one heartbeat, desire hit with a dizzying rush. The sudden hitch of her breath told him she felt it, too.

He lifted his hand to tuck her damp hair back and couldn't seem to help but let his touch linger on the soft, delicate shell of her ear. Of their own accord, his fingers slipped into her hair, burying deep.

She held his gaze steady as she pushed up and swung a leg over to straddle his thighs. He drew in a ragged breath, his body throbbing with need as he wished she'd settled a few inches higher.

Clenching his fingers ever so slightly in her hair, he drew her forward, his gaze zeroed in on her lips. Even with the move, he made one last token effort at doing the right thing.

"You know there are all kinds of reasons why this is a bad idea."

"Maybe." Hands braced on his shoulders, she leaned in until her lips were less than an inch from his. "But in this exact moment, there isn't a single one I give a damn about. You?"

Reyes couldn't even remember them, much less give a damn about them.

He answered with a little tug to close the distance between them and melded his mouth with hers. When her lips parted on a sigh, he angled her head and deepened the kiss with a bold stroke of his tongue. Her soft moan only drove him deeper, until they were both desperate for air. He sucked in a lungful while trailing his lips down the curve of her throat.

He reached for the buttons on her shirt—*his* shirt—his heart thudding hard at the anticipation of revealing what lie underneath. Raine eased back, her hands lightly trailing over his forearms as he worked his way down. He caught her swift glance at the bedside lamp at the same time he realized she'd removed her bra earlier, too.

Sweet Jesus.

"So, um, do you usually just leave the light on all the time then?"

He was busy taking in the exposed curves of her breasts. "Usually."

"And no one's minded?"

Reyes stopped on the second to last button and looked up. "Do *you* mind?" She shook her head, but he noticed the corner of her lip caught between her teeth. "Raine, you can be honest."

"I don't," she insisted. Then she rolled her eyes with a slightly sheepish smile. "I guess I'm just curious if other women you've been with have been okay with sleeping with the light on. What do you tell them?"

He tried to avoid answering by teasing, "Really? Right now, you're curious about other women?"

She frowned, and ducked her head. "I'm sorry. That was stupid to ask."

"No." He tucked a knuckle under her chin and raised her gaze to his. His heart thumped hard as he admitted, "I don't know if other women would be okay with it because I haven't been with anyone since before it happened."

Her eyes widened. "In three years?"

He lifted his shoulders, then let them droop as nerves rushed in. Until this moment, he hadn't really thought about how long it had been. Well, he had, but now he was suddenly worried about how long he'd last.

Raine palmed his face with a soft smile, then leaned in to gently press her lips to his. He started to lean into the kiss, but she eased back a couple inches.

"Do you trust me, Reyes?"

The suddenly serious question prompted a solemn nod—until she leaned over and switched off the lamp. His pulse revved like crazy, and three years of conditioning had him tensing beneath her.

She leaned in again, her lips brushing his before raining soft kisses over his face. After a moment, his breathing eased, and he began to anticipate where the next one would fall.

"You good?" she whispered.

"Mm-hm."

"Good." *Left eye.* "Don't think of the dark." *Scar.* "Just feel." *Forehead.*

By now, she had his full attention, and with her body against his, that was an easy order to follow. He parted the sides of her unbuttoned shirt and skimmed his hands up her rib cage to her breasts. He loved the weight of the firm globes filling his palms, and when he circled her hard nipples with his thumbs, her mouth settled over his again. A throaty hum vibrated her lips against his before he opened to the probe of her tongue.

He loved that she wasn't shy, and as she arched over him, her hips riding his as he sucked on one breast, then the other, he asked, "What do you want, Raine? What do you like?"

Her fingers clenched in his hair, and she widened her legs, bearing down over his erection. "I want you," she breathed. "All of you."

His body pulsated in eager response, but if he buried himself in her right now, he'd likely be finished in a few desperate strokes.

So he stripped off the shirt and her panties, then flipped their positions. As he bent his head to swirl his tongue around one nipple, she skimmed his T-shirt up his back, her light touch a torturous tickle. A quick reach dragged it over his head, and he tossed it aside.

Her hands moved to his chest and he enjoyed the sensation of her exploring fingers before it became impossible to resist the temptation of her body laid out beneath him. Her muscles were firm and toned from years of riding, yet her skin seductively silky soft.

He took his time worshiping her breasts, then kissed his way farther down, past her navel, to the sweet spot that had her moaning his name minutes later. He wished he could see her face as she came apart beneath him, but wouldn't trade a moment of this with her for anything.

She drew in a deep breath when he moved up to lie beside her. "I'm not complaining, but I think you got that backwards."

Despite the smile in her voice, Reyes paused mid-reach for a condom in his night stand. "Things haven't changed that much in three years, have they?"

She laughed. "I was supposed to give *you* a good memory of the dark. Something to help after I..."

His chest clenched at where that sentence had been going before she trailed off. "After you're gone?"

Her soft sigh was full of regret. "Yeah."

He took it back. He would trade this one night for a lifetime of forever with her.

But that wasn't an option. She had to get back to her life, and a career that included riding for Olympic gold. He would never ask her to give up her dream.

Reyes brushed his knuckles over her cheek before kissing her with all the pent-up longing of the past few weeks and what was to come in his future. Somewhere in there they stripped off his sweats and boxer briefs, and she nearly killed him with the soft explorations of her hands.

As her fingers circled his flesh and caressed up and down, his hips bucked in response. He reached down to close his hand around hers, applying torturous pressure before pulling her away.

"I need to be inside you," he rasped.

He rolled on the condom, then positioned himself at her entrance. In the faintest of light filtering in from the outside yard lights, he saw her lips part on a soft gasp when he slid into her tight heat. A low groan of pure pleasure rumbled from deep in his chest as he buried his face in her hair.

Holy fuck, I don't remember it ever feeling this good.

A soft laugh whispered over his ear. "I'd love to take the credit, but that's just because it's been a few years."

"Did I say that out loud?" he asked.

"Yeah." Raine arched beneath him, her hips urging him to move.

After a few strokes, another moan left his lips when she matched his rhythm. "Take the credit—it's truly all yours."

Her hands in his hair drew his mouth back to hers. "How about it's ours?"

He didn't agree or disagree as a tingle started at the base of his spine, urging him faster. He fought hard to hold on until she came first—or with him—but his control slipped fast. "Raine...I...I can't..."

"It's fine," she bit out, her nails biting into his back. "I'm good. Oh, God, Reyes, *so good.*"

Her inner muscles tightened around him. His climax barreled through him, and he let go as it carried him over the edge with her.

His pulse still beat crazy fast as he shifted to the side moments later. With her arms wrapped around him, her fingers threading through his hair at the nape of his neck, she made a negative sound and kept his weight over her body.

Emotion swelled in his chest, and he knew without a doubt he'd failed despite his best efforts. She'd given him this memory to hold onto in the dark, and in turn, she'd take his heart with her when she left. He wasn't so sure the exchange was fair—but he wouldn't take it back for anything.

Now, he just had to figure out how to live with only the memory as she rode her way to gold.

CHAPTER 17

Sunday morning, Raine woke briefly when Reyes murmured he was going to feed the horses, and then a short while later, he slid back under the covers with her. She couldn't remember the last time she'd stayed in bed past eight, and certainly not with a man. But he'd woken her with a kiss that quickly turned into so much more.

She wished she could spend the whole day with him right here, but reluctantly lifted her head from his chest to check the clock on the nightstand. "Brunch is in an hour. I should get back to the guest house to shower and get ready. You want to meet me up there?"

There was a beat of silence before he pressed a kiss to her shoulder, then rolled over to sit up on the other side of the bed. "I'm not going to brunch."

Raine sat up, holding the sheet to her chest. "You're not?"

Back still to her, he shook his head as he pulled on his briefs and a pair of jeans. "I got other stuff to do."

Surprised by his short tone, she frowned in disappointment—and hurt—while reaching down for the button up shirt he'd given her in place of her wet top. As she slipped it on and secured the buttons, it took all her willpower to not demand exactly what *stuff* was more important than making the most of the time they had left?

"You want coffee?" he asked on his way to the door.

In what, a to-go cup?

Biting back the snark, she said, "Sure. Thanks." Then she sat dumbfounded after he left, wondering what the hell had happened in the past thirty seconds?

Life had made a seismic shift last night and then settled into a new reality this morning. But maybe it had only been for her. Maybe he hadn't felt the same connection when they made love, and she was the only one who wanted to use the rest of her stay to figure out how they could have a future together.

Swallowing past the lump in her throat, she pulled on her panties, grabbed her bra and now dry jeans, and headed for the bathroom right next door to his bedroom. She shot Reyes a quick look in the kitchen. He had his back to her, his hands braced on the counter in front of the sink, his shoulders hunched as he stared out the window overlooking the white-fenced pastures. As if the weight of the world was suddenly resting on those broad shoulders.

She wanted to ask what was wrong, but chickened out and turned back toward the bathroom—until she spotted her top from the night before draped over one of the island stools to dry. Probably better to wear that across the lawn, just in case any of her cousins arrived early and saw her crossing from the barn to the guest house.

She was halfway across the living room to retrieve the shirt when footsteps pounded up the stairs from the barn. She jerked to a halt as a loud knock rattled the door.

"Rey? You in there?"

He spun around from the sink at the same time the door swung open. His brother pulled up short when he saw the both of them.

"Geezus, Dev, you could wait for me to get the door," Reyes grumbled as he came around to the other side of the counter.

"We were looking for Raine," he shot back, his gaze swinging from one to the other.

Heat seared her face as he clearly took in the whole picture with Reyes in just jeans, and her in just his shirt.

"You two really should answer your damn phones."

Hers sat on the island counter, completely forgotten after their trip down to check the horses. "My battery died."

"Mine, too," Reyes said.

"You should've charged them as soon as the power came back on," his brother advised. He shifted his attention back to her as more footsteps sounded on the stairs. "Shelby's been trying to call you since last night, and your *father* is looking for you."

Her stomach dropped out from under her at the same moment her dad appeared in the doorway. When had he gotten here?

Relief etched his features as he entered the apartment. "Thank God you're okay, honey. No one could reach you after the storm, and I didn't know what to think when you weren't at the guest—"

He stopped and broke off abruptly, his gaze sweeping down to where Reyes' shirt ended at mid-thigh as she clutched the rest of her clothes in her hands. Heat prickled along the back of her neck as her dad's expression darkened.

Reyes had moved to stand in front of the counter, and her dad pivoted to glower at him. "What the hell is going on here?"

Raine took a step forward. "Dad—"

He cut her off with a jerk of his hand. "I wasn't talking to you."

Her eyes widened at his furious tone. She went from feeling the need to explain to being royally pissed off. "Well you should be," she retorted.

Dev backed toward the door. "I'm just going to go let Shelby and her parents know you're okay."

Her dad's glare didn't waver from Reyes. "You sonofabitch. I paid you to be my daughter's trainer, not sleep with her."

Reyes stood stiff as a board. "With all due respect, sir, you haven't paid me a dime."

"Is that supposed to make this better?"

"No, but—"

"I'll have your job for this."

Raine's heart lurched as she took a quick step forward. "Knock it off, Daddy. Reyes didn't do anything wrong."

"He took advantage of the situation."

"He certainly did not." She shot a glance at Reyes to see his jaw clenched as tight as his fists. "I am a grown woman. I make my own choices."

"Looks to me like you're still making the same *bad* choices. I would've thought you'd learned your lesson by now."

White-hot heat speared through her at his words. She couldn't believe he would throw that in her face in front of Reyes—in front of *any*one. It had been years ago. She'd been eighteen and naïve. She *had* learned her lesson, which is why she knew what she and Reyes had was different.

Her gut clenched when she saw him frowning at her, and she shook her head at her dad. "That's not fair."

"I don't give a damn what you think is fair." He pointed to the door. "Put your clothes on and go pack your stuff. We're going home."

Disbelief spiked her anger. "I'll go home when I'm ready."

His furious brown gaze bored into hers. "Are you still having trouble with the jump?"

"No. Reyes helped me work through it and—"

"Then you're ready. Besides, it's time you got back to competing. There's an event in New York in two weeks. I have you all signed up."

She blew out an irritated breath. "You should've asked me first."

"Why? This is your job. It's time you got back to it."

"You're the one who made me come here, so don't blame me for being away." She stole a glance at the still silent Reyes and then faced her dad once more. "I don't want to leave yet."

"Because of him?"

Yes. Him, and so much more. "Because it's *my* life. You're my dad, not my boss."

He gestured to the door. "Go pack, Raine. *Now*. I will meet you at the guest house after I've spoken with Mr. Torrez."

"No. And I'm not going to New York, either."

He stared at her for a long moment, his frustration palpable. "Who the hell do you think pays for everything? As long as my name is on the checks, you will do as I say."

"Fine, then I quit." The moment the words left her mouth, shock reverberated through her system. Her stomach fell like a lead balloon. Where had that come from? She'd always pushed back to some extent, but usually gave in after token protest.

Her dad's dark eyebrows shot toward his hairline. "Excuse me?"

A few simple words would take it back.

No.

Not this time. This is too important.

The eye-opening revelation slammed home. Nothing had ever felt this momentous. For once, she knew exactly what she wanted —*Reyes*—and she wasn't backing down.

A flood of relief buoyed her heart with joy and shored up her determination. She breathed deep, then lifted her chin while meeting her father's gaze. "I said, *I quit*. I'm done with competing. No more events. Find someone else to boss around, because I'm done."

Her dad gaped at her in shock. "What about the Olympics?"

Uncertainty skipped her pulse, but then it steadied. If giving up the Olympics was what it took to be with Reyes, so be it.

"Raine," her dad implored, "You can't do this."

"Watch me." And she marched out of the apartment to cross the lawn in nothing but Reyes' shirt.

CHAPTER 18

Reyes stared dumbfounded as Raine swept from the room. She didn't mean that. No way could she just give it all up. In fact, he was pretty sure she hadn't meant to say something so drastic at first—he'd seen the surprise on her face before she'd doubled down.

"This is your fault."

He shifted his attention to her father. The man's furious gaze threatened to incinerate him on the spot. "Sir—"

"Cut the bullshit, son. If you had an ounce of respect for me or my brother, you wouldn't have seduced my daughter."

He did his best not to flinch at the accusation. It had been the other way around from the second he'd met her—even all those years ago—but he wasn't about to tell her father *that*. Besides, she hadn't done any of it on purpose.

"She's a fully consenting adult," he said stiffly.

"You took advantage of your position with her."

"It wasn't like that at all." He shifted his stance and glanced out the door before meeting the man's gaze once more. "I care for her, sir."

"Isn't that nice," he sneered. "You'll be happy to know she has a history of *caring* for her trainers, too."

The implication sunk deep to sour Reyes' gut. He frowned in the direction of the guest house. Was he just another guy on a list of guys for her? Was this something she did despite her proclaimed aversion to casual relationships? Or, had that simply been a line?

"Didn't know that, did you?" Mr. Diamond asked.

He clenched his jaw at the man's superior tone. Doing his best to ignore the crushing hurt bearing down on his chest, he asked, "What do you want from me?"

"End whatever it is that's going on—and end it for good. You've seen her ride. She's got gold in her future."

"I agree."

"Then you can't let her quit." The man's voice took on a desperate tone. "It's been her dream to ride in the Olympics since she was a little girl. If she gives that up because of some foolish notion there's something between the two of you, the time will come when she hates you for robbing her of that dream."

Wow. The guy knew how to get right to the heart of it, didn't he? And yet, Reyes couldn't disagree with one word he said, or the apparent place it came from in the man's heart. It was hard to fault him for protecting his daughter's dream.

Besides, he'd been struggling with how to distance himself so he could deal with her leaving. Didn't this just provide the perfect fucking opportunity?

"Do this," her father added, "and I won't ask my brother to terminate your position. I'll even add a nice bonus to your paycheck."

Reyes jerked his gaze up. "I'll talk to her, but not because you just threatened my job, and most definitely not for your fucking money. You can get the hell out now."

Surprise flickered in the man's eyes, but then he left with a solid thump of the door.

As soon as he was alone, Reyes scrubbed his hands over his face and then turned to pound his fists on the counter, stopping just short to lightly tap the surface. So many emotions danced right in front of him, fighting for the upper hand. Anger, frustration, hurt, disbelief.

One rolled into the other until they coalesced into a howling cyclone that made it hard to breathe, much less think. The only thing that made sense was getting it over with sooner rather than later.

After a shower, he pulled on a T-shirt, jeans, and boots, then saddled Taz before heading up to the guest house. He knew without a doubt he was going to need some therapy the moment he walked away from her.

His heart thundered in his ears as he approached the door with heavy feet. When Raine answered his knock, the distress in her hazel eyes stole what little breath he'd sucked past the vice pinching his chest. He barely managed a gruff, "Hey," as he handed over her forgotten phone.

"Hi. Thanks." She stuffed the phone in her back pocket with a strained smile and stood aside to let him in. "I am so sorry about earlier."

"You don't owe me any apologies."

"I'm still sorry you had to go through that. My dad was a jerk."

No argument from him—though he very grudgingly admitted he understood the man's motivation even though he'd offended the hell out of him with the execution.

Raine shut the door and turned to face him. He couldn't keep his gaze from devouring her shower-damp hair and the beauty of her makeup-free features. She wore a filmy, peach-colored shirt, and a pair of white shorts that left her legs bare. Barely an hour ago, they'd been wrapped around him as he selfishly stole one more memory to hoard for later.

"Can you frickin' believe my father?"

Reyes grimaced as he glanced at the floor, then raised his gaze to hers. "He's right. You can't quit."

Surprise whisked across her face. "I can, and I did."

He shook his head. "You can't give up on your dream."

"What if it's not *my* dream?"

"What?"

She shrugged, her gaze shifting toward the French doors leading to the pool. "I don't know. When I think about the Olympics, I'm not sure who wants it more, me or my dad." She gave a short laugh. "Actually, my dad does, because I quit."

A spark of hope flared bright. If it was her father's dream, did he really have to do this?

Yes. She'll end up hating you.

The spark sputtered out. "I've seen how hard you work, Raine. You have to follow this through. Maybe your dad does want it more than you, but you still want it."

"I'm not so sure about that anymore."

And that right there cinched it for him. She wasn't sure she wanted it, but that also meant she wasn't sure she didn't. "You have to go home."

She shook her head with a frown. "I want to be here with you."

His heart kicked in his chest at her declaration. He hadn't wanted to use the next thing, but didn't see any other way. "Is that what you say to all your trainers?"

"What?" Her eyes widened, then narrowed. "What did he tell you?"

"That you have a history of...getting involved."

"It happened one time—*one*—and it was years ago. I was young and stupid, and he *did* take advantage."

"Your dad made it sound like more than that."

"Of course he did. He wants me to go home, remember?" Fury shook her voice. "I dated some after that, and had one somewhat serious boyfriend about two years ago, but that's it. That makes you the third guy I've ever been with, so whatever my dad told you, it isn't true. I would hope you'd believe me over him."

His heart soared, then took a dizzying nose-dive. *Shit.* That blew that angle. Which left him with the worst option of all. The one that would hurt the most.

Before he could form the words to send her away, her expression softened as she moved closer and took his hands. She tipped her face up, her eyes full of a warmth that squeezed his chest and made it hard to breathe.

The corners of her mouth trembled before she declared, "I love you, Reyes."

His heart lodged up in his throat. The emotion shining in her eyes matched what had been building inside him and solidified last night when she loved him through the darkness.

"I've had a thing for you since the summer we visited when I was fifteen, but these past few weeks, getting to know you, and last night..." Her cheeks flushed, and she ducked her head with a sheepish, almost shy smile. She squeezed his hands and looked up again. "I've always done what is expected of me. What my dad wants. But now it's about what *I* want, and that's to stay here and do the horse rescue with you."

He closed his eyes as one second of pure joy was swallowed up by black misery.

Years from now, when she realizes what she gave up, she will blame you.

He could not be the one to steal her dream.

Reyes pulled his hands from hers and stepped back. "You're reading too much into last night," he said gruffly.

A tiny frown marred her brow. She stared long enough to make him squirm, then shook her head with defiant bravado. "I don't believe you didn't feel our connection. Look me in the eye and tell me you didn't feel anything last night. Right now. I dare you."

She could dare all she wanted. He wasn't a Diamond.

He forced a shrug. "It was good, of course, but it was never going to be more than the one night." No matter how much he wanted it to be.

Her expression fell. "How can you say that?"

"I never made any promises."

"No, but..."

Her eyes went all shiny, and she blinked hard as she spun away from him. He fisted his hands at his sides. He had to get out. Now.

To keep from reaching out for her, he strode over to open the door. "Go home, Raine. Go ride like you're supposed to."

"Is he paying you?"

He froze halfway through the doorway and saw she'd faced him once more. "You know me better than that."

"I sure thought I did." She swallowed hard. "Especially since you said you don't sleep around."

The next words made him sick to his stomach, but he forced them out anyway. "Well, as *you* said, there's a first time for everything."

He hated himself the moment he saw the utter devastation in her eyes. Guilt spurred his feet out the door and back to the stables. He galloped Taz across the land moments later, wishing he could outrun the blackness chasing after his soul.

He'd had to do whatever it took to get her to go for the gold... even if it ripped both of them to shreds.

CHAPTER 19

"Rey?" his dad called across the arena shortly before five p.m. "I'm heading out. You almost done out here?"

Reyes reined Willow Moonlight over a set of four caveletti and brought the mare to a halt at the fence. His parents had returned from their month long Europe trip a week ago. The day after Raine had gone back to Texas with her father.

"I'm going to work with her for a little longer, then get some time in on Stimpy."

His dad took off his Denver Broncos baseball cap, scratched his head, then resettled the cap. "You should come over for dinner tonight."

"I got some stuff to do around here."

"You said that the past three nights. Your mother is worried about you."

So was his dad. He could see it in his eyes, and it was there in the tone of his voice. Because he wasn't putting much into maintaining the happy-go-lucky façade of the past few years. What was the point? He was miserable, and it wasn't worth the effort to pretend otherwise.

But that didn't mean he wanted to talk about it either. Any of it.

His parents knew some of what had happened in their absence, but not all. Dinner would only bring questions he wasn't ready to answer.

"Maybe tomorrow night."

"No more maybes," his dad warned.

Reyes shrugged and backed up Willow. "Tell Mom I'm fine."

"You know I don't lie to your mother."

He didn't say anything else as his dad left and he wheeled Willow around. He would be fine—in about fifty years, when he was dead and didn't have regrets plaguing him every second of every day.

Since Raine had left, he worked from sunup to sundown. Then he lay in the dark in his bedroom, fighting for air until her memory slipped in to ease the tightness in his chest. He relived every moment of that night with her in his arms until he fell asleep—which brought on a whole other form of torture.

His subconscious brought her to life in his dreams. He heard her laugh, saw her beautiful smile. That flicker of annoyance in those greenish-brown eyes of hers when he pushed her buttons. The flash of desire when he pushed *other* buttons. He filled his senses with the subtle flowery scent of her shampoo. Felt the silk of her pale skin as he caressed her curves. Tasted the sweetness of Raine on his lips and his tongue.

He inevitably woke up hard, his body pulsating with need as reality rushed in to chill his soul for another day.

After Reyes had finished in the barn, the sun was long gone, and he wearily climbed the stairs. He ate a bowl of cereal standing by the sink with the TV playing on the other side of the room. Then he grabbed a beer and slouched on the couch. The show on the screen didn't interest him in the least, so he lifted the remote to shut it off. A few minutes later, he drained the beer and set it on the end table before reaching to turn off the lamp.

His breath gave that familiar, hated catch in the darkness, but he sought out Raine in his mind. Therapy and torture all in one.

Instead of that last night they'd spent together, his memory took him to their first day in the ring.

"I'm done. I'm going home."

"So, you're not only afraid of the jumps, you're afraid of me, too."

"I'm not afraid of you, I just can't stand you."

"Whatever you gotta tell yourself."

"You were a jerk last summer, and you've been a jerk since I got here last night. It's taking everything I have not to smack you right now."

His surprised laugh echoed in his head. *"Really?"*

"Yes, really."

"By all means then, go ahead. I dare you."

And she'd taken the dare and smacked him. Hard enough that the memory made his cheek sting even now. He raised his hand to his face as her unapologetic voice echoed in his head.

"Don't dare a Diamond, 'cuz we don't back down."

Another scene flashed—this time as they floated only inches apart from each other in the pool.

"How about we compromise? Tell me why you don't like the dark, and I'll tell you about the accident."

Another leap; another memory. At the pool again, but after that inferno of a first kiss that nearly made him lose his mind.

"You're seriously mad? I'm trying to do the right thing."

"The right thing would've been to not make me think you wanted this in the first place."

"I do want you, Raine. More than I've ever wanted anyone before. But I need this job. I need to be here."

But did he really need to be *here specifically* anymore? He was sitting in the dark by himself. And though he felt uptight and restless, he knew it had more to do with the subject of his thoughts than not being able to see.

Dealing with the dark had gotten easier each day—missing Raine had not.

"Don't dare a Diamond, cuz we don't back down."

Well, neither did a Torrez—unless he was a complete idiot.

His stomach churned with a sinking feeling just as a sharp rap on the door made him jump.

"Rey?"

Recognizing his brother's voice, he sat up straighter as he called, "It's open."

The door swung inward. With the light from the stairs at his back, his brother's front was in shadows. "I didn't think you were here."

"Then why'd you come up?"

"Saw your jeep." Dev leaned a shoulder against the doorjamb and crossed his arms. "You're in the dark."

"Can't put nuttin' past you, bro."

After a beat of silence, his brother repeated, "You're *in the dark.*"

As if he hadn't gotten the significance of the words the first time around. Because, you know, it was only *his* PTSD.

"Yes, I'm in the dark, Dev. Apparently in more ways than one."

"What does that mean?"

He winced. "Nothing." Schooling his features, he shifted to flip on the light, then arched his brows at his brother. "What are you doing here?"

"Dinner with the Diamonds."

"Hmm." He rose and swiped up his empty bottle to go toss it in the recycle. "Want a beer?"

Dev shut the door and raised his hand in a staying gesture. "No, thanks. We're heading home soon. I saw the lights off and the jeep here, and thought I'd check in."

Reyes moved forward to brace his palms on the island. "You've checked. All good."

His brother walked over to face him across the counter. "Or somewhat better, it would appear."

"Sure."

"Except I got a call from Dad earlier. He said you've been burying yourself in work. Like when you first got home."

So Dad sent Dev.

He wanted to be annoyed. Instead, his chest tightened at the fact they cared. Not that he ever doubted they did.

"Thing is," Dev continued, "unless you've started seeing a therapist about your PTSD, the only thing different I'm aware of in the past month is a certain Diamond up here for training."

Reyes dipped his head, staring at the counter as he traced his finger along one of the black veins in the marble-like top. He didn't want to admit his stupidity, but it was going to come out sooner than later.

"She told me she loved me."

"And?"

He glanced up. "And I sent her home."

"That much is obvious. I meant, and *how do you feel about her?*"

"I love her."

"Then why send her away?"

"She was going to stop competing. Give up her dream of riding in the Olympics. I couldn't let her do that. She would've come to hate me."

Dev nodded. "Maybe. So why didn't you go with her?"

"I didn't think it was an option." He gave a wry smile. "At the time anyway."

"And now?"

"It's definitely an option."

His brother smiled. "Good." He pulled his phone from his pocket, typed a message, and then reached to put it away again. "I'll take that beer after all. Let's sit down and figure this out."

~

One week later, Reyes followed Shelby and Dev into the arena complex in New York. A myriad of people milled about near concessions on the right, and through a wide opening front and center, he caught a glimpse of sand and jumps. Riders trotted and cantered past as they warmed up their mounts.

"Uncle Matt said he'd meet us by the left side—there he is."

Reyes had already spotted the signature Diamond dark hair. His brother's hand landed on his shoulder for a quick squeeze. "Good luck."

He gave them a nervous smile, then strode over to where Raine's father waited. The man's expression tightened when he made eye contact, and his whole body followed as he stiffened.

Reyes willed his pulse to settle down while extending his hand. "Mr. Diamond, we haven't been formally introduced. Reyes Torrez."

He looked down, hesitated, then accepted the handshake. "Matt's fine."

The older man's tone sparked surprise. It wasn't anywhere near as confrontational as his rigid body language suggested it would be.

"What are you doing here?" Matt asked.

Her father stood a good two inches taller than him. Reyes lifted his chin slightly to meet his gaze. "I love your daughter, sir."

"And she loves you."

"That's what she told me."

He frowned toward the arena. "So you're here to take her back with you."

A statement, not a question, and it was full of resignation.

Reyes shook his head. "I'm here to support her in whatever she wants to do."

Matt's gaze met his once more, surprise mingling with hope. After a long moment, he nodded. "She's about to ride. Let's see how she does."

CHAPTER 20

Raine hadn't spoken one word to her father on the way home to Texas, nor any time they crossed paths in the two weeks prior to their flight to New York for the Grand Prix event in which he'd signed her up to compete. She almost didn't go, but having sought solace with Diamond Fire for countless hours out on the open Texas range to keep herself from wallowing, she felt closer to her mount than ever before.

He deserved the chance to jump. A ride of redemption.

She knew it sounded ridiculous—he had no such awareness—but she wanted to show the world they were stronger than ever after their fall. With a wry twist of her lips, she tugged at the hem of her fitted black jacket and smoothed a stray hair back into the severe knot at the nape of her neck. So, maybe it was better said as *her* ride of redemption.

And, based on the nervous excitement tingling in her body, a way to test herself as well. After they'd arrived last night, she'd taken a good hard look at her life and realized she needed to figure out her future for herself. She didn't want to just go with what her dad expected, or ride because Reyes had broken her heart and she had nothing else to do. She certainly wasn't going to ride because *he* told her to.

No. It was time she decided exactly what *she* wanted.

Reyes.

She ignored the whisper of her aching heart and refused to allow thoughts of him to mess with her focus. Having already warmed up in the schooling ring after last minute advice from Charlie, she sat astride Fire to watch the other jumpers with a critical eye while waiting for their turn.

She knew most of them from the Grand Prix circuit last year, and they were all so good. No, they were better than good. The best of the best.

Her stomach got a little queasy with the realization she used to be one of them.

No—I still am.

The affirmation resonated deep in her soul, which meant she had a lot to prove to everyone today.

Seeing they were up next, Raine closed her eyes and visualized the course walk-through again. Once they made it over the vertical at the mid-way point, they'd be fine. She just needed to make sure she didn't seize up before then. Or more importantly, *at* the jump.

"Do you trust Fire? Let him take you over it."

Her pulse skittered at the vibrant sound of Reyes' voice in her head. She did trust Fire. And, despite Reyes breaking her heart, she still trusted his advice when it came to her horse. They'd get through this as a team.

A deep breath quieted the white noise in her head enough for her to register her name and number had been announced. Diamond Fire pranced his way into the arena with an excess of energy that stirred the crowd. Raine mentally blocked out the noise, leaned forward with a murmured, "Let's do this, boy," and off they went.

She let years of practice and experience take over, and the second Fire cleared the first jump, a surge of exhilaration cleared her nerves. She'd argued with Reyes she wasn't so sure she wanted the Olympics, but all it took was that one set of rails here in competition to cement her certainty.

She wanted gold as much as she still wanted him.

Moments later, they sailed over the vertical as if it were mere inches, and after the final combination, the crowd roared as Fire cantered over the line. A quick glance at the board revealed no time or jumping faults. She pumped a fist in the air as the announcer confirmed she'd move on to the jump off with the current leader, and any additional riders who qualified.

She exited the arena and dismounted as Charlie took hold of the reins.

"Great job out there."

"Thanks," she undid the strap of her helmet and handed it over to hug Fire's neck. "He did amazing, didn't he?"

"You both did," her father's voice said from directly behind her.

Her stomach gave a little lurch as she turned to face her dad.

"I'm proud of you, honey."

Her anger over Colorado had dulled some, and now her certainty during the ride confirmed he'd done what he thought was best for her. Then she noticed tears in his eyes and emotion clogged her throat as she stepped forward to wrap her arms around his waist. "Thanks, Dad."

"I'm sorry about the last few weeks." His hand smoothed over her hair as his chest expanded on deep breath. "Whatever you decide to do, Raine, I'll support you."

She leaned back with a frown of confusion. "Whatever I decide to do?"

He loosened his hold and stepped aside. "Someone's here to see you."

She followed his gaze past the people milling about. When she saw Reyes leaning against the back wall, her heart lodged up in her throat and swelled with joy. It took a moment to register that Shelby and Devante stood with him. Her cousin offered a smile and a wave as they started forward without Reyes.

Her heart raced the whole time she gave them each a tight hug and distantly accepted their congratulations on the ride. All the while, she was hyper aware of the tall, gorgeous man a mere twenty feet away instead of however many states lay between New York and Colorado.

A stolen glance skipped her pulse at the sight of his tousled, dusty brown hair, those dark eyebrows, and his intense green gaze locked on her. He should've been nondescript in a plain black T-shirt and worn jeans, but Reyes Torrez was not a guy that would ever fade into the background. Not for her, anyway.

"She's not even listening to us," Shelby groused to her fiancé.

Raine turned her guilty gaze back to her cousin. "I'm sorry."

"Don't be." She jerked her head toward Reyes with a grin. "Just go."

She gulped back a surge of nerves and started toward him, her heart thudding hard with anticipation. As she got closer, words from the last time she'd seen him started to pour into her mind. Her feet grew heavy and a lump of renewed pain formed in her throat.

"You're reading too much into last night."

"I never made any promises."

She'd handed him her heart, and he'd shoved it back at her with no concern for the damage he caused.

Stopping in front of him, she crossed her arms. "Why are you here?"

He straightened from the wall, but left his hands in his pockets. "You and Fire looked great out there. It was an amazing ride."

"Thanks." She lifted her chin slightly as the announcer called the next rider. "You were right. I *do* want gold, and I'm not giving up until I get it."

"Good." He nodded solemnly. "I'm glad."

Someone bumped into her from behind, and she murmured a quick acknowledgment for their apology before turning back to Reyes. "You flew all the way here just to tell me you're glad?"

A crooked smile appeared and was gone just as quick. "I came to tell you I'm sorry, and that *you* were right."

About what? The anxiety in his eyes made her heart beat faster as she tilted her head and waited.

He eased closer, his gaze never wavering from hers. "I came because I love you, Raine, and I want to be here for you in any way you need me. Any way you *want* me. Because I pray to God you still want me."

The gruff emotion in his low voice weakened her knees, but she managed to keep from throwing herself into his arms. He didn't deserve for her to make it too easy after she'd spent weeks with an ache in her chest that had made it hard to breathe at times.

Arms still crossed, she dropped her gaze to his chest while shrugging her shoulders. "Maybe you read too much into my words that day."

"Really?" he asked. "How does one not read everything into *I love you*?"

"You tell me," she shot back. "You're the one who told me to leave and walked away."

The hurt he'd inflicted seeped into her voice. She couldn't help glancing up to see his reaction even as she clenched her jaw at the revealing words.

Anguish darkened his eyes. "I thought it's what I needed to do." He grimaced slightly. "It *was* what I needed to do—I just wish I hadn't hurt you doing it."

"Why?"

"Because I knew I loved you then, but I could never ask you to give up your dream. I didn't want you to end up hating me someday."

"Better I hate you *that* day instead of letting me make my own choice?"

"I was damned either way." The frustration in his voice sent his hand up to rake through his hair. "If we'd had more time..."

If her father hadn't shown up they'd have had another week. But that would've only made it harder for her to leave. Or, Reyes might have let her stay, and she very well may have ended up blaming him for the loss of her dream when it would not have been his fault.

Letting her think their night together meant nothing to him had been awful, but it sank in what he'd been willing to give up for her. It made her want to...smack him.

And kiss him.

CHAPTER 20

"More time wouldn't have mattered," Raine said with a shake of her head.

Reyes was dying to reach out for her, to take her in his arms and kiss away the hurt or whatever else was keeping the distance between them, but he was also afraid to push too hard. He didn't know what he'd do if she couldn't forgive him.

Desperation nipped at his nerves, but he forced it back down. Like with the thoroughbreds, he needed to be patient.

"Everything was so…raw that morning," he said quietly. "But if we'd had more time, I would've realized you didn't have to stay. I could go with you, instead."

"But I'd never ask you to leave the place that brings you peace after what you've gone through. I know how much you need to be there."

Hope flared at the empathy in her words. At her use of present tense, not past.

"Not after you." He finally gave in to his need to touch her, reaching for her arm, pulling her hand free to capture her fingers with his. "I haven't slept with the light on since you left."

Her soft smile added a splash of gasoline to his hope.

"I don't need the light anymore, but I do need you. If you'll still have me, that is."

She sighed and dropped her gaze to their joined hands, as if searching for the words she wanted to say. When she tried to pull her hand free from his, he panicked and held it tight while grabbing for her other one.

"I dare you to love me again."

"Really?" she laughed. "You think that's going to work?"

She lifted her gaze then, and his heart jolted at the tears in her eyes. "Don't cry. Please, Raine, I'll do whatever it takes," he vowed. "I'll even get on my knees to beg your forgiveness if you want."

She arched her eyebrows. "I'm going to want you on your knees at some point, but not right now."

Her teasing words sunk in and brought a flood of relief. They swept his mind to a place that sent his blood racing through his veins, and the sass in her eyes turned up the heat a good ten degrees.

"As for your dare..."

"Diamonds don't back down," he reminded.

When she pulled her hands free from his, his heart sank. But in the next instant, she reached up to lay her palms against his cheeks. "No we don't, but I can't take a dare to love you again when I never stopped in the first place."

This time, finally, the relief was complete. He rested his hands on her hips, allowing a small smile as he swallowed past the emotion in his throat. "I'm so sorry I messed everything up."

She rose up on her tiptoes. "You're forgiven. And guess I should thank you for making me figure out for myself exactly what *I* want."

"Gold."

"Definitely gold. And it'll be that much sweeter if you're with me when I win it. If you were serious about that."

"Dead serious. I'll be right by your side." He slid his hands up to pull her flush against him while touching his forehead to hers. "I love you, Raine."

"I love you, too," she whispered back.

Happiness swelled in his chest as she wound her arms around his neck. He captured her lips with his and kissed her with everything he had.

Moments later, the announcer over the loudspeaker made him break the kiss. He cupped her cheek with one hand while grinning down at her. "You've got a jump-off to get ready for."

"I've got a jump-off to win," she corrected as they walked hand in hand to where everyone waited by Diamond Fire.

A half-hour later, he watched her do just that.

And then a year later, he blinked tears away as his wife of two months stood at the top of the Olympic podium with her fellow US equestrians while the Star Spangled Banner played for the gold medal winners.

And one month after that, after they made love in their new bed in their newly purchased eighty acre ranch in Colorado, Raine gave him the second best gift he ever could've asked for besides her heart—a due date of March 28th.

Thank you for reading! I hope you enjoyed ***Don't Dare a Diamond*** and any reviews for it, or the whole anthology would be greatly appreciated.

If you'd like to check out the rest of the **Must Love Diamonds** series, you can find links to all retailers here: https://staceyjoynetzel.com/all-books/

Hearing from readers is the best, so let's connect, and feel free to pop in and say "Hi!" at any time!

Website - www.STACEYJOYNETZEL.com - check out all my books here

JOIN Stacey's Newsletter - new releases, fun stuff, exclusive excerpts and special sales

BookBub - get notified whenever I have a new deal!

Facebook - @StaceyJoyNetzelAuthor - general fun and book stuff

Thank you & happy reading!
~Stacey~

New York Times bestselling author Stacey Joy Netzel lives in Wisconsin with her husband and kids, and enjoys hiking, canning, painting, and visiting her parents in NE Wisconsin (Up North), at the family cabin on the lake. Traveling anywhere to the mountains to do some hiking is a bonus she wishes she could do much more often than every couple years.

She writes steamy romantic suspense & small town contemporary romance with sexy, rugged heroes, and strong, resilient heroines. Colorado, Wisconsin, and Italy are favorite settings, and you can find them in her Must Love Diamonds, Romancing Wisconsin, Italy Intrigue, Welcome to Redemption Series, and Colorado Trust Series.

ONCE A FOOL

DONNA MARIE ROGERS

Donna Marie Rogers

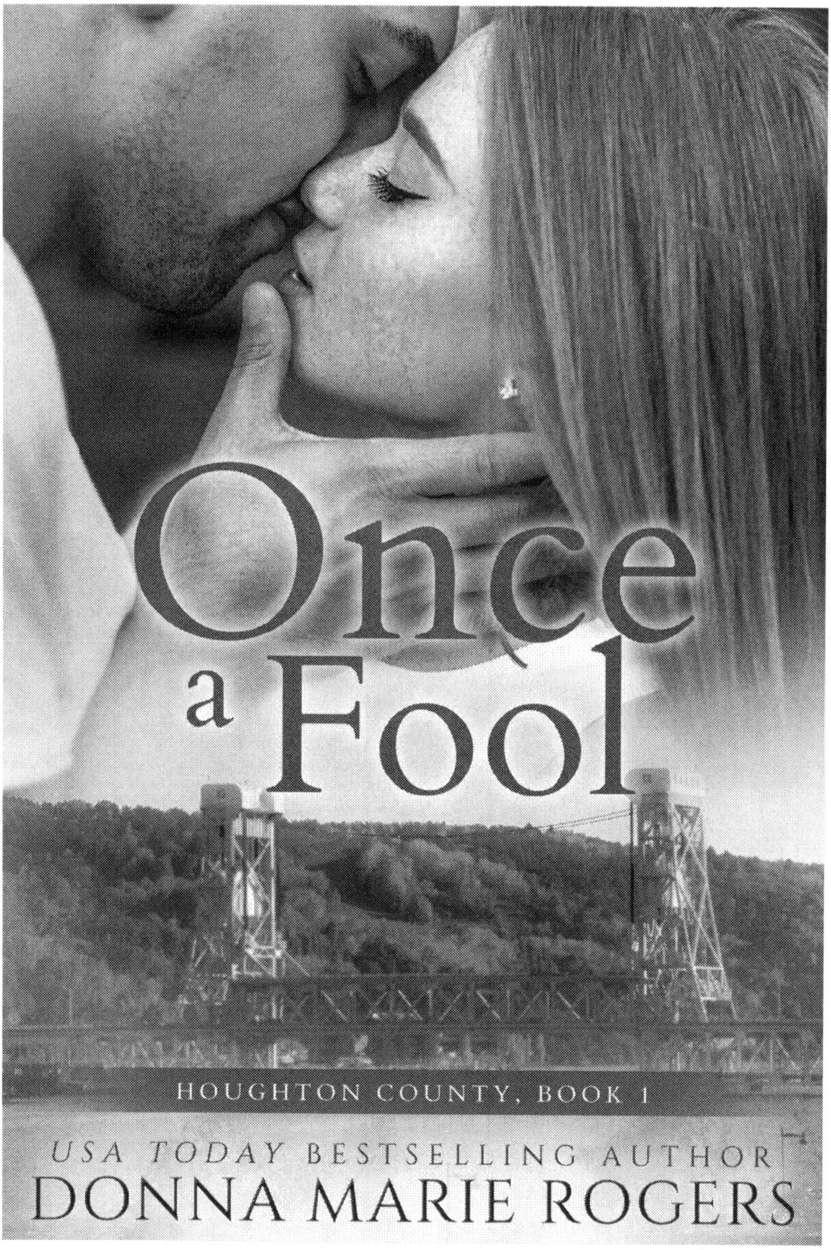
Once
a Fool
HOUGHTON COUNTY, BOOK 1
USA TODAY BESTSELLING AUTHOR
DONNA MARIE ROGERS

CHAPTER 1

Harley Lawson yelped in surprise as a flash of lightning and explosion of thunder simultaneously lit the storm-darkened sky, rattling the roof of the library. With a nervous laugh, she headed for the door, watching as the last glimmer of sunlight faded away, blanketing the small Upper Peninsula Michigan town in complete darkness. The power had gone out in the area about ten minutes earlier; the only lights she could see appeared to be headlights.

A loud crash in the back room made her cry out and spin around in fear, her heart pounding as if she'd just run a marathon. She was alone in the building. Dropping her purse from her shoulder to the crook of her elbow, she rummaged around with shaking fingers until she found her cell phone. She crouched down beside the check-out desk and dialed for help.

"9-1-1, what is your emergency?"

"My name is Harley Lawson, and I work at the Portage Lake Library," she whispered, her heart pounding so hard she could feel it all the way down in her toes. "I'm alone, and I heard a crash in the back room. Sounded like glass breaking."

"Miss, I've just dispatched a police officer. He should be there within minutes. Please remain on the line until he arrives. Are you in a safe location?"

She swallowed and narrowed her eyes, trying to make out any kind of movement in the pitch-black room. "Yes," she whispered.

"Good. Just keep calm and the officer should arrive shortly."

"Thank you." The woman's calm tone helped to ease her nerves a bit.

"You're welcome."

The wind pummeled the building, causing all sorts of spooky rattling and clanking in the walls and roof. It seemed an eternity passed before headlights shone through the front door of the library. She took a deep breath and rose, slowly, before making her way over to peer out into the darkness, anxious to see another human being—and preferably not one brandishing an axe.

Had he gotten out of his vehicle yet? The slamming of a car door answered her question, and she blew out a silent breath as she rushed forward to let him in. Remembering she was still on the line with emergency, Harley pressed her cell back to her ear. "He's here. Thanks again." She disconnected without waiting for a reply and unlocked the door. As soon as she twisted the knob, the wind tore it from her fingers, and icy-cold rain pelted her in the face. "Holy shit!"

The officer clicked on his flashlight and shined the bright beam past her into the darkened expanse of the library, running it back and forth before stepping inside and forcing the door closed behind him. "That about sums it up."

Was that humor in his tone? Sounded like it, though his stern expression made it impossible to know for sure, especially with his eyes shadowed by his hat.

"Miss Lawson, my name is Officer Nichols. Can you tell me what's going on?"

She slipped her phone back in her purse. "I was just getting ready to head home when I heard a loud crash in the back room, like maybe someone broke a window. I immediately called 9-1-1."

He lifted his flashlight again and lit the book-lined pathway that led to the back of the library. "I'm going to go take a look around. Please stay here until I return, understand?"

She nodded, her heart in her throat.

He headed off; the beam of light bouncing around the large room until both disappeared from sight. She strained to hear something, anything, as she waited for him to return. The crunch of broken glass reached her, and her pulse sped up. A huge fan of horror movies, her mind was imagining all sorts of grim scenarios, from a serial killer, to zombies, to spastic vampires, like in the movie *30 Days of Night*. Was the entire town about to become victims of a clan of blood-sucking fiends? She almost laughed out loud over her ridiculous thoughts.

Officer Nichols returned, the stream of light from his flashlight preceding him as he headed back her way. The man was tall, definitely over six feet, and broad-shouldered, though that was about all she could make out in the darkness. He continued to run the beam around the room as he approached.

"I've checked all the windows, none were broken. The noise you heard was a large framed poster that fell off the wall. It was hung on a plastic hook, which broke off. I'd chalk it up to bad timing."

"Thunder shook the building seconds before it fell. Could that have done it?"

"Possibly. If the hook was already cracked, anything could've caused it to break."

She grinned as she recalled her fanciful thoughts of a few moments ago. "Well, I guess I'd better go clean it up. I'm off the rest of the week, and I don't want to leave it for someone else to do."

"I'll help you, then walk you to your car."

No complaints on her end. His deep voice was sexy as hell. "I'd appreciate that, thanks."

They made quick work of cleaning up the shards of glass, Harley sweeping up as much as she could while Officer Nichols held the flashlight in one hand so she could see, and the dustpan in the other. She finished by wiping up any tiny pieces they might have missed with damp paper towels.

Once she had the door locked behind them, Harley, grateful to see the rain had dissipated into a light mist, and the wind had calmed down a bit, led the way to her vehicle, a silver, 1999 GMC Jimmy that had belonged to her father. She had planned to buy a newer vehicle once she settled in, but driving her dad's cherished old truck helped her miss the old man just a little bit less.

She unlocked the driver side door, slid inside, and turned the key in the ignition. Nothing but a weird grinding noise. She turned it again, but the same thing happened. Casting him a quick look, mortified beyond words, she tried it again, and...more grinding.

Officer Nichols opened her door and leaned in. "Sounds like your starter's shot. Don't think any of the shops are open this late. If you want to lock 'er up, I can give you a ride home. You'll have to call for a tow in the morning."

"I...that would be great. Thank you." She didn't have to work tomorrow, so at least that was in her favor. Harley locked up her car and stepped back out onto the wet pavement. Having never been in a police car, she felt compelled to ask, "Do I have to ride in the back?"

His brow creased as if he wasn't sure whether she was joking or not.

She wasn't. She truly had no idea.

"No, Miss, you'll ride up front with me."

The laughter in his tone put her at ease.

Just as he was pulling out of the parking lot, the power came back on, and for that she was grateful. Toby didn't do well during thunderstorms.

"So, where do you live?"

"Not far from here. I'm over on Dosier." Which was a dead-end street, one of its selling points. Neighbors only on one side.

He cast her a sidelong glance. "My parents live on Dosier, second house on the right. It's where I grew up."

Eager to learn more about him, Harley turned to skim her gaze over his shadowed profile. "No kidding."

He nodded, and she thought he was about to say something else, but he fell silent.

"I got the house at a really great price," she announced, hoping to get the conversation moving again.

"That's because six people were murdered in it last year."

"What?" She nearly choked on her tongue. "Are you serious? Please tell me you're joking, that I'm not living in the fricken Lutz house."

He made a right onto to Dosier, then shot her a curious sidelong glance. "The Lutz house?"

"Yeah, like in the movie, The Amityville Horror. Based on a true story where this guy killed his entire family, then the Lutz family moved in and were terrorized by ghosts and demons."

"You like scary movies?" He sounded pleasantly surprised.

"Yes, and please answer my question. Am I really living in some...murder house?"

He turned his head slightly to the left as the road curved, and she could make out the lower half of his face. A small grin curved those perfectly shaped lips. "Nope."

The air whooshed from her lungs as relief settled in. "What the hell?"

"Sorry. Couldn't resist."

"You're an ass," she informed him, the words out before she thought better of them. But, hey, he *was* being an ass.

"I've been called worse. So, you must be new to town."

"What makes you think that? I know they say everyone knows everyone in a small town, but Houghton isn't *that* small."

"Because my mother hasn't tried to set us up yet."

CHAPTER 2

Now what the hell possessed him to say that? Cameron cleared his throat as he pulled his cruiser into her driveway. The two story, wooden farmhouse style home was freshly painted and looked well-maintained. When he was a kid, his friend, Gabe, had lived in that house, and because his parents had both worked and were rarely home, they'd spent a lot of time here.

"I take it your mom's a bit of a matchmaker?"

"Something like that." He unbuckled his seatbelt and swung his door open. "I'll walk you to the door."

"I'd appreciate that, since you're the reason I won't get any sleep tonight." She got out of the police cruiser and hurried around, her steps slowing as she made her way up the walkway that led to the front porch.

Cam laughed softly as he followed behind. "Sorry. And to be clear, no one's ever died in this house. At least, not that I'm aware of."

She shot an incredulous look over her shoulder. "*Not* helping." She unlocked and opened her front door, then reached in to turn on the porch light.

He finally got a chance to study her face, and damn if she wasn't even more beautiful than he'd thought. Those light blue eyes and long, coppery hair was about the sexiest look on a woman he'd ever seen.

Down, boy. The librarian didn't seem like the casual sex type, so it would be best to just keep his distance.

An odd purring reached his ears, and he watched with curiosity as she crouched down to scoop up whatever had been making the noise.

"How's my little man? Were you afraid of the storm, sweet boy?" She cooed at the little fuzzball as she nuzzled it against her cheek. It was all he could do to keep from rolling his eyes.

"What the hell is that?" Definitely didn't look like any cat he'd ever seen.

Her head snapped up. "What do you mean, what is it? He's a dog."

A laugh burst forth before he could tamp it down. "Seriously? Looks more like a squirrel."

"He is a full-blood Pomeranian, Officer Nichols. And he looks nothing at all like a squirrel." Her indignation was sexy as hell.

For some odd reason, he wanted to hear his name on her lips. "Cameron."

"What?"

"My name is Cameron. Most people call me Cam."

She stared at him for a moment, and he started to wonder about his sanity. He should have simply said goodnight and been on his merry fucking way. He had zero interest in dating, even if his mom refused to give up hope. After everything his ex-wife put him through, he had no intention of wading into those fickle waters again.

"Seems a little disrespectful. You're an officer of the law."

"It would only be disrespectful if I hadn't just given you permission to use my name, Miss Lawson."

She eyeballed him with something akin to annoyance before

setting her *"dog"* back down on the hardwood floor. It purred, spun around, and skittered off out of sight.

"I have to be honest, I've never heard a dog purr before."

"He was *growling*," she informed him, crossing her arms over her chest. "At you."

He narrowed his eyes as he contemplated that. "Touchy little thing. Just like his owner."

Her hands dropped to her denim-clad hips. "Thank you, *Officer Nichols*, for everything you did tonight. I appreciate it."

He flattened his lips and gave a quick nod, recognizing a dismissal when he heard one. Not that he didn't deserve one after needling her the way he had. Unconscious self-preservation? "Just doing my job, *Miss Lawson*. Take care."

With that, he spun on his heel and hotfooted it to his car, resisting the almost overwhelming urge to look back and see if she was watching him. Seriously, it hadn't been that long since he'd gotten laid.

Then again, maybe it had.

He backed out of the driveway, and caught a glimpse of her still watching him from the door as he put the cruiser in Drive, her silky hair whipping around her face, and those gorgeous blue eyes… No doubt they'd make an appearance in his dreams later that night. *Fuck*.

A quick glance at his dash told him he had about forty minutes until ten o'clock, when his shift ended. Since he didn't have to work tomorrow, maybe he'd see if his sister, Joss, and the boys wanted to take a ride up to the copper mines and spend the day exploring.

A young widow with three boys under ten, to say Joss had been dealt a rough hand would be an understatement. Her husband, Brandon, had died almost four months ago at the ripe old age of thirty-one after a very short battle with cancer. And since his family hadn't approved of her, they'd been little to no help. Hell, she hadn't heard from the boys' other grandparents since the day of his funeral. He knew they somehow blamed Joss for their son's death, as absurd as that was, but the real mystery was them abandoning their own grandchildren over it.

Joss was handling it all as best she could, and she had an amazing support system in their own family. But he knew it weighed heavy on her that the boys weren't part of their father's family. She told them the older couple were grieving the loss in their own way, but she'd admitted her fear to Cam and the rest of the family that they might be gearing up to sue her for custody. And while it seemed preposterous a judge would take three young boys away from their mother for no reason other than she was now a single parent, anything was possible.

Cam had learned that the hard way four years ago after catching his ex-wife fucking the downstairs neighbor in their own bed.

Not that he still harbored any feelings for the fickle woman. He just needed a reminder, every once in a while, that women couldn't be trusted.

Okay, since he knew Joss had loved and adored her husband, and their parents had been happily married for over thirty years, not all women fell into that category. But he'd be damned if he'd ever put himself out there again on the slim chance he'd find someone who knew what the hell commitment meant.

Forcing his thoughts back to work, he pulled into his space in front of the station, and headed in to start his paperwork. He made quick work of it, clocked out, and headed home.

He'd been back in Houghton County almost four years now, and frankly, he'd never been more content. He owned a somewhat secluded cabin on Portage Lake, which was close enough to see his family whenever he wanted, while far enough away to keep his sanity.

After parking his cruiser in the two-stall garage he'd had built last summer, he hurried inside to put an end to Cleo's impatient barking. Thankfully, his neighbors were far enough away on both sides that it hadn't yet caused a problem. Remembering Miss

Lawson's odd-looking dog made him grin as compared its purring rumble to Cleo's ferocious growl.

"How's my girl?" Now *this* is a dog, he thought as he patted the black and tan German Shepherd on the head before setting his keys and hat on the table beside his front door. Cleo whined and shimmied with excitement as she waited for him to change into sweats and a T-shirt, grab a beer from the fridge, and lead the way out back so she could do her business, and he could enjoy his nightly ritual.

Cam loved to sit on the pier for a half-hour or so to unwind before heading in to bed. The breeze came in off the lake, carrying all the familiar scents that eased and calmed him after eight hours on the job, dealing with everything from kids throwing rocks at a passing boat, to feuding neighbors squabbling over a tree that hung just a little too far over the other's fence, to a possible B&E at the public library.

And meeting the first and only woman who'd piqued his interest in four years.

Tilting the bottle to his lips, he watched as Cleo raced back and forth along the shore. After being stuck in the house all day, she had boundless energy. He gave his head a shake as she lapped at the water, dug her nose into the sand and whined at whatever it was she unearthed, before finally heading over to join him on the pier.

As he scratched her behind the ears and neck, his thoughts returned to the pretty librarian, and it suddenly struck him that he couldn't remember her first name. The incident hadn't required him to file a report, and he'd been so busy trying not to drown in those mesmerizing blue eyes he hadn't thought about much else. The thought both alarmed and frustrated him.

He took another pull off his beer before digging his cell from his pocket. He'd better text Joss before it got too late.

Busy tomorrow?

After about ten minutes, she still hadn't responded, and he

figured she must have hit the hay a little earlier than usual. But just as he stood to head inside, his phone beeped.

Probably heading to Mom's to do laundry. My washing machine died this morning.

Cam knew she could barely make ends meet, let alone afford to replace her washer.

Better idea, Copper Harbor. The boys can let loose, get ice cream, lunch. You wash your clothes here and spend the night, sound like a plan?

A thirty second pause.

Lonely or avoiding Mom? lol

Missing my nephews...their mother not so much

Lol

He gulped down the rest of his beer and waited.

Well??

Well what?

As if he hadn't had enough grief tonight. *Forget it*

Geez just messing with u. Sounds great. Thank u. I love Mom but I need a break, and the boys miss their fav uncle

He glanced at the time, five to eleven.

I'll be at your place by 8:30. We should get to Copper Harbor around 10.

Sounds good. I'll have the boys ready. Nite & thanks

Nite

Cam slipped the phone in his front pocket and whistled for Cleo. Once she was inside, he locked the door and headed into the kitchen to set the coffeemaker. Since Joss and the boys lived in the same neighborhood as his parents, he set the alarm on his phone for seven-thirty, and headed upstairs to bed. Just before drifting off, he wondered if his mom had met the new neighbor yet.

CHAPTER 3

Though sleep had eluded her most of the night thanks to a certain gorgeous man in blue, Harley still managed to roll out of bed at six. It took three cups of coffee, and a bagel with cream cheese to exorcize Mr. Tall, Dark & Gorgeous from her thoughts, but when she finally felt like she could function, she started making calls.

First, to a local towing company, who recommended an auto shop just down the road from them that opened early. She called said shop to let them know her vehicle was being dropped off and why, and they told her going by what she'd described, it would take at least a couple of days and to expect a call later in the afternoon with a quote. Her next call was to a car rental place on the other side of the bridge, and her last was for a cab to drive her to the car rental place. Not that she wanted to rent a vehicle when the truth was, she probably should start looking for one to buy. But she had plans for the day, and had no intention of changing them. This had waited long enough.

She quickly showered and brushed her teeth, eager to get started in her search.

Harley hadn't been sure what she'd wanted to do after her Nana passed away last year. The dear old woman had been her last living relative, and since Harley didn't have anything—or anyone—tying her to Green Bay, she'd made the decision to sell the house and start fresh somewhere else. The only question had been where.

But the answer had come when she found an old bible while packing up her grandmother's things. On the inside cover was a family tree, and directly next to Harley's name was *Baby Boy* with his birth year, which was a few years before hers. No 'Died' year like most of the others, which could only mean one thing—she must have an older brother out there somewhere?

Stunned by the discovery, energized with excitement, she'd started a thorough search of the house, looking for anything that could give her answers, or at least a place to start looking. She came across a few letters her father had written to his mom while at college, up in the UP of Michigan. Oddly enough, she'd had no idea her father even attended a university. She guessed because she was so young when he'd died, they'd never gotten around to talking about higher education.

Her mom, who had bounced around from foster home to foster home, and had no known family, died of cancer when Harley was just an infant, so, sadly, she had zero memories of her, and only a handful of photos. But she'd been eleven when her father had been killed in a motorcycle accident while on his way home from a job in Milwaukee, and that day was forever etched into her memory.

Her phone dinging to announce the arrival of her cab, pulled her from her musings. After a quick check to make sure Toby had food and water, she grabbed her purse, slipped into her sandals, and hurried out the door.

Harley made it out to the college by nine, eager to start her search, even if she wasn't exactly sure what she was looking for. She'd already combed through all the public records she had access to through the library, but had come up empty. With only a year to go on, she knew locating her brother would be no easy task.

It's not like she could call the surrounding hospitals and ask the names of all the babies born in a particular year. Her last hope was to search the college records and pray she could find something that linked her father to a female student.

Paging through one yearbook after another, plus any and all photos she could find, articles, and the school's entire website took up most of the day, but just when she'd about given up hope, she came across a picture of her father with a young woman in one of the newsletter archives. It appeared to have been taken at some sort of party. Unfortunately, it was more of a side profile as they were facing each other, and the picture itself was sort of blurry. It also didn't have a caption, so no names.

After taking a couple of snapshots of it with her cell phone, Harley returned the yearbooks and other media she'd found during that timeframe, and headed out. She needed to get home to take Toby for a walk, and she also needed to figure out what she wanted to do about supper. She smiled ruefully over how pathetic that sounded, as if it were some important decision.

Once home, she checked the freezer and decided to make a frozen pizza. But first, she needed to take Toby for his evening walk to the end of the block and back.

Though she hated to admit it, Harley was curious about the parents of Officer Nichols. Cam, as he'd invited her to call him.

Somehow, the name suited him. And she was certainly attracted to the handsome cop, though she knew men weren't usually interested in her type of look—red hair and freckled—so she wouldn't hold her breath on any mutual attraction. But...he had seemed sort of flirty, in an odd way. Unless he just had a really morbid sense of humor—which wasn't exactly a deal-breaker.

She had just made it to the end of the block, and turned to come back when she saw a middle-aged woman coming down the driveway of the house Cam noted belonged to his parents. Wearing jeans and a purple fitted T-shirt, her slightly graying, light brown hair pulled up into a bun, she stopped at the bottom and slipped something inside the mailbox, then put the flag up.

She turned and stopped when she saw Harley. A huge smile curved her lips as her blue-eyed gaze landed on Toby. "Well, hello there. Aren't you just the cutest thing?"

Harley stopped, and, little playboy that he was, Toby pranced right over to introduce himself.

The woman knelt down to pet him, cooing and laughing as he graced her with a chin lick. She glanced up and Harley was struck by the familiar nose and strong chin. This had to be Cam's mom.

"Are you the new neighbor down the road, last house on the left?" She gave Toby one last scratch behind the ears, then rose to her feet with a delicate groan.

"Yes, I moved in last month. I'm Harley Lawson."

"It's so nice to meet you, Harley. I'm Marianne Nichols. My husband and I have lived here for, goodness, almost thirty-five years now, raised four kids. It's a wonderful neighborhood."

"I love it here so far. Everyone has been very nice, very welcoming." So, Cam had three siblings. She wondered if he was the oldest, youngest, or fell in the middle.

"Do you live in that big house all by yourself?" Her face screwed up. "Sorry, that was nosy."

Harley grinned, remembering Cam's comment. "It's fine. Yes, it's just me and my little Toby here. I'm from Green Bay originally, but when my grandma passed, I decided it was time for a fresh start."

"Well, I sure am glad you chose Houghton County, though I am a bit surprised. Lovely young woman like yourself, I'm surprised you didn't head somewhere warmer, like California, or Florida."

She shrugged and admitted, "I'm a bit of a loner, and I like the Midwest. My nana was my only family, and since my dad went to college up here, I decided to come check it out. I'm glad I did."

"Have you found employment yet? Because I happen to have an in at the police station." She winked.

Harley had to hide a grin. "Actually, I was lucky enough to get hired on at the library. I work Monday through Thursday, ten AM to close, and I really like it. The quiet suits me."

Marianne clapped her hands together with purpose. "So, listen.

My younger son, who happens to be a police officer—and single—is on his way over for supper, and it would be great if you could join us. I made chicken and noodle casserole, green beans, which I can myself, and biscuits, which I popped out of a can."

The older woman's eyes gleamed with humor, and Harley couldn't help but laugh. She was tempted. The look on Cam's face would be priceless. And he'd have to be on his best behavior in front of his mom, right?

"If you're sure, I'd love to. I just need to run Toby home and feed him his supper."

The pleasure on Marianne's face was comical. "That'll be perfect, give me time to get the biscuits in the oven. And for my son to arrive."

"Thank you. I'll be back in a few minutes."

As Harley led Toby back to the house, she couldn't help but wonder if she were losing her marbles. Why would she subject herself to more time in that man's company?

Because he's gorgeous, her libido reminded. *And you've barely been able to stop thinking about him since he dropped you off last night.*

She picked Toby up when she reached her driveway, and carried him up the walkway and into the house. After putting a small scoop of kibble into her little man's food bowl, Harley ran into the bathroom to brush her hair and teeth, then spritz on her favorite body spray.

She locked her front door this time and headed back down the street, her steps slowing as she watched a police cruiser pull up in front of the Nichols' driveway. As she approached, she realized the officer who got out of the car wasn't Cam. The officer was about the same size, but his coloring was different, as was his uniform. This guy, no doubt Cam's brother, had lighter hair, and younger features. A twinge of disappointment surprised her. She'd been looking forward to seeing her annoying rescuer again.

She made the edge of their driveway just as he did. A warm smile set her at ease. "Hi. Are you here to see...my parents?"

"Uh, yes. I just met your mom and she invited me to dinner. My name's Harley and I'm new, just moved in down the road."

"Nice to meet you, Harley." He held out his hand. "I'm Logan." He gestured for her to precede him up the driveway. "Come on, I'm sure my mother is chomping at the bit to see us together."

"Yeah, I had heard she's a bit of a match maker...and I assume you're single?" Liking the younger Nichols brother immediately, she smiled and walked ahead of him to the front door.

"And ready to mingle, as they say." He grinned before hurrying around to open the door for her.

Harley stepped inside the homey, and spotless living room, her gaze taking in the polished coffee and end tables, the gleaming mirrors, and brass wall art. She glanced down at the lush light beige carpeting, and wondered if she should take her shoes off. When Logan slipped out of his, she had her answer and followed suit, though she wished she'd thought to put on socks and her Adidas instead of her sandals. Thankfully, she'd recently painted her toes, though the bright blue polish seemed to stand out like a beacon against the light carpeting.

Drawn to the wall of framed pictures, she couldn't resist stepping up to take a closer look. Several family photos graced the walls, as well as school pictures of the four children—two boys and two girls. She grinned when her gaze landed on one of a Cam with a big, toothy smile, where he couldn't have been more than nine or ten. The youngest, a girl, had light brown hair like their Logan and their mother, but with their dad's piercing dark brown eyes.

Cam had those same eyes.

A picture of the older daughter, who had reddish brown hair and blue eyes, with her own family caught her eye—a handsome dark-haired, olive-skinned, studious-looking type Harley assumed to be her husband, and their three boys. A very nice picture, and all of them gave her a glimpse into the Nichols family, which made her feel a little bit more of a connection to the town. These people clearly had strong roots in the area. She hoped to grow such roots herself one day.

Maybe even with a long-lost brother, who she hoped resided here in Houghton County.

Marianne strode in, an older gentleman right behind her. Though he was a little shorter than both his sons, his presence was just as imposing as Officer Cameron Nichols.

"Oh, good, I see you and Logan have met. Harley, this is Cam Sr., also known as our chief-of-police. Most people just call him Chief." Her smile widened. "Told you I had an in at the police station."

"That you do." Her gaze took in father and son both. "Which I'll keep in mind in case the library gig doesn't work out."

Chief Nichols stepped forward and held out his hand. "Nice to meet you, Harley. Glad you could join us for dinner. Mari's casseroles are all delicious, so I promise you won't be disappointed. Do you cook?"

She barely held back a laugh at the very pointed question. They wanted to know if their son would starve if they happened to start dating. "I do. My Nana was an amazing cook, and she made sure I knew how to make all her recipes. I use my crock-pot four or five times a week and do a lot of freezing."

"A hard worker, and you can cook," Cam Sr. said, casting a knowing look in his wife's direction. "Sounds like a catch to me."

"Me, too," Marianne chimed in, stepping forward to give Logan a hug.

She thought she caught Marianne and the chief exchanging knowing smiles, and bit her bottom lip to hold back a grin. Their tag-team matchmaking was rather sweet, and Logan was certainly pleasant enough, in demeanor, and on the eyes. But...he didn't give her that same ping of excitement—and frustration—that his brother had.

Not that it mattered since her looks weren't exactly popular with the opposite sex. She'd learned that lesson the hard way in high school. Once dinner was over, and Harley headed home, Logan would no doubt let his mother know he wasn't interested.

"I have the table set, so come on, let's eat." Marianne walked ahead to lead the way, her husband casting Harley a quick, enigmatic smile before following after his wife.

Once they were out of sight, Logan leaned in close. "Sorry. They mean well, and because they're so sickeningly happy, they want all their kids to,"—he made air quotes—"find the kind of happiness we all deserve."

"That's so sweet."

He cocked a brow. "It's also embarrassing as hell. Do you have any idea how awkward it is to go anywhere with those two? If they aren't engaging in PDAs, they're throwing every single woman they can find at me and my brother, hoping one will stick."

She laughed at the mental image.

"We heard that," came the tart reply from another room.

Logan grinned. "No shit. I didn't exactly whisper."

He escorted her into the dining room, which was much more extravagant than she'd been expecting. The focal point was a huge, cherrywood table that sat—she did a quick count—ten people, its matching sideboard set against the far wall. Her grandmother had a similar piece that she'd inherited from her own mother, which now graced Harley's dining room. Though it wasn't nearly as fancy as this one.

Mrs. Nichols had set the four placements at one end of the table, so at least they wouldn't have to shout at each other. Though she did notice a stack of extra plates and some silverware beside it. Cam Sr. sat in the end seat, his wife to his left. Logan pulled out the seat two spots over from his father's right, before taking the spot between them.

Marianne lifted the cover off one of the big casserole dishes, and swept a cloth napkin off the bread basket. Harley's mouth watered as the heavenly scent of freshly baked biscuits and the creamy chicken bake filled the room. "Wow, you may be sorry for inviting me. I'm starving, and this all smells wonderful."

The older woman laughed. "Oh, eat up, there's plenty. I made a second pan. My two oldest are coming by with my grandsons, though I'm not sure when they'll be here."

As if on cue, the slight creak of a door swinging open was followed by a mix of voices. A woman's voice and several younger ones she was pretty sure must be the grandsons.

Then came the deep, sexy baritone that had kept her up half the night.

CHAPTER 4

Cam lifted Jacob, his six-year-old nephew, onto his shoulder, and let four year old Jeremy hang onto his neck as he galloped through the living room, past the kitchen, and into the dining room where he knew everyone would be busy eating. He saw his brother, and then stopped short. Sitting right beside him was their parents' sexy new neighbor. She looked up and smiled, and damn if she wasn't even more beautiful in the light of day, with the gorgeous coppery hair flowing freely around her shoulders.

He carefully set both of his nephews on their feet, who immediately raced around to get a hug from their grandma.

"Hey, how was Copper Harbor?" Logan asked as he got up to give Joss a hug. She had her youngest, Jarrod, on her hip.

"Perfect timing, by the way," his mom announced before planting loud, playful kisses on both boys' cheeks. She rose from the table and announced, "I'm going to go grab some more cups, and the iced tea."

"Will everybody please take a seat so we can eat supper," the old man pleaded. He cast a conspiratorial wink at the librarian before adding, "Some of us are starving."

Miss Lawson turned a lovely shade of pink, which only made those icy blue eyes... Ah, hell. With a silent groan, Cam helped the boys get settled, then took the seat directly beside the object of his recent wet dream. Lord only knew why he was torturing himself, but part of him wanted to smell that intoxicating scent he hadn't been able to get out of his mind.

"Can you grab the milk, too, Mom?" Joss called out as she came around to sit beside Cam. But Mom was already gone, so she thrust Jarrod at him. "Here, would you mind holding him for a minute? I'd better go help her."

Cam had no sooner gotten the little stinker settled on his lap when he felt him lean over and announce, "Pretty!" before grasping a lock of the redhead's hair in his chubby little fingers.

But to Miss Blue Eye's credit, her yelp sounded more like a laugh as she gave the little guy's cheek a soft pat.

His dad leaned in, that familiar scheming smile setting Cam's teeth on edge.

"Son, have you met our new neighbor yet? Harley, this is Cam Jr., our oldest. He's also an officer here in Houghton County. Cam, Harley bought your friend Gabe's old house."

Harley, huh? Not even close to the names he'd been testing in his mind. Somehow, the prim and proper-looking librarian struck him more as a Mary, or Martha, or Elizabeth. He met her gaze, and was pretty sure she was hiding a grin. "We actually met last night after she placed a call to 911."

"What? Is everything okay?" his mother demanded as she strode back into the room carrying a tray of cups and a pitcher of iced tea, Joss right behind her with the milk. "Why is this the first I'm hearing of it?"

"Because this is the first time we've spoken since Miss Lawson and I met."

"He told me I lived in a murder house," the sassy redhead archly informed his mother, as if tattling on him as retribution.

Oddly enough, it only made her more attractive. Damn, he wanted to kiss those perfectly pink lips.

"He swore he was joking," she added, casting him a teasing, sidelong glance.

And he was pretty sure his mother's eagle eye picked up on everything. He racked his brain for an excuse to get the hell out of there, but nothing came to mind. Hell, who was he kidding, he didn't want to leave. After a quick glance at his playboy brother, he knew who he *did* want to leave, though.

"Of course, he was," Mom assured her with a nervous laugh.

He could easily read her mind as her gaze slid back and forth between him and Logan. It suddenly dawned on her that her matchmaking skills might be aimed at the wrong son, so she was making a mental switch and adjustment. "Cam has a wicked sense of humor, always has. I remember when he was no older than six or seven-"

"Woman, can we *please* eat already?" the old man groused, his patience, as great as it was, wearing thin. No doubt he hadn't eaten a thing since lunch as Mom had him on a fairly strict diet.

"Geez, keep your shirt on," she countered with a roll of her eyes.

Whatever she'd been about to say must have been swiftly forgotten as she scooped a decent size portion of everyone's favorite casserole onto his plate. And thank God, because Lord only knew what horrifically embarrassing story she'd been about to share.

Within minutes, everyone's plates were loaded, and the usual 'oohing' and 'aahing' commenced. When Joss reached for Jarrod, Cam waved her off.

"Eat, I got him. Right, Buddy?" He let his nephew hold a spoon with a couple of creamy noodles, and chuckled as one made it into his mouth, while the other landed in Cam's lap.

"Wow, you sure are good with him."

He cast Harley a sidelong glance, her astonished tone grating. "You don't have to sound so surprised."

She laughed softly. "I didn't mean to...I...sorry."

"Cam's been wonderful with the boys," Joss told her, sporting what he feared to be the same hopeful interest as their mother. "He'll make an amazing father someday. By the way, I'm Joss."

"I'm Harley. Nice to meet you."

"Nice to meet you, too, Harley."

Cam nearly rolled his eyes, recognizing the lilt of interest in her tone. He cleared his throat, uncomfortable to realize all three women were staring at him.

"Someday in the *far* future," he finally responded, his emphasis on 'far' an attempt to change the subject. He caught his father and brother exchanging glances, their grins only partially hidden as they chewed like they hadn't eaten in days.

Thankfully, the old man asked the boys about their afternoon up north, and everyone listened with rapt attention as they explained, in great detail, every minute of the day, including from the time they woke up, the incident where Jeremy had an accident in the park, which he denied even though he'd had to have his pants changed, to who ate their ice cream faster, who swung the highest at the park, and on and on and on.

To her credit, Harley hung on their every word with wide-eyed interest, and all three boys seemed just as smitten with the fire-haired beauty as their uncle.

Fuuuck.

Logan suddenly reached into his breast pocket and pulled out his phone. "It's the station," he announced before slipping out of the dining room.

Bored with dinner, Jarrod wriggled to be free. Cam set him on his feet, then finished his food, and gulped down a full glass of the sweet tea. He let out a whopper of a sigh and leaned back in his chair seconds before his dad did the same. His mom, who was the slowest eater on the planet, smiled around the table as if this were the best night of her life.

Harley surprised him by also blowing out a satisfied sigh. She took a sip of her tea, and then wiped her mouth before saying, "Marianne, this was absolutely delicious; the best meal I've had in a long time. Thanks so much for inviting me. I'll have to return the favor one day soon."

"You are so welcome. And we look forward to it, right, Chief?"

His father smiled with genuine delight. "I do love to eat, so count me in."

"Great." She cast a sidelong glance up at Cam before adding, "You're all invited. Maybe next week?"

"Next week would be perfect," his mother cooed.

It took all his strength not to roll his damn eyes. He loved the woman, but she was starting to be a real pain in the ass with this matchmaking stuff.

"Am I invited?" Logan asked as he stepped back into the room.

"Absolutely. Friday or Saturday, just let me know which night works best for everyone." Harley's smile nearly lit up the room, casting some sort of spell, it seemed, over his entire family. Even his father seemed enthralled.

"I have to head back to the station," his younger brother announced. "It was nice meeting you, Harley. I look forward to dinner." He winked at their new neighbor, kissed Mom on the cheek, and strode out the door.

"He's so nice." Harley turned to meet his gaze head on. "And I bet he wouldn't make fun of Toby."

"What?" His mom looked at him, a small frown furrowing her brow. "Did you make fun of that adorable little boy?"

"Tattle tale."

The smug librarian shrugged, mirth lighting those light blue eyes.

"Harley, you have a son?" Joss asked, fixing him with a scowl of her own.

"Good Lord, it's a dog. Or so she says," he teased, giving her a dose of her own medicine. "I'm still not convinced."

Instead of the pouting anger he expected, she surprised him with a grin. "He *is* a dog. He's just very small. Though he thinks he's the size of a mountain lion. Poms are a dominant breed, so Toby's pretty fearless."

"He's also absolutely adorable," Mom told Joss, who nodded as if she suddenly understood.

"Cam has a German Shepherd named Cleo, and she's the apple of her daddy's eye."

"You have a dog?" Harley asked him, almost as if in accusation.

"Yeah. She's the puppy of one of the dogs I worked with in Afghanistan. Well, not such a puppy anymore, she'll be two in October."

"Cam is an Army veteran, like his father," his mother explained, reverence in her tone. "He served eight long years, and I have the gray hairs to prove it."

"I had no idea," Harley said, with the same admiration in her tone as his parents. She looked from his dad back to him. "Thank you both for your service."

She was looking at him as if her entire perception of him had suddenly changed. Growing uncomfortable under her respectful gaze, Cam gave a curt nod. He cleared his throat and refilled his iced tea, feeling as if all the oxygen had been sucked out of the room.

"Cameron, why don't you walk Harley home while I get started on your laundry."

As luck would have it, he'd discovered that morning that his own washer was leaking, so he'd sent Mom a text making sure he and Joss could both bring their laundry with. "Joss has more to do than I have, you should let her get hers done first."

"Nah, it's fine. Mom invited the boys and I to sleepover, so I'll get ours done tomorrow. I'm off 'til Tuesday, so I'm in no hurry."

"Listen, I don't want to be a bother," Harley told his mother. "It's still light outside, and I'm only a few houses down. Thanks again for dinner. It was nice to meet you all." She smiled and rose from the table.

Worried she might have read his hesitance for indifference, Cam rose with her. He even managed a smile. "I'd be happy to walk you home. Never let it be said Cam Nichols isn't a gentleman."

His mother bestowed him with a look of whole-hearted approval, while Joss gave him two thumbs up. He'd have returned her two digits with a single one of his own, but their mother was watching.

Placing a hand on Harley's shoulder, he said, "Come on. I'm eager to get another look at that so-called dog of yours."

Her blue eyes did a roll and her lips pursed with what he hoped was feigned disproval.

Mom gave Harley a quick hug on the way past—Cam rolled his eyes—then Harley waved at Joss and blew each of his nephews a kiss, finally placing a hand on his father's shoulder as she headed out into the hallway.

"You be nice," his mother whispered as he strode past. "I really like her."

Cam liked her too, much as he wanted to fight it. And he could tell by the laser-focused intensity of her gaze, the crafty older woman knew it, too.

Harley had stopped at the front door to slip on her flip-flops, and strangely enough, he found himself fascinated with her feet. He'd never thought much about feet before, but Harley's were petite and perfectly-shaped, her bright blue toenails sexy as hell.

Holy balls, did he have a foot fetish? The thought had him choking back a laugh. Thank God the woman couldn't read his thoughts.

He followed her outside, and as soon as he and Harley reached the bottom of the porch steps, she said, "I really like her, too. You have an amazing family, Officer Nichols."

He let out a silent breath. "So, we're back to *Officer Nichols*, are we?"

She slowed down to grin at him. "I guess that'll depend on how you treat my *dog* this time."

He returned the smile as they walked side by side down the sidewalk toward her house. It was a weird feeling, and not just because he'd spent more time inside the two-story, split-level home than she had. But he was eager to see what she'd done with the place, not that he expected some huge change. He found himself curious to know what she liked, if she was a 'less is more' type, or if the walls were already brimming with picture paintings, mirrors, and whatever else women liked to hang.

He was also curious to know what kind of music she listened to, which was her favorite fast food place, what her family was like. If she'd ever been in a serious relationship.

The latter thought frustrated him. Last thing he wanted to do was spend even more time thinking about the sexy librarian than he already had. All night until he'd finally fallen into an exhausted sleep, and then all day while trying to keep his attention focused on Joss and the boys. He hadn't felt this kind of interest in a woman since he first started dating his ex-wife—and he was determined to keep it that way.

Even if his dick didn't seem willing to cooperate.

They walked in silence, mostly because he had no idea what to say, and he guessed she wasn't all that eager to strike up a conversation after his jokes about murder, and insulting her dog. When they finally reached her driveway, she turned to face him, her expression inscrutable. "I appreciate you walking me home, but I know you only did it to please your mother. So, no worries, I'll tell her you were a wonderful escort, blah, blah, blah, and she'll get off your back."

His brow dipped. "What the hell are you talking about?"

She gave an exasperated eye roll. "It's pretty clear your mom was hoping to hook us up. At first, I thought it was your brother she was trying to set me up with, but as soon as you arrived, her focus definitely shifted."

He waved that off. "She tries to set us up with every single woman she comes across. Believe me, we've gotten used to it. I walked you home, Miss Lawson, because I wanted to."

She let out a soft snort. "Uh-huh, sure. And let me guess, you dreamt about me all night, too."

Damn, if she didn't hit the proverbial nail on the fucking head. "I was tired, fell right asleep."

"Me, too," she quickly countered.

Her tone was hard to read, though something told him she seemed...hurt?

He blew out a hard breath, propped his hands on his hips, and decided to start the conversation over. "So, I'm curious what the old house looks like. Haven't been inside since I was seventeen. Don't suppose I could get a tour...?"

She crossed her arms over her chest and tilted her head to the side as if considering his request. "Sure, why not."

He chuckled over her lack of enthusiasm as he followed her up the porch and into the house.

CHAPTER 5

The thought of this man in her home, curled up on the sofa with her watching a movie, or sitting across from her at the breakfast table wasn't something Harley wanted to dwell on too much. His interest in her was cursory at best. And at worst? She'd end up with another broken heart—a lesson learned the hard way, and one she wasn't all that keen on repeating.

One guy she'd dated for all of two weeks told her she reminded him of the school teacher on some old show that took place after the Civil war—just what every woman wants to hear from the guy she's hoping to sleep with. She repressed a grimace at the thought.

Toby came running up just as Cam stepped through the door. He closed it behind him, then turned and gazed down at her little furball, his expression hard to read. She assumed he'd never seen a toy Pomeranian before, which would explain his less than tactful reaction last night. And now that she knew he liked dogs, maybe just not small ones, she felt a smidge better about him.

She picked up Toby, who immediately started licking her face. She laughed as she failed to dodge his spastic little pink tongue.

Wanting to make a proper introduction, she held him against her side so he was facing Cam. "Toby, I'd like you to meet Officer

Cameron Nichols. I'm pretty sure he's a nice guy. He's an Army veteran, an officer of the law, and he's clearly an amazing uncle. But for some odd reason he's not that fond of...petite dogs."

He regarded her through narrowed eyes, but instead of responding to her teasing introduction, he reached out and gave Toby some slow scratching behind his ears. "Hey, boy, nice to meet you. Sorry about last night. I was a little distracted by a certain blue-eyed redhead. I stuck my foot in my mouth, and I'm afraid she's holding a grudge."

He'd noticed her eyes? A wave of pleasure washed over her. "Lucky for Officer Nichols, I've never been a grudge holder. And I appreciate his apology."

He returned the smile, and it was her turn to notice how gorgeous those amber-flecked, whiskey-brown eyes were. They gazed at her with such intensity she started to grow warm.

More than a little anxious, she set Toby down, and waved Cam inside. The house was clean enough, and while she had hung a few things on the walls, she'd always hated clutter, so the décor was minimalist at best. Unlike her grandmother, who had covered every wall in her home with every painting, sconce, framed needlepoint, or photo she could find. The woman had loved rummage sales, and Harley had, too, when she'd been a kid. But the thrill definitely wore off by the time she reached high school when on the first day of freshman year, she was cornered in the bathroom by a trio of popular girls who started chanting, "Thrift Store Harley." She'd cried her eyes out in one of the stalls until a teacher happened upon her and brought her to the office.

Ah, good times.

Cam stepped into the living room and looked around, his lopsided smile made her wonder if he was thinking about a specific memory, or a childhood full of them.

He glanced up the staircase, then back at her. "Which bedroom is yours?"

A surprised laugh nearly choked her. "Um, I'm not giving you a tour of my bedroom."

"Can't blame a guy for trying."

He shrugged and continued to glance around, but she caught his grin.

Harley headed into the kitchen, leaving him behind to reminisce. "Can I get you a beer, or a soda? I also have some wine coolers. I had planned to have a couple drinks and watch a movie or two."

She heard something, and looked back to discover him right behind her. "Whoa!"

Cam chuckled. "Sorry, didn't mean to scare you. And a beer sounds great, thanks."

She took a deep breath, and let it out slowly in an effort to calm her racing heart, then pulled two Buds from the fridge and handed him one. They twisted their caps off at the same time, and she held out her hand for his so she could toss them both. He headed back into the living room and did a complete three-sixty, his gaze moving around as if he still couldn't quite believe it. She followed behind, sipping her beer as she watched him.

Finally, he cast her a sheepish glance. "Sorry, you must think I'm nuts. It's just, this place was my second home growing up. Gabe and I spent more time here than anywhere else, playing video games, and eating a lot of frozen pizza."

She thought of the pictures she'd seen on his parents' walls, and a smile broke free as she imagined him as a young boy. "Sounds like fun. My childhood was pretty boring. Spent most of my time with my grandma." She gestured for him to have a seat on her sofa. Thankfully, Nana had taken good care of everything she owned, so Harley was able to bring the majority of the furniture with her to Houghton County.

"What about your parents?" He sat down and tilted the bottle to his lips. Harley had to drag her gaze away before it became obvious she was staring. But those lips...she wanted nothing more than for him to kiss her. Lord knew she'd never work up the nerve to make the first move herself. She sat down, leaving space between them.

"I didn't know my mother, she died of cancer when I was a baby."

"My God, I'm so sorry."

She waved her hand in a 'don't worry about it' gesture. "I don't mean for this to sound heartless, but since I have no memories of her, and she had no known family, I've never had any real connection to her. I have pictures, and my father sure did love her, told me she saved him, but never would tell me how. It devastated him, losing her."

"I bet it did. So, does he live in Green Bay?"

She twisted her lips. "My dad was killed in a motorcycle accident when I was in seventh grade."

"Jesus."

"Nearly killed my grandma. I had to be strong for her, you know? Never really was able to grieve for him. He's actually the reason I chose Houghton County. After grandma passed, I discovered my dad had gone to college up here. Figured it was as good a place as any for a fresh start." Not quite ready to tell anyone her real reason for moving up here, she shrugged and took another sip of her beer.

"So, you're an orphan, in a sense. I can't imagine losing either one of my parents, I..." He gave his head a shake and set his beer bottle down on the coffee table. "Hell, talk about insensitive. And just when you probably didn't think I could be a bigger ass, hey?"

She laughed softly. "It's fine, no worries. You've always had your parents in your life, of course you can't imagine losing them. And I've met them—they're wonderful people."

He gave a nod of thanks, then picked up his beer and polished off the rest.

Harley did the same and stood. "Can I get you another?"

He rose, too. "I'd love that, but I think I should probably get going. You do have plans to get drunk and watch a movie, if I recall."

"I never said get drunk," she corrected as she took his empty bottle. "And I wouldn't mind some company. I mean, unless you're not big on movies."

Now, why the hell couldn't she have just kept her damn mouth shut? She knew he was just being nice to please his mother, which actually made him a pretty nice guy. And here she was taking advantage of his—

"I love a good movie, if you're sure...?" He made a teasing face. "Wait. You're not gonna make me watch some sappy love story, are you?"

She laughed. "Relax. I was thinking horror or comedy. And I'll tell you what. I'll let you have the final say."

"Now, that's a plan I can get behind. I'll just text Joss so they don't send out a search party." He pulled his cell from his front jeans pocket and sat back down, legs slightly spread, one muscular arm draped across the back of the sofa, while he typed in a message to his sister. If he wasn't the sexiest sight she'd ever seen, she didn't know what was.

Harley hurried into the kitchen for two fresh Buds, feeling like a teenager with her first crush.

When she returned, he'd already turned on the TV, and was busy flipping through the apps on her Firestick. She handed him the beer and sat, again, leaving plenty of space between them.

"Thanks. So, comedy or horror? How about...*The Amityville Horror*?"

"Smartass. I'm fine with anything. I am a horror buff, but I love a good comedy, or action...or both. Have you seen the new Ryan Reynolds movie? I've been meaning to rent it."

"No, who else is in it?"

"Samuel Jackson and Salma Hayek."

He waggled his brows. "Sounds great. I'm in."

She rolled her eyes as she took the controller from him.

"What?"

"Nothing," she said with a soft chuckle.

"I happen to think Sam Jackson is dreamy," he informed her. "Got a problem with that?"

She laughed so hard she spilled a little beer on the floor. "Shit."

"Sorry." He set his down and reached into his front pocket, pulling out what looked like a wad of napkins. "Didn't mean to make you wet yourself."

"Cute. And why do you just happen to have a pocketful of napkins?" she teased through narrowed eyes.

"We stopped for ice cream in Copper Harbor. I don't know if you have any experience with little kids, but here's a tip: Always grab a shit-ton of napkins."

"I don't. And thanks. I'll keep that in mind."

Once she had the beer wiped up, Harley curled up in the corner of the sofa and purchased the movie. They laughed themselves sick, pausing once for a bathroom break and to grab a couple more beers. At some point, Toby started scratching at the sofa for her to pick him up, and Cam surprised her by scooping him up and giving him the tummy scratching of a lifetime. Truthfully, the little traitor was so content his little leg started kicking, something he rarely did. And if she were being honest with herself, she was a little jealous—she'd sure love to feel those strong hands on her.

And be the one in his lap.

Whoa, girl. Just because his mother is practically shoving him at you, doesn't mean he's interested. Probably just being nice to get her, and his sister, off his back.

"You okay?"

She realized he was staring at her. "Fine, why?"

He shrugged, his hands continuing their gentle rubdown on her little furball. "You look like you swallowed glass or something."

Harley let out a nervous laugh and took a quick pull off her beer. "Sorry. Just a little tired. Which is pretty pathetic considering it's only eight o'clock."

He gave Toby one last pat before polishing off his beer and rising to his feet. "Never let it be said I can't take a hint."

"Oh, no, I didn't mean—"

"I'm just teasing. But I do need to get my laundry washed as well. If you can believe it, Joss' washing machine died, so I invited her to do laundry at my house only to discover mine is leaking water like a sieve. Thankfully, the curse hasn't hit my parents yet."

She smiled, wanting him to stay, but understanding why he had to go. And frankly, it was no doubt for the best.

Before she did something really stupid, like kiss him.

"Well, thanks again for walking me home, and hanging out for a while. You are officially my very first guest."

He nodded and looked around uncomfortably before heading for the door. Harley followed after him and tried not to let her disappointment show as he stepped out onto the porch. She flipped on the light. "Have a good night. And please thank your parents again for dinner. That casserole was amazing."

"It was, and I will. But don't think you're getting out of cooking for us. I'm dying to know if you can actually cook, or if I'll find a stack of take-out boxes in your kitchen."

She swatted at his shoulder, and he grinned. They stared at each other for nearly twenty seconds in silence before laughing. Good Lord, talk about awkward.

Just when she thought he would turn and head on his way, he cocked his head and asked, "You planning to go to the Strawberry Festival? It starts next weekend?"

Was he...asking her out on a date? *Relax, act casual.* "I don't know. We have posters hanging in the library, but to be honest, I hadn't really looked at them too closely. What about you?"

"Joss and I talked about taking the boys while we were in Copper Harbor. I know they'd all love it if you joined us. Mom and Dad, too. They go every year."

Okay, so not a date. Just taking pity on the lonely, new neighbor to keep his mom off his back. She swallowed down a bubble of disappointment. "Can I ask you something without sounding too nosy?"

He cast her a curious smile. "Sure, what's up?"

"Is Joss divorced, or separated from her husband? No one's mentioned him, and from what I gathered, she and her boys seem to spend a lot of time with you and your parents. Not that there's anything wrong with that," she amended. "You're all so supportive of each other, which is wonderful."

"Joss' husband, Brandon, was one of the best guys I knew. He died of cancer about four months ago. It was so aggressive he passed only a few months after his diagnosis."

"My God...I am so sorry." Though she'd lost her mother from the same deadly disease, the circumstances couldn't have been more different. She couldn't even imagine how hard the loss must have been for Joss, and the boys. At least, the older two.

"It's been hell on her. She loved him, and now she has to raise those boys without his support, both emotionally and financially. So, I've been stepping in as much as I can. Logan, too."

She twisted her lips with remorse. "Now I feel like a jerk for asking."

His brows pulled down. "Why? It's a fair question."

"Well, I'll say it again, you are a great brother. Joss is lucky to have you."

"I appreciate you saying that. I love those boys. My sister, too, though she can be a real pain in the ass sometimes."

He grinned, probably to make sure she knew he was teasing. Which he seemed to do a lot for someone who otherwise seemed quite serious. Though now that she knew he was an Army veteran, as well as a police officer, it made sense.

"I'd better get going," he said. "Think about the festival. I know everyone would love for you to come."

But would you? she wanted to ask. Instead, she said, "I will. Thanks for the invite, and...everything else. I guess I'll see you around?"

"I'm sure you will. 'Specially if Joss and my mom have anything to say about it. 'Night."

His gazed dropped to her lips for a pulse-pounding moment, but then he turned and made his way down the steps.

Disappointment burned in her chest, though she didn't know why. She was used to men dismissing her. Not that she hadn't dated, had a couple of short-lived relationships, but—

Without warning, Cam cursed, spun around, and ran back up the porch steps. Before she could react, he grasped her face with both hands and kissed her. It took only a heartbeat for her to melt right into his embrace.

His lips were firm, yet softer than she could have imagined, as Cam proceeded to kiss her as if she were the tastiest of sweets. But just when she would have wrapped her arms around his neck to deepen the kiss, he pulled back with another muttered curse and gazed into her eyes.

"I'm sorry. I shouldn't have done that, I...sorry."

And then he was gone again.

Tears burned her eyes as she watched him hurry down the block.

Harley had no idea if the kiss was born out of curiosity on his part, or to try and please his mother. But one thing was certain...if he'd enjoyed it, he wouldn't have run off as if the hounds of hell were nipping at his shoes.

CHAPTER 6

Three days later, and Cam still couldn't get the damn kiss out of his mind. Of course, as soon as he'd walked in his parents' front door that night, his mother and Joss had done a tag team interrogation that would have made the old man proud. He'd opted not to tell them he made a complete fool of himself, and could only hope Harley did the same.

He still wasn't sure what possessed him to kiss her. He hadn't felt that particular urge in years, not that he'd been celibate. But kissing was personal, and while he had normal urges like any other man, he hadn't really *kissed* a woman since...

Nope, he wasn't going to go there. Though it had taken a while, he was well over that fickle female and didn't want to waste even another second thinking about her.

Oddly enough, the searing bitterness he normally felt when his thoughts turned to his ex-wife wasn't there. He felt...nothing. A good sign, even if it didn't mean he was ready to jump into anything serious. But at least he didn't feel like he needed to fight his quickly growing feelings for a certain copper-haired, blue-eyed librarian.

He pulled out his cell phone to make sure he hadn't gotten the time wrong. Logan had texted him this morning to see if he wanted to meet for an early dinner, which they did when their schedules meshed. But since they were working different shifts this month, he could only assume Logan had something he wanted to talk about.

Harley?

Probably. If it was a family matter, he would have simply called. If little brother wanted a face-to-face, there had to be a reason for it.

He got out of his cruiser and slid on his sunglasses. Logan had said Birdie's, their favorite diner in all of Houghton County, so he closed his car door and headed inside. A familiar, slightly graying brunette waitress approached with a glass of water and a menu tucked under her arm.

"Well, hello Officer Nichols. Can I get you some coffee?"

"That'd be great, Britta, thanks. Logan's joining me, he should be here any minute."

"I'll bring two cups," the older woman said as she strode away.

Cam slid into one of the open booths and took off his sunglasses, dropping them into his breast pocket as he did a quick yet thorough scan of the small restaurant. Britta returned with two mugs and a pot of coffee just as Logan stepped inside. His little brother also took off his sunglasses and glanced around, nodding when he saw Cam.

"Hey, Britta," Logan greeted as he sat down across from him. "I'm starving. Can I get a double cheeseburger, no onion, extra mayo, and ketchup for my fries, please?"

She set a glass of water in front of his brother, poured them both a cup of the steaming brew, then set the pot on the table and turned to Cam. "And what can I get for you?"

He did a quick scan of the menu, not that he needed to since he knew the damn thing by heart. "I think I'll have the same, only can you bring me a little cup of barbecue sauce?"

"You bet." She winked at Cam, and gave Logan a soft pat on the arm with the menu on her way past.

He watched as his brother guzzled most of his water, then leaned back and propped his left arm across the top of the booth. Yep, something was up.

"Is this about our lovely new neighbor?"

Logan's surprise shown on his face before a slow grin stretched his lips. "So, I'm not the only one who's been thinking about her."

It wasn't a question. Cam hated the jealousy that bubbled up, like acid reflux.

"I had hoped I was wrong about the interest I saw when you looked at her. Then Joss confirmed and told me to back off. I figured it was just Mom egging her on, but wanted to talk to you before I ask her out."

His brother laughed, and Cam couldn't help but grin. Joss and Mom were both convinced Harley was his soulmate. After meeting her one damn time. The absurdity of it made him shake his head. While he could admit to a strong attraction—the woman was, after all, drop dead gorgeous—Mom and little sister had definitely romanticized it into something more.

"So?" Logan prompted. "Am I free to pursue our new neighbor, or should I back off?"

Cam made a decision he hoped didn't come back to bite him in the ass. He grinned. "Back off."

As far as brothers went, Logan had always been a stand-up guy, and loyal to a fault. Hell, his whole family was amazing, the most supportive bunch he'd ever known. And his brother no doubt wanted the same for him that the entire family wanted—for Cam to finally move the hell on and find love again.

The thought scared the fuck out of him, but not like it had since returning from active duty and having his whole life flipped upside down.

After dinner, Cam had two calls from the station. The first, to the grocery store, where a young female worker was being harassed by an ex-boyfriend having a hard time letting go. The second was to a bar on the east side of town called The Haven. A brawl had broken out between some women, and by the time he arrived, a couple of their boyfriends had joined the fray.

At six foot three inches, two hundred-twenty pounds of muscle, and in uniform, Cam knew he struck an intimidating figure. Which came in handy when he was outnumbered as he was. Thankfully, none of the knuckleheads were drunk enough to give him trouble, which meant he was able to diffuse the situation fairly quickly and send everyone on their merry way.

Ready for a break, he drove through a fast food drive-thru for two large coffees, made sure to ask for creamer and sugar packets, then headed for the library to see the blue-eyed reason he hadn't been sleeping well.

The lot was surprisingly full, and he had to park in the row furthest away from the door. Seemed odd for a Monday night...or any night, really. Maybe the pretty new librarian was a big draw.

An unreasonable surge of jealousy filled his chest, which he quickly tamped down. What the hell was wrong with him?

With a rueful shake of his head, he got out of his cruiser, a cup of coffee in each hand, and headed into the library.

He saw her as soon as he stepped through the door. She was busy helping a couple of teen boys, her smile genuine as she pulled a book from the shelf, then another, handing them to the boys, talking in that animated way of her. He watched as they followed her to the desk to be checked out. That's when she looked up and saw him...and her smile faded.

Well, shit.

Clearing his throat, he forced his legs to keep moving until he was standing before her.

"Hi. Thought I'd stop by with a peace offering. Not that I have any clue why you seem to be upset with me."

When she didn't take the proffered cup, he set it on the counter and glanced around the library, taking in everything as he mulled over what he should say next. For such a small woman, she could be oddly intimidating.

"If you didn't know I was upset, then why bring a peace offering?"

"It didn't start out as a peace offering, it was just an excuse to come see you."

She glanced away, uncomfortable, or because someone was

approaching, he wasn't sure. She smiled, waved, then turned back to face him. "Why?"

A simple enough question. Why indeed. "Right about now, I'm not sure."

Harley did some lip twist thing before glancing around and lowering her voice. "I get humoring your mother by walking me home, even staying for a bit. But why the kiss when she wasn't there to see it?"

He almost laughed, but the obstinate woman looked dead serious. "Why else would I kiss you? Because I wanted to."

A family walked by, and he nodded while Harley smiled at them. Once they were out of earshot, she demanded, "Then why did you apologize? I mean, the look on your face...like you were disgusted by it."

Stunned, he could only stare at her. "I was feeling a lot of things that night, but disgusted was *definitely* not one of them. And I apologized"—he took a quick glance around before lowering his tone—"because I was afraid I might have been a little rough."

She cocked her head like Cleo did when she heard a noise outside. "Haven't you ever read a romance novel? Women like it when a man grasps her face before...what is so funny?"

Her smile faded again; she crossed her arms over her perfectly shaped breasts. This woman would certainly keep a man on his toes.

"I don't know. I guess I assumed you'd read Stephen King, or someone like that, not romance novels."

"I *do* read Stephen King," she proudly informed him, her outrage sexy as hell. "I also read mysteries, sci-fi, fantasy, and yes, romance."

"I never said there was anything wrong with it. My mom's been reading those things since I was a little kid. Joss reads 'em, too, when she has time. I bought them both Kindles for Christmas last year." Now, why did he feel the need to toss that out there?

A reluctant smile finally chased away her frown. "That was a very thoughtful gift."

"What can I say? I pay attention." He leaned his hip against the counter, and finally remembered the coffee. "Still hot," he told her as he took a sip of his own, which had creamer, no sugar. Though he had both in his pocket if she needed them.

She grasped the cup and smiled with genuine gratitude. "Thank you. Black, I hope?"

He nodded, took another sip of his coffee, then bit the bullet and asked, "Any chance we can have a redo of the other night?"

After a thoughtful sip of her coffee, she glanced up at him, those spectacular blue eyes brimming with unease. "Are you sure this isn't about your mom? Because I won't be anyone's charity case."

"I don't even know what to say to such a ridiculous question," he slowly admitted, striving to keep his annoyance in check. The woman was certifiable...which made him nuts for even contemplating getting involved with her.

Hey, whoa, buddy. Just a date, that's all we're talking here. A fucking date.

Her shoulders slumped, and those long lashes blinked a little faster than normal. "I suppose you wouldn't. Good-looking guy like you was probably a popular jock in high school who had every girl panting after you."

Okay, this conversation had officially gone off the rails. "I was neither a jock, nor all that popular in high school, not that I have to explain myself to you, or anyone else. And I've never dated anyone my mom tried to fix me up with—I'm not sure why I decided to start with you."

She visibly flinched, and Cam immediately regretted what he said. *What the hell's wrong with you?* Christ, they hadn't done more than share a quick kiss, and already he was losing his mind.

She opened her mouth to respond when a woman with a couple of elementary school-aged kids approached the counter and set down a pretty big stack of books. The mother gave them both an uncertain glance before pulling her card from her wallet and setting it next to her books.

"Thank you, Officer," Harley said before turning to her customers, effectively dismissing him.

Cam snatched up his coffee, took a quick look around, then strode out the door.

Crazy female.

He must have been out of his mind to even consider spending more time with her.

CHAPTER 7

Torn between furious indignation, and reluctant regret, Harley forced thoughts of the insultingly ornery man from her mind as she slid into her rental car and headed home. Her Jimmy wouldn't be ready until Friday as she'd decided to have some other work done as well. She knew she should—and could afford to—buy a new vehicle. But she just wasn't quite ready to give up her last real connection to her father.

She glanced at the clock on the dash—eight-twenty pm, and man, was she hungry. Looking forward to the pot roast dinner simmering away in her slow cooker, Harley wove her way through the light, evening traffic, eager to get home. As soon as she finished dinner, she planned to clean out all the boxes she'd found in the cubby beneath the staircase. She'd only discovered the semi-hidden closet by accident yesterday while sweeping. The latch had been painted white, so it blended in with the wall, which you had to crouch over to see anyway.

As always, Toby was waiting by the door to greet her, his hoarse little bark never failing to bring a smile to her face. She scooped him into her arms, and was showered with kisses as she kicked off her shoes and headed into the kitchen to check on her dinner. The aroma was enough to make her mouth water, and as she tucked Toby under one arm and lifted the lid, she had to close her eyes, the smell simply orgasmic.

Or maybe she was just that friggin' hungry. Having skipped lunch, she'd be surprised if she didn't eat the entire crock of fall-apart tender roast, potatoes, and carrots in one sitting.

Now that her greeting was officially over, Harley set Toby down, his little nails clacking on the tile floor as he skittered away. She put the lid back on the slow cooker, then ran upstairs to wash up and change into shorts and her favorite Harley Davidson T-shirt, one of many she owned that used to belong to her father. Though it had been washed many times over the years since his passing, somehow, she could always smell him when she wore it.

She'd just reached the bottom of the stairs when someone knocked on her door. Hard. Toby went nuts barking, and she paused for a minute as several ugly scenarios played through her mind. A second set of hard knocks had her rushing over to peek out the window. When her gaze landed on Officer Annoying, she huffed out a sigh and opened the door. His shift must have already ended as he was in jeans and a black T-shirt—which stretched tautly over his broad shoulders and muscular arms. She barely held back a schoolgirl sigh as she opened the door. "What?"

"Geez, nice greeting."

Harley crossed her arms over her chest. "Look, I just got home, I'm starving, and I have things to do, so can you please just tell me why the hell you're here? And if it's to throw some more insults at me, save your breath."

He stared at her for a moment, with any luck, running his words over in his mind before allowing them to leave his lips. Last thing she wanted was more verbal sparring. She didn't like to fight, and it seemed this man was always ripe for it.

Well, to be fair, she might have jumped to the wrong conclusion based on past experience, and taken his abrupt departure the other night the wrong way, especially considering he *had* tried to extend an olive branch earlier with the coffee. But she'd already been in a somewhat pissy mood thanks to her co-worker calling in sick, leaving her to work the entire ten-hour shift alone.

"I came here to apologize. There seems to be a bit of miscommunication between us, and I admit I tend to speak before I think."

"No shit."

He chuckled. "Believe it or not, what I said earlier was supposed to be a compliment. It just...came out wrong, and I stuck my foot in my mouth." A boyish grin transformed his handsome face. "Fair warning, I'm sure I'll do it again."

Damn, just when she'd all but decided to stay away from the moody cop, he goes and turns into a nice guy, taking all the blame. Hell, she could be difficult, too, and well knew it.

When she didn't respond—mostly because she didn't know quite what to say—he leaned in and sniffed the air. "Damn, something smells good." He met her gaze with barely concealed excitement. "Beef stew?"

"Pot roast." When he continued to stare expectantly, she silently lamented having to share her dinner, even though she knew there was plenty. "Would you like to join me?"

"Since my supper was going to be a couple peanut butter and jelly sandwiches, hell yes." His brow lifted. "But I don't want to intrude. You mentioned having things to do, and it's already eight-thirty."

"It's fine. I was hoping to clean out that small closet beneath the staircase. The last owners forgot to empty it."

"Well, since you so graciously offered to feed me, how 'bout I help you clean it out?" He stepped past her into the foyer. "Gabe and I spent a lot of time in that closet. It was like our clubhouse when we were kids."

She smiled over the nostalgia in his voice. "If you're sure, I'd appreciate it. A couple of the boxes are pretty big." She led the way into the large kitchen and motioned for him to take a seat at her grandmother's prized cherrywood dining room table.

"Can I help with anything?"

He stood beside the table, looking a little uncomfortable with the prospect of being waited on. Since he did live alone, she understood. She'd felt the same way when having dinner at his mother's house.

"Sure. Would you grab me a bottle of root beer from the fridge, and whatever you'd like?"

"Sounds good. I love root beer."

Harley piled two plates with pot roast, carrots, and potatoes, and carefully carried them to the table, then retrieved forks and knives from the silverware drawer.

They ate in virtual silence, just a few mmms and hmms here and there. She figured Cam must have been just as hungry as she was, which worked in her favor since she had no interest in table conversation.

He finally cracked open his bottle of root beer and took a long pull, ending with a hearty "Ahhhh. Man, did that hit the spot." He finished his plate, scraping up as much gravy as he could with his fork before setting it down and leaning back in the chair. "That was delicious. I think pot roast just might be my favorite meal."

"Me, too. And thank you, though I have a feeling your mother's pot roast puts mine to shame."

His eyes narrowed playfully. "If you tell her this, I'll deny it with my dying breath, but no. This even beats my mom's. Hers is great, too, don't get me wrong. But she uses cream soup and onion soup mix, which is how my dad likes it. You make it old school, which I prefer. Tried to make it myself once, but let's just say even Cleo wouldn't eat it."

Harley laughed softly as she twisted open her own soda. "Since most dogs will eat anything, I guess that's saying something." She stood and picked up her plate and fork. "I'll just get these in the dishwasher, then we can get started on the closet. There isn't too much in there, so it shouldn't take long."

He stood and picked up his own plate. "Can I help?"

"I've got it. You can get started on the closet by pulling that huge box out of there. I'm guessing it's a Christmas tree."

"I'm on it." He handed her his plate and practically raced into the living room.

She figured he must be reminiscing about all the fun he'd had in this house when he was a kid, and the thought brought another smile to her face. Since she'd never really had a close friend, she could only imagine how he was feeling. He certainly looked eager.

As she put the plates and forks in the dishwasher, Harley tried not to think about how good it felt to have someone—a man she was interested in—enjoy a meal she'd prepared. Truth was, she'd never dated much, and had little experience when it came to the opposite sex. She'd had one short-lived boyfriend in high school, who'd dumped her as soon as his friends started teasing that she was ugly, and her freckles were gross. Her first job after school had been at a car dealership, and she'd dated one of the mechanics for about three months—her first lover. Until he'd gotten a new job, and didn't bother to tell her, just disappeared from her life. Two months later, they had an awkward run in at the mall, where he'd casually introduced her to his new gorgeous girlfriend, and acted as if they barely knew each other. Rat bastard.

She'd only been with one other guy since and had been the one to break things off after it became clear he was nothing more than a freeloader, hanging out on her couch all day while she was at work, eating her food, never contributing a dime toward living expenses or chores. Boy, did that shit grow old fast. She decided to stay single for a while after that, which was almost two years ago now.

But something about Officer Nichols made her want to give the whole dating thing another try.

Probably need my head examined.

She heard the distinct sounds of boxes being slid across the floor, and headed into the living room to see what he'd unearthed.

"You're right," he said as he straightened. "It's a Christmas tree. And a pretty nice one from the looks of the box."

"When did your friend's parents sell the house?" she asked as she knelt down to read the box. *Pre-lit, six-foot Classic Blue Spruce.* If the lights worked, that would save her from having to buy one.

Nana always insisted on real trees, while Harley thought they were a lot of work, and the branches were never strong enough to hold many of her ornaments. Not to mention real trees could be fire hazards. "I never met the owners, but my realtor said they were a younger couple who'd only lived here a couple years, then got divorced. I figured the tree belonged to them, but maybe not…?"

"Gabe's stepdad died shortly after we joined the Army, and his mother sold the house almost immediately, moved back home to Iron Mountain. That had to be about ten years ago."

"Oh, wow. I'm so sorry. He must have been pretty young." Her own father had only been thirty-four when he died.

"Yeah, he was in his late forties, I think." Cam pushed the big box aside and crouched down to head back inside as Harley followed suit. "This tree is too new to have been theirs. And I believe two other families have lived here as well, so no telling who it belonged to."

It only took about twenty minutes to go through everything in the small closet—though it felt longer crawling around the small space with Officer Sexy. Damn, did the man smell amazing.

Besides several smaller boxes full of glass ball and other Christmas ornaments, four plastic bags stuffed with garland in silver, gold, and red, and a handful of boxes full of other holiday décor, they found several board games, a box filled with carefully folded tablecloths and napkins, and one holding an entire set of dishes for eight.

Most of the stuff Harley would donate to a local charity, but she decided to keep the tree since, once they opened the box, it appeared to be brand new. And she was fairly certain no one would be stopping by to collect any of these things.

Harley was about to slip out of the cubby when something on the floor in the corner caught her eye. She picked it up, and her pulse stuttered as she stared at a face so familiar it made her chest ache. Only…it couldn't be him. *How* could it be him? The thought was crazy. And yet…the teenage boy in the picture was the spitting image of her father. But this picture was too recent. The calendar hanging on the fridge was clearly visible, and it was the same year her father had passed away.

And then she recognized the second teenage boy in the picture, now the grown man busily moving the boxes they'd just gone through out to her foyer.

Once out of the cubby and in better lighting, she looked to the photo again, examining it through narrowed eyes. Yep, no question, the other boy was none other than Cam, which meant the ginger-haired kid had to be his friend, Gabe.

Could it really be possible that the house she'd purchased completely by random was the very same house her half-brother had grown up in?

CHAPTER 8

Cam stacked the boxes Harley planned to drop off at Goodwill by the front door. He was fairly certain none of it belonged to Gabe's mom, but he'd text him tonight just to make sure.

He realized Harley was staring intently at something she held in her hand. A picture? "What'cha got there?"

She jumped a bit, as if he'd startled her, then slowly held it out. He cocked a brow as he took it from her.

Cam recognized the photo immediately, and even remembered the day it had been taken. And no wondered she looked horrified. *Holy pizza-face, Batman.*

"This was Gabe's fifteenth birthday." He grinned as he met her curious gaze. "He'd gotten a new game system. We ordered pizza and stayed up all night playing video games."

She stared at the picture a bit more before smiling. Might be his imagination, but the curving of her lips seemed a bit forced.

"So, this is the infamous Gabe." She seemed to shake off some invisible funk before adding, "I didn't have a best friend growing up. I didn't have many friends at all, really."

Now he understood why her mood had altered a bit. He glanced back at the picture, a little unsure of what to say. "Joss didn't have many friends in high school either. She was a bit of a loner. Still is."

"What about your younger sister? Aren't she and Joss close?"

He shrugged. "Mel's the baby, a *"very nice surprise,"* as our parents like to say. She's only nineteen, so she and Joss are eight years apart. They get along, but Mel's sort of a free-spirit, while Joss is a homebody. Plus, Mel attends college in California, so we only see her on major holidays."

"Well, I look forward to meeting her some day."

Feeling a bit awkward, Cam wasn't sure if he should stay until she kicked him out, get to know her a little better, or take his leave before he somehow managed to stick his big-ass foot in his big-ass mouth. Again.

"So, are you free this Saturday night? I was thinking about inviting your family over for that dinner. I found my Nana's recipe for baked chicken and rice, and she always made green bean casserole with it and Rhode's bread."

"Rhode's bread? Sounds fancy." He loved the fact she wanted to spend more time with his family.

Which also worried the shit out of him. Puzzling, to say the least. As was the sudden urge to kiss her.

She grinned. "It's a brand of frozen bread dough. You just thaw, rise, and bake, and you have a hot loaf of bread. Nana would make it for dinner at least once a week, and for breakfast, too, alongside scrambled eggs with green peppers, onions and cheese, and thick-cut bacon."

"That sounds really good." *Man, those blue eyes are gorgeous. And her perfectly bowed lips...* "I love thick-cut bacon."

"Maybe I'll make it for you sometime."

Unable to resist her a moment longer, Cam set the picture on the small table beside the couch before grasping her hands and gently tugging her forward. He gently gripped her waist, and was lost in those glacial pools of blue as she gazed up at him with uncertainty.

"I'm not doing anything for breakfast tomorrow," he informed her in a low tone before leaning in and capturing her mouth. A soft gasp surprised him, so he pulled back slightly, then brushed his lips across hers with just the slightest pressure.

A soft whisper of sound escaped her as she leaned in and pressed her mouth to his. A surge of emotion took him by surprise. He cupped her face, remembering what she'd told him, and slanted his mouth across hers.

Her lips were silky smooth, and he touched his tongue to the seam, seeking entrance, wanting to taste her so badly he was damn near dizzy with it.

Another soft sigh, and then she opened for him. Cam didn't waste a second slipping inside. She touched the tip of her tongue to his, then slid her arms around him. Cam grunted his approval. It had been so long since he'd kissed a woman, truly kissed her.

He moved his hands around to cup the back of her head, running his tongue along hers, tasting, stroking, flicking, her hesitant response the sexiest thing he'd ever experienced.

His pulse thrummed in his veins as he crushed her in his arms, molding her against the hard proof of his desire while deepening the kiss. He wanted her, more than he'd ever wanted another woman. The thought scared the shit out of him, even while he prayed she felt the same. The thought of having to leave, of having to walk out that door right now, was something he couldn't even fathom.

She whimpered in his arms, her hands moving to clutch his forearms as she tore her lips free. Disappointment settled in his gut like a lead boulder.

"I'm sorry," she said on a breathy whisper.

"No, I'm sorry." He brushed his thumb across her cheek, then dropped his hands and took a step back. "Seems I have little control where you're concerned."

"I liked it. The kiss. And I like you, despite the voice in the back of my head telling me to run for the hills. It's just... Look, I'm not the casual sex type."

He recaptured her hands, retaking the step to bring them toe to toe again. "There is nothing casual about the way I feel about you, Harley."

The most beautiful smile transformed her face, smoothing away the worried lines on her brow. He realized he was falling fast for the gorgeous redhead, and the thought scared the shit out of him. It also filled his chest with something he hadn't felt in a long time—anticipation of the future.

Harley pulled both pans of her Nana's chicken and rice casserole from the oven, her body humming with a combination of both excitement and nervousness. She wanted tonight to be perfect. She really liked Cam's family, but more importantly, she really liked Cam. She hadn't been able to think about much else since he left the other night. And while he hadn't stopped by again to see her, he had been texting her every morning and night. Sweet texts, like *Good morning, beautiful*, and *Sweet dreams*.

Truth was, the moody cop was turning out to be a great guy. Part of her was afraid to buy into it, to believe he was truly interested in her for more than just sex. But the hopeful part of her argued she deserved happiness as much as anyone else, and why wouldn't he want more from her than just a good time?

Head spinning, she gave it a shake in an effort to dismiss the frustrating thoughts. She'd made a nice meal for him and his family, and she planned to enjoy the evening.

After covering the pans with foil, she slid the two loaves of bread into the oven. They'd take about thirty minutes to bake, and she'd put the green bean casserole in beside them in about ten minutes.

She glanced into the dining room at her table, so pretty set with Nana's favorite rose print dishes, and the card table next to it, which she'd set up for the boys with the smiley face plates and vintage Looney Tunes jelly glasses from her own childhood. She'd loved playing with her food on those plates, and hoped the boys would as well.

Harley had just pulled the freshly-baked bread from the oven when the doorbell rang. She tossed the pot holders on the counter and rushed into the foyer, swinging the door open with a genuine smile of excitement. The entire family, minus the youngest sister, Melanie, stood on her porch. And since there was no vehicles in her driveway, they must have all walked down together.

"Come on in," she urged, waving everybody inside.

Cam gave her a wink on the way past, and she had an overwhelming urge to kiss him right in front of everyone. But she didn't dare. It was much too soon. Heck, she didn't even know if they were dating. She didn't know what they were doing, though she hoped to find out later tonight. He had already asked if he could stay for a movie once his family headed home. And she had a feeling he'd let her know exactly what he wanted once they were alone.

"It smells wonderful in here," his mom announced as she looked around with interest. "You may have to give me this recipe."

"I would be happy to," Harley assured her.

Her home was similar in style to theirs, so they all headed into the dining room just off the kitchen. Jacob and Jeremy spotted the second table immediately and raced around to take their seats, oohing over the plates and glasses, just as she had at that age.

"Where would you like us to sit?" Joss asked as she adjusted Jarrod on her hip.

"Anywhere you like. In fact, I have a space set at the card table for Jarrod, if you think he'd prefer to sit with his brothers? I have a couple of pillows on the chair so he can reach."

"Me, too! Me, too!" Jarrod insisted as he wriggled to be free.

Joss laughed as Logan swept him from her arms in a move that would make the Packers proud, spinning him once before setting him in the pillow-lined chair, and adjusting him so that he could reach the table. "How's that, Buddy?"

As Logan took the seat next to his sister, Cam surprised her by asking, "How can I help?"

She caught the looks that passed between his parents and sister, and it was all she could do to hold back a smile. “Since you know what everyone likes, maybe you could pour the drinks while I get the food on the table? I made a pitcher of iced tea. I hope it’s sweet enough.”

“Oh, I’m sure it is,” Marianne assured her before rising back to her feet.

Harley waved the older lady back down. “Please, relax. It’ll just take me a minute to get everything situated.

Just as she’d hoped, everybody loved Nana’s chicken and rice casserole, even the boys, who made a spectacular mess on the table and floor in their enthusiasm. Both loaves of bread she’d put out disappeared within minutes, and Harley couldn’t have been happier. She offered the leftovers to Joss, who happily took them. There was just enough for her and the boys to have lunch the following day.

After fawning over and enjoying the chocolate éclair torte she’d thrown together for dessert the night before, the entire family hot-footed it out the door as if their shoes were on fire—or as if they’d been instructed to make a speedy exit.

“Dinner was amazing, Harley,” Marianne cooed as she hurried down the porch steps.

Cam stood beside her in the doorway, waving to his quickly departing family. Harley almost laughed as she caught the wink his dad sent him.

“You kids enjoy your movie,” Logan tossed over his shoulder as he grasped Jeremy’s hand and followed the rest of the clan down the sidewalk back to their parents’ house.

As soon as Cam closed the door, she spun around in feigned outrage. “You planned that. For them to leave right after the meal.”

One brow hiked up as he slid an arm around her waist. “No shit, Sherlock. I’ve been waiting all week to get you alone again, and I know my mom and Joss. They’d have interrogated you all night if I hadn’t taken matters into my own hands.”

“Maybe I *wanted* to chat with them a bit,” she demurred, spinning away and heading into the kitchen to load the dishwasher. "I like them both very much—your father and brother, too. And those boys are adorable. It's a little uncomfortable knowing you actually asked them to leave so we could—"

Two arms snaked around her waist from behind, making her yelp. Suddenly surrounded by the most delicious warmth, Harley could barely breathe—or form a coherent thought.

"So we could what?" he whispered against her temple. "What is it you think we're going to do?"

His lips skimmed along the shell of her ear, her cheek, until he was nuzzling the sensitive skin just below her jaw. She closed her eyes and leaned into his embrace, her head lolling back as she offered him the expanse of her throat.

"I have to clean up," she protested in a near whisper.

"It can wait," he countered. "The dishes aren't going anywhere."

She turned in his arms and twined hers around his neck. She wanted him, so much, but wasn't quite sure she was ready to sleep with him. "A movie?"

He met her gaze, and she easily read the disappointment in his eyes. But to his credit, he smiled as if it were the best idea he'd ever heard.

"Whatever you want. How about something scary?"

"I'm game. There's a couple of new ones on Netflix."

Once they were snuggled up on the couch, Harley started to relax a bit. She was lying across his lap, his woodsy, masculine scent a sexy backdrop to the slow massage he gave her, one hand stroking her from shoulder to hip, giving her love handle a soft squeeze before trailing down to the inside of her knee, and then caressing a leisurely path back up to her shoulder, over and over until she felt limp as a cooked noodle, her skin tingling with anticipation.

By the time the movie ended, Harley was rethinking her earlier reservations. She was single, lonely, and God, how she wanted him. Seriously, why should she deny herself? It's not as if she was looking for anything long-lasting, but that didn't mean she couldn't enjoy the sexy cop's company.

"I should probably get going. While I still can," he said, his voice gruff. He gave her hip a quick squeeze.

Making a decision she hoped she didn't later regret, Harley rose to her knees and straddled his lap, facing him. The hard ridge pressing into her backside was unmistakable. "I bought some thick-cut bacon today," she informed him, her heart thumping with nervous exhilaration. "Thought maybe I could make that breakfast for you…in the morning."

CHAPTER 9

His hands settled on her hips, those bedroom brown eyes gleaming with unadulterated male appreciation. "You sure?"

She leaned forward until she was but a breath away from those sexy lips. "I'm sure."

"Thank God," he muttered before crushing her in his arms and slanting his mouth beneath hers.

Harley couldn't remember the last time she felt so...so *alive.* Their mouths meshed as passion took over, Cam's wet tongue teasing the seam of her lips, seeking entrance. Harley opened with a soft sigh, meeting his tongue with only a moment of hesitancy before the slow, sexy drag of his drew her in. She ran her palms down the hard planes of his back before yanking his T-shirt free from the waistband of his jeans, eager to feel his warm skin beneath her fingers.

He tore his mouth free to nip at her earlobe. "Should we move this to your bedroom, or are you okay with doing it on your sofa?"

She laughed. "Doing it? Wow. Such a romantic."

"It's your fault for being so damn sexy," he countered with a lop-sided grin. "I can't wait to get you naked."

"Yeah, maybe you should quit talking before you kill the mood." She playfully rolled her eyes. "And I'm definitely okay with sofa sex, though I'd rather save that for another time."

He stood so quickly she almost spilled from his arms. She grinned as she wound her arms around his neck and clamped her legs around his hips.

Cam gave her ass a squeeze before heading for the stairs. "Which room is yours?"

"First door on the right," she murmured against his throat before giving his earlobe a reciprocal nibble.

He surprised her with a chuckle, but didn't stop his ascent.

"What's so funny?"

"That's Gabe's old room."

Hmm, had she somehow sensed her brother when she'd chosen his room for her own? She almost laughed out loud at the ridiculous thought. As if she were psychic or something. The room had the best view, and that's why she'd chosen it.

Cam used his shoulder to push the door open, and she gazed around her bedroom through new eyes as the fading sun bathed the walls in luminous streaks of orange and red. When he set her on the blue, black, and white striped comforter, the heady floral scent of her fabric softener wafted up, making her very glad she'd thought to wash her bedding that morning.

As he kicked off his shoes, and toed off his socks, her nerves kicked in. She reclined back on her elbows and tried to calm her racing heart. Everything she'd fantasized about since first meeting the sexy cop was about to become reality, and she closed her eyes for a moment, as eager as she was anxious. Cam had no doubt been with plenty of woman—what if he found her lacking? Or boring?

Harley glanced up when she didn't feel the bed dip, and found him watching her with pulse-pounding intensity. "Is...something wrong?"

He gave his head a slow shake. "You're so fucking beautiful," he finally muttered, his voice thick.

Her heart tripped with his overwhelming declaration. Anticipation started a slow throb between her thighs as he lied down next to her and skillfully reclaimed her lips.

The man was magnificent—so handsome, so sexy. He smelled like spicy heaven, and tasted faintly of the rich chocolate frosting she'd made. Wrapping her arms around his broad back, she hooked one leg over his hard thigh, and delved into his hot mouth. He rumbled low in his throat as his tongue stroked hers, slow, erotic drags as they touched and explored. His solid weight pressed her into the mattress as he deepened the kiss, and she couldn't resist moving against the hard ridge wedged against the apex of her thighs.

Eager to run her fingers across the hard planes of his back, she grasped the hem of his T-shirt and worked it up his chest. He broke the kiss and leaned back to help wrestle the tight-fitting shirt off his muscular frame, then pulled her to a sitting position and deftly swept off her own shirt before tossing them both on the carpeted floor. Their gazes met and held. Harley pulled her bottom lip between her teeth as he reached behind her and unhooked her lacey black bra. He slid it down her arms, the silky straps like a soft caress across her heated flesh. His eyes darkened as he looked his fill of her naked breasts. Her nipples hardened under his smoldering scrutiny.

"You're stunning," he said, his tone low, sensual.

"I'm covered in freckles," she needlessly pointed out. Though very small and light, she'd always felt like an oddity because of them.

"I know. They're the sexiest damn thing I've ever seen." Grasping her face between his big palms, Cam brought his lips to hers, plundering her mouth while expertly maneuvering her onto her back and blanketing her with his huge frame.

God, how she loved the feel of his weight crushing her into the soft mattress. And he kissed her with such single-minded focus, such passion, she could barely breathe. Every inch of her tingled as his hands gripped and searched, kneaded and caressed. Never had she felt so wholly desired, and she suddenly believed he truly did think she was beautiful.

She wanted to feel his mouth on her more than she'd ever wanted anything in her life.

As if reading her mind, his hand trailed down the length of her throat and down between her breasts before cupping one with gentle pressure. He finally released her swollen lips to press soft, wet kisses along the same path his hand had taken. When his mouth closed over her pebbled nipple, she gasped and twined her fingers into his thick hair.

He took his time licking and laving, swirling his tongue around and around, then nipping lightly with his teeth before closing his lips over the swollen peak and sucking with gentle pressure. She arched into his hot mouth with a soundless sigh, her fingers stroking his scalp with silent encouragement.

Cam let go of her wet, throbbing nipple with a soft sucking noise and gazed up at her through hooded eyes. "You okay?"

His deep voice, rough with concern, surprised her. Attempting to sound sexy and reassure him at the same time, she cooed, "Never better." But the words came out as more of a squeak, and her face prickled with embarrassment. *Dumb ass.*

He grinned. "Good to know."

A quick nip at her bottom lip, then he resumed his sweet torture, switching over to give the same loving attention to her other breast. She closed her eyes, which only served to increase the erotic sensations. She grew wet at the thought of what he might have planned next. Foreplay. Not something she had a lot of experience with. The only two guys she'd slept with had both been more interested in their own pleasure than hers.

Thankfully, Officer Sexy was unlike any man she'd ever known before.

He pressed his lips to the spot just below her ribcage, then lower, trailing a slow, scorching path down her belly to her navel before dipping his tongue in, surprising a sharp gasp from her. He splayed his palm across her belly, glanced up and caught her gaze.

Then he slipped his fingers beneath the elastic waistband of her leggings and slowly peeled them down. Those amber eyes gleamed as he stared down at the scrap of black satin that barely covered the apex of her thighs. He did the same slow drag down her legs as he removed her thong, the light friction practically setting her flesh on fire.

And then she was lying before him in all her freckled, naked glory, wearing nothing but the shimmery purple nail polish on her fingers and toes.

His hot gaze raked over her, slowly, warming every single inch of her. She missed the slow stroke of his hands, his wet tongue on her aching breasts. Her inhibitions started to melt away as her desire for him amplified. She grew bolder and rose up onto her knees, eager to take the reins. Reaching for one of the belt loops on the waistband of his jeans, she slipped a finger in to playfully tug him closer.

He watched through heavy-lidded eyes as she unbuttoned his jeans and pulled the zipper down with deliberate laziness. He stood with a muttered curse and shucked his jeans, then his boxer briefs. Harley's mouth went dry as his impressive erection sprang free. He knelt back on the bed and they came together in a rush of need, lips meshing, hands stroking and squeezing.

Cam pushed her to her back, and after one last kiss, dragged his mouth down her torso, licking and lipping her sensitive flesh until he reached the neatly trimmed ginger curls.

"Spread your legs," he gruffly commanded, running his palm along her inner thigh, urging her to open for him.

She let her knees fall apart, hyper aware she was already wet for him. He dragged his fingertips through her slick folds, caressing and stroking before sliding one thick finger inside her. Her inner walls clenched, and her nipples tightened painfully as he leaned in to run his tongue across her swollen clit. Harley dug her heels into the mattress and fisted the comforter as he stroked in slow rhythm with his tongue. The throbbing intensified, building to a crescendo as she realized she was about to come. He closed his mouth over her swollen nub and sucked, making her whimper with need. She twined her fingers in his hair as she rocked her hips against his mouth and fingers.

"My God...I think, *Cam...*" Neck arched back, body tight as a strung bow, she exploded with a lusty cry.

Cam licked and laved until she collapsed into a puddle of satisfaction. He gave her one last tongue stroke, and a playful nip on the inside of her thigh before leaning over to grasp his jeans and dig a condom out of his wallet. She watched through lethargic eyes as he tore the wrapper open and quickly sheathed himself. Though still quivering from aftershocks, she couldn't wait to feel him deep inside her. And his self-satisfied smile only made her want him even more.

He leaned over and captured her mouth. Harley spread her legs wide, grasped his hard length, and guided him to her. He entered her slowly, groaning low in his throat as he slid home, and she nearly sobbed her relief when he was seated deep inside. She planted her heels in the mattress as she met the stroke of his tongue, their mouths mimicking the slow, steady thrusts of their bodies.

Cam dragged his open mouth across her cheek, playfully nipping her throat, then her shoulder. That delicious tension built again, and she marveled at the thought of orgasming a second time.

She slid her fingers through his hair and clenched tight. "*Faster.* Oh, my God, *faster.*"

"*Geezuz.* I hope you're close," he growled before bracing his forearms on either side of her and increasing the speed of his thrusts.

Harley came so fast it startled her. She gripped his lower back with both hands and rocked against him as a second climax rippled through her. Cam's strokes grew frenzied until a hoarse shout tore from his throat. They undulated together until their breathing relaxed, and their pulses slowed. He collapsed on top of her with a gruff chuckle. A small giggle escaped, and they both laughed as he rolled them to their side and gathered her in his arms.

"Damn, I thought my fucking heart was gonna blow." He heaved a shaky breath while stroking his hand up and down her back.

Afraid of what might fall from her lips if she tried to speak, she closed her eyes and snuggled into his warm, hard chest. The heady, lethargic feeling of being held in this amazing man's arms after being pleasured so thoroughly and completely—twice—was something she'd never thought to experience.

A yawn escaped. Then another. Cam's soft chuckle was the last thing she heard before sweet dreams claimed her sated mind and body.

CHAPTER 10

Cam woke from a light doze and stretched, careful not to wake the sleeping beauty in his arms. Harley had nodded off almost immediately, and he had to admit, he'd felt ten feet tall. The woman was incredible. Sexy, funny, sassy. And damn, those freckles were hot as hell. He was becoming more entranced by the day. The fact he was still lying in her bed instead of heading home to his own was what really threw him.

Though it didn't surprise him since he'd thought to bring Cleo with him to his parents' house. Just in case things went his way... and damn, did they go his way.

Harley stirred, the hand lying over his heart sliding down to rest just below his navel—and a hairs-breadth away from his dick, which hardened in anticipation. He'd thought she was sleeping, but then those silky fingers slid down farther and cupped him with gentle pressure. A quick glance assured him she was awake, and peeking up at him through the thick fringe of her lashes.

"I owe you one," she explained, her voice slightly sleep-raspy.

Then those delicate fingers closed around his straining erection. Words failed him as she stroked her way down to the base, then back up, slowly, down and up, his cock hardening to full-length within seconds.

When she leaned in to press her lips to his, her hot tongue seeking entrance, lust gripped him. Hard. Rolling on his side to face her, he palmed the back of her head and delved into her hot mouth. Once he had her shapely, slim leg positioned over his hip, she guided him to her slick entrance, and he entered her with a slow, deep thrust. She moaned, her fingers clenching his back, her nails digging into his flesh as they surged together.

Cam grasped her ass and drove into her welcoming heat with a grunt of satisfaction. He tried to take it slow, a little afraid of embarrassing himself, but Harley was having none of it, and moved her hips against him—hard, fast—until she cried out. He watched her face as she came, her pleasure heightening his, his heart racing so fucking fast he feared it might burst. A curse tore from his throat as he imploded with the force of a freight train.

Once their hips slowed, and he was able to draw air into his lungs, he gathered her in his arms and promptly passed out.

The next time Cam woke, blinding, morning sunshine filled the room. He groaned, stretched, and reached for Harley, only to discover himself alone. The aroma of bacon frying reached him, and he smiled, remembering her promise of the night before.

He crammed his legs into his jeans and hurried down the steps, as eager to see that beautiful face as he was for a cup of coffee. She stood at the stove stirring what he hoped was scrambled eggs, and when she looked up and saw him, a huge smile lit her face. For him. He walked up behind her and slipped his arms around her waist. Cam knew the powerful level of happiness he was experiencing should scare the shit out of him. Oddly enough, it didn't. In fact, the prospect of heading home to his empty cabin suddenly didn't appeal.

She turned in his arms and grinned. "Morning. Wanna taste?" She held a small pile of fluffy scrambled eggs on the edge of her spatula.

"I'd love one." But instead of eating the proffered eggs, he kissed her. Then he ate the eggs.

She laughed. "Sassy. Go ahead, sit. I have a carafe of coffee on the table and that black mug is for you."

"Yes, ma'am."

Damn, it felt good to have a woman cook for him. Other than his mother. The thought made him grin. Seemed like that was all he did lately, smile like a fool. Not that he was complaining. While he wasn't quite ready to examine his growing feelings for the sexy redhead, he *was* finally ready to move out of the past and into the present. That alone felt amazing.

He poured himself a much-needed cup of coffee and sipped while he watched her fill two plates with scrambled eggs, several slices of bacon, and toast. "You didn't have to go to all this trouble," he told her as she set a plate in front of him. His mouth watered as he picked up a slice of the thick-cut bacon. "Not that I'm complaining. Thank you so much."

"I like to cook." She sat and refilled her own cup. "I'm nowhere near my Nana's level—she could make a flip-flop taste good. But she taught me all the basics."

"Well, you're a great student 'cuz everything you've made has been delicious." He scooped up a forkful of the eggs—which were chockfull of diced green peppers, onions, and mozzarella cheese, and shoveled it into his mouth.

"Mmm. Damn, this is good. You probably cook every day for yourself."

"I do like to go out for lunch, or dinner, *once* in a while." She met his gaze as she took a bite of her toast.

Now, there was a hint if he'd ever heard one. "In that case, since I've yet to take you out on an official first date, whad'ya say to dinner one night this week?"

"Sounds good to me." She flashed a small smile of satisfaction before adding, "And maybe we can head back here for a movie afterward. Assuming the date goes well."

She cast him a mischievous grin. The date would go very well, of that he had no doubt.

He polished off his eggs and bacon in record time, then his toast, which she'd managed to get just right—a teensy bit on the dark side. "There's a supper club not far from my place that has amazing broasted chicken. I also know a great Italian restaurant in Houghton. Mexican, too, if you prefer that. El Puerto. Their steak tacos are the best, I can eat like twenty of 'em."

She cupped her tummy as if in protest. "Well, Officer, that's a contest you'd win. I can eat three, maybe four, but that's because I usually get filled up on the chips and salsa."

"Hell, if I skip the chips and salsa, I could probably eat thirty."

She let out a half-laugh, half-groan. "Well, maybe you should save some room this time. For dessert."

He smiled so wide he could hardly contain it. "So, El Puerto, then?"

"Definitely El Puerto," she confirmed with another of those impish grins.

Unable to take his gaze off her, he watched as she got up to retrieve a napkin covered plate from the counter beside the stove. The rest of the bacon, which he happily helped her polish off.

Once they finished breakfast, and she got up to put the plates in the dishwasher, he realized the photo of him and Gabe they'd found was sitting on the table beside her coffee mug. He picked it up and gave his head a rueful shake.

"I should probably burn this damn thing."

"Not a chance, I love that picture. And technically, it's mine since I found it in my house."

An interesting argument. "Why would you even want it? You don't know Gabe, and let's be honest, this isn't the most flattering picture of me. I'd forgotten how bad my acne was."

Her brow dipped. "You look like most of the kids I went to school with," she assured him as she topped off his coffee then sat back down and took the picture from him. Her features softened as she gazed at it. "So, got any fun stories you can share? Were you and Gabe good kids, or troublemakers?"

He took a sip of the steaming brew, then leaned back in his chair, surprised by her interest. "We kept out of trouble, for the most part. Only strayed to the dark side a handful of times."

She rested her elbow on the table, chin in her hand. "*Dark side*, hey? You've piqued my interest, Officer Nichols. So, let's hear it. What's the worst thing you and Gabe ever did?"

He laughed. "Eager to hear about my childhood humiliations?"

Her brow dipped, but then those sky-blue eyes sparkled with mirth. "Just making polite conversation."

"In that case, why don't you share first? What's the worst thing *you've* ever done, Miss Lawson?"

Judging by her thoughtful frown, he wasn't sure she'd take the bait. Or maybe she couldn't think of anything she wanted to share. Finally, a sheepish smile curved her lips.

"Okay, so when I was a kid, the elderly couple who lived directly behind us grew a little garden every year behind their garage. I used to sneak over the fence at night and steal whatever was ripe. Tomatoes, cucumbers, pumpkins. I'd give them to Nana, and tell her my friend's mom sent them over."

He stared at her for a full ten seconds before letting out a bark of laughter. "Seriously? The worst thing you've ever done is steal tomatoes from the neighbor's garden? That's like...picking a flower from the neighbor's rose bush."

Her lips thinned. "Okay, so what high crimes did you and Gabe commit?"

He polished off the last bite of his bacon and washed it down with a gulp of coffee. "Well, one night we stole his mom's car so we could go to a party over the bridge."

Face tilted to the side, she seemed slightly impressed. "Definitely worse than stealing veggies from the neighbor," she admitted. "How old were you guys?"

"Fifteen."

Her eyes widened. "How much trouble did you get in?"

"Plenty. My dad pulled us over on the way home. I swear, I almost pissed myself when I saw those flashing lights."

Her mouth rounded into a perfect 'O'. "Which one of you was driving?"

"I was. Gabe got shit-faced at the party."

Concern etched her face. "Does he have...a drinking problem?"

Her odd question took him by surprise. "Of course not. He was playing Quarters with a bunch of other kids, trying to show off for some girl, and I was playing video games in another room. I had no idea until someone came in and told me he'd passed out in the bathroom."

Expecting her to laugh over their youthful stupidity, he was taken aback by her worried frown. Hell, she looked ready to cry. "You okay?"

She cleared her throat and smiled—sort of—then waved away his concern. "Sorry, I... My dad was killed by a drunk driver."

Ah, fuck. "Harley, I'm so sorry. I had no idea."

"Oh, I know you didn't," she said, waving away his concern. "I'm not sure why I reacted like that. It's been years. I'm just glad nothing serious happened. Well, other than getting pulled over by your own father. I bet you were grounded forever...?"

"Two months," he confirmed with a self-deprecating laugh, remembering how fucking scared he'd been. Gabe, too, once he'd sobered up. "He also took us to the police station and tossed us in a cell. Made Gabe drink like two pots of coffee before calling his mom. Dad still teases him about it once in a while. In fact, I don't think Gabe is much of a coffee drinker to this day."

He grinned; she grinned back, and thankfully, the mood lightened.

"So, what are your plans for today?"

Harley took a thoughtful sip of her coffee before giving a one-shoulder shrug. "I don't really have any. Maybe take Toby in to be groomed, if they have an opening. You?"

"I was thinking about doing a little fishing. Don't suppose you'd be interested...? You can bring Toby over to meet Cleo. He'd have a blast running down by the lake."

Worry suddenly etched her face. "I don't know. Toby's a little guy, I wouldn't want any accidents—"

"Cleo wouldn't harm a hair on his head. She's a lover, not a fighter."

He winked, and she rolled her eyes.

"All right, sounds like fun. I haven't been fishing in years, though, so I hope you have something simple in mind."

"We can do a little casting off the pier, or perch jerking. If you prefer fishing off a boat, I own a pontoon, and a fishing boat. Trolling is nice and easy. When my parents would take us kids fishing, my mom always had a rod in one hand, and a book in the other."

"Somehow, I can totally picture that."

Her seemingly genuine interest was a nice surprise. While his mom loved to fish, neither of his sisters much cared for it.

"How long 'til you're ready?"

"Thirty minutes. I need to shower first."

"Don't suppose you'd like some company?"

Harley started toward the stairs, tossing over her shoulder, "Long as you don't mind washing my back."

"Hell, sweetheart, I'll wash both your back *and* your front. But we'll definitely need more than half an hour."

Her steps quickened, and so did his. He caught her around the waist, and she squealed as they raced up the stairs. Cam couldn't remember the last time he'd felt so...content.

CHAPTER 11

After more than three weeks of getting to know each other, of making love nearly every night, of watching him interact with his family, especially his nephews, who adored him, Harley was fairly certain she'd fallen in love with Cam.

Having never experienced that particular emotion for the opposite sex before, she could be confusing lust with love. Her plan had been to take things slow. If she and Cam were meant to be, she wanted it to happen slowly, organically.

But she just couldn't seem to get enough of the big, sexy cop.

Or him of her.

Remembering the last time he'd slept over, a delicious shiver ran through her. He'd bought a bottle of wine to go with dinner, which they polished off while watching an erotic thriller, before spending half the night making love on her incredibly comfy sofa. Her eyes drifted closed, her nipples tingly with awareness as she recalled the way he'd loved her, first with slow anticipation, then fast with need. He was generous, yet demanding, funny, and the sexiest man alive. Those few nights he hadn't slept over, Harley found herself struggling to fall asleep. Which seemed ridiculous considering they'd only been dating a few weeks.

The question she couldn't seem to vocalize was, were Cam's feelings for her just as strong? She didn't know much about his relationship past, but he seemed to be open and loving, romantic, even. Had he been seeing anyone serious before her? Had he ever been engaged? Or married?

After her second cup of coffee, Harley showered, dressed, and put on a little mascara and lip gloss. She decided to wear a pair of cutoff shorts—which Cam had called Daisy Dukes—and a well-fitted, purple Harley Davidson T-shirt, which she knew looked good on her. He was due home soon, and she wanted to look her best. Something she'd never much cared about until falling for the handsome police officer.

Whoa...home? It had certainly started to feel like Cam lived with her. She missed him more than she ever thought possible, not that she planned to admit as much. Heck, they were still very much in the 'getting to know each other' phase, and she definitely wasn't ready for it to end.

Cam had headed off on a pre-planned fishing trip with Logan and the chief Monday morning, and were due home today. Hopefully, sooner rather than later. He'd texted her each morning with a fishing progress report, and called every evening to say goodnight, but she still missed him liked crazy.

His mom and Joss had invited her out to lunch, which had been a nice surprise. They'd eaten at a great steakhouse and shared a bottle of wine while getting to know each other better. Well, in their case it had been more of a subtle interrogation. Which was funny since they'd both been a bit tight-lipped when it came to Cam, mostly just sharing funny family stories. But she understood their reluctance to share anything personal with her.

Not like she'd been completely honest about her reason for moving to Houghton.

Regardless, she enjoyed both women's company very much, and was pretty sure they felt the same about her. Cam had such an open, wonderful family, which really helped on the days when she was missing her Nana.

She also wondered if it was time to talk to Cam about Gabe. Though it seemed crazy to believe the guy was her long-lost brother based off one picture, the resemblance was so striking, she truly did. She'd even started to wonder if meeting Cam hadn't been accidental at all. Maybe fate had played a hand in bringing the three of them together.

A familiar, brisk knock at her front door had her jumping up with excitement, and Toby barking like a fool. She'd hurried over to unlock the door, and the moment she pulled it open, Cleo raced inside and headed straight for her little friend, who did his cute little doggy dance as the Shepherd fell onto the floor and rolled to her back. Harley missed the rest of the show as she was promptly pulled into Cam's arms and hoisted up for a kiss.

She wrapped her arms around his neck, happier than she'd ever thought possible.

After kissing her quite thoroughly, he whispered, "Miss me?" then set her on her feet and stepped inside to close the door.

"Maybe a little," she demurred, unable to wipe the smile from her face. "Are you hungry?"

"Starving." He dropped his duffle bag on the hardwood floor and waggled his eyebrows, his meaning clear. "But it'll have to wait until tonight. We're supposed to meet my family in less than an hour."

Her brow creased. "Oh. Are we going to your mom's for lunch or something?"

"The Strawberry Festival starts today. Don't tell me you forgot...?"

Holy crap, she *had* forgotten! "Sorry, I've had work stuff on my mind. Good thing I'm already showered and ready to go, hey?"

His gaze raked her up and down. "And you look as great as you smell."

"I bought a new body mist," she informed him with a playful batt of her eyelashes. "I was hoping you'd like it."

"Oh, I like. And I worry every man who gets within two feet of you will like as well."

She grinned. "Well, the only other males I plan to get that close and personal with are all in single digits, so I hope you're right."

He grasped her hand and pulled her back into his arms. "So, how are you at frying fish?"

She gazed up at him in feigned outrage. "Are you serious? Where I come from, it's a crime to not be able to fry fish. Nana was a bit of a stickler about those Midwest traditions. The deep fryer sat on our counter year-round."

He chuckled. "Good to know because I probably have enough fish in my freezer to eat every Friday for the rest of the year. Mostly crappie and perch, but I also caught three huge walleye, and six Northern."

His excitement was so palpable she couldn't help but laugh. "Guess I'd better start printing out recipes."

"Sounds good."

He pressed his lips to hers, his mouth soft as he kissed her, though carnal need flamed quickly between them, as it always seemed to do. Harley was on the verge of asking if he wanted to run upstairs for a quickie when someone else knocked on her front door.

Cam broke the kiss, frowned, and swung his head. "I swore Mom said they'd meet us at the fair."

"Maybe they changed their minds, wanted to all ride together?"

He strode over and opened the door, and when Harley realized who was standing on her porch, her pulse sped into triple time.

Gabe.

She knew this day would be coming, but figured she'd at least have time to prepare.

"Hey, man, come on in!" Cam told his friend, stepping aside. "I thought you said you couldn't make it this year?"

"Thankfully, I was able to switch weekends with Bushnell." He walked inside—his stride almost identical to her father's—and exchanged thumps on the back with Cam while looking around with barely concealed interest. "Your mom told me you were here, and I couldn't resist stopping by. I hope that's okay...?"

He gave her a quick onceover, then stepped forward and held out his right hand. "You must be Harley. I'm Gabe. Glad to finally meet you."

Harley stared at him in stunned silence as she perfunctorily shook his hand. *Holy shit*. Not only did he walk like her dad and look like him, with his neatly shorn ginger hair and muscular physique, but their voices were nearly identical. Which screwed with her in a way she wasn't expecting. Made her heart ache. She couldn't remember the last time she missed her father like this. Her eyes burned as she fought back the urge to cry with everything she had. Sure, she was probably seeing what she wanted to see because she was desperate for a familial connection. But her gut told her no way could this guy be anyone *but* her brother.

Until she was sure, though, she'd have to continue to keep her suspicions to herself. If it turned out Gabe was her brother, he likely didn't know.

When she realized Cam and Gabe were eyeballing her expectantly, she cleared her throat and forced a soft chuckle. "I'm sorry. It's just...you look like someone. Guess it took me by surprise."

"Anyone I should know about?" Cam asked, his tone teasing, but his eyes alight with something else. Jealousy perhaps? Did he think she was talking about an ex? She'd never had a guy show jealousy over her, so it was a bit of a novelty. Of course, she could be completely misinterpreting his response.

"My father, actually."

Gabe laughed. "I look like your dad? I have to say, that's a first."

Her face grew warm. "I just meant your coloring."

"Obviously, you look like him as well," he pointed out, still smiling.

Harley managed a reciprocal grin. "In coloring, yes, though I have my mother's facial features."

A familiar ring had Cam digging his phone from his pocket. "It's a text from Mom. They're at the fairgrounds and want to know where we are." He typed a reply, then closed the distance between them and gave her a kiss. "You ready?"

"For strawberry shortcake? Hell, yeah."

He grinned, then asked Gabe, "You wanna ride with us?"

"You bet." He cast her a wink, which had Cam rolling his eyes.

They headed out, and the guys chatted a little about the fishing trip. It seemed so strange to her, thinking that this funny, outgoing guy could be her brother. She just hoped she could get the info she needed from him without coming across like some nosy busybody, as her Nana would say. If Gabe was her brother, she'd find a way to prove it, even if she had to run a DNA test—assuming it was legal. But she wouldn't say anything, to either of them, until she knew for sure.

Which led her to something else she hadn't thought too much about until now. Could it be her father had cheated on her mother, and that's why he hadn't wanted the child? It seemed unlikely, knowing him to have been a good, hard-working man. But he'd also been human, so anything was possible.

Heck, Gabe could very well know who his biological father was, but never had any interest in meeting him—or, by extension, her. She sure as hell hoped that wasn't the case.

God, how she wished she had someone she could talk to about this. Cam was a great listener, but for obvious reasons he wasn't an option. Same for Joss, and their mother.

"About stopping by without calling first," Gabe suddenly said from the backseat of Cam's Jeep Cherokee. "I got the distinct feeling my timing wasn't the greatest."

"Your timing sucked," Cam confirmed with a grin.

Harley gave his arm a playful slap. "Your timing was fine. We were just about to leave for the festival anyway."

Cam laid his right hand on her thigh and cast her a sidelong glance that reminded her of exactly where they'd been heading when Gabe arrived, his heated look so full of promise a slow throb started between her thighs. She squeezed them together and carefully kept her gaze focused straight ahead.

"So, Cam tells me you're a librarian," Gabe said. "That sounds..."

"Boring as hell?" she finished for him with a grin. "Believe it or not, I love it. I've always been a huge reader, and I prefer my nice, quiet workspace. What do you do for a living?"

"I'm a police officer down in Iron Mountain."

She craned her head to look at him. "Seriously?"

He and Cam both laughed. "Seriously."

"I don't know whether to feel safe, or nervous," she teased, thinking how proud her dad would be of his son, wishing he could have met him.

"I'm curious, were you named after the motorcycle, or the comic book supervillain?"

"The motorcycle. My dad used to ride."

"Used to? He doesn't ride anymore?"

"Harley lost her dad when she was a kid," Cam explained, grasping her hand and giving it a supportive squeeze.

Her heart swelled as she fell even deeper in love with her handsome cop.

"I'm sorry. I had no idea."

She turned to meet Gabe's remorseful gaze...so much like her father's. "It's fine, you couldn't have known. He died in a motorcycle accident when I was twelve."

"I lost my dad, too. But I was an adult by then. Must've been really hard losing him at such a young age."

"It was. My mom died when I was a baby, so I never knew her. Then I lost my Nana last year."

"Christ." He was silent for a moment. "Is that why you moved to Houghton? Do you have family here in town?"

She knew Gabe was only making small talk, but his interest warmed her heart. "I...maybe. I found an entry in the family bible after my Nana passed that I decided to follow up on. I also discovered my dad went to Michigan Tech, so I figured Houghton was as good a place as anywhere to start over."

Cam made a right onto Highway 41, then glanced over at her. "If you have a name, I can look them up for you."

"Thanks, but...I'm still getting used to being on my own. I'm not quite ready to go down that road yet." Harley hated lying to him, but she needed to know for sure if Gabe was her half-brother before she said anything to either of them. If it were true, big brother might not be as thrilled to discover the truth as she would be.

Cam parked near the pavilion, and then escorted them over to where his family was waiting. Everyone lost their minds when they saw who was with them, and all three boys raced over—well, Jarrod toddled—to say hello to "Uncle" Gabe, who whisked Jarrod up in his arms before giving Jacob and Jeremy head ruffles and hugs.

She noticed Joss hung back a bit, her eyes alit with feminine interest as she gazed wistfully at her brother's friend.

Huh. Very interesting.

She glanced at Cam, who was hunched over chatting with his mother. When Marianne looked up and smiled, Harley suddenly knew exactly what they were talking about.

Her. Or more accurately, her and Cam.

She returned the older woman's smile before deftly turning to sweep Jacob into her arms. Joss' oldest seemed to have taken a liking to her, and frankly, she adored the little charmer right back. All three boys were amazing, but she'd quickly developed a special bond with Jacob.

"I want strawberry shortcake!" he announced once she set him back on his feet.

Joss reached them and smiled indulgently at her oldest boy. "Don't worry, little man, we're not leaving until they have to roll us out of here." She met Harley's gaze and added, "You may have to roll Cam out as well. Big brother can eat."

Harley laughed. "I know, right? It's a miracle he's so fit."

"It runs in the family. Mom's slim, and Dad didn't start to put on weight until he hit fifty."

Gabe walked over and handed Jarrod to Joss. His eyes lingered on the widowed brunette a little longer than necessary. Was something going on between Cam's widowed sister and his best friend?

Or was Harley simply adding a romantic plot to an innocent friendship? They had to have known each other since they were kids.

Cam and his mom finally joined them. He slipped an arm around Harley's shoulders and gave her a gentle squeeze. "Dad and Logan will be here soon. The old man had an eye appointment, and Mom asked Logan to drive him in case they give him those drops that make your pupils huge."

"I hate those," Joss said. "Turns everything into Chrome City."

"I'm hungry!" Jeremy announced, yanking on his uncle Cam's leg.

"Me, too, buddy." He swung his nephew up onto his shoulder and cast Harley a wink. "Ready to eat yourself sick?"

She cast one last glance at Gabe, then grinned. "Lead the way, Officer."

CHAPTER 12

It had been a long day of power eating, and one activity after another, and everyone was finally starting to wind down, getting ready to pack up and head home. Cam was pretty sure he'd spend most of the following day in a food coma, but it would be worth it. They hit half the food booths before the parade, and several afterward, sampling pasties, burgers, brats, pizza, and plenty of strawberry dishes, including everyone's favorite—strawberry shortcake. The boys participated in tons of games, arts and crafts, face-painting. The women danced with the kids to live music in the park, while Cam, Gabe, Logan, and Dad enjoyed the festival's famous trout boil. And his coworker's oldest daughter won Strawberry Queen, which was a great moment for the proud papa.

For Cam, the best part of the festival had been watching Harley interact with his family. She, Joss, and Mom all got along famously, and Dad kept winking at him—the universal sign of approval. She and Gabe had really clicked as well...though if he were the jealous type, he might have been a little insecure about how much time she'd spent with him. Whether they were playing with the boys, or huddled together in animated conversation, his girlfriend and his best friend had spent a lot of time together. Truth was, they were quite a bit alike, and that worried him on some level. Gabe had always been the more outgoing of the two, while Cam could be quiet and moody on occasion.

Boring, even, according to Joss.

His ex, Portia, had tired of him fast enough, if she'd ever loved him at all. Not that he gave a shit anymore. Hell, he wasn't entirely sure he'd ever truly loved her. But they'd dated the last couple years of high school, and when he'd decided to enlist, getting married before he deployed had seemed the next logical step. The thought of his loving wife waiting at home for him was what got him through a lot of rough days.

Then he'd come home for good, ready to start a family, only to discover her pregnant with the neighbor's kid.

Harley isn't Portia, he reminded himself. She'd been nothing but loving and giving, and he'd been happier than he had in years. But they hadn't made any declarations yet. Hell, they'd only been dating a few weeks.

Though he was pretty damn sure he was in love with her. Pretty. Damn. Sure. And while Harley was the most amazing woman he'd ever known, he had no fucking idea how she felt about him. What he did know is that they had great sex, liked a lot of the same things, and both his family and dog adored her.

He watched as Harley embraced his entire family, one person after another, and gave each of his nephews a kiss on the cheek to boot. And then she hugged Gabe, her eyes closed, her smile widening just the tiniest bit. His gut clenched as she embraced his longtime friend a second or two longer than necessary. When she pulled back, her eyes seemed a tad bright.

Christ...was she falling for his friend?

His insecurities kicked in again as he remembered how friendly Portia and their also-married neighbor had been, almost from the day they'd moved into the building. Hell, he'd been friendly with the guy, too, thinking it was nice to know Portia would have friends to help support her while he was deployed. He hadn't suspected a damn thing, and had been completely blindsided by their infidelity. No way in hell was he going through that shit again.

But this was Gabe, dammit. No way would he go after his woman, of that he was certain. And Harley was friendly with everyone. He was letting his self-doubt crowd his brain, and that could only lead to trouble. Maybe the loss of his longtime friend, and the woman he was falling in love with.

He gave himself a mental shake as Harley rushed over and slipped her arm through his. She gazed up at him, and the excitement shining in her eyes erased his doubts.

"Hey, man," Gabe called out. "Logan and I are gonna stop at Paddy's for a beer, and I'll just crash at his place, grab my truck in the morning, if that's all right?"

Before he could respond, Cam's cell buzzed in his pocket. He pulled it out and saw that the station was calling. Out of his peripheral he saw his father and brother both pull out their cells as well.

Logan and Gabe rushed over, Dad on their heels. "Looks like we have a hostage situation in the Bridgewater apartment complex," Logan said. "Since we're short-staffed, all available area officers have been called in. Even the chief here. I figure the three of us can ride together, and Mom can take Joss and the boys home."

Cam gave a curt nod as he slipped his phone back in his pocket. Tamping down what he knew were baseless worries, he met Gabe's gaze. "Since you have to head back to pick up your truck, would you mind driving Harley home?"

The question was rhetorical. He pulled out his keys and tossed them to his friend before turning to Harley. "I don't know how long we'll be, could be hours."

"Just be safe. And don't worry about Cleo, I still have some of her food from her last sleepover."

He smiled and kissed her, hard. "I'll text or call as soon as I get a chance."

The hostage situation involved an angry ex-husband who had been holding his ex-wife and their four children by gunpoint, and threatening a murder suicide. It took close to three hours to talk him down, with Logan doing most of the negotiating. First, he'd released the kids, and then finally broke down and released the children's mother. Fearful he would kill himself once alone, Cam had quickly slipped inside via an open bedroom window and was able to disarm him just as he squeezed off a shot.

The bullet grazed the back of the guy's head instead of entering his brain. He'd collapsed on the floor, sobbing while Cam called for an ambulance. The husband was taken to the hospital, while the woman and her children were taken to the Hancock police station, where a family member—the woman's mother—met them and took them to her home.

Once the paperwork was filled out, the three of them finally headed home, with Logan dropping Cam off first. Gabe's truck was still in Harley's driveway, and the lights were all out. Since she had given him a key to her front door the week before, he decided not to wake either of them up, and simply let himself in and locked the door behind him.

He was met by Cleo, who led him into the living room where Gabe was sprawled out on the sofa.

His friend sat up and wiped at his eyes. "Hey, man. So, what happened?"

Cam gave him the short version as he sat in the wing chair and stroked Cleo's head and back. "The desperation and just...pure heartache in the guy's eyes really took me by surprise."

"You saved his life."

He shrugged, not feeling much like a hero. "So, why are you still here instead of down at my parents' house? Not that I mind, but I'm sure Mom already had the guest room ready for you. Much comfier than this couch."

"Your lady was a bit freaked out, didn't want to be alone. We talked for a little while, then she offered to make me breakfast before heading up to bed." He grinned. "She chose my old room for her own."

For the first time since meeting his oldest friend on the playground in first grade, Cam had to force a smile. She'd offered to make him breakfast? "Yeah, I got a kick out of that as well. Listen, man, I'm beat. Has Cleo been out lately?"

"Had her out a couple hours ago," Gabe confirmed.

"Appreciate it. I'm heading up to bed. See you in the morning."

After a very quick shower, he slid into bed next to Harley.

She immediately snuggled her backside against him, spoon-style. "Everything turn out okay?" she whispered.

He slid one arm beneath her, and the other around her, pulling her as close as he could, needing her warmth. "As okay as it could be. I'll tell you about in the morning. Right now, I just want to hold you, and sleep as long as Cleo lets me."

She cuddled even closer, her sweet ass oh-so tempting. But with Gabe within earshot downstairs, he decided to save his last iota of energy, closed his eyes, and gave in to his exhaustion.

CHAPTER 13

"Here, let me help with something."

Harley was making a huge batch of banana pancakes and sausage patties, her father's favorite breakfast. When she'd suggested it to Gabe, he'd nearly floated off the ground with excitement. Could something like that be hereditary, liking the same foods? While she doubted it, the thought warmed her, bringing a smile to her face she almost couldn't contain. Not that she wanted to. This was the happiest she'd been in a long, long time.

The man she'd fallen madly in love with was sleeping soundly up in her bed, while his best friend—and more likely than not, her half-brother—was helping her make breakfast. It was all she could have hoped for and so much more.

She handed Gabe the rubber-coated tongs she used to turn the patties, then flipped two more perfectly golden-brown pancakes onto her Nana's ancient, blue and white-flowered platter. The coffee carafe was full and already on the table, as was maple syrup, butter, and a big bowlful of fresh blueberries and strawberries.

After setting the platter in the middle of the table, she spun around, and the kitchen tilted as her stomach roiled, sending her reeling. Gabe caught her around the waist just before she hit the floor. She clutched onto him for dear life, wrapping her arms around his neck as the dizziness overwhelmed her.

"Don't let me interrupt."

Harley glanced up in surprise, the sudden movement causing a fresh round of nausea and dizziness. She grasped the back of the chair, and Gabe assisted as she slowly slid onto the padded seat. What the hell…?

Cam stood frowning down at her, his arms crossed over his bare chest. "What's wrong? You don't look so good." He knelt down beside her and peered into her face. Talk about mortifying.

"I don't know." She swallowed, hard, then took a deep breath and let it out slowly. "I set the platter on the table, turned to go back for the sausage, and got super dizzy. Almost like I was going to faint. Thank God Gabe caught me."

He cast a quick glance behind her. "Yeah. Thank God." Cam pulled the chair next to her over and sat facing her. He grasped her hand, which took the sting out of his odd reaction. For a second there, she thought he was actually mad at her for getting sick. "Maybe we should run you in to Urgent Care, have you checked out."

She tried to wave his suggestion off, but the dizziness hadn't quite dissipated yet. "I'm sure I'm fine. I had a lot to eat yesterday, maybe something didn't agree with me."

He shook his head slowly, as if unconvinced. "I don't know. Seems like you would have been sick hours ago if that was the case."

"It can actually take anywhere from about four to twenty-four hours for food poisoning to take hold," Gabe informed them.

Cam's frown deepened.

After a few more deep breaths, the nausea passed, though Cam's strange reaction had her puzzled. "Seriously, I'm fine. Just a little dizzy spell. Maybe I have vertigo or something. Now, can we please enjoy the breakfast Gabe and I made."

"As if I did much of anything." He grinned at Cam. "She let me turn the sausages, suddenly I'm a master chef."

Cam chuckled. "Anything's an improvement over that slop you call chili. I swear, last time, some of the chunks of meat looked like roadkill—"

"Oh, my God." Harley shot to her feet and raced up the stairs into the bathroom, barely making it to the toilet in time. She vomited everything in her stomach, shocked by how quickly the nausea returned, and how intense.

When she was sure nothing else was coming up, she brushed her teethed, gargled with mouthwash, and washed her face with cool water, which felt amazing. Moving much slower, she made her way downstairs, careful not to meet the gazes of her two stunned guests as she took a seat at the table and topped off her coffee. She brought the mug to her lips, but her stomach churned as soon as she got a whiff, and she set it back down with a soft thud. Dammit, coffee was one of her favorite smells.

Cam and Gabe both took their seats at the table, but neither reached for any food.

She eyeballed both of them with frustration. Tears stung her eyes, but she quickly blinked them away. "I worked really hard on this breakfast. I don't want it to go to waste."

They shared a look of concern, which, for some reason, set her teeth on edge.

"Honey, are you sure you're okay?" Cam asked. "I still think—"

"I'm fine," she stubbornly insisted, even as a niggle of suspicion burrowed into her brain.

Her period had always been like clockwork, and if she'd done the math correctly, she was just over a week late. Not exactly uncommon in general. But still, the dizziness, the vomiting? As soon as she could get these two out of the house, she'd run to the drugstore for a pregnancy test. Just to eliminate that theory. They'd used protection every single time so she couldn't—

Wait. *Shit.* Except for that very first night. They'd made love twice, and hadn't used a condom the second time.

Cam and Gabe were both staring at her as if she'd grown horns. She knew her emotions showed on her face, and promptly effected a reassuring smile. She realized, thankfully, that her appetite seemed to have returned, so she picked up her fork and speared the top two pancakes. The sausage didn't seem like a good idea, but suddenly her mouth was watering for banana pancakes with fresh berries and maple syrup. After piling on both, she cut off a section with her fork and stuffed it in her mouth.

The two men shared another look, Cam shrugged, and they both started filling their plates. Harley ran that night over in her mind while the guys made small talk and ate with relish. She'd almost forgotten they hadn't used protection that second time, and doing the math, it had been right in the middle of her cycle. If she and Cam had been dating longer, she wouldn't feel so...unsure. But a month? Hell, she didn't even know how she felt about it, let alone worrying about Cam's reaction.

"Hey, you with us?" he asked, surprising her.

"Of course. You guys were talking about the best time of day for trolling. Gabe thinks just before dawn, you insist it's when the sun's at its peak."

She grinned, and they both burst out laughing.

As soon as breakfast was over, Gabe headed home to Iron Mountain, and, after making her reassure him she felt well enough for him to leave, Cam took Cleo home with a promise to return for supper. He needed to check in at the station, get the paperwork finished from the hostage situation, and then check in with his family.

Harley didn't waste any time and drove over the bridge to a drug store out of the way, just in case. With her luck, she'd run into Cam's mom, or Joss, if she headed to the local grocery store.

Once home, she headed up to the bathroom, read the instructions, and took the test. Those few minutes seemed to last forever, and she ran downstairs at one point to pour herself a glass of iced tea.

Truth was, she was afraid to look at the results. If she was in fact pregnant, her whole world would completely change. Again. The last time her life did a backflip, she'd lost her grandmother. This time, she'd be welcoming a child.

Cam's child.

A peaceful warmth coursed through her at the thought. She could easily envision a little boy who looked just like his father... though maybe with a few freckles. Any kid of hers would at least have some, even if his father didn't have any.

Cam a father. He would be amazing, of that she had no doubt. Starting a family with the man she loved would be a dream come true for most women, and Harley was no exception. But after only a month of dating? She wasn't only worried about how Cam would react, but what about his family? It killed her to think they might not be happy about it. They were wonderful people, and she knew they were as fond of her as she was them. But a baby after only a few weeks of dating?

Giving herself a mental kick in the pants, she forced herself back up the stairs to face her future.

She didn't realize she was holding her breath until her eyes landed on the stick, and it expelled from her lungs in a rush.

A blue plus sign. *Pregnant.*

Collapsing onto the edge of the tub, she picked the test up and stared at it. She knew these things were highly accurate, though she'd take the second one in a few hours, just to be sure. All the signs were there. Even her breasts were oddly tender.

A surprise surge of happiness nearly overwhelmed her. She wanted this baby. Wanted it more than she ever could have imagined.

Harley palmed her flat tummy and wondered if she would have a little boy like the one she'd been imaging, or maybe a little girl with her own ginger locks and freckled complexion. *Maybe both,* she thought, since her Nana had been a twin. Would Cam have a preference? He sure did love those nephews of his. Having a little girl would certainly throw him for a loop.

The thought brought a smile to her face and tears to her eyes.

Okay, so tonight, after dinner, she'd tell him. It seemed a little prophetic that she was making the chicken and rice casserole she'd made the night they'd first slept together. The night they'd created the little one growing inside her. Could it be a sign Cam would be just as happy as she was?

Harley sure hoped so.

CHAPTER 14

Cleo raced out of the house and straight for the Jeep, her enthusiasm to see that squirrel-sized little playboy almost as strong as his to see Harley. Cam had barely gotten the passenger door open before she squeezed in past him and jumped up onto the seat. He laughed as he shut the door and strode around the vehicle. It was about quarter to seven, so they still had a couple hours of sunlight left, and he enjoyed the view of the lake as he drove down Highway 41 into town.

Harley's place, like his parents', was only about a ten-minute ride, and as always, he couldn't wait to lay eyes on her. Man, did he have it bad. Which scared the hell out of him since he couldn't seem to get it out of his mind how she'd fawned over Gabe. He wanted to have full confidence in the woman he was quickly falling in love with, but he knew he hadn't imagined the way she gazed at his friend. Almost wistfully.

He was hoping they could talk tonight, clear the air and settle any misgivings he had. Trust was the one thing he still grappled with, and he wanted to trust her, wanted to believe this woman was worth fighting for. Though, who was he really fighting but himself? Gabe would never do anything to hurt him, of that Cam had no doubt. But he'd known Gabe for years—decades, actually—and he trusted him like a brother. It was his beautiful redhead who had him feeling all kinds of insecure.

He pulled into her driveway, and before they'd even reached the porch, the front door flew open. Harley stood there as beautiful as always, wearing jeans and a turquoise blue T-shirt that fit her to perfection. Her coppery hair hung down past her shoulders, and she swiped it back as Cleo reached her and waited to be acknowledged before running inside to see her friend. He almost sighed like a teenage dork as he climbed the steps.

She threw her arms around his neck and grinned up at him, her happiness infectious, and doing a lot to assuage his doubts.

"Guess what I made?"

He hoisted her up and carried her inside before giving the air a sniff. Damn, it smelled good. His brow dipped. "Is it that chicken casserole you made for my family?"

"Yep. And I made a loaf of the bread, and green bean casserole as well. I remember how much you liked it."

Cam gazed down at her, his heart full. He kissed her, hard, making her giggle.

"Save it for later, Officer, my dinner's getting cold."

He laughed and gently set her on her feet. "Sounds good. I'm starving."

"You're always starving," she pointed out as she led the way into the kitchen.

Cam sat in what had become his unofficial chair. He felt comfortable here. He always had, but now it was in a completely unexpected way. Harley sat across from him, and scooped a big helping of the fragrant casserole onto his plate, then some green beans. When she buttered a slice of bread for him, he grinned. She'd make a great mother someday.

Fuck. Kids. Not a subject he was ready to deal with. Thankfully, that conversation shouldn't come up for a while.

His phone vibrated. He pulled it from his pocket and glanced at the screen—Anna Harrison, Gabe's mom. "Hello?"

"Cam, Gabe's been shot. He's in surgery right now and I'm scared, he looked so pale, so—"

He froze, his blood running cold. "Anna, he's going to be fine," Cam insisted, refusing to believe anything else. He met Harley's concerned gaze, as he said, "I'll be there as soon as I can." Iron Mountain was a good two hour ride from Houghton. "I thought he didn't have to work until Monday?"

"It didn't happen at work. He was picking up burgers at that sports bar on the corner when a fight broke out. Gabe tried to break it up...and he was shot in the chest."

The last word came out as a sob, and Cam shot to his feet. "Anna, listen to me, he's going to be okay. I'll be there in a couple hours." With that Cam ended the call and crammed his phone into his front jeans pocket.

"What happened?" Harley asked, her voice a near whisper.

"It's Gabe." Christ, he could barely get the words out. His mouth felt dry as dust. "He was shot. I'm sorry about dinner, but I have to go. His mom...she's all alone."

Her hands flew to her mouth; her eyes widened, reddened. "Oh, my God. Is he...is he okay?" She stood and gripped the edge of the table.

"He's in surgery. He was shot in the fuckin' chest." His arms started shaking and he fisted his hands in an effort to remain calm, not lose his shit.

"Oh, my God," she repeated, her voice cracking. She raced over and threw her arms around him.

It shook him to realize she was sobbing. He crushed her in his arms even as he puzzled over her reaction. But he didn't have time to worry about any of that, he needed to get on the road. "I'm sorry, but I have to go."

She tore away from him, rubbed at her eyes, and grabbed her purse off the chair before hurrying past him to the front door. He quickly followed and found her slipping into her white tennis shoes.

"I'm coming with you."

She met his gaze with that determination he'd come to know and dread.

"It's a two hour ride, one way. I'm sure I won't be home until late, if not tomorrow. And what about the dogs?"

"I have pads down by the back-patio door, and I'll drop my key off with your mom. I'm sure she'll take care of the dogs tonight if we need her to." With that she strode out the door.

Dropping her key off gave him the opportunity to fill his parents in on Gabe, whom they loved like a son. With a promise to take the dogs out before bed, they hurried him off to go to Gabe and be by his mother's side.

They arrived at the hospital a few minutes after nine, and Mrs. Harrison was waiting for him just inside the ER doors. She looked tired, her eyes red-rimmed and a fresh flood of tears spilled down her cheeks as he approached.

Anna wiped them away with a clump of tissues, then cast Harley a curious glance before reaching for him.

"Cammy, I'm so glad you were able to come."

He gave her a quick hug, then pulled back to gaze down at her. "What's going on? Is he still in surgery?"

She gave her hand a frustrated wave. "I have no idea. I assume so. The nurse said the surgeon will come talk to me as soon as they're done."

"He's gonna be fine, you know. Tough as nails, just like his mother."

Just as he'd hoped, a small smile curved the older woman's lips.

"And as stubborn as his father."

Cam felt a hand slip into his, and realized he hadn't introduced Harley. He kissed her palm and apologized with his eyes. "Anna, I'd like you to meet my friend, Harley. Harley, this is Gabe's mom, Anna Harrison."

He heard sniffling and realized Harley was in tears again. She'd been more emotional than he'd expected, and as much as he hated such insecurities, he couldn't help wondering why she was so upset. Of course, it was a terrible situation, and anyone would feel sympathy. But she was acting as if...as if she'd known Gabe for years, when she'd only just met him the day before.

She stepped forward and gave his friend's mom a hug. "I'm so sorry," he heard her whisper with a quaver in her voice.

"Thank you, Harley." Anna attempted a smile, for his benefit, he had no doubt. "I appreciate you coming. I know Cam can use the support. Gabe told me all about you. He seemed quite smitten."

Harley wiped at her eyes and smiled. "I really like him, too. He's a great guy. Charming and handsome. And really funny."

He clenched his jaw as the green-eyed monster reared its ugly head. Dammit, his best friend was fighting for his life, and here he was thinking petty thoughts.

Anna cast him a curious sidelong glance. "He's definitely all those things and more." She cleared her throat, then waved toward the waiting room. "Why don't we sit. I'd love to talk, about anything. I need to keep my thoughts positive or I'll drive myself crazy."

Cam walked them both into the waiting area, but didn't want to sit after two hours in the car. "I'm gonna grab a soda. Can I get either of you anything?"

"I've already had a couple cups of coffee, but thanks."

He looked at Harley, who was staring at Anna as if trying to solve a mystery.

"Harley, can I get you a soda, or bottle of water?"

Her brow cleared and she met his gaze. "Water would be great, thank you."

Needing a minute to get himself under control, Cam went in search of a beverage vending machine. He was worried about Gabe, and when he returned, a tall, reedy guy in scrubs was already speaking with Anna. She grasped his hand, her expression hard to read. "He's out of surgery and in recovery."

Cam looked to the doctor to elaborate.

"Officer Harrison was very lucky. The bullet passed straight through his lower chest, missed his kidney and liver. He lost quite a bit of blood, but the damage was minimal. We'll know more once he wakes up."

"How long will that take?" Anna asked.

"Between thirty minutes and an hour is my best guess. We'll let you know as soon as he's awake." He gave them a reassuring smile and then strode off.

Cam gave Anna a hug. "It's good news."

"He lost so much blood, though. I got here as they were wheeling him in to surgery. He was unconscious, didn't even know I was there."

"He knew. And he's strong as an ox. He's going to be fine, Anna. I'm absolutely sure of that."

Harley approached, slowly, as if she didn't want to intrude. Anna wrapped an arm around her, and the three of them hugged. Cam leaned down and gave his thoughtful librarian a kiss on the lips. Her eyes widened as she cast a meaningful glance at Anna. If Gabe had told his mom about Harley, then she already knew the gorgeous redhead was his girlfriend.

Cam led them back over to the padded chairs by the coffee station. He sat between them and scrubbed his fingers through his hair. "I can't believe this happened at Hogan's. It's a freakin' cop hangout."

Anna shrugged, as if just as stunned. "It was Jack who called me. At first, I thought he was joking." Jack was a fellow officer in Iron Mountain police department, and she and his mother were good friends.

She twisted the straps on her purse, the strain of the situation showing on her face as she struggled to keep her composure.

He gave her a quick side hug. "He's going to be fine."

The older woman gave a tremulous smile and leaned her head on his shoulder. He made eye contact with Harley, who had been surprisingly quiet. He realized her eyes were red and swollen; she'd been crying, emphasized by a clump of tissues clutched in her hand. He tamped down his worries and twined his fingers with hers. She laid her head on his other shoulder. That's how the nurse found them a short time later.

"The surgeon asked me to tell you Officer Harrison is awake," she informed them with a big smile. "He'll come get you as soon as he finishes his evaluation."

"Thank you," Anna said, relief lightening her tone.

With a grateful nod, Cam forced his doubts to the back of his mind, but knew he'd have to talk with Harley as soon as they were alone. Either he was losing his mind, or his lovely librarian was falling for his best friend.

CHAPTER 15

Harley's breath came out in a rush at the news, her relief nearly doubling her over. Terrified of losing another possible family member—the brother she'd only just found—she been out of her mind with worry. But he'd made it through surgery, and was awake, thank God, so she felt as if she could finally breathe again.

Gabe had already been transferred to a room by the time the surgeon returned. It was hard holding her emotions in check, but somehow she managed as first Anna wept softly over her son, who held her hand and attempted to smile, and then Cam, whom she'd never seen so emotional before. It warmed her to see just how close the two men were, and assuming she was right about Gabe being her half-brother, Harley would forever be a believer in fate.

While Anna fawned over her son, who still had a breathing tube inserted, Cam came over and hugged her, the warmth of his embrace making her feel safe and content. To quote a sappy movie, he completed her.

And baby makes three.

In an instinct as old as time, her hand moved to her stomach.

She decided she would still give him the news tonight. Good news to sort of balance out the bad.

Miraculously, as there had been no real damage to Gabe's lungs, the surgeon was able to remove his breathing tube within the hour. He also predicted a full recovery in four to six weeks.

Cam had stepped out of the room to answer a call, and Anna went in search of a restroom. When she looked at Gabe, she realized he was motioning her forward with a wave of his fingers. She approached the bed slowly, her heart clenching as fresh tears stung her eyes. She could have lost him, just like that. One minute they're sharing breakfast, getting acquainted, the next, he's in a hospital bed with a bullet wound in his chest.

Her facial expressions always gave her away, so she forced a smile and came around to stand next to the bed. "You've looked better." she teased, managing to keep her voice level.

He smiled, which quickly became a grimace. "I've felt better. Seems I was pretty lucky."

"*Very* lucky," she confirmed. "I thought Cam was going to break the speed of light getting us here."

"Are you pregnant?"

Stunned over the question, she almost bit her tongue. "What? Why—"

"It's summer, not really the time for viruses," he explained, his words coming out slowly, his voice raspy from the anesthesia. "And food poisoning seemed a stretch after your appetite returned. Pregnancy seemed the next logical conclusion."

She considered denying it, having not even told Cam yet, because it seemed unfair for Gabe to find out first. But she knew her eyes had probably already answered his question for her. "I was planning to tell Cam tonight, after supper, but then we got the call and..." She shrugged; they both knew what call she was talking about.

"Don't change the plan on my account." His smile was weak, but bright. "Believe me, he's going to be thrilled."

She stared at him, hope filling her chest. "You think so?"

"I know so."

He sounded confident, and he certainly knew Cam better than she did. All she could do was hope he was right.

Anna returned to the room and came over to stand on Gabe's other side. She felt his brow and then his cheek. "How do you feel?"

"Like I got shot in the chest with a .22 caliber handgun. I'm just glad the punk didn't have a 9mm."

His mother pursed her lips. "Not funny."

He chuckled, then grimaced.

"See? That's what you get for trying to be Mr. Comedian."

Harley had to force herself not to react. Good Lord, she'd been an emotional basket case all day. Pregnancy hormones?

The door swung open and Cam strode in. "Looks like someone is feeling better."

Gabe waved his friend over. "Can you do me a favor? Take Mom home, then you and Harley head home as well. I've got a lot of sleeping to do if I'm going to be out of here anytime soon."

"Gabriel, we both know I'm not going anywhere. Besides, I have my car here." She slanted a look at Cam. "But I agree about you and Harley heading back to Houghton. It's late, and I'm sure your mother doesn't want to have to scrape that neurotic dog of yours off the ceiling when you don't come home."

Harley bit back a grin over the visual.

"Believe it or not, Cleo is an angel for my mom. I think she's just scared of you." Cam winked at Harley, then asked Anna, "Do you need me to run to the house for anything before we leave? Maybe feed Queenie?"

"No, Cammy, but thank you. Her dishes were both full when I left, and all I need is a pillow and blanket, which the hospital has plenty of in stock."

He nodded, then walked around the bed to lay a gentle hand on his friend's shoulder. "I'll be back tomorrow afternoon, no doubt with the whole family."

Tears stung Harley's eyes again, and she blinked like a madwoman, not wanting to worry Cam.

Gabe gave his head a weak shake. "I appreciate it, but it's not necessary. I'm gonna be just fine."

"Mom and Dad will drive themselves if I don't bring them, you know that. And Joss and the boys will no doubt come as well. But don't worry, I won't let them climb up on the bed."

"Good luck with that," Anna teased.

Harley moved in and gave Gabe's arm a rub. She wanted to pull him into a hug, but knew she'd have to explain everything, and this certainly wasn't the time or the place for that conversation. She gave him one last lingering look, then turned and wiped at her eyes.

Cam nodded at his friend, gave Anna a quick hug, then walked out of the room without so much as a glance in Harley's direction.

She knew he was scared for his friend, even though the doctor assured them Gabe would make a full recovery, so she tried not to take it to heart. He was waiting for her at the elevators, and as the doors opened, she grasped his hand.

The first ten minutes of the drive, Cam was unusually quiet, but then this was no usual situation. Though the outcome had been best case scenario, his dearest friend had been shot in the chest and could have died.

Deciding to trust Gabe's assessment of how Cam would take the news of his impending fatherhood, she took a deep silent breath and grasped his hand. "We need to talk." Crap, not exactly the way she'd planned to open. "I have something to tell you."

He cast her a quick glance, his preoccupation evident. He was still worried about Gabe. Hopefully, once she told him her news, and they had time to talk about it, make some decisions about the future, he'd feel better.

"What is it?"

He seemed he had a death grip on the steering wheel.

Deep breath in...and release. "Cam...I'm pregnant."

He swung his head and gaped at her. "What did you say?"

Her pulse sped up—he didn't sound the least bit happy. But

Gabe knew him, was sure he'd be thrilled. Maybe she was reading too much into his initial response.

"Look, I know it doesn't seem possible, we've only been together—"

"How do you even know it's mine? We've been dating for five minutes."

She froze. Pulled her hand from his. She couldn't have heard him right. "What the hell did you just ask me?"

He swiped his fingers through his hair, cursed under his breath. "We always use protection, how—"

"I thought the same thing," she bit out, her emotions doing a sharp turn. "Apparently, we both forgot about that first night. We didn't use a condom the second time."

He was silent, which broke her heart. He honestly didn't think the baby was his. How she hated him at that moment. She'd been so full of hope, imagining a wonderful future together where they got married, had three or four kids.

Cam tried to grasp her hand, but she pulled it from his reach and crossed her arms over her chest. Tears started slipping from her eyes, and she quickly swiped them away, hoping to God he hadn't seen them. But she knew he had. She could see him glancing at her in her peripheral vision.

"Do you have feelings for Gabe?"

She swung her head, stunned. Where the hell did that come from? "What in the world are you asking me?"

He cast her a sidelong glance. "You were practically flirting with him at the festival. I told myself you're just a friendly person, but when I told you Gabe got shot... You've only known him for two days, but you were emotional as if"—he threw up a hand in frustration—"someone you love got shot or something."

Harley almost laughed, and would have if her heart wasn't breaking. How he could actually think something so absurd infuriated her. The rational side of her brain reminded that, regardless of his prophetic comment, Cam had no idea she and Gabe might be siblings. And yes, she had been talking to him a lot, getting to know him, hoping for a tidbit of info that might confirm or deny her theory. She had thought Cam a bit quiet yesterday, but she never dreamed it was jealousy over her spending time with Gabe.

He tried to put his hand on her leg, but she flinched away from his touch. "Maybe I was upset because I care about you, and you'd just found out your best friend was shot." Just thinking about that moment made her blood chill in her veins. And while there was more to her visceral reaction, she *had* been upset on his behalf, as well as her own personal reasons.

Cam was quiet after that, which was fine with her. She just wanted to get home and crawl into bed. Alone. But when he pulled into her driveway over an hour later, he got out of the Jeep and followed her to the front door. She heard deep barking and remembered then that Cleo was inside.

She unlocked the door and reached in to flip on the light in the foyer. Cleo jumped up to greet Cam, just as Toby ran into her arms. The familiar gesture almost made her weep, and she wasn't sure if it was her hormones, the events of the last two hours, or both. All she knew was that she was exhausted, both mentally and physically, and hoped he would leave without trying to talk things out.

"Look, we need to talk about this."

Of course, he did. She wanted to scream, but knew it would only lead to crying, and she'd done enough of that for the night. Frustration warred with exhaustion. "No, we don't. I'm tired and want to go to bed."

"Maybe I reacted badly," he pressed, "but you *were* flirting with Gabe. I'm not the only one who noticed."

Hurt, she waited for him to elaborate, but the truth hit her almost immediately. "Joss?"

"She only mentioned you seemed a little infatuated with him."

"That's funny coming from her."

He frowned. "What's that supposed to mean?"

"Nothing. None of your business." She knew she sounded petty, but didn't really give a shit. She'd done nothing other than engage in conversation with Gabe, and if Cam—or a jealous Joss—saw that as flirting, that was their problem. With the exception of his youngest sister, his entire family had been there, including his mom and dad, for God's sake. He honestly thought she was the type to hit on his friend right in front of his parents?

Her eyes burned as tears pooled in her eyes again, and she spun around in frustration. Damn hormones! She heard him move a second before his hands settled gingerly on her shoulders.

"Sweetheart, I'm sorry. I'd have to explain my failed marriage to you for you to understand why I said what I did. And I'd much rather spend the night holding you."

So, he had been married before, and it obviously didn't end well. But that had nothing to do with her. "I don't give a damn about your ex, and how dare you compare me to her. If I'd done the same, assumed you were going to do what one of *my* loser exes did, I wouldn't have even told you about the baby. I would have simply waited for you to leave me when someone prettier came along."

"Well then you must've dated nothing but idiots. You're the most beautiful woman I've ever known. Inside and out."

God, how she wanted to believe him. "You're not wrong about the dating idiots part." She turned to face him. "And just to be clear, you're the only man I've slept with in well over a year. So yes, I am *positive* this baby is yours."

She started for the stairs, but stopped in her tracks as her eyes landed on the picture of Cam and Gabe she'd discovered in the cubby, which she'd tacked onto the wall. *Dammit*. She needed to tell him the truth about Gabe. Or what she'd come to hope was the truth. After a quick glance in his general direction, she turned back around and knelt in front of her Nana's antique coffee table to retrieve one of her cherished photo albums. She laid it on the table and flipped through several pages until she found the photo she was looking for. After plucking it from its pocket, she walked back to Cam and handed it to him.

His brow lifted in curiosity as he took it from her. The picture had been taken at Great America in the late eighties, when her father had been about fifteen. Cam stared at it, his eyes shifting from the photo, to her, then back to the photo again. "I don't get it. This looks like Gabe, but...where did you get this?"

"That's my father. William Lawson. The reason I came to Houghton County was to search for my half-brother. A brother I never even knew existed until my Nana died, and I found her old bible with an entry below my father's name and next to mine that said 'Baby Boy Lawson' and the year he was born. The only lead I had was my father attended Michigan Tech, which is why I decided to move here. When I found that picture of you and Gabe in the cubby under the stairs, I was stunned."

After one last look, Cam handed her back the photo. "Gabe's middle name is William." He propped his hands on his hips. "Why the hell didn't you just tell me?"

Her shoulders slumped with relief over finally having this out in the open. Especially now that she knew he'd completely misinterpreted her interest in Gabe.

"Because I had no idea if it was true, or just wishful thinking on my part. I mean, I end up buying my half-brother's childhood home? It sounds insane. And if it *is* true, but Gabe doesn't know, I didn't want to disrupt his life. And I didn't want to put you in that position either. You would have felt obligated to tell him."

"This is...nuts." He combed his fingers through his hair and blew out a hard breath. "Look, it's late. Can we please go upstairs and get some sleep? Tomorrow, you can head back to the hospital with me and talk to Anna privately."

"I had planned to head back there to do just that. But I'm not sharing my bed with you. Go home, Officer. I need time to myself."

"Harley—"

"Please."

He swallowed, gave a curt nod, then whistled for Cleo and strode out the door.

She locked it behind them, collapsing against the wall as exhaustion settled in. She loved him, but the man had issues with trust. And the last thing she wanted to do was pay for another woman's mistakes.

But they were going to have a baby together, so she couldn't just walk away from the situation.

As a host of emotions assailed her, Harley dragged her butt up the stairs and slid under the comforter. Tomorrow, she'd figure everything out. Tonight, she just wanted to sleep.

CHAPTER 16

Harley had woken up early despite sleeping like the dead for a few hours. She'd decided to drive to Iron Mountain alone, knowing Anna would be by her son's side. When she'd stepped off the elevator, she had been lucky enough to catch the older woman pouring herself a cup of coffee at the nurses' beverage station.

"Good morning, Harley." Anna smiled, then glanced past her, no doubt wondering why she was alone. "Cam miss the elevator?"

"No, I'm here by myself. How is Gabe?" She filled a small plastic cup with water from the dispenser.

A curious smile lifted one corner of Anna's mouth. "He's tired and sore, but very happy to be alive. Thanks for asking. Is there something I can do for you?"

"I was hoping we could talk."

"Um, sure." She snapped a plastic lid onto her coffee cup. "Of course. What's on your mind?"

"Was Gabe's biological father's name William Lawson?"

The color drained from Anna's face, and just like that, Harley had her answer.

"How did...how could you possibly know that?"

She glanced around to make sure they didn't have an audience. "Can we go sit down so I can explain?"

The older woman nodded, her expression guarded as she walked past her into the empty waiting room.

Harley decided not to waste time. "William Lawson was my father."

"Was?"

"He died years ago in a motorcycle accident." As always, just saying it made her heart ache.

Anna covered her mouth and blinked several times as if fighting back tears. Had she loved her dad?

"I'm so sorry. I had no idea he'd passed."

"Thank you. It's been a long time, but I miss him every day."

Harley took a sip of her water as they shared a moment of awkward silence.

"I never knew my mother," Harley finally continued. "And last year I lost my grandmother, who was my last living relative." She explained how she'd come to learn of Gabe's existence, and how Michigan Tech had been her only lead.

Anna closed her eyes for a moment, then took a cautious sip of her coffee before setting the cup on the table and meeting Harley's gaze.

"Will and I met freshman year. We had a computer science class together. One night, we were studying in his room and...we slept together. Just the one time. When I found out I was pregnant, well, it wasn't exactly the best news. We were both so young. Deciding to give the baby up for adoption was a hard decision, but we weren't in love or anything." She shrugged. "It seemed the best solution for both of us. But...as the months went by, I realized I couldn't do it. I couldn't give up my baby. I was about four months along when I dropped out of school and headed back home to Iron Mountain."

"I'm not judging," Harley began, choosing her words carefully. "But why didn't you just tell my dad how you felt?"

"Harley, I don't want to say anything unkind about your father. I respected him; he was a really nice guy. But he was adamant that if forced to support a child, he'd have to drop out of college. We were both eighteen, so young, and I didn't want to burden him like that. The day I gave birth, I called to tell him, promised our son was with a good family...and that was the last time we spoke."

Harley was silent as the story came to an end. She was grateful Anna had decided to keep Gabe. That one action was what eventually led her here to Houghton County, to her half-brother—and to the man she loved. She slid a hand to cover her stomach. In that moment, she understood how Anna must have felt.

But Cam wasn't an indebted, teenaged college student. He was a grown man, an Army veteran, an officer of the law. A responsible human being. He was also an idiot, but she could forgive him for that. And he'd been right, they needed to sit down and talk things through so they could make plans for the future.

But first, she was really hoping to get an official introduction to her brother.

"Does Gabe know any of this?"

"He knows everything except Will's last name. I was afraid Gabe might try to look him up one day." A smile had lit up her face. "But maybe it's time for him to meet his sister."

Her chest swelled with anticipation. At that moment, Harley was as happy as she'd ever been. "I would really like that."

"I don't know what the fuck's wrong with me," Cam admitted as he gazed out his friend's hospital room window.

"I wouldn't even know where to begin with that one," Gabe teased, his voice still a bit raspy. He definitely sounded better this morning, and some of his color had even returned.

Cam had stopped at Harley's place in the morning only to discover her gone. Since it was only eight a.m., a moment of panic set in. But then he heard Toby barking his heart out, and knew she'd never leave her beloved 'little man' behind. Had she driven down to Iron Mountain to speak with Anna? He knew his parents planned to head down in the afternoon, so he hopped in his Jeep and headed south on US-41. Thankfully, his hunch had been right, and she'd been in Gabe's room sitting beside his bed, sharing a story about their father.

Well, until Cam arrived. The feisty redhead quickly excused herself as soon as she glanced up and saw him.

"I realized how comfortable you two were with each other," Cam confessed. "How she seemed to fawn all over you, and all I could think about was Portia and the neighbor."

"Portia was an unfaithful bitch," Gabe bluntly reminded. "She cheated on you in high school, and you forgave her, something I never understood. And it wasn't just that. She was selfish, mean, never gave a shit about you or anyone else."

Cam nodded, knowing his friend was right. He'd been a fool, and that was on him. With Portia, the signs were always there. Unfortunately, his dick had ruled his head back then.

"I'm an idiot, I get it. I'm sorry I doubted Harley, but even more, I'm sorry I doubted you. It's just...Harley is beautiful; fucking stunning. Anyone would be attracted to her, and that scared me."

"You didn't notice how much we look alike?" Gabe cocked a brow. "I think the real question here is—have you secretly had the hots for me all these years?"

Cam flipped him off, and his buddy chuckled—which was followed by a grimace.

"Good, you asshole. And it was a perfectly legit question."

"It was an asinine question coming from a perfectly asinine idiot. As if I would ever do something like that...and to *you* of all people." He sighed. "I still can't wrap my head around it. I have a sister, and she's dating my best friend."

Cam blew out a hard breath. "Yeah, I'm not sure if that last part's true anymore."

"Buck up, man. She'll forgive you. It's pretty clear she's crazy about you. Funny that you thought she was flirting with me at the festival, when all she did was talk about you. I almost got a damn toothache listening to her go on and on and on."

That gave him a glimmer of hope.

"So, I suddenly feel like it's my job to say this...but you're going to marry her, right?"

Cam met his friend's gaze, and it suddenly struck him just how much his life had changed in such a short amount of time. He was in love, and...he was going to be a father. The thought brought on such a rush of happiness in nearly brought him to his knees. "She told you about the baby?"

"I was a little curious how she could be sick as a dog one minute, then scarf down pancakes the next. Then Mom mentioned she kept holding her stomach."

"She's not even speaking to me," Cam pointed out. "Not sure how I'm supposed to propose if she won't look at me or talk to me. And hell, we've only been dating a little over a month. She'll probably tell me to go scratch."

The ass grinned. "Maybe. But if you don't screw things up again, I think I might have an idea."

Cam hoped it was a good one since his future might well depend on it.

When Harley returned to Gabe's hospital room, Cam and Anna were both gone. Disappointment settled in her chest like a boulder. She hadn't known what to say to him when he'd first arrived, and a wave of nausea had hit at that moment, buying her a little time. But she hadn't expected him to be gone by the time she got back, especially after a two-hour drive. Was he really that desperate to get away from her?

"So, what should I call you? Sis? Sissy?"

She took a sip of her bottled water and forced a smile for Gabe. "Harley will be just fine. What about you? Do you prefer Bro? Broman?"

He grinned. "You'll be calling me Uncle Gabe soon enough."

She glared over the reminder. "I don't want to talk about it."

"Do you love him?"

"I…don't know. I thought I did, but…" She stood and went to gaze out the window at nothing in particular. "Cam actually asked me if the baby was his." She spun around and glared at her newly found brother. "How could he ask me such a thing?"

Gabe's gaze was kind as he waved her back over to sit. "Has he told you anything about his ex?"

Harley plopped back down and shook her head before casting a hopeful glance toward the door. "He mentioned her last night, but we haven't had a chance to talk since then. I thought we might talk today, but he obviously didn't want to." She muttered the last part under her breath.

"Cam met Portia in high school. I never really cared for her, but that's another story. She wasn't happy when he told her he'd enlisted, so he proposed, figured it would make her happy. Too bad she wasn't nearly as worried about *his* happiness."

"She sounds awful."

He laughed. "That she was. Worse, she was a cheater. When Cam retired from the Army, he came home and found her in bed with their neighbor. And she was pregnant. It crushed him, Harley. Took him a long time to get over it. The humiliation more than anything else, since I'm not sure he ever really loved her."

Her heart broke for Cam as she imagined what it must have felt like to come home from serving his country only to discover his wife pregnant by another man. Suddenly his ill-timed question made sense. It still hurt, but to be fair, they'd only been together such a short time. For all he knew, she could have been pregnant when they met. Maybe that's where the question came from, not that he thought she'd been sleeping around Houghton.

"I feel like maybe I overreacted. It just…it hurt for him to ask me that."

"Because you love him."

She did. More than she'd ever thought possible. "It seems crazy considering we really barely know each other, but I do love him. And I had envisioned such a different scenario when I told him about the baby, like him proposing or something." She laughed softly at her unbelievable notion.

Gabe's smile faltered as a grimace wracked his face.

Harley stood and hovered over him. "What is it? Is something wrong? Are you in pain?"

He waved away her concern, though she could tell he was just trying not to worry her.

"I'm okay. Probably just need a nap. Christ, I feel like an old frickin' man."

"Is there anything I can do?" She glanced at the door, curious to know where Anna had gone.

"Mom went in to work for a few hours," he said, reading her mind. "But knowing her, she'll be back by lunch. Why don't you head home, get some rest? I don't mean to seem ungrateful after you drove all this way to see me, but I'm beat, and I don't want you to hear how badly I snore."

"Too late." She gave a sheepish grin. "You were snoring when I got here." Harley hooked her purse over her shoulder. An odd thought struck her that once the baby was here, she'd have to put away her stylish, black handbag for a tote bag. A smile tugged at her lips. "Okay, big bro. You get some rest, and once I get home, I'll do the same." She gave his arm a gentle pat, and then headed out.

She owed Cam an apology, and she sure would love a second chance to tell him about the baby. A do-over. And since the fastest way to a man's heart was his stomach, she'd attempt to invite him over and knock him on his ass with a delicious pot roast dinner, then sit him down for a hard talk—find out how he truly felt about her. And their baby.

With the sun high in the beautiful blue, cloudless sky, the drive home seemed a lot faster than the one to Iron Mountain. Maybe because she felt hopeful again. Her thoughts had been so negative when she'd left for the hospital early that morning. She'd been worried about Gabe, heartbroken over Cam, nervous to talk with Anna.

But now, she knew for certain Gabe would make a full recovery.

And while he'd been astonished by his mother's announcement that Harley was his sister, he couldn't have been happier and more welcoming. Anna, too, had been amazing. Harley hadn't known what to expect when she'd first started the conversation. But as they talked about her father, the older woman turned to gaze out the window, and Harley was reminded of that picture she'd discovered at the college. Anna and her father may not have been in love, but she truly believed their coming together had been fated.

Because she wasn't alone in the world anymore.

She rested her hand on her stomach. Her family was suddenly growing by leaps and bounds, and if she and Cam could work things out, maybe she'd have even more family one day...

By the time Harley pulled into the driveway, she was feeling good, in both body and spirit, the earlier nausea having finally passed. She unlocked the front door and opened it—and nearly jumped out of her skin when she realized she wasn't alone. Thankfully, it was Houghton's sexiest cop who stood in her living room, and he was holding Toby.

Her little man was barking and wriggling to be free, and Cam finally set him down. As Toby raced toward her, that's when she noticed he was wearing a baby bib that read, *Will you*, which looked like it had been written in black marker. Her gaze moved to Cleo, who also wore a bib, and hers read, *Marry my daddy*.

Harley covered her mouth, and promptly burst into tears.

CHAPTER 17

Stunned, Cam rushed to Harley's side and wrapped his arms around her. An odd thought struck him that she was even beautiful when she cried. "That wasn't exactly the reaction I was hoping for. Are you okay?"

She nodded against his chest, then used his T-shirt to wipe her eyes. He laughed aloud at that, loving the quirky redhead more and more by the minute.

Harley's gaze moved back and forth between the dogs, and then a beautiful smile transformed her face. She looked up at him, then back at Cleo and Toby. "Was Gabe in on this by any chance? He did seem eager for me to head home."

"Maybe. He's your brother and thought I should make an honest woman out of you."

Her smile faltered and she took a step back. "So, this is about you trying to please Gabe?"

"No! Of course not. Sweetheart, I'm crazy about you. I *love* you. I was in a bad place in my head last night when you told me about the baby, and I said something I will be forever sorry for." He stepped forward and placed his palm over her tummy. The realization that his child grew inside her filled him with an inner peace, as if this moment was healing the past. "I have no doubt this baby is mine, and I want to marry his or her mother because I love her. I love *you*. Both of you."

More tears spilled down her cheeks. She wiped them away with the back of her hand before gazing at him with a watery smile. "I love you, too."

Cam crushed her in his arms as a sense of contentment nearly overwhelmed him. It was all he could do to keep from losing his shit and bawling like a baby. Home, hearth, and a family of his own were all in the cards for him after all, and suddenly he wholeheartedly believed in destiny.

"Does your family know?" she asked as she pulled back to take another glance at the dogs.

"Yeah. I hope that's all right. I actually borrowed the bibs from Joss."

"Well, you'll have to replace them because I'm saving these. In fact, we should get some pictures of those two." She grabbed her purse and pulled out her phone.

"I already did." He pulled her back into his arms. "Does this mean you'll marry me?"

She twined her arms around his neck. "Yes."

Cam laughed, happier than he'd ever thought possible. Once a fool, always a fool? Not this guy.

He picked her up and sealed their future with a kiss.

ABOUT DONNA MARIE ROGERS

JAMISON FAMILY SERIES

Nothing is more important than family...

There's Only Been You, Book 1

Foolish Pride, short story

Meant to Be, Book 2

LAKE SHELBYVILLE SERIES

That Magic Touch, Book 1

Heartland Magic (Summer 2020)

HOUGHTON COUNTY SERIES

Once a Fool, Book 1

DOUBLE M RANCH SERIES

Golden Opportunity, Book 1

Golden Dream, Book 2

WELCOME TO REDEMPTION SERIES

A hometown series full of sexy romance, humor, and heart...

A Fair of the Heart, Book 1

The Perfect Blend, Book 3

Home Is Where the Heart Is, Book 5

Never Let Me Go, Book 7

Say You Love Me, Book 9

(Books 2, 4, 6, 8, 10 written by Stacey Joy Netzel)

About Donna

USA Today bestselling author Donna Marie Rogers inherited her love of romance from her mother, who devoured romance novels like they were Fannie May candies, and never missed an episode of Little House On the

Prairie. And though it wasn't until years later Donna would come to understand her mother's fascination with Charles Ingalls, Donna's love of the romance genre is every bit as all-consuming.

A Chicago native, Donna now lives in beautiful Northeast Wisconsin with her husband and children.

She's an avid gardener and home-canner, as well as an admitted reality TV junkie. Her passion to read is only exceeded by her passion to write, so when she's not doing the wife and mother thing, you can usually find her sitting at the computer, creating exciting, memorable characters, fresh new worlds, and always a happily-ever-after.

Visit Donna at:

www.DonnaMarieRogers.com

Subscribe to Donna's Newsletter:

https://mailchi.mp/9ce32e22e5f4/t2mnen5tjm

ENGULFED

RACHEL RIVERS

RACHEL RIVERS
Feeding the Darkness
RACHELRIVERSAUTHOR.COM

AWARD WINNING AUTHOR
RACHEL RIVERS
This time, neither of them can walk away.
ENGULFED

PROLOGUE

Keeley Summers wasn't looking for love when it nipped her on the jaw. Startled, she pulled back, not wanting the connection, but as she stared into those chocolate brown eyes, she knew she was a goner.

"She adores you."

Keeley rolled her eyes and handed the wriggling puppy to the man standing beside her. "If she doesn't stop chewing on my shoes, I'm going to take her right back to the pound."

"No, you won't. You adore her as much as she adores you."

Keeley watched, amused and oddly aroused by the way Owen rubbed his nose against Sura's. God, what a picture they made, the all-star college baseball player and the mutt he'd rescued. Owen's dark hair curled at the nape, causing Keeley's fingers to twitch in an effort not to reach out and grab it.

They turned to her, two pairs of deep brown eyes staring into her soul, and Keeley was sunk. Laughter erupted from her chest when Owen opened his mouth to mimic Sura's lolling tongue and crazy puppy pants.

"You're both insane," she chortled.

"You wouldn't have it any other way." Owen leaned in to press his lips softly against hers. Sura squirmed between them, but Owen deepened the kiss, slowly encircling her tongue with his.

Keeley's blood boiled as he rubbed a stubble-covered cheek across hers. Amazed he could incite this newfound fire within her, Keeley bit back a moan as she eased into him. The sound morphed into a yelp when Sura's wet tongue slapped against her throat.

"See?" Owen asked huskily. "She adores you, just like I do."

Knowing she was grinning stupidly, but too enthralled to care, Keeley pulled Sura from his arms and crossed the cramped dorm room to place the puppy on her bed. "Stay," she ordered, more than a little surprised when Sura obeyed.

Facing Owen once again, she marveled at the rock-hard planes of his body, outlined by the black and white baseball tee and slim jeans worn white at the knees. Though they'd been dating less than a year, she knew every ripple of muscle, every hard-earned callous, every ropy vein criss-crossing his disciplined body.

"Why don't you come over here and adore me?" Keeley asked as she lowered to the plaid throw covering the narrow bed.

"Best idea I've heard all day," Owen murmured.

Fire burned in his eyes as he reached for her.

The door thudded open, and life poured in.

"Man, you will not *believe* what just happened! You know how I've been crushing on Maddie, right? Well, we just happened to run into each other at the eatery and I mentioned our upcoming game this weekend and she was totally stoked for it so I asked if she wanted to chill after and she said that'd be great and asked for my number and everything." Sean barely had time to draw a breath before plowing on. "So I gave it to her and told her I'd walk her back to her dorm so I did and she told me she'd been building up the courage to ask me out so I told her I'd been building up my own courage, then she leaned in and kissed me. *Man*, that girl can kiss!"

Smiling despite the interruption, Keeley stepped out from behind Owen and studied the gangly guy with hair the color of a carrot and a face only a mother could love. "Sounds like a good start."

"Sounds like you'd have hated to be interrupted," Owen growled.

"Yeah, man, that would have totally blown!" Oblivious to the dig, Sean beamed at them. "I'm starving, wanna order a pizza?"

"You go ahead," Keeley laughed. "I should get home, I need to study."

"Party pooper."

Bending to scratch Sura's head, Keeley felt another tug on her heart. The puppy looked up at her with such trust Keeley found it hard to walk away.

As if sensing her torn emotions, Owen placed a hand on the small of her back. "Why don't we take Sura for one final walk before you go?"

Heart thundering, Keeley nodded and scooped the pup into her arms. "Why don't we?"

Leash in tow, Keeley and Owen left the dorm and headed for the closest park.

"Are you sure I shouldn't keep her at my place?"

"Your place is hardly bigger than mine," Owen responded. "Besides, she was my idea. You didn't want her, remember?"

"It's not that I didn't want her; we're both just so busy right now, it didn't seem feasible. You're smack in the middle of the season, and I'm swamped with course work and the gym."

"Do you want to take her back?" Owen asked as he paused to let Sura sniff the base of an oak tree.

"Of course not," Keeley scoffed. "I'm simply saying maybe we let her stay at my place where she'll have a balcony to sit on during the day."

"If you want her at your place, just say that."

Keeley rolled her eyes. "Fine. I want her at my place."

"No."

Laughing, Keeley punched him in the arm. "Why do I like you?"

"Because I'm irresistibly good-looking and charming."

"And arrogant."

"Confident," he corrected as he slung his free arm over her shoulders. "I think she should live with both of us."

"What, like a joint-custody arrangement? I get her four nights a week, you get three? Every other month we swap weekends?"

"Not exactly." Owen stopped short.

Keeley turned to him, taken aback at the sudden fierceness in his eyes. "What, exactly?"

"I think we should move in together."

Stunned, Keeley gaped at him. "Move in? Together? Us?"

"Yeah. It makes sense, right? You already have a place, I could just move in. Or we could find a new place. Our place."

Keeley's jaw moved up and down soundlessly before she found her voice. "But don't you have to stay on campus? I thought the entire team had to live in the dorms."

"Only for the first year. I stayed on because Sean and I get along so well and I didn't have any reason to move. Now, I do."

Keeley's heart thudded painfully against her rib cage. She'd known he cared for her, but to share a living space was a step they'd never discussed, much less acted on. Sure, he stayed over a couple nights a week, but he didn't leave clothes or toiletries behind. Hell, she'd only recently started stocking his favorite beer, and that was only because it had become *her* favorite beer, too.

"I don't know what to say."

Grinning, Owen tugged her ponytail. "I know you need to think it over, plot out all the pros and cons, consider all the variables."

"Making fun of me isn't a great way to get me to say yes."

"I'm not making fun," he chuckled as they continued down the street. "Your analytical brain is one of the things I love most about you."

Keeley's feet felt detached from her body. Only her trust in physics had her confident she wouldn't fall flat on her face with each step. Her legs had turned to a disconcerting mixture of jellied cement, hindering her ability to walk smoothly. Dammit, she hadn't seen this coming. Owen was right, Keeley was a planner, a meticulous detailer, an annoying perfectionist. Everything had its place. Everything.

Now she had to figure out where Owen and Sura fit in.

They turned and walked back toward the dorm. The air was warm but dry, a welcome change from the usual humid cloak of wet heat that came with spring in eastern Texas. Breathing it in, Keeley grasped at the reasons they shouldn't move in together. They were too much alike, too type-A, too aggressive. They'd fight all the time about the "right" way to do things. God, would he expect her to do his laundry?

"Now that you've had time to dwell on all the things that could go wrong, how about considering what could go right?"

"I wasn't dwelling," Keeley grumbled, tugging her long ponytail in annoyance. Dammit, this was another prime example of what could go wrong. He knew her too well. How irritating would it be to have someone who knew your moods using them against you?

The wail of sirens pierced the air. Sura scrambled, terrified, as the ladder engine raced toward them. Owen picked her up, snuggling her close to his chest as the truck tore past, followed closely by two police cruisers. Curiosity turned to dread as the vehicles turned onto campus and arrowed toward the dorms.

"It's probably just a fire alarm." Owen stroked Sura's head. "Nothing to worry about."

"No, the cops wouldn't respond to a fire alarm." A sickening ball of dread settled in her gut as she quickened her pace before fully sprinting toward the dorms. The expected acrid scent reached her just as she made the final turn, before she saw the plume of smoke rising above the burning dorm. Her father's voice echoed in her head, cataloging the activities as she scanned the scene.

Half a dozen fire trucks formed an impromptu wall in front of the building as firefighters poured into and out of them like worker ants, hauling gear and hoses over the concrete. Her mind recited the movements of the well-trained firefighters, and with each motion the fear within her unwound its tentacles and threaded them throughout her whole being.

Keeley sucked in her breath as she counted the floors and windows and realized Owen and Sean's room was consumed. Flames licked out the shattered window, crackling like paper caught in the wind. Keeley knew in her gut if Sean had still been in the room, he was dead. The angle of the flames, the direction of the smoke, left no doubt as to the intensity of the fire raging inside. Even if he'd managed to avoid the initial inferno, the combination of chemicals in the smoke would have poisoned him.

Owen's curse had her spinning, planting herself in front of him. He shoved his phone back in his pocket and Keeley could see by the sheer terror on his face that Sean hadn't answered. "There's nothing you can do."

"The fuck there isn't. Move, Keeley." He shoved Sura at her, tried to step around her.

Keeley pivoted, hooked his foot with hers, essentially locking him in place. "You can't go up there."

"I said move, god damnit!"

Keeley merely looped Sura's leash around his forearm, securing the dog to his body. From the corner of her eye, she saw the cop moving toward them. Stall, she just had to stall a few more seconds. "You'll die if you go in there."

"Sean is dying now! MOVE!" He shoved her back a full two steps, Sura whining in terror.

Instead of doing as he demanded, Keeley made a decision she knew would shatter their relationship forever. Remembering the one self-defense maneuver her dad and his buddies had taught her when she'd entered high school, she spun around to Owen's back, planted her foot at the back of his knee, and forced him to bend. Now that their heights were even, she wrapped an arm around his neck, her elbow notching into his throat. Bringing her other hand behind his head, she locked him into the restraint and squeezed.

Tears poured down her face as he struggled, fighting to free himself, but Keeley held on. The choke worked in seconds, and by the time the cop reached them, she'd awkwardly lowered Owen to the ground, rolling him so he lay flat on his back.

Panting from the effort of simultaneously holding the choke in place and controlling his collapse so he wouldn't faceplant, Keeley raised to her knees and faced the officer. "Arrest me if you need to, but I couldn't let him go in."

Pity lit the officer's dark eyes as he met her tear-streaked face. "You probably saved his life."

Briskly rubbing Owen's shoulder, Keeley braced for what she knew would be an ugly scene.

Within seconds, he was awake, slightly dazed, but quickly regained his bearings. "What did you do to me?" Pushing off the ground, he managed to make it to a seated position before the officer put a firm hand on his shoulder.

"Stay down a second, son."

"I can't stay down, my friend is in there." Owen stared numbly at the men and women rushing in and out of the dorm. "He's in there."

"Let the professionals do their job. Your girl saved you some serious injuries by keeping you from charging this place."

Owen's eyes turned to Keeley, all warmth and care long gone. "She's not my girl."

CHAPTER 1

Something was burning.

Lieutenant Keeley Summers bolted out of her chair and headed for the unmistakable stench of smoke. Long legs ate up the short distance from her office to the station kitchen. Rounding the corner, mentally prepared to grab the fire extinguisher beneath the double sink, she came to an abrupt halt at the sight in front of her.

Her entire crew crowded around the stove. "Happy Birthday!" they chanted as one.

Surprise couldn't overtake the drive in her belly. "What the hell is burning?"

Juan Gomez, resident driver and womanizer, grinned sheepishly. "Your cake."

"Not to worry," Jillian Martin said as she elbowed Gomez aside. "There's still ice cream." The petite blonde held out a carton of Rocky Road along with a spoon.

Shaking her head to clear it, Keeley stepped forward to take it. "While I appreciate the gesture, I'm confused. How did a room full of firefighters burn the cake?"

"Some dumbass set the oven timer to five hours instead of fifty minutes," boomed Frank Carlisle, the oldest and meanest of her crew.

Nodding, Keeley cracked open the carton and dipped her spoon in. "I see. And no one did a buddy check on the oven?"

For once there was dead quiet in the kitchen. Then all hell broke loose.

"Well, what happened was—"

"It's really Gomez's fault—"

"If Jillian hadn't had a wad of gum in her mouth—"

"I only took three minutes to check the score—"

"Enough!" barked Keeley. "I don't need to know about wads and scores." *What the hell did a wad of gum have to do with anything, anyway?* "I appreciate the sentiment, even though the execution failed." Studying the men and women staring sheepishly at her, Keeley held up the ice cream carton. "Is this all we've got, or is there enough for everyone?"

Hours later, Keeley sat at her desk once again and rubbed gritty eyes. Dammit, she needed sleep. Not the 'catch a snooze in the bunk' sleep, the real deal. Thanks to a vicious stomach bug making its rounds, she'd pulled double shifts to ensure the men and women under her weren't running short staffed. Now she wanted nothing more than to crawl into her own bed, pull the duvet over her head, and crash for a solid twelve.

As the alarm rang out and dispatch squawked overhead, Keeley knew her dream would remain just that – a dream. Sprinting to the bay, she listened as the call details boomed over the station's PA system. Four vehicles were involved, one crunched beneath another while the other two had spun out of control and stalled in the roadway. Limited access meant incidents on the interstate were always difficult, but when the dispatcher paused to take a breath, Keeley knew it would be bad. Sure enough, dispatch informed them two people were currently trapped inside the pinned vehicle while a third person had been ejected from a pickup truck.

Keeley donned her turnout gear alongside her team and less

than sixty seconds after the alarm sounded her crew was ready. "Let's roll," she commanded as she climbed aboard the engine and settled into her front seat. As doors slammed around her and Juan steered them out of the garage, the heavy-rescue equipped squad truck close behind, she was struck with how lucky she was to have a team so in-sync with each other. She rarely had to give commands, never worried if everyone would pull their weight; her team just did their jobs, and did them well. Tugging on the headset, Keeley radioed to their sister station, confirming they were less than two minutes out.

Keeley lifted the microphone away from her lips and breathed deeply, preparing herself for the gruesome scene they were quickly approaching. She'd become a firefighter to study and fight fires, not respond to medical emergencies and car crashes. She did all of those, but her stomach still rolled at the sight of blood and brain matter splattered over pavement.

Closing her eyes, she imagined standing in the surf of a black sand beach, overlooking the melodic crashing and receding of waves. The sun beamed warm on her face while a gentle sea breeze playfully teased her hair. It was so real she felt the grains of sand beneath her toes, smelled the salt and brine of the ocean. She hadn't risen to Lieutenant by letting her weaknesses show, and she sure as hell wasn't going to let them show with Captain within reach. After a few moments of forcing her breathing to steady, she once again felt calm and collected, then she opened her eyes and focused on the task at hand.

The engine's siren wailed as Juan navigated the ramp leading to the interstate, and Keeley began mentally listing possible scenarios and the steps she and her team would need to take once they arrived on-scene. At just after eleven PM, traffic was light, but what vehicles had been traveling through the innards of Dallas sat at a standstill. Juan blasted the horn and rode the right shoulder to where their sister engine idled ahead. Before the engine had even fully stopped, Keely opened her door and dropped to the ground as all her planning blew away.

Dammit! Dispatch hadn't advised that an eighteen-wheeler was involved. The massive truck had fishtailed at some point, sending a red SUV into the guardrail while a black pickup sat facing the wrong direction in the right-hand lane. If that had been the extent of the damage, Keeley would have been fine – but it wasn't. A tan sedan rested beneath the tractor trailer, its entire front end crushed accordian-style into the front seat. Keeley's heart galloped in her chest, but she gritted her teeth and ran to assist the men attempting to cut off the driver's door.

She didn't hear the conscious female screaming from the passenger seat, didn't smell the antifreeze and oil that steadily gushed onto the ground. Her entire focus centered on the male whose lower body was jammed beneath the steering wheel. Keeley didn't need a medical degree to know the guy was in bad shape. The top of his skull had been shorn off during the impact, revealing shiny bone amid the dark blood and gray brain matter.

Keeley's stomach revolted, but she shut it down and jumped into action, grabbing loose debris and tossing it out of the way. Knowing the specialized team had the extrication under control, Keeley directed her crew to work on the female.

Juan and Jillian dropped their medic bags at the rear of the sedan as they began to address the screaming woman. Judging from the angles of her legs, Keeley assumed she'd shattered both tibias. Juan yanked open the back door and crawled into the backseat while Jillian gently placed the neck brace on the woman, speaking in soft, soothing tones. Juan reached around the headrest to secure the brace in place as Keeley pulled splints from one of the bags.

The wail of the approaching ambulance broke Keeley's concentration as it screeched to a halt. The doors slammed open and Keeley breathed a sigh of relief as she recognized the two paramedics jumping from the truck. Petite and curvaceous, Chantel Romiro may look like Ms. Argentina, but she was as brilliant as a Rhodes Scholar and as mean as a black mamba. She also just so happened to be Keeley's closest friend. Her partner Robbie

Sinclair was as steady as they came, and together they were a dynamic duo.

Movements quick and practiced, they unloaded the gurney and rushed it over.

"Happy-fucking-Birthday to you," Chantel said, her words as punchy as the riotous curls exploding over her headband. "What have we got?"

"The driver is obviously trapped," Keeley said, ripping the Velcro from the splints. "The passenger appears to have multiple lacerations and broken bones. Possibly a neck or head injury."

"Brutal." Chantel snapped her latex gloves into place. "Let's make some music."

Keeley followed Chantel's sharp commands, taking no offense to the clipped words and bossy tone. Her friend was the best, and to get in her way would be purely egotistical. And stupid. Keeley assisted Frank with the backboard, getting it into place and holding it steady as Juan and Jillian maneuvered the woman onto it. On the count of three, they lifted it onto the gurney.

Staring down at the tear-streaked face, Keeley's heart sank. The woman wasn't a woman at all; she was a girl no older than sixteen or seventeen. Clumpy glitter coated her fake eyelashes and smeared across her cheeks.

"Am I going to die?" She looked straight at Keeley, cracked lips trembling.

"Not today."

"What about Boone?"

"Is that the driver?"

"Yes, he's my brother. Is he okay?"

Keeley glanced over at her counterparts. Lieutenant Marty Shire shook his head, the hard lines around his eyes doing nothing to detract from the hollow sadness in their depths.

Glancing back down at the girl, Keeley steeled herself. "We're doing everything we can to help him."

"That's a no. I know that's a no." The girl began to sob in earnest, rending Keeley's heart with every pitiful cry. She'd promised herself long ago that she'd never give a victim or family member false hope. She'd be gentle, she'd be thoughtful, but she'd be honest. Keeley had kept that promise for more than a decade and though her heart begged her to lie to this poor girl, she couldn't.

"What's your name?" she managed to ask over the clog in her throat.

"Bethy," the girl whispered.

"All right, Bethy, you listen to me. The best of the best are working on him. If anyone has a chance of saving him, it's them."

Bethy tried to nod but the neck brace stifled her movements. "Please. Please save him. He's all I've got."

Chantel pushed Keeley aside, knowing her well enough to see the anguish she was trying to hide. "Okay, babydoll, we're gonna cut open your shirt to attach some wires. No big deal, yeah?"

Keeley didn't hear Bethy's reply as she stepped back and allowed Chantel to do her job. As she glanced about, searching for the next task to focus on, the scene blurred and stretched out around her as everything downshifted into slow motion. Additional paramedics had arrived and were busy checking on the other drivers involved in the hellacious crash. A woman stood outside the SUV, attempting to hush the screaming toddler in her arms. A middle-aged man crouched outside the pickup truck, an EMT kneeling by his side.

Two Texas Department of Transportation trucks had arrived, their drivers busily setting up cones and barricades to block off the crash scene. The tractor trailer driver spoke to a police officer, wringing his blue hat in his hands like a dishrag. The helplessness on his weathered face ripped at Keeley's soul. She didn't know exactly what had happened, but no matter who was at fault, lives would be forever changed.

All around her, her fellow first responders slowly brought order to the chaos strewn across the interstate. Juan had climbed into the back of the ambulance, helping Robbie run the IV tubes while Chantel spoke rapidly into the radio mounted on the side panel.

Jillian hauled medical bags back to the engine as Frank dumped a sand and clay mixture over the fluids running in rivulets along the asphalt.

Eyes inevitably drawn back to Boone, Keeley watched Marty assist his guys in draping a tarp over the driver's door. Heart heavy, Keeley kept silent as the firemen stepped back, away from the boy they'd been unable to save. He'd wait there, in the chair of his death, until the Medical Examiner arrived and conducted an investigation.

Over the din of noise, Marty found her eyes and held them as time finally returned to normal. Keeley didn't cross to him, didn't have to. An unspoken understanding ran through them, the leaders of their crews. *Take care of your own.* Once they arrived back at the station, Keeley would hold a debrief, but for now, there was still work to do.

Keeley hopped down from the front seat, legs heavy with fatigue. The drive to the station had been silent save for the groans and clunks of the engine as it meandered back to the bay. No one spoke, no one joked, no one hurled insults. The resulting quiet had been deafening.

"Let's take thirty then meet up in the kitchen," she ordered.

Her crew merely nodded before dispersing. Weary, Keeley climbed the stairs to the upper floor that housed the bunks. Walking past the narrow room with its standard twin-sized cots, Keeley headed for the bathroom.

Shutting the door, she sank onto the toilet and let the tears fall. She could hear her dad's voice, asking if she was sure she wanted to be a firefighter. *"You'll see some really hard stuff."* Keeley had answered yes, absolutely, but she hadn't understood her dad's warning, not really. Teddy Summers had spent thirty years at the department, rising to the rank of Deputy Chief prior to retiring. He'd supported Keeley's decision to follow in his footsteps, but not without cautioning her of the horrors she'd witness. When she'd made Lieutenant, he'd beamed brighter than the sun at her promotion ceremony, then taken her out for beer and nachos. He'd leaned close and told her that she had a duty not only to the city, but to the men and women under her supervision. *"Don't forget where you came from, and prioritize your people. Always,* always *put your people first."*

Now was the time to do that. Making a mental note to call and check on him, Keeley scrubbed her hands over her eyes. Not one to show emotion in public, she rose and splashed water on her cheeks until they returned to their naturally tanned shade. Studying her reflection in the aging mirror, Keeley wondered how many firefighters had done exactly this over the years – washed away all evidence of the turmoil they felt day after day.

Drying her hands on a towel, she stepped back and squared her shoulders. Now that she'd had a good cry, she felt better. Not great, not good, but better.

She entered the kitchen to find Jillian sitting at the table, ice cream piled in a bowl in front of her. "I made one for you, too. It's in the freezer."

"Thanks." Keeley grabbed hers, pulled out a chair, and sat. "Talk to me."

Jillian lifted her eyes from the melting Rocky Road. "I don't have anything to say."

The youngest in the crew, Jillian still felt she had something to prove. She worked doggedly, manning the hoses and running the routes with the best of them, but females were still in the minority and they knew it. Jillian didn't want to be seen as a *female* firefighter – she wanted to be seen as just a firefighter. Keeley remembered feeling the same way, so she let the defensive tone slide.

"You've worked for me long enough to know that won't cut it."

Sighing, Jillian let the spoon fall with a clatter. "I don't know how I feel about it."

"That's fair." Keeley brought the spoon to her lips, but the usually sweet treat tasted bitter on her tongue. "You did well."

Jillian's eyes snapped to hers. "Thanks."

"I mean it. You're always willing to jump in and handle more than your fair share of the weight. I appreciate it, and I know the guys do, too. I'm glad you're on my crew."

A small smile tugged the corners of Jillian's lips. "That means a lot."

Juan trudged in, followed by a surly Frank. "I didn't do it on purpose," Juan was exclaiming, arms spread wide. "Jesus, take a chill pill."

"Purposely or not, you fucked up."

"I said I'm sorry! I'll buy you another one."

Frank opened his mouth to reply when Keeley broke in. "What's going on?"

"Lover-boy over there broke the tip off my nose-hair trimmer."

Stunned, Keeley sat back in her chair. "He did what?"

"Snapped the tip off my goddamn nose-hair trimmer!" Frank roared. "Clumsy little shit."

"I'm not clumsy, Grandpa—"

"Whoa, whoa, that's enough." Keeley stood, hands held out as the remaining members of her crew funneled into the kitchen. "Juan, buy Frank another trimmer and be more careful in the future. Frank, I'm sure that trimmer meant a lot to you, but Juan apologized and will replace it. Can the two of you move on? For the love of all that's holy, *please*?"

Frank slapped a hand on the table as he sat. "Fine, but it better be the exact same model."

Juan rolled his eyes and sat on the opposite side of the table. "Whatever, I'll make it right."

Keeley shook her head at the vastly different personalities in front of her, grateful the others hadn't chimed in and taken sides, as was the usual practice when an argument broke out. She'd never imagined leading a crew would be easy, but some days she wanted to toss her bars on the captain's desk and ask for a demotion back to basic firefighter. Drawing a deep breath, Keeley opened her mouth to speak when the alarm blared once again.

Cursing, Keeley led her crew back into the bay. As the dispatcher updated them on the fire alarm going off at a local business, Keeley thanked her lucky stars this was actually a fire call and not another crash. Between the last one and her crew bickering like siblings, she could use a fiery distraction.

CHAPTER 2

Owen Prescott cursed as he spotted the fire engine idling outside Kore K9. The alarm company had woken him from a sound sleep brought on by too many restless nights and too much crossfit. Owen had jerked awake the moment they'd said the fire alarm had been triggered, then hauled his ass to the building he'd recently purchased.

A breath he hadn't realized he'd been holding exhaled loudly at the realization the building hadn't actually burned to the ground. As he drove closer, he squinted. In fact, it didn't look damaged at all. Parking in front of the entrance, he grabbed Sura and eased her to the ground. Ever loyal, she trotted behind him as he searched for the firefighters.

Turning the corner, he stopped in his tracks. The ponytail and kickass stance identified her better than a DNA test ever could. She was the one woman he'd never forgotten and hoped to never see again. His traitorous heart tripped in his chest as he studied her long frame and noted the name stamped on the tail of her turnout jacket. *Summers. Well, fuck.* Steadying his breathing, he shoved his hands in his pockets as a younger fireman approached him.

"You the owner?"

"Yeah, I'm Owen Prescott."

"You'll be happy to know we didn't find a fire anywhere in the building. It looks like you may have a wire or two shorting out and it's causing the alarm to go off."

As if on cue, a loud shrieking pierced the quiet night.

The fireman shrugged and jerked his head toward the building. "Since we're here, we might as well check again, just to be sure."

Owen nodded as the young fireman was joined by an older, stern-looking man. As the two headed into the building together, Owen's attention reverted to Keeley. She didn't turn as she spoke into her handheld radio, agitation apparent in the way she tossed her head. Long forgotten but all too familiar sensations thrummed along his fingers as he watched her characteristic hairstyle whip about with her movements.

Without warning, Sura ambled toward the woman who was obviously in charge. Owen could have stopped her, but he waited, curious how Keeley would react. Sura's stubby tail wagged furiously as she rubbed against Keeley's leg.

Owen saw the instant Keeley recognized the brown eyes gazing up at her, full of adoration and love. Lowering her radio, she spun around slowly, meeting his stare. She didn't move, didn't so much as flinch, but the change in her attitude struck Owen like a fist to the face.

Taking his time, he crossed the parking lot to stand at arm's length from the woman he'd once loved. "Hi."

"Hi."

Her voice was stronger than he remembered and he wondered what she'd experienced to turn a free-loving girl into a tougher-than-nails woman.

"Thanks for coming out."

"That's the job." Though her words were short, she bent down and stroked a hand along Sura's dark fur. The dog wiggled closer, eager for more scratches. Keeley smiled, and the light of it struck Owen in the heart.

"Hey LT, we can't find anything." A petite blonde strode out of the side door, pushing her hat out of her eyes as she approached. "Do you want us to make another round?"

Turning a questioning eye to Owen, Keeley paused. "Do you want us to check again?"

Owen's stomach pitched at her question. Suddenly he was staring at his dorm, watching smoke pile out of the windows, Keeley holding him back from rushing inside.

"Owen?"

Blinking, Owen found Keeley's eyes and held them as he returned to the present.

"You okay?" she asked.

Shaking himself, Owen struggled for normalcy. "I'm good. There's no need to check again, I think it's a glitch in the system. I'll have someone out to check it in the morning."

"Sounds like a plan." Keeley bent to give Sura a final rub before turning to leave.

"Keels, wait."

At the use of her pet name, Keeley jerked to a halt, the petite blonde almost smashing into her back. Sensing something was up, the woman skirted around her boss and busied herself with the truck as Keeley turned to him, those intoxicating whiskey eyes on his once more.

"What?"

Crossing his arms, Owen faltered. What could he say to her? He'd always assumed he'd never see her again. *Don't fuck it up.* "So, do you come here often?"

God, he'd fucked it up.

"Really?"

"That was a terrible line. Let me try again. How are you?"

"Busy."

"I can see that. Lieutenant, huh? Your dad must be proud."

Her face softened enough for Owen to see the girl he used to know. "He is. Incredibly."

When she turned to leave again, Owen instinctually reached out, taking her by the arm. "Have coffee with me."

"I beg your pardon?"

"Has your hearing faded over the years? I asked if you'd have coffee with me."

"No, you commanded I have coffee with you. There's a difference."

"Fine, will you have coffee with me?"

"No."

Owen wasn't sure whether to laugh or curse. "Listen, I'm new to this part of town. Cut me some slack and clue me in to what's-what around here."

"There's an amazing piece of technology that can do that for you – it's called the internet, you should look it up."

"I've missed your smartass mouth."

"I can't say the same."

"Bullshit. Some people change, but you don't, and you're not a liar."

Keeley's eyes turned cold as her hands settled on her hips. "You walked away from me, Owen. Or did you forget?"

"How could I when I regret it every day of my life?"

Obviously thrown, Keeley stared at him. "What?"

"Have coffee with me. Please," he added.

"I don't drink coffee."

Emboldened by the fact she hadn't flat-out refused, Owen used the one thing he was sure would get her. "Okay, how about a walk in the park with me and Sura?"

Eyes narrowing, Keeley pursed her lips. "A walk in the park? That's it?"

"Unless you're interested in something more."

"A walk is plenty."

Owen grinned. "I work tomorrow, but how about the next day? Are you off?"

"Yes."

"Great, I'll see you at River Legacy around ten?"

"Why not go to one of the city parks?"

"They don't have miles of trails."

Keely gave Sura a pointed look. "I don't think the old girl is up for miles of trails."

"True, but it's the prettiest park around, and she does love the pretties." Owen winked. "Why do you think she loves you?"

Keeley rolled her eyes and turned on her booted heel. "Jesus, that's pathetic."

"Doesn't make it any less true!" Owen called over the rumble of the engine.

Keeley merely shook her head as she climbed into the passenger seat of the big truck. Owen grinned like a schoolboy as it pulled away.

Whistling for Sura, he pulled open the glass-fronted door leading to Kore K9, turning on the lights as he strode past the small desk housing a new Mac, printer, and a smattering of pens and papers. The disorganized mess reminded him that he needed to hire a receptionist, but the thought was just as quickly forgotten as he reached the entrance to the training area.

Whereas the rest of the building may be sparse, here he'd spared no expense. The slate gray floor alone had cost an arm and a leg, but he'd demanded top grade for the space named after his military buddy killed in action.

Walking the expensive floor, Owen nodded approval at the custom shelves lining the walls. The local carpenter had nailed the project, ensuring every slab of wood served a purpose. Rubber balls, lengths of rope, boxes of varying sizes were stacked neatly. In the far corner, pyramid stairs, round rings, and narrow tunnels were tucked away discreetly. The effect was exactly what Owen wanted in the school – no frills, all business.

Korey would be proud.

Rubbing his tired eyes, Owen allowed his friend's face to fill his mind. Korey had always loved watching Owen train with Turbo, Owen's working dog in the Army. Hell, Korey had donned the bite sleeve more times than Owen could count, willing to let the canine practice chewing on him. He was the best friend Owen had ever known, and in the span of a heartbeat, he'd lost him.

Feeling the firestorm brewing within, Owen knew he needed to get out of the school, go home, and work off some frustration and guilt. When his brain started betraying him, re-playing the moment Korey had died, he shut it out. He didn't need a constant reminder of why he'd opened this place, or who it was named for. Looking at the silver bracelet on his wrist, he could hear Korey's brawling tone telling him to toughen the fuck up and get on with it.

So he did.

Whistling for Sura, he turned out the light and headed home. Once there, he moved quickly, mixing dry and soft dog food for Sura, dumping it in her bowl, and freshening her water. Only then did he move to his bedroom to release Kore.

The Belgian Malinois stared at him, silent and alert, as Owen approached the kennel. Ears perked, teeth slightly bared, the dog resembled one of the hounds of hell. Speaking softly in German, Owen unlatched the lock and stepped back from the door.

Kore had never bitten him, but it wasn't for lack of trying.

Owen hadn't wanted another Malinois, not after leaving Turbo behind when he'd left the Army, but when Korey's parents showed up on his doorstep, dog in tow, Owen had been a goner. Even without hearing the Malinois's story, Owen would have taken him. Looking at the hard eyes staring at him out of the crate, Owen had felt an instant bond snap into place.

The feeling had *not* been reciprocated.

The damn dog had snapped at Owen the moment he'd stepped close to the cage.

The Malinois had washed out of K9 training, not having the "correct temperament" for a working dog. Within minutes of meeting the mean bastard, Owen realized they'd actually meant the dog was too Type A – too dominant, too damn violent for the program. When Korey's parents told Owen they thought the snarling beast would be a good companion dog for Owen to train as a service pet, Owen had fought the urge to laugh out loud. But he hadn't turned him away, and had, in fact, named him for the soldier they'd all lost overseas.

It had taken two hard weeks of constant commands, curses, and channeled anger before Kore willingly allowed Owen to snap the leash in place. Now, six months later, their relationship was steady, but still somewhat rocky.

Kore stepped out of the kennel, hackles lowering as he shook out his fur.

Maintaining the distance between them, Owen fisted his hands on his hips. "Okay, big boy, we're going for a run."

The word 'run' sent Kore's tail into overdrive. Careful to keep the dog in view as he lifted the leash from its hook on the wall, Owen snapped the command in German. "Hier."

Kore obediently trotted to circle behind Owen's feet, then dropped his rump to the floor with a solid thump. "Good boy."

Owen snapped the leash in place, proud at how well Kore stayed at his side. When they passed Sura in the kitchen, bent over her bowls, Kore growled softly. Sura merely shot him a disinterested look and went back to her chow. Kore sniffed, dismissing her, and sat while Owen settled a bud in one ear.

"We'll be back, sweetheart. Don't wait up."

Sura's attention never wavered as she systematically devoured her food.

Owen and Kore stepped into the soothing quiet of pre-dawn. The sun hadn't yet risen and the moon shone bright and bold over the quiet suburban neighborhood. Unlike most of the newer developments on the outskirts of the city's limits, this one had been around for generations. None of the houses looked alike, and the yards ranged from small and neat to rambling and overgrown. Owen liked the consistency of the inconsistent, the stamp of character and individuality of each of the plots.

He took off at a jog, Kore keeping pace at his side. Morning runs had become more than exercise for the pair. Over the past months, they'd developed an easy rhythm rarely exhibited elsewhere. After the first week, Kore hadn't even struggled against the leash, so happy to be out in the fresh air stretching his legs.

Owen increased the speed, ignoring the twitch in his knees.

Jumping out of helicopters and airplanes for damn near a decade destroyed joints and tendons alike. Pushing past the pain, Owen found the speed they both craved, caught somewhere between painful and exhilarating. Kore's tongue lolled to the side, eyes darting back and forth as they crossed a four-way intersection. A squirrel darted in front of them and Owen braced for impact – but none came.

Praising the dog for keeping his focus, they ran on, breaths exploding in pants, twin images of effort and masculinity. At the turn-around point, Owen let his mind wander. Unsurprisingly, it arrowed straight for Keeley. God, had it really been twelve years since he'd seen her? The fist in the gut was no surprise, she'd always had that effect on him, but the cool disinterest in her eyes had shaken him more than he cared to admit.

If he were honest with himself, a small part of him had harbored hope they'd one day run into one another. Though, for it to happen in Dallas was more unexpected than the chance meeting itself. When they'd talked about the future, they'd tossed around the idea of moving to Tennessee, to live in the South where old men still dipped Bruton and young girls still rode their bicycles on the street. Fate had laughed and intervened. He and Keeley would never grow old beneath a weeping willow surrounded by a brood of kids and a gaggle of dogs.

The thought made him sigh as he and Kore rounded the final corner to home. He'd given up everything when he'd walked away from Texas A&M all those years ago. Keeley, his baseball scholarship, the comfort of knowing who he was and what he was doing. He'd dove face-first into a pile of shit and somehow came out standing on top. He'd come home from his last deployment angry, hurt, and ready for a change. The years of combat and death had dulled the need for adrenaline-pumping action, and in its place honed the desire for steady, even monotonous days. Easy days. Predictable days.

Glancing down at the dog slowing beside him, it dawned on him he'd ended up taking on something as adrenaline-seeking and spastic as the things he'd left behind. Kore was anything but easy. Slowing his pace, he remembered the coldness on Keeley's face, and realized his civilian life was turning out to be anything but predictable. Wincing, he didn't think Fate had finished laughing yet.

CHAPTER 3

Keeley studied her reflection, more than a little irked she gave two damns how she looked. It was just a walk in the park, anyway, so why did it matter if she wore her teal running tights or jade leggings? And he wouldn't notice if her black top scooped into a low V in the back, so why worry if it exposed too much skin?

Disgusted with herself, Keeley slammed the closet door with its full-length mounted mirror and turned away. Grabbing her wallet off the bed, she left the house with a definite agitated gait. Slamming into the driver's seat, she peeled out of her driveway.

God, what was she doing?

She had no interest in anything to do with Owen Prescott. He'd shattered her heart, shredded the fabric of her dreams so she'd had to sew the jagged edges back together with nothing but grit and determination. Now, over a decade later, it was appalling to realize he could still send her hormones into overdrive simply by breathing.

So why the hell had she said yes to his asinine request for a walk in the park? Maneuvering the traffic jamming the city streets, she rolled down the window and sighed as fresh air slapped her face. While she loved the crowded innards and stress of the city, at heart she still craved the wide-open space and serenity of the countryside where she'd been born and raised. Thanks to work, she rarely managed to escape to her roots, so she'd take the air whooshing in her window as a measly compromise.

Her heart began to pound when she saw the pitched roof of the park's pavilion, lush grass and dense trees spread out around it, with trails meandering through the serene landscape. Flowering bushes dotted the green, spewing reds and purples and yellows into the air. Owen was right, it was the prettiest park in the area.

Forcing herself not to slam the car door, she stepped back and stretched her arms over her head. Dammit, she should be sleeping, not fending off the pathetic advances of a man using his dog to get to her. Muscles bunched and lengthened as she rounded her back. Double dammit, she'd never have been able to resist Sura, and Owen knew it.

A happy bark caught Keeley's attention. Turning, she saw the eager dog moving slowly, her elderly legs bowed as she trotted forward. Keeping her eyes deliberately down, Keeley refused to acknowledge the man standing nearby, but she couldn't stop the surge of love as she knelt to rub that smooth belly.

"Hello, sweetheart."

"Hello, yourself, darling."

Keeley rolled her eyes. "I was talking to Sura."

"Oh, I thought you were addressing me."

Straightening, Keeley squared her shoulders. "Let's get something straight – I'm here for Sura. Not you, not our past, not whatever you may want in the future. I'm not interested in picking up where *you* left off. Got it?"

"Did you practice that speech in the car?"

When Keeley moved to open her car door, Owen swore. "Jesus, you're a tough shell. I'm sorry for that."

"For *that*? That's what you're sorry for?"

Owen had the dignity to wince. "That came out wrong."

"Everything you've said has come out wrong."

"Not everything." Whistling for Sura to fall into step, Owen set off for the nearest trail. "I was right to ask you to come out today."

"Why did you?"

"Honestly, I'm not entirely sure."

Angling her head, Keeley kept Sura between them as they meandered down the paved path. "Okay, that may be the first right thing you've said."

Owen shoved his hands in his jean pockets. "I never thought I'd see you again."

"Ditto."

"I was hoping I wouldn't."

"Again, ditto."

"You make me feel too much."

Keeley paused. As much as she wanted to see Owen ground into dust for the pain he'd caused her, she wasn't cruel enough to shrug off what she knew was sincere honesty. "I know you blame me for what happened that night."

"I used to, that's for damn sure. It was easier to blame you than myself."

Surprised, Keeley glanced at him. "Why would you blame yourself?"

He kept his eyes averted, avoiding her gaze. "It was my idea to get this dumb mutt in the first place, even though I knew I shouldn't keep her in the dorm."

"That's just dumb. I pushed for her, too."

"No, you didn't. You didn't want the responsibility."

Sighing, Keeley pushed her sunglasses on top of her head. "You're right, I didn't, but I fell for her just as hard and fast as you did."

Owen met her eyes then, a cocky grin on his mouth. "I told you you would."

Keeley rolled her eyes again, but a smile tugged her lips. "Whatever."

They walked in silence for a moment, falling into an all-too familiar pace. Keeley may not have wanted to be attracted to him, but she failed to see how any hot-blooded woman could look at him and not have heart palpitations. His loose t-shirt didn't disguise the honed muscles amid his rangy arms. Ropy veins still ran beneath the skin along his hands, but the smoothness had been marred by small scars and nicks.

She briefly wondered where he'd gotten them but refrained from asking. It was none of her damn business. Resuming her study, she was shocked to realize there was no hair beneath his Braves baseball cap. Had he shaved the luscious locks he'd once pampered like a Pantene model? Who was this man?

The stark changes piqued her curiosity and she despite her wariness at seeming too interested, she needed to know. "How was the Army?"

Owen drew in a long breath as he pondered his response. "A strange combination of heaven and hell."

"You don't have to tell me."

"Then why did you ask?"

"I probably shouldn't have. I'm sure you saw...things," she broke off lamely. "Don't feel obligated to talk about it."

"I never feel obligated to talk about it." Owen shielded his eyes as they rounded a corner and caught a face full of the sun's rays. "There's not much to tell. I enlisted, went to boot camp, had some additional training, became a K9 handler, deployed a few times, and got out."

His tone may have been light, but the hand still bunched in his pocket was rigid. Keeley knew him well enough to know that wasn't all of it, not even close, but she didn't push. Hell, she wasn't sure she even wanted to know. Knowing meant understanding. Understanding meant empathizing. Empathizing meant caring. She really, *really* had no interest in caring.

"You were made for it."

Surprise had Owen finally meeting her gaze. "Why do you say that?"

Keeley shrugged. "You were a great baseball player, but I always figured you'd eventually get bored with it. It was a game to you, one you excelled at, but still a game. You're not the type of guy to spend his life merely playing."

Owen stopped in his tracks, not noticing when Sura kept pace with Keeley. "Why the hell didn't you tell me that years ago?"

"You didn't need to hear it years ago," Keeley called over her shoulder. "Come on, catch up."

Owen did, his long legs eating up the distance quickly. "No, seriously, if you knew I would grow bored playing baseball, why didn't you say something?"

"You'd have figured it out for yourself eventually, but fate intervened. Prematurely, if you ask me, which she doesn't."

Reaching out, Owen grabbed Keeley's arm, turning her to face him. "You knew I was angling toward the major leagues. Did you plan to tell me this before I signed?"

Sighing, Keeley studied the face she'd once known so well. The boy was gone, completely replaced by the man in front of her. He was harder than she remembered, but also...softer? How the hell was that possible? The realization didn't sit well, so she took a big emotional step back while flinging the truth in his face.

"Yes. I loved you too much to let you make the wrong decision."

Dark eyes searched her face, but for what, she couldn't say. The intensity of his gaze caused nerves to snap along her spine as oily snakes coiled in her belly. After what seemed like a lifetime, he started walking again. "Apparently not."

"What does that mean?"

"We were young, Keels. I don't think either of us made the right decisions back then."

She wanted to ask what he'd have done differently, but she bit her tongue. It didn't matter. There was no changing what had happened, and even if she could, she wouldn't. She liked who she'd become, dammit, and she knew without a doubt that she'd never have been so driven if Owen had stayed.

Focusing on the trees around her, Keeley reminded herself she could stop this walk at any time. She wanted to – god, she wanted to – but she felt an undeniable draw she couldn't resist. There was something in his eyes, something haunted and hollow that hadn't been there a decade ago. It spoke to her, much like the fires she fought. It was physical, true, but it was deeper. *He* was deeper.

She tried telling herself it had nothing to do with the urge to pin Owen against the nearest pine and ravage that tight mouth with hers. Flexing her fingers in irritation, she practically felt his body against hers.

"You okay over there?" Owen asked, his voice slightly amused.

"Fine," she lied.

"You don't look fine."

"Thanks, asshole."

Laughing, Owen tossed back his head. "I only meant you look stressed."

"I have a stressful job."

"I'm proud of you."

Nothing could have stunned her more. Mouth agape, she stared at him. "I beg your pardon?"

"Why are you so surprised that I'm proud of you?"

Possible answers screamed through her head. *Because you never supported me being a firefighter. Because you couldn't control me. Because you hated me for reading the fire that killed your best friend.* Rather than speaking any of those, she slowly shook her head. "You're not what I expected."

"Is that good or bad?"

"I don't know yet."

"I'll take it."

"Excuse me?"

"You know, Keels, I've never seen you so flustered before. I think I like it."

"Well I *don't* like it."

Owen sent her a cheeky grin. "Oh, I'm well aware."

Fisting her hands on her hips, Keeley glared at him. "Why did you ask me to come today? To assuage your ill-placed guilt?"

Owen's eyes lost their joking light, hardened. "You know nothing of my guilt."

"You're right, and I don't want to." Turning on her heel, Keeley started back to her car. Dammit, *dammit*, she'd known this was a bad idea.

Before she'd taken three steps, Owen grabbed her arm and yanked her to him. "This is what I want."

Suddenly his mouth was on hers, plunging her beneath the onslaught of emotions too vast to name. She thought she may have moaned as her head fell back in abandon, but she was too busy warring her tongue with his to be sure. When his teeth nipped her lower lip, she thought she'd come where she stood.

If she'd been able to think, she'd have been pissed at how demeaning it was to tremble for a man who'd tossed her aside. But she couldn't think, not with his hands sliding up her ribs to stop just beneath her breasts.

"In case I haven't been clear," Owen said against her lips, "I want you."

Slapping a hand on his chest, Keeley pushed him away. "Oh, you're crystal, pal. I just don't want you back."

"Liar," he crooned.

"Okay, fine. My body responds to you, just like it always has." More, she thought. God, so much more. "But that's not the point. My brain doesn't want you, and I tend to think before jumping into the sack with men these days."

"Just how many men have you been jumping lately?" he asked, scarily quiet.

"None of your damn business," she tossed back. "My hormones may be on fire right now but my head is cool, and it's telling me to walk away from you."

"Go ahead," he challenged. "I'll just come after you."

Exasperated and more aroused than she wanted to admit,

Keeley pulled at her ponytail. "Why are you doing this? We've already proven we shouldn't be together."

"That was then. This is now."

"Thanks for the physics lesson, Einstein."

"I mean it. We're different people now. You were right, we couldn't handle each other before. We needed to grow on our own, to experience life without each other."

"I still have a lot of life to experience."

"I sincerely hope so," Owen agreed. "And I think I'm starting to realize I want to be there while you do."

Keeley's mouth dropped open. She slammed it closed; reconsidered her position. It was obvious Owen was too caught up in the moment to see reason. "Look, we've both admitted we never wanted to see each other again. We shouldn't lose sight of that because we've spent the last half hour on a walk."

"I know what I shouldn't lose sight of," Owen said with a determined gaze. Reaching out, he took her hand. "Invite me over for dinner."

"No! What part of this don't you understand?" Panic set in as she tugged her hand out of his. "I meant what I said. I have no interest in picking up where we left off."

"I don't either. I'm not saying I want a fresh start, but I want to see where this could go."

"Well, I don't."

"Well, I don't plan to walk away again."

"You don't even know me anymore."

"But I want to." Owen said flatly. "You know how I get when I go after something I want."

Keeley's eyes narrowed to slits. "Is that a challenge?"

"You always did love a good challenge."

Throwing her hands in the air, Keeley stalked to her car. "I'm done with you."

"I think I like seeing you flustered."

The satisfaction in his tone put Keeley on the defensive. The fact he could see just how much he affected her had her seeing red. "Go jump off a cliff."

"Since you're a first responder, wouldn't you just have to jump after me?" he called out.

"Fat chance," she grumbled as she wrenched open her car door. But as she backed out of the narrow parking space, she couldn't stop the shiver of anticipation as he stood, a panting dog at his feet, staring after her with a smug smile on his handsome face.

CHAPTER 4

Owen's focus never wavered from the poodle currently chewing its leash. "Aus," he commanded. The pup, aptly named Quagmire, merely re-angled his head and gnawed the fraying fabric. "Aus," he repeated, this time with a firm hand to emphasize the order.

Quagmire released the leash, earning Owen's praise. He'd no sooner drawn up the slack in the leash when the pup began running in circles. "Sitz," he commanded, but Quagmire was having the time of his life spinning over the slick floor.

Sighing, Owen considered throwing in the towel. Why the hell had he agreed to obedience training? He was a combat K9 handler, responsible for the apprehension of multiple subjects of interest, the detection of too many bombs to count. He'd have been mortified if his guys could see him now, unable to convince a goddamn poodle to sit.

After fifteen minutes of hard, sweaty work, Quagmire sat. Owen wanted a fucking beer. Or twelve.

Calling it a day, he released Quagmire to his owner, a busty redhead whose high-pitched squeals annoyed him more than the dog ever could. Fighting the urge to toss them both out of his school, he gritted his teeth. "Have you been re-enforcing the commands at home, Ms. Grande?"

"How many times must I insist you call me Leesa?" she chided. "Of course we practice at home, don't we Quaggy Baby?" She smiled up at Owen, squeezing her arms across her impressive chest to push her tits further out of the skimpy pink top. "We work on it every day, just like you said."

"In that case, I should be seeing improvements by now."

"Well, I may be a bit soft on him," Leesa giggled, arching her painted brows. "I tend to give in to men of the opposite sex."

"He's not a man, he's a dog, and he needs a firm hand."

"Which is why I'm here." She batted impossibly long lashes at him, and Owen couldn't help but wonder how long it took her to glue those suckers on. "Maybe we should come twice a week?"

Owen's breath caught in his lungs at the prospect of dealing with them more than once every seven days. Truthfully, he wouldn't have taken them on at all, but she was the friend of one of the wives of his A&M buddies, so he'd felt obligated, which only irritated him more.

"It wouldn't do any good to come in more often if you're not going to practice at home."

"Ooh, that's it!" she clapped her hands together. "You should come to my place to give him lessons!"

Seeing the trap, Owen backpedaled. "I'm not a vet; I don't do house calls."

"I'd double your rate."

"It's not the money, Ms. Grande, it's simply my policy."

"And you can't flex," she cooed, "just this once?"

"Afraid not," he answered flatly, "but I can give you the names of other trainers, if that's what you're looking for."

On a huff, Leesa rolled her eyes. "I don't want anyone else; I'm told *you're* the best."

"Then I'll see you here, same time, next week."

"Fine," she purred. "I'm looking forward to it."

Owen didn't watch her leave but busied himself righting the

equipment he'd used for Quagmire's training session. The pounding behind his eyes only inflamed his temper. The conniving woman always succeeded in giving him a headache, not only with her pathetic overtures, but also with the punch of perfume swirling around her perfectly curled hair.

"She wants to eat you alive," said a voice behind him. "Two big bites and you'd be a goner."

Turning, Owen flipped his old teammate the bird. "I hate you."

Laughing, Ty Morrell stepped closer. "Come on, man, she's raring to get a taste of you. You should let her." The Texas Ranger's starting third baseman had a glint in his eye that told Owen exactly what he thought Owen should let Leesa do.

"She's not my type."

"You don't have a type."

Insulted, Owen shoved a ball back on its shelf. "Of course I do."

"O-Man, you've been avoiding women like the plague since you moved to town. Being a concerned friend, I've taken it upon myself to remedy that little mistake."

"It's not yours to remedy," Owen ground out, "and it's not a mistake. Besides, I'm seeing someone."

Owen winced the instant the words left his mouth, and as Ty's face split into a wide grin Owen wished he'd kept his mouth shut.

"Well, hell, you should have said something! Who is she?"

Shrugging, Owen refused to meet Ty's eyes. "Just a woman."

"Uh uh, you don't have women. Spill."

"Why are you here, anyway?"

"Cat wanted me to invite you over for dinner."

Owen planted his feet and stared Ty down. "Is your phone broken?"

"Nope, but I knew Leesa would be here, so I wanted to stop in and see how it was going."

"So you're no more than a nosy bastard?" Owen nodded. "Got it."

"Come on, Cat's been worried about you. So have I."

"Why?"

The smile faded from Ty's eyes. "I know you saw some shit in the sandbox, O. I may play dumb when it benefits me, but I know you came back with more scars that those on your hands."

Drawing a deep breath, Owen paused. Ty might come across as flighty, but he was as solid as a damn rock. Still, he didn't feel like ripping open wounds best left patched.

"It's Keeley."

Ty's eyes bugged wide. "Keeley? *The* Keeley?"

"The one and only," Owen muttered as he grabbed a roll of paper towels.

"Holy hell, I haven't seen her in years! What's she doing up here? How long has she been in town? How did you run into her?" Ty paused for a brief second. "And why aren't your legs broken?"

Owen looked up as he bent to wipe slobber off the floor. "Why would my legs be broken?"

"You did her wrong, and you know it. She's not the type of woman to forget it."

Owen's shoulders tightened. "Would you stop with the types shit?"

"Spill it."

"She's a firefighter. A damn lieutenant. Isn't that a kick in the balls? She responded out here when my fire alarm was going off the other night."

"No way. No fucking way. Cat is gonna love this. She and Keeley always got along." Inspiration struck, winging Ty's eyebrows into his hairline. "Bring her for dinner!"

"No, no, hell to the no. She wants nothing to do with me, so the last thing I need is to bring her somewhere that'll dredge up old memories best left buried."

"Uh uh, that's your mistake. You can't let that shit fester, man. Get it out in the open."

"What do you know about women? You've been with the same one since high school."

"Exactly." Ty brushed his shoulder. "I know how to keep 'em happy."

Laughing, Owen walked his friend to the front lobby. The more he thought about it, the less he liked the idea of dinner with Ty and Cat. For all her gruff exterior, Keeley was an emotional female. Sometimes *overly* emotional. He wasn't sure what she'd feel when faced with the couple they'd run with thick as thieves back in their college days. "I'll talk to her."

"Uh huh. You do that." Ty slipped aviator sunglasses over his tan face. "I know she's more of a football fan, but you should see if she wants tickets to Sunday's game. I have field seats with your name on them."

Owen crossed his arms. "Just the two of us?"

"Well, I'll either be on third or inside the dugout so I don't know who else you expect."

"Just making sure this isn't a setup."

"Would I do that to you?"

"Yes, you absolutely would."

With a cheeky grin, Ty saluted as he sailed out the front door. Shaking his head, Owen skirted around the desk and closed himself in his office. He had thirty minutes before his next client, and he intended to make the most of his time.

Paperwork could wait.

Crossing to the stack of boxes in the corner, he drew a deep breath, preparing himself for the onslaught of images. Carefully opening the first box, he gingerly removed the bubble wrap from the photo frame. Five men stared out at him, cocky grins on beard-covered faces. Dressed in fatigues with a dusty tank behind them, they had no idea what awaited them. It was their first deployment as members of the 2nd Ranger regiment. It would be the only deployment for three of them—they had returned home in boxes.

He unearthed photo after photo, each as gut-wrenching as the last. Soldiers crowding around a group of solemn-faced village elders; a gaggle of school kids kicking a soccer ball across the barren Afghani landscape; Turbo and Flash, two of the best goddamn bomb dogs Owen had ever encountered, lying obediently at their handlers' feet.

He arranged some photos around the office, then took the others to the lobby where he hung them with care. He'd loved the military. The rules, the expectations, the predictably unpredictable fuckery. He'd craved deployments, ready to cross the ocean to join his buddies in their hunt for bad guys. He wasn't naive enough to believe he'd joined the Army solely out of a sense of duty for his country; he was a realist, and man enough to admit he'd joined out of a desire to escape, for someone else to call the shots, and quite possibly, for the chance to unleash his anger and guilt on dudes he'd deemed expendable.

God knew he wasn't proud of his early intentions, but months of therapy had aided him in realizing he'd been fighting on two fronts – the war on guilt within, and the war on terror without. Though he may not have joined for the "right" reasons, once in his unit, he'd embraced the combat lifestyle, loving his fellow teammates like brothers, training like a damn fiend to complete the missions set out before him. Until the final one.

Unearthing the last box, he paused, fighting back grief so potent it pooled in his gut like lead. Trembling fingers pulled the battered lid apart. Reaching down, Owen removed the frayed dog leash, its name tag dulled with dirt he couldn't bring himself to clean off. The swift slice of regret kicked him in the balls, as harsh and unrelenting as the first day he'd felt it. Beneath the leash rested a pair of dog tags. Korey's dog tags.

The site of them transported him to a different world. A bloodier, more ruthless time and place.

The grime of ever-present sandy dust coated his mouth. The compound loomed in front of them, its insides shielded by walls twelve feet high. It was eerily silent. No birds sang, no traffic hummed. The compound was still—too still. Adrenaline spiked through Owen's veins, sharpening his vision, his hearing. The only break in the quiet was the squawk of the radio as the platoon sergeant requested confirmation from the support fire squad.

"Bravo, confirm fire squad ready."

"Roger that."

"Alpha, stack on position."

"Roger."

Owen watched his teammates line up around the corner from the entrance. Four deep, they flanked the sharp edge, waiting for Rob, their resident bomb-guy, to slap the explosive on the door. Whichever villager had installed the sheet of metal had been looking at their bottom line. Rather than detaching the door from the frame, they'd installed it in one massive piece, extending the metal shards until they'd become embedded in the mud and cement making up the walls of the shitty compound.

Rob ran up to the door, peeling the backing off the double-sided tape as he approached. In one swift move he stuck the dip can onto the metal then quickly backpedaled, running the detonation cords between his hands as he eased around the breach team. Taking his place behind the fourth Ranger, he waited for the command.

Owen heard the radio traffic, second nature by now. Rob pulled the ring from the green plastic stick, lighting the explosive inside the det cord. Within half a second, the C4 inside the dip can ignited, blowing debris more than a hundred feet in several directions. The breach went off like a well-choreographed play. The four-man team moved as one body, pausing only long enough for the rear man to take lead. With a powerful kick, the door was open. The rear man pivoted, slamming his back against the wall to allow the other three Rangers entry. Once they moved in, he followed.

Owen and his remaining teammates moved up to the wall and awaited their order to enter. Seconds passed agonizingly slow as the breach team cleared the area immediately past the door. Owen checked his breathing, checked Turbo. The dog, calm as a seasoned soldier, panted quietly. Muscles bunched and quivered, yet he sat on his haunches, patient and deliberate, until Owen told him differently.

"Courtyard north clear," the team leader stated over the radio.

Gathering the slack in the leash, Owen grinned down at his loyal partner. "Time to play."

. . .

The bark behind him snapped Owen back to the present. Pivoting, he couldn't stop his body from lowering into a defensive crouch. Raising his hands, he shielded his face with one arm as he attempted to draw a pistol that didn't exist. A tall, dark-skinned man stared at him, eyes wide, as a Belgian Malinois on a studded leash sent up a series of barks loud enough to piss off the neighbors.

"Mr. Prescott? I apologize, I didn't mean to startle you."

Heart pounding in his ears, Owen slowly raised to a guarded standing position. He counted his breaths, in and out, until his heart didn't feel as if it would gallop out of his chest. The man across from him stood stock still, having finally gained control of the Mal so it sat obediently at his feet. It took Owen a few additional seconds, but he finally placed them.

"Marcus, good to see you." Shifting his attention to the dog, he smiled. "Rock, you're being a good boy. Well done."

Going through the motions, he moved Marcus and Rock into the training room then excused himself. Shutting the door to his office, he perched on the edge of the cheap desk and let his face fall into his hands. It had been a long time since he'd fallen that deep into a memory. He'd worked long hours with his therapist to minimize their occurrences. He'd packed them over a year ago, when he'd packed up to leave Fort Bragg. They'd remained sealed, locked away, until he'd decided to use their contents at his new school. Now, he could see he should have taken it slow, and he definitely should have waited to unpack them in private, when he wasn't expecting anyone.

Rubbing his hands over his face, he rose and grabbed a bottle of water from the mini fridge in the corner. The plain liquid tasted like ashes on his tongue, but he forced himself to swallow. His skin was clammy, and he knew without looking that his face was pale. Breathing through his nose, he pitched the empty bottle in the recycle bin and forced himself to square his shoulders.

There were several forms of courage. It had taken his teammates physical courage to breach that compound that day. Now, faced with hours of training a dog that looked like the one he'd given up, he realized it would take a truckload of moral courage to get through. Bringing Turbo's face into the forefront of his mind, he calmed. His hands regained their normal dexterity, his heart rate finally slowed. Focusing on the tan and black face, he opened the door.

CHAPTER 5

Keeley blew stray wisps of hair out of her eyes. She'd taken a backstage role, letting her guys work the problem, but dammit, she wanted in on the action. She listened as they asked, ordered, and finally, attempted to barter. Seeing they were getting nowhere, Keeley stepped in.

"Mr. Burch, what really happened today?"

The elderly gentleman turned surprisingly fierce blue eyes in her direction. "I've already told these pestering young folks what happened. I ain't gonna say it again."

They stood in the center of Mr. Burch's room. The small space was dominated by a narrow bed, its soft sage comforter centered with military precision atop the mattress. A dresser stood in one corner; its edges chipped from numerous moves. It was bare atop the shiny surface, save for an ivory statue of the Virgin Mary and a pack of Marlboros. Keeley didn't bother to roll her eyes at the presence of cigarettes inside the oxygen-ridden room.

A squat TV sat in the opposite corner, hooked up to a decrepit VCR that hadn't seen a store shelf in two decades. *Dances with Wolves* played on the ancient screen, a young Kevin Costner astride a gorgeous horse galloping among a herd of buffalo. Turning her attention to the not-so-young man on the edge of the bed, Keeley knelt down, so they were eye level.

"The staff say you've been making suicidal statements the past couple of days."

"I've done no such thing. They want me out of here, the heathens. They're stealing my belongings, right from under my nose! They hope I die so they can pawn the rest of this!" Motioning with one feeble arm, the man attempted to stand, but collapsed back down. "You're not doing anything about it, either, are you?"

Keeley looked over her shoulder to see the officer behind her, eyes sad as he studied Mr. Burch. Looking back at the feeble man, Keeley steeled her voice. "Mr. Burch, I'm not here to talk about your stolen items. If you'd like to talk to Officer Dunn about that after I leave, that's up to you. For now, I'm here to figure out why you overdosed on your medication."

"I took it exactly as I've been instructed."

"You're lying," Keeley said flatly. "You've been pretending to swallow your pills, then spitting them back out, hoarding them until you had enough to kill you."

Mr. Burch's face turned a scary shade of puce. "Those are serious allegations, madame."

"Attempted suicide is a serious business, Mr. Burch." Keeley leaned in until she could smell his mouthwash. "My bars are a testament to what I've experienced while at this department. The highs, the lows; the happy times, the painful ones. I'm not a spring chicken, and you're not going to pull the wool over my eyes like you did with my crew. I know you were trying to kill yourself. I'm not here to tell you that's wrong, or that life is worth living. I don't know your situation, but I do know that feeling lonely and hopeless and scared must be terrifying. I wouldn't want to live that way, either."

Keeley paused as tears gathered in Mr. Burch's eyes. "I also know I have a job to do, and I'm damn good at my job. I care about you, whether you believe it or not. I'd really appreciate your honesty here. Tell us what you took."

Mr. Burch stared at her, the internal struggle obvious on his paling face. His lips twitched, twin slashes of wrinkled paper. Finally, he sighed, pulling off thick bifocals and rubbing them on his plain white t-shirt. "Do you know what I used to do, Ma'am? Who I used to be?"

"Why don't you tell me?"

"I was a fighter pilot in the US Navy. I've flown planes in conditions you wouldn't believe, fought enemies you don't know exist. I've tested aircraft that never saw public approval, been in countries we've never admitted to. Now I lay in my own piss until someone can get around to changing me. I haven't seen the outside of this blasted facility in over two years, haven't seen anyone I care about in double that. You tell me, young lady, do you think this is a life I have any interest in living?"

Keeley's heart ached, but she kept her voice firm. "I can't answer that, Mr. Burch. I can say I'm grateful for your service and we should never forget the men and women like you who fought for us. We take you for granted and that's our mistake. There's a lot to be learned from your generation, your strength. The only way we can do that, though, is if you're still alive."

"No one cares enough to do that. Not anymore."

"I'm doing it now, aren't I?"

"You're one person. What difference can one person make?'

"You tell me," Keeley said softly. "What difference did you make?"

Mr. Burch's eyes cleared and a hint of humor lit them. "You're right. You are good at your job."

"What did you take, Mr. Burch?"

He told them, down to every last pill. Before he'd finished, the paramedics were already loading him onto the gurney, radioing ahead to the nearest hospital's cardiac unit. He was still talking as they strapped him down and wheeled him out of his sad little room inside the assisted care facility.

"I'm glad it was you," he bit off as Keeley stopped at the open door of the ambulance. "I never thought women had a place in combat, but I can see I may have been wrong about that."

"I can tell you you're absolutely wrong about that," Frank admonished him as he heaved the paramedic's bag into the bay. "These two women are worth their weight and then some when the shit hits the fan."

"I just might believe that," Mr. Burch whispered as he leaned back against the thin gurney pillow. He closed his eyes and proceeded to lie quietly as Keeley shut the doors and stepped back.

"Some calls rip out your heart," Jillian murmured from behind Keeley.

Turning, Keeley nodded once. "They remind us why we do this."

"He just needs someone to talk to. I wish I knew someone."

Jillian walked back to the firetruck, leaving Keeley staring after her. Sighing, Keeley realized she did know someone. In fact, it may do both of them good. Pulling her phone from her jacket pocket, she shot Owen a quick text.

Come by the station if you have time.

Before she could slip the phone back into its normal spot, he responded.

I'll make time.

Shaking her head, she helped load their gear back onto the truck, then hopped up into the passenger seat. Her crew's voices were a blur around her as she settled back for the drive to the station. Dammit, her pity for Mr. Burch was going to bleed over onto Owen, she just knew it. What must it be like to do the things military men and women did while overseas, then come home to a society that didn't understand it and couldn't replicate it? Sure, some of those men and women leaving the service joined professions like law enforcement or the fire department, but not all.

How did they cope? How did they adjust? Feeling her animosity toward Owen softening somewhat, she sighed. He *had* seemed sincere on their walk the other morning. Deep down, Owen had always been a stand-up guy. Honest, faithful, kind. True, he'd speared her straight through the heart, but he hadn't been malicious—he'd been hurting.

Keeley didn't know what had happened in the military to give him that hard edge, but she knew it wouldn't be pretty. Owen was the type of guy who wouldn't settle for less than the hardest, toughest road possible. She was sure he'd followed it, right to the end of the damn line.

That was the problem.

Gomez backed the truck into the station bay, and Keeley jumped down, ignoring the protest from her ankles at the sharp smack of boots on concrete. Over a decade on the job took its toll on the joints, muscles, and psyche. She treated each one carefully, deliberately. Maybe it was time for a round with her masseuse.

Headed for her office, she detoured only long enough to check on her sister station. Ensuring they were snug in their own station, she peeled her sweaty tee off her chest and grabbed her shower gear. The stall was old but spacious, allowing her plenty of room to stretch weary muscles beneath the stingy spray. She made a mental note to contact maintenance again about the water pressure as she lathered her loofah. Unable to suppress the moan as she scraped off a layer of skin with the porous sponge, she washed everything, twice, until she no longer smelled the underlying sickly-sweet odor of the elderly, disinfectant, and death in her nostrils.

Finally satisfied she was clean, she rinsed the soap and simply stood, soaking in the peace as much as the water. She loved her job, really, she did. She'd never once regretted becoming a firefighter. She'd been accused of being single-minded, demanding, and ruthless. She didn't argue with the first or second, but rather than ruthless she deemed herself...problem oriented. A lieutenant over a squad didn't have time to ask twice or play nice. She was responsible for lives, and she took that responsibility very, very seriously.

She didn't normally hang with her crew outside of work. Her dad had explained the ins and outs of supervision would force her to draw lines in the sand where they hadn't been while she'd been the low girl on the totem pole. She didn't regret wearing the brass, never had, but sometimes it weighed heavy.

Grabbing her towel from the hook outside the stall, she

wrapped the thin material around her body, wincing when it didn't quite cover her ass. Hell, she'd grabbed the wrong towel. Again.

Stepping out of the shower, she shrieked at the man standing in the doorway. "Fucking fuck! What are you doing in here?"

Owen's eyes were as wide as hers. "Jesus! Sorry! They told me to come on up. I couldn't find you, and this is the only door I hadn't opened."

"It didn't occur to you to *knock*?"

"I did! When you didn't answer, I got worried." Crossing his arms, he leaned a hip against the doorjamb. His gaze shifted from surprised to aroused. "You've filled out."

"Are you calling me fat?"

"Never. Unless it's PHAT."

Rolling her eyes, Keeley motioned him out. "I'll be dressed in a minute. You can wait in my office."

"Which is where?"

"Down the hall to the left."

With one final sweeping gaze, he winked at her. "Damned if you don't still do it for me."

Huffing out her breath, Keeley stared at the door he'd shut at his back. Damned if that wasn't true for her, too. Refusing to be distracted by it, she quickly donned a fresh gray tee, thin-knit pants, and socks. Shoving her feet into sandals, she refreshed her ponytail and headed for her office.

He stood at the window overlooking the bay beneath. His shoulders appeared wider than she remembered, but maybe that was because she was no longer distracted by the wave of hair that used to graze his neckline. Hands thrust in his pockets, he looked exactly as she'd expected – hard, sexy, and out of place.

"This isn't a social call," she said, a bit harsher than she'd meant to.

Turning, Owen raised a brow. "Then what is it?"

"I need a favor."

Owen raised his other brow. "I was intrigued, but now I'm fascinated."

"Don't be trite."

"I've been called many things, but I don't believe trite has made the list."

"Now it has. Have a seat."

Humor passed over his face. "Used to giving orders, huh? It suits you."

Years of training prevented her from grinding her teeth. "Please take a seat."

"Oh no, I like the orders."

"Shut it and sit down."

"Careful, I may not be able to refrain from tossing you on this desk and ravishing you."

Laughing, Keeley didn't know whether to punch him or jump him. Looking at her desk and realizing she'd never again see it without imagining herself bent over it, she leaned toward punching him.

As if sensing her inner turmoil, Owen cut her a break and sat. "Seriously, how can I help?"

The simplicity and sincerity of the offer struck her. It was so typically *Owen*. "I answered a call today of a retired Navy pilot. He's the one who needs your help." She outlined the situation, skimming over the attempted suicide, but knowing Owen would cop to it without her spelling it out.

Sure enough, he was nodding before she'd even finished speaking. "Which hospital?"

She told him, then sat back and studied him. He studied her right back, those probing eyes pulling out emotions she'd buried deep. She didn't like it, didn't appreciate it, and didn't want it. None of that seemed to matter as the man across from her sparked a fire within her by simply breathing.

"That's all," she clipped.

A slow smile spread across his handsome face. "I don't think so."

One second he was seated, the next he leaned across the desk, face inches from hers. She liked to tell herself she couldn't have stopped him, but the terrifying truth was she could. Easily. He did what he'd always done – set her alight. His lips brushed hers, a sensuous tease that promised pleasure. Breathing in his heady scent, she purred in pure female response. The sound snapped her back to reality. Shoving away from the desk, from *him*, she pushed to her feet.

"You're out of your mind," she ground out, desire sliding uncomfortable claws into her belly.

"You've always made me crazy."

"I've already told you we're not picking up where we left off."

"What's it going to take to convince you that's not what I want, either?" The first slips of frustration edged his voice. "Dammit, Keels, we need to talk about this. Fate put us back in each other's lives for a reason."

"I don't believe in fate."

"Then you're a fool," he said softly. Raising up, he turned from her. "Come with me to watch Ty play this weekend."

Thrown by the abrupt shift of gears, Keeley shook her head. "Ty? Ty Morrell?"

"He's in the big leagues now, plays for the Rangers." Owen's face melted into a proud grin. "I always knew he had it in him."

"When do they play?"

"Sunday. You working?"

She could have lied, told him she was. But that would have been cowardly, and she was no coward. "No."

"I'll pick you up at noon."

"I haven't agreed to go."

Owen's smile turned sly. "But you will. You know you want to."

He didn't wait for her response, whistling jauntily as he strode out of her office. Legs suddenly weak, she flopped back into her chair. Couldn't he see she couldn't just forget what he'd done? He'd shredded her heart, tossed her love in her face. She'd accepted it, even forgiven him, but forget...she couldn't. Hell, she didn't want to. It wasn't that she held it to her chest in defense, but she hadn't made it to where she was by allowing others to treat her like a fucking doormat.

Frustrated anew, she leaned back and kicked at the desk leg. Missing, she plowed her shin into the fidget bar she'd placed beneath the desk. A shriek of pain escaped before she could stop it. Cursing life in general, she bent to rub the skin.

"You okay in here, LT?"

Jillian's face peaked around the corner of the door. Motioning her in, Keeley grit her teeth. "My own stupidity."

Jillian's eyes sparkled. "Does it have anything to do with the hunk who just left?"

"I didn't see a hunk."

Jillian's eyes widened before she caught herself. "Okay."

Yanking on her ponytail, Keeley allowed herself a rare moment to vent. "Who does he think he is? Assumes he'll just waltz back into my life and because we *used* to tear up the sheets I'll go right back to it? Arrogant putz."

"If you defined 'tear up the sheets' I may be able to imagine him there and answer that question."

Choking out a laugh, Keeley rubbed her eyes. "It was rhetorical."

"You know, I've never even heard you mention a guy." Taking advantage of the opportunity for girl talk, Jillian perched on the edge of the seat Owen had just vacated. "We all assumed you had a bad breakup or something, because a woman who looks like you doesn't stay single unless she has some baggage."

"You all assumed?" Keeley asked softly.

Sensing her blunder, Jillian plowed on. "I mean look at you. You're smart, determined, gorgeous, and in charge. What man wouldn't want that?"

"You'd be surprised." Keeley rolled her shoulders. "Anyway, he's getting under my skin, and I don't like it."

"I do," Jillian said simply as she stood, earning her a hard glare from her boss. "I think it's time someone did."

"I'm not sure how I feel about that."

"I know." Shooting her a quick grin, Jillian backed toward the door. "Knowing you, if you've given someone the power to make you unhappy, it means they matter."

She dashed out before Keeley could open her mouth, which was just as well since Keeley found herself unable to think of a response. She'd told Owen she didn't believe in fate, but after having Owen shoved in her face time and time again, she was starting to reconsider.

CHAPTER 6

Spring in Dallas meant an abundance of rolling greenery and sprouting flowers. Prior to joining the military, Owen wouldn't have given them a second thought. Spring had been crunch time, filled with practice and ice baths and games, not marveling at fields rioting with wildflowers. Now, he took the time to not only see it, but appreciate it.

He stopped at a sidewalk stand for a bouquet of assorted blooms, their colors and textures a testament of spring. They reminded him of Keeley, of all her fascinating facets and precise demands. At once both wild and tamed, she'd only grown more appealing over time.

Never wanting to run into her again had been purely selfish. It was his own pride he'd attempted to spare a beating, not hers. She deserved an apology, and an explanation. But not today. Today was for fun at one of his favorite places in the entire world.

Keeley had texted him Saturday and told him she'd meet him there. Some men may have been disappointed, but not Owen. Knowing Keeley, he was just glad she hadn't flat out refused to go.

Cradling the flowers in one arm, he checked his watch. Ten minutes to spare. He'd just turned the corner, heading for the gate, when he saw her. It was as if the jumbotron had crashed on his head at the same moment a fastball struck him in the chest. Never one to worry about fashion, she wore a three-quarter sleeve Rangers shirt with cropped jeans. Her long tail gently swung from the back of a maroon A&M cap, and sunglasses covered a good portion of her face.

Flowers forgotten, Owen crossed to her and pulled her into his arms.

"Hey, whoa, wait!"

Owen ignored her, breathing her in as he drew her close, pulling her up on her toes as he wrapped his arms around her. After a tense moment she relaxed and slid her arms around him. Only then did he release her. Pleased to see she was just as affected as him, he grinned at her.

"If those were for me, you owe me another bouquet."

Glancing down, he realized he'd smashed the blooms when he'd gathered her in his arms. "It was worth it."

When he moved to toss them into a nearby trash can, Keeley grabbed them. "Give me those! What are you thinking?"

"You said to get you more."

"I was kidding." Tucking them under her arm, she motioned him forward. "Shall we? I need a beer."

They moved through security, then proceeded into the inner perimeter of the stadium. Fans of both teams mingled, talking, shouting and laughing good-naturedly. The scents of popcorn, pretzels, and pizza pierced the air. Owen breathed deep, savoring the smells of his childhood.

"Where are our seats?"

Drawn out of his head, he slid his sunglasses up onto his forehead, and grinned wickedly at her. "We're in a field suite, baby."

"Get out."

"Seriously, Ty wanted us to be comfortable."

Stopping abruptly, Keeley squinted up at him. "You told Ty you were bringing me?"

"Yep."

"Why would you do that? He's going to think we're together."

"We are together."

"You know what I mean. I don't want people thinking we're dating."

Refusing to rise to the bait, Owen tapped a finger on her nose, an old habit that had her snarling. "This is supposed to be a fun day. Don't spoil it." Taking her arm, he aimed her toward the entrance for the field suites. "Besides, if I was really trying to impress you, I know better than to spring for the fancy seats."

"What would you spring for?"

Cagey, Owen chose his answer carefully. "An all you can eat crab leg buffet followed by Rocky Road ice cream and a horror flick."

Snorting out a laugh, Keeley shook her head but didn't respond. Owen hoped the memory he planted would grow and fester. He hoped she would remember the date when they'd done just that. She'd felt sick, but Owen had waited her out, rubbed her down, then fucked her senseless.

A sideways glance told him she was remembering the night, too. The creamy skin along her throat was tinged pink, a sure sign she was riled. Riding the feeling, Owen stroked the arm tucked into his. Shaking her head in denial, she removed her arm and motioned for him to lead the way. Stepping through the doorway and onto the patio, Owen breathed in the scent of baseball.

Behind him, Owen heard Keeley's shocked gasp. He couldn't blame her. Situated between the dugout and home plate, they were face level with the field, an elegant subterranean box. A tall round table sat in one corner, ringed with bright red seats. A bar made of earthy woods ran the length of the box, more snazzy red chairs perched beneath it. Four glossy seats sat right against the field, more like expensive office chairs than any stadium seat he'd ever seen. There was only one other couple in the box, and it was obvious they were more into each other than what was happening on the field in front of them.

Owen stepped right up to the fence, heart pounding as he

watched players warmup by throwing a ball or swinging a bat. Standing there, he could all but taste the dip in his mouth, shooting that calming nicotine throughout his body. He could feel the hardness of the bat beneath his hand, hear the hard smack as the ball sailed into his glove.

He loved baseball the way most mothers loved their newborn. Uncontrollably, wholly, and somewhat exasperatedly.

"Sir, can I get you a drink?"

Owen turned to the woman standing near his elbow. He hadn't heard her come in, absorbed in his own thoughts. Forcing a smile, he ordered a tall beer, unsurprised when Keeley did the same.

Placing the crushed flowers on the bar, she moved up to stand beside him, her gaze riveted to the grass and dirt in front of them. "It's good to see you here."

Now he was surprised. "Why do you say that?"

"Baseball has always been more than a passion for you. I'm glad to see your time in the military couldn't take that away from you, too."

Struck, Owen stared at her. "What do you think the military took from me?"

"Peace," she answered softly, then smiled widely as a player approached their box. "Well, well, if it isn't the man of the day himself. Hello, Ty."

"Keeley, I'm glad you decided to take this sucker up on my offer." Eyes shaded behind mirrored sunglasses, he jerked a finger at Owen. "Truth be told, I didn't know if he'd have the cajones to ask you."

"Having cajones has never been his issue," Keeley replied.

Ty threw back his head and laughed. Owen realized the boxes around them had gone silent; everyone's attention suddenly riveted to the beloved Ranger.

"I've always liked you," Ty told Keeley.

"Ditto. How's Cat?"

"She's great, big as an orca."

"I beg your pardon?" Keeley planted her hands on her hips, a sure sign she was about to take someone's head clean off their body.

Recognizing the threat, Ty shook his head. "She's eight months pregnant."

Keeley's stance relaxed fractionally, but her eyes remained hard. "I'm thrilled for you, but I doubt she'd appreciate being called a killer whale."

"It's an inside joke," came a quiet voice from behind them. Owen spun, a grin springing to his face as Ty's wife waddled into the box, a toddler's hand clenched tightly in her own. Hair black as midnight was braided along the side of her head in a complicated loop, and exotic eyes set deep in a face smooth as satin and dark as coffee gave her the look of an ancient fertility goddess. "Chad thinks I'm kin to the monstrous dolphin."

The little boy at her side nodded his dark head earnestly. "My baby brother makes her belly stick out just like an orca."

"It's true. Go stand with Uncle Owen a minute."

Chad raced to Owen's side, and he bent to pick up the grinning toddler. Dressed in a miniature version of his dad's jersey and dark blue shorts, his still-pudgy hands were already sticky with what appeared to be chocolate. Smears of it ran along his chin and coated his upper lip. Mischievous eyes twinkled at Owen and he was struck, as always, that his friend had helped create a helluva good-looking kid.

Cat moved to embrace Keeley, holding her tight. "It's so good to see you."

Keeley wrapped her arms around her old friend, hands splayed across her back. "I can absolutely say the same."

"I didn't think I'd be able to make it today, but the heat's going to stay at bay long enough for me to enjoy at least the first few innings."

"Make her put her feet up," Ty broke in. "She's too damn stubborn for her own good."

"Too damn stubborn!" Chad piped up.

Cat merely rolled her eyes as she indulged in that long circular belly rub pregnant women seemed to need. "Can't take these two anywhere."

"Did Owen tell you I had to save him from a client's wiles the other day?" Ty asked Keeley.

"He did not," Owen interrupted as he shifted Chad in his arms, "and doesn't plan to."

Ty only grinned wider. "Make him. It's hilarious."

"Unless you're the one getting wiled," Owen bit off.

"Boys," Cat chastised softly, "behave. Chad, this is Ms. Keeley, Keeley, my first-born, Chad."

"It's nice to meet you." Keeley smiled at the boy whose arms had loped around Owen's neck. "How old are you?"

"I turn this many next month," he said proudly, holding up three chubby fingers.

"Happy early birthday."

"Thanks!" He shot her a disarming grin. "Maybe you'll buy me a present."

"Chad! You don't need any more presents." Cat sighed deeply. "Sorry, he's obsessed with toys right now."

Someone on the field yelled and Ty snapped his head around to listen. Nodding, he started backing away from the fence. "I gotta go. Enjoy the game, guys." Puckering his lips, he smacked them in a quick kiss. "Cat, Chad, Chase - love you to the moon." Saluting them, he turned and jogged to the dugout.

Chad started squirming, a sure sign he wanted down. Abandoning Owen without a qualm, the boy crossed to Keeley and held up his arms. Surprise flitted across her face, but she bent to pick him up.

"You're pretty," he told her.

"So are you."

Watching the fair-haired firefighter and the dark-haired toddler interact, Owen felt an unexpected tug in his gut. He didn't know what it meant and didn't really care to find out, but it was there, strong and sure.

Moving to one of the seats at the bar, Cat eyed the flowers.

"Those are also pretty." She hoisted her front-heavy body up, her lightweight coral dress swirling around her ankles as she propped her sandaled feet on the seat rung. Nodding to the pair studying the grassy field, she sighed. "That's quite a picture, isn't it?"

"Quite," Owen agreed.

Patting the seat next to her, she shifted as the attendant placed a bottle of water in front of her. "Come sit. It's been too long since you've come to the house."

"I've been busy." Owen nodded his thanks as the woman placed his beer on the bar.

"Haven't we all?"

"True." Easing onto the seat, he listened with half an ear as Chad and Keeley debated whether the tyrannosaurus rex or ankylosaurus would win the title of King of the dinosaurs. The breeze drifted lazily into the box, bringing with it the chorus of yells and whistles and claps that were baseball personified.

"You miss it," Cat observed.

"Terribly."

"Ty was serious when he said he'd talk to the manager about letting you try out."

"Nah, that stage of my life has passed." Owen lifted his beer. "At *this* stage, I'd rather sit in an expensive box with a beautiful woman and drink to my heart's content."

"Mmhmm," Cat agreed half-heartedly and met Owen's gaze head on. "She's more than just a beautiful woman."

"You're telling me."

Cat's eyes laughed as she sipped from her water bottle. "She always has been a handful for you."

"Make that two handfuls and you'd be right."

Grinning, Cat turned her attention to the field, where they were preparing for the National Anthem. "It makes my heart happy to know it's the truth."

Standing for the patriotic song, Owen watched Keeley remove her hat and place it over her heart, the other hand clutching that of the young boy as smitten with her as Owen was.

CHAPTER 7

Leaning back in Owen's passenger seat, Keeley fingered the flowers in her lap and had to admit she'd had fun. She hadn't expected to, but she also hadn't expected to run into Cat. Chad was just the icing on the cake. Sharp as a tack, the kid had kept her on her toes the first five innings.

After he and Cat left, Keeley found herself surprised to actually be enjoying Owen's company. No, that wasn't true. She'd always enjoyed his company; she just didn't want to.

She hadn't resisted when he asked if he could drive her home. Now they rode in silence, each deep in their own thoughts. *What was she doing?* True, she'd thought she'd never see him again, but she'd had plenty of time to settle. So why hadn't she? He kept throwing her off her stride, which didn't make her primal reactions to him any easier to swallow.

Risking a sideways glance at him, she ground her teeth as he appeared totally relaxed, fingers tapping the steering wheel in time to Janis Joplin. Meanwhile she was a boiling pot of resentment and anger, laced with arousal. Not a good combination.

He pulled into her driveway and turned to her, eyes clouded. "Are you going to ask me in?"

"No."

"Can I walk you to your door?"

"No."

"How about a good night kiss?"

"N-"

Before she could answer, he'd pivoted in the seat, grabbed her shirt, and hauled her over to his side. His mouth was an assault on hers, tugging her lips with his teeth as his hands skimmed up her sides. How could the man shoot her from coolly logical to a raging inferno in the span of a heartbeat?

All thought stopped as his hands slipped under her shirt and raced along her ribs. Rough and hard, he showed none of the poise she knew he possessed. She didn't care as desire stabbed between her legs, causing her to throb and ache for more.

One hand remained beneath her shirt, fingers tugging at her nipple through her bra as the other retreated to gently squeeze her throat. Unable to fight, she moaned and leaned closer.

"You're sure you don't want me to come in?"

No, god dammit, she wasn't sure. But the question snapped her back to reality. Pulling back, she yanked his hand from under her shirt and grabbed blindly for the door handle. "Thanks for the game."

"I'm not playing a game."

Blinking at him, twin flickers of humor and smugness snapped. Eyes sharp, he looked just as disoriented as she felt. "I meant the baseball game."

"Oh. Yeah. You're welcome."

Pushing open the door, she clutched the freshly crushed flowers to her chest and stumbled out of the truck. Shaky legs carried her to the porch and fumbling fingers finally managed to insert the key into the deadbolt.

She stepped inside, turning back once more to see Owen staring at her, hands clutching the wheel. Even from this distance she could see his whitened knuckles. Good. He deserved to be just as rattled as her.

Slamming the door behind her, she locked it, dropped the flowers on the table, and kicked off her shoes. Looking at the bruised blooms, she sighed, picked them back up, and trundled into the kitchen. She dug around for a vase, settling for a large Aggies cup when she couldn't find anything fancier.

Dropping the stems into the water, she carted the cup into the living area and plopped it on the side table. The bedroom was too intimate – the last thing she needed was another reminder of him in her personal space. Slipping the hat from her head, she tossed it on the love seat and flopped on the couch.

Dammit, her lips still tingled from being ravished and she could still feel the fires he'd created as his fingers raced along her skin. Hell, sex had never been a problem for them. They'd torn up the sheets, literally, during their bouts of sweaty foreplay. Imaginative, god, the man was creative with positions, and his stamina...oh, boy.

She'd never admit it to his face, but no other man could hold a flame to him in the sack. No wonder she was floundering, searching for balance. The man was the best lay she'd ever had, it made perfect sense she'd have trouble resisting him.

Feeling marginally steadier, she rose from the couch just as her phone pinged. Digging it out of her back pocket, she read the display.

Feel lk shit. Nd grl time. Bsy?

She translated Chantel's shorthand easily enough and shot back a reply.

Just got in. Come on over.

B rgt thr.

Shaking her head, she quickly changed clothes then—knowing her best friend—retrieved a metal shaker from the cabinet. Reaching up, she chose a clear bottle of tequila and another of orange liqueur from the row of bottles lining the top of her fridge. Keeley rarely drank anything other than beer, but Chantel was a different breed.

She selected a lime from the bowl on the counter and deftly sliced it in half. Adding the juice to the cocktail, she tossed in some ice and quickly shook the contents. She'd no sooner started pouring the liquid into a frosted glass when she heard Chantel's key in the lock. Moments later her dull living room was filled with color and sound.

"Oh my god, you won't fucking believe the day I've had."

Biting the inside of her cheek to keep from smiling, Keeley turned, margarita in hand. "I want to hear it, anyway."

"You're a saint, you know that? A fucking saint." The cocktail sloshed against the salted rim as Chantel pulled her in for a one-armed hug. "This is exactly what I needed." Eyes narrowing, she glanced at the empty shaker. "Where's yours?"

Opening the fridge, Keeley pulled out a beer. "Spill."

Chantel opened her mouth, and every tiny detail gushed out. Keeley felt the last of the tension flee her body under the barrage of exaggerated movements and facial expressions accenting the story of betrayal and deceit. Chantel didn't pause except to take healthy gulps from her glass. Less than five minutes in, Keeley was fixing her friend another.

"So I told him to get out, he'd lost the privilege of putting his slimy, lying, two-timing hands anywhere near my body."

"What did he do?"

"The pig grabbed me, tried to 'make me see reason.'" Chantel's dark eyes flashed. "Oh, I saw reason, all right. Enough reason to punt his balls into his throat and deliver a rather magnificent hook to his scummy face."

Keeley winced. Chantel may look like every man's wet dream, but she was also a second-degree black belt in kickboxing. "How long did it take him to get up?"

"Long enough." Smile feral, Chantel polished off her second cocktail. "God, this is just what I needed." Leaning back against the couch cushions, steam released, Chantel finally relaxed. Eyes slitted, she scanned the room, sitting up abruptly as they lighted on the flowers in the corner. "What are those?"

Following her gaze, Keeley shrugged. "Flowers."

"No shit, Sherlock, where did they come from?"

Wincing, Keeley took a drag from her bottle. "Owen."

"Owen? The I-fucked-you-up-good-then-left-you-Owen?"

Sighing, Keeley closed her eyes. "That's the one."

"WTAF?"

Chuckling despite the stress that had jumped back between her eyeballs, Keeley shrugged. "The actual fuck of it is that I ran into him on a call." She briefly explained what had happened, followed up by their walk with Sura, Owen dropping by the station, and finally, the baseball game. Less animated than Chantel, it only took a matter of minutes.

"Wait, so you've willingly seen him three times now and this is the first I'm hearing of it? Wow."

Recognizing the hurt in her friend's voice, Keeley debated pulling her own hair. "Look, I didn't deliberately hide it from you. I'm still working it out for myself."

"How the hell can you do that by yourself? You're too close to it, too deep." Chantel motioned with her empty glass. "That's why we bounce things off each other – detached perspective."

"You don't stay detached long," Keeley grumbled.

"Fucking A, I don't." Chantel pushed her hair off her shoulders. "Okay, let's look at this like grown-ass women who habitually punt men's balls into their throats."

Keeley raised a brow. "I'm pretty sure you're the only one in this room who does that."

Ignoring her, Chantel pressed on. "After you ran into him, obviously unintentionally, you've accepted his invitation to meet up with him *and* the dog you adopted together, invited him to your station, your *home*, and accepted an invitation to a baseball game, which is totally a thing you used to do together, yeah?"

Blinking, Keeley stared at her. "That sums it up."

"So it's your turn."

"My turn to what?"

"Invite him to do something."

"Whoa, whoa," Keeley set her beer on the table with a snap.

"Aren't you supposed to be reminding me that he broke my heart and left me bleeding?"

"Why should I? You remember that clearly enough."

"But that's the whole point of the bashing, right? You tell me I'm too good for him, he doesn't deserve me, blah blah?"

"Oh, honey," Chantel sighed. Setting her glass beside Keeley's beer, she took her friend's hands. "If this was some casual fuck, absolutely. But this is *Owen*. I get it, I didn't know you when you two had your falling out, but I know you now. You've never gotten over him. It's why you can't move on. Personally, I think fate has given you a second chance. Ride it out, see what happens."

Dumbfounded, Keeley shook her head. "What the hell is up with all this fate talk? This isn't what I expected."

"The bastard broke your heart, but I'd say he more than paid for it." Chantel paused, choosing her words carefully. "Have you talked about it?"

"No. What's left to say?"

"Probably a lot, but I can't answer that. Look, it's obvious the guy is still hung up on you."

"You can tell that from a couple of day dates and a cup of crushed flowers?"

"I can tell because he's risking a whole helluva lot by putting himself out there."

"What does that mean?"

Chantel tsked. "You're so naive it's oddly cute." She released Keeley's hands, clasped them dramatically over her heart. "Do you think he saw combat overseas?"

"I'm sure he did."

"Do you think it haunts him?"

Unsure where her friend was headed, Keeley dipped her head. "I'm sure it does."

"Would you let him shut you out?"

Exasperated, Keeley stood, ripping the band from her hair and raking her fingers through it. "Just say what you're getting at."

"Facing you not only means he has to face what he did to you, but also what he went through on deployment."

Incredulous, Keeley whipped her hair back into the band. "How do you figure that?"

"You won't let him hide from you. You'll hold him accountable for how he treated you, how he walked away. And when he starts to close off due to the horrors he's witnessed, you won't let him. You may not force him to talk about it, in fact you shouldn't, but you'll make him remain open with you. He knows that, honey, because he knows *you*. Yet he still seeks you out. That tells me all I need to know about him."

Dumbfounded anew, Keeley lowered to the couch. "You really believe that?"

"With my whole, ball-punting heart." Chantel studied her with a mix of pity and envy. "Now, I could use another drink."

"Then you're staying the night."

"Obviously."

They spent the remainder of the night watching old Halloween movies and debating the scariest villain of all time. At one point they'd realized they were ravenous and ordered pizza. The half-eaten Hawaiian sat between them, the crusts removed and lying forgotten in the box. Empty beer bottles lay scattered on the table and the room carried the unmistakable aroma of lime.

Sometime after midnight, Michael Myers hacked at a screaming female as Keeley draped a blanket over a softly snoring Chantel. Gauging her balance, she attempted to stand on one foot, failed miserably as she toppled into the wall. Chantel didn't move.

Shaking it off, Keeley snagged her phone and headed for the master bedroom. Turning down the duvet, she dropped onto the sheet fully clothed and studied her phone. *Don't do it,* she chided herself. Dammit, she'd failed the balance test, which in turn was her drunk text test. She tried to tally up the pros and cons of texting Owen in this state, but she couldn't keep them straight in her head. Hell, it was so late he probably wouldn't get the message tonight. Still, she pulled up his text thread.

I should have let you come in.

Settling back against the pillows, she placed the phone on the nightstand and turned off the lamp. Closing her eyes, she'd started to drift when her phone pinged. Eyes flying open, she reached blindly for her phone.

I can come now.

Snorting, Keeley smiled.

It's late and I'm drunk.

You've always been an entertaining drunk.

You've always been a poor liar.

I've never lied to you.

Point proven.

There was a pause and Owen sent the confused emoji.

You really ARE drunk.

Told you.

Let me see you tomorrow.

It was Keeley's turn to pause. She'd opened this can of worms, she might as well see it through.

Come over for dinner.

You're cooking?

She could all but hear the fear in his voice but laughed.

Hell no, I'll order Chinese.

Deal. I'll pick it up on the way.

Six o'clock sharp. And bring Sura.

Done.

Torn whether to leave the conversation there or add a good night, Owen answered the internal debate for her.

Dream of me.

Not likely.

Pity. I hope I dream of you.

Shaking fingers hovered over the keys. Dammit, dammit, dammit! She hoped she dreamed of him, too.

I hope I'm kicking your ass in the batting cage.

Is it any wonder I've never gotten over you?

Unable to think of an appropriate response, she flicked the

phone to silent, set it on her nightstand, and pulled the sheet over her head. She couldn't answer for him, but she was beginning to realize she'd merely masked her hurt with anger. The truth, combined with the greasy pizza and bubbly beer, made for a rough night.

CHAPTER 8

After a grueling day in the training room, Owen sported a nasty headache and an even nastier disposition. All he wanted was a few blessed hours of quiet and a dark room. Instead, he headed to Keeley's place with a bag overflowing with steaming Chinese food on the seat beside him.

He could admit her text had surprised him, then planted a seed of hope. She thought of him, even when she didn't want to. That had to mean something. God knew he thought of her, more than any human should think of another.

A wet nose pressed into his neck and he grinned. "Almost there, girl. And before you start begging, I'll remind you, you've already eaten your dinner."

Sura circled the back seat, anxious. While she'd normally be up front, it had only taken one mishap to learn she couldn't be trusted near human food. Letting her ire be known, she growled, one long, low sound, as Owen parked in Keeley's drive.

The house surprised him. A single-story rancher on a corner lot, it was the epitome of everything Keeley hated. Small yard, no privacy, and a horde of cookie-cutter houses in close proximity. It was just another example of how she was still the girl he'd known, yet she'd changed. He couldn't wrap his mind around it; because it couldn't make sense. Could it?

Shrugging off the irritating mood, he climbed out of the truck, released Sura, and hoisted the plastic bag of white takeout boxes. He didn't have a chance to knock before the door swung open and his heart dropped to his feet.

Keeley wore a simple blue dress, the hem hitting right above the knee and thin straps covering bare shoulders. It was rare she left her hair down, but she'd done so tonight. It flowed down her back, a single braid pulling the bits away from her face while leaving the rest of those golden strands loose. She'd dispensed with shoes and he could see her toes were painted a soft rose. He wanted to shut Sura in a room with the food while he feasted on the woman in front of him.

"Right on time." Stepping back, she smiled at Sura. "Hello, pretty girl."

Sura rubbed against Keeley's thigh, teasing the blue fabric higher.

"Where's my hello?" Owen asked, his voice gruffer than he'd intended.

"Hello."

"Minx."

"Heathen."

Grinning, Owen held up the food, continuing their one-word conversation. "Hungry?"

"Ravenous."

Keeley led the way past a simply decorated living space, filled with furniture in muted bronzes and greens, to a spotless kitchen. He knew the appliances and surfaces weren't gleaming because Keeley had recently scrubbed them. She just didn't use them.

Setting the food on the shiny counter, he cocked his head. "Got any beer?"

"Help yourself." Always hungry, Keeley had already turned her attention to dishing the food onto plain white plates. Owen chuckled as he opened the fridge. A half-empty carton of orange juice, a single stick of butter, two apples, and a six-pack of beer graced the nearly empty shelves.

"You're low on provisions."

"With my work schedule it doesn't make sense to buy in bulk."

"Please, your work schedule has nothing to do with it. You'd live off beer and ice cream if you could get away with it."

"You're not wrong." Keeley opened a drawer and dug out two forks. "You only live once."

By the time she'd carted the food onto the tall two-seater dining room table, there was barely enough room for their drinks. Piles of Kung Pao chicken, rice, lo mein, egg rolls, wonton soup, and crab rangoon covered every inch of the small surface.

"Eyes bigger than your stomach?" Keeley asked.

"Yeah, right. I remember how much food you can pack away."

Shrugging, Keeley swirled lo mein onto her fork. "Food is fuel."

"And you hate running on empty."

"Doesn't everyone?"

Owen split his focus between his own plate and her face. She'd added a touch of makeup, another anomaly. Was it wishful thinking, or was she actually trying to look nice? Not that she didn't always, but she rarely took the time to mess with cosmetics.

Emboldened, he slathered his egg roll with soy sauce. "Tell me about being a firefighter."

Keeley's fork paused briefly on its way to a crab rangoon. "What do you want to know?'

"What do you like about it?"

"It's multi-faceted. When people think of firefighters, they automatically assume we're relegated to only fighting fires. While it's a logical assumption, it's wrong."

"What else do you do?"

"At our core we're first responders, so we respond to car crashes, medical calls, alarms, door breaching, etc."

"Door breaching?"

"Sure." Keeley sipped her beer. "The police department calls us when they need to get inside a house but don't want a lot of residual damage."

"The police call you?" Images of explosives on metal doors pierced his mind, curling dread in his gut. "That's fucking weak of them. Are you trained to handle that kind of action?"

Confused, Keeley squinted at him. "I'm not talking about serving warrants, I'm talking about welfare checks where someone hasn't heard from their grandmother in a few days and think she may have fallen and can't come to the door. The officers don't want to break her damn door, and they know we have the equipment to make a softer entry."

"Oh." Reigning in the emotions sparked by imagining her breaching a door, Owen shook his head. "Sorry, breach means something else in my world."

"Tell me about it."

"Uh uh, you first." He wagged his fork at her. "You didn't answer my question."

"Which was?"

"What do you like about it? You said it was multi-faceted," he pushed on before she could interrupt and accuse him on not listening, "but what does that mean?"

"I'm drawn to fire. It...speaks to me on some crazy, nonsensical level. I can't explain it, but when I'm near the flames, I can read them. Where they're going, how hot they're burning, what they'll destroy next. It's exhilarating and terrifying. All the other stuff, responding to medical alerts and overdoses, that keeps me balanced."

"Like Mr. Burch?"

"Exactly like Mr. Burch. Have you seen him?"

"Twice. After I left your station the other day, then again this morning."

"How is he?"

"Better. I've spoken with his social worker and we're trying to get him into a VA-run home for veterans."

Keeley's eyes softened. "You're working with his social worker?"

"He doesn't have any family left, so someone needs to."

Keeley pushed rice around her plate. "When I asked you to go talk to him, I didn't mean for you to feel obligated to do anything other than talk."

"I know." Nerves taut, Owen cradled his beer between two fingers. "I don't feel obligated."

"You can be a nice guy."

"Oh, great," Owen huffed. "Fucking perfect."

"What's wrong with being a nice guy?"

"Nice guys always finish last. Always."

"If they're considerate of their girl, they do."

Thrown, Owen opened and closed his mouth while Keeley stared at him. Finally, he tossed back his head and laughed. "Touché."

Smiling, Keeley reached down a hand to pat Sura's head. The dog had abandoned her dutiful owner for the pretty blonde and sat beside Keeley's seat, a polite distance from the food. Owen's heart ached as Sura turned her head and licked Keeley's hand from fingertip to wrist. Keeley merely smiled at her, then returned to eating.

"I want you back."

Keeley didn't meet his eyes as she scooped up a piece of chicken. "I'm not ready for that."

"I didn't ask you to come back, I'm just letting you know where I stand."

"I hear you, loud and clear."

"What are you going to do about it?"

Keeley swallowed, set down her fork. "Tell me about the Army."

On an irritated sigh, Owen sat back in his chair. "You're evading."

"No, I'm not. I need to know about your time in the military."

"It's in the past. What does it have to do with now?"

"Everything," she said softly. Meeting his eyes, she held them, gaze strong and true. "You don't expect me to jump into the sack with someone I don't know, do you? Is that the girl you remember? Because if it is, your memory is faulty."

"I didn't say anything about jumping in the sack."

"Stop deflecting."

"I'm not deflecting, I'm clarifying."

Rather than the spark of temper he expected from her, she smiled sadly. "Owen."

Dammit, he didn't want to share those years of his life with her. Not her. He'd shield her from them, from his mistakes, from his regrets. That part of his life had no bearing on where they were now or where he wanted them to go.

But looking at the determination in her eyes, he knew she wasn't going to let it go. The damn woman was worse than Kore when she had a bit between her teeth.

"The gist of my military career is unexciting. I was a handler for an MWD, military working dog, attached to a Ranger battalion. I was stationed out of Fort Bragg, North Carolina. I deployed to Iraq twice, Afghanistan three times. When I came home the last time, I was ready to get out."

Even to his ears it sounded dry and rehearsed, like a kid giving their spiel to judges at the science fair.

Keeley ran a lazy finger along the side of her beer. "Okay, now I understand the frame of the picture. Paint its interior for me."

He should have known she wouldn't settle for just the facts, but he wasn't ready to tell her all of it. Not yet. Maybe not ever.

Choosing his words carefully, he stacked the empty boxes to give his hands something to do other than shake under the table. "On my final deployment, we were tasked with detaining and questioning a high value target. Our intel guys narrowed his location to a compound in the middle of fucking nowhere. We had to move quickly because the bastard was known for hopscotching around the damn country. Later we'd find out he fed us the information, rigged it so we'd move in the daylight rather than waiting for the cover of darkness."

Owen paused, refusing to acknowledge the ghostly taste of dust coating his mouth. "We went into the compound, then all hell broke loose. We lost three men that day. Three, out of a team of eight."

Keeley reached over, covering the hand still clutching a white box. "Thank you for telling me."

"I'm an open book."

Bitter regret joined the gritty memory of sand in his mouth, but Keeley's hand remained firm and warm on his. "There may come a day when I have to ask how you cope with it. I won't now, it's none of my business, but my greatest fear is losing one or more of my guys on a scene. If that day comes, I'll be looking to you for guidance." She smiled, a real smile, smoothing out some of the rougher edges of Owen's guilt. "Until then, you can wash the dishes."

An answering smile tugged his lips. "I brought the food."

"I provided the beer and the plates."

"Why don't we do them together?"

It didn't take long to remember why he should have just done them himself. While he gathered up the boxes, she dumped the plates into the dishwasher, remaining grains of rice and all. Shaking his head, he followed up behind her, rinsed the dishes in the sink, then stacked them neatly in the racks.

Grinning ear to ear, she cocked a hip against the counter and fingered her braid. "Told you, you could wash the dishes."

"I rinsed them. There's a difference."

Rolling her eyes, she crossed to the fridge and pulled out two fresh beers. "So you always said."

"What else did I always say?"

Slowly twisting the caps off the bottles, Keeley eyed him warily. "I don't remember."

"I do." He couldn't say why, but the nerves playing over her face pleased him immensely. He reached for his beer, sliding a finger along the back of her hand in the process. "I always said we complimented each other nicely."

"Uh huh." She snatched her hand back as if stung. "I can't recall."

"Our nonverbal communication spoke volumes," he pressed on. "And when I was inside you, it felt like you'd been made for me. Just for me."

"That I remember." Eyes glazed, she shook her head as if to clear it. "Some things are best left to memory."

"And some aren't," he argued. "You can't stand there and tell me you feel nothing. You can't even stand for me to touch you, and it isn't because you're repulsed."

"I do feel something. A lot of somethings," she corrected. "I can't get a handle on all of them, so I'm taking it slow."

"I've already told you what I want."

"I said I hear you, loud and clear," she shot back. "You walked out on me, remember? As long as we're taking this stroll down memory lane, let's check the facts. *You* blamed *me*. You wanted nothing to do with me. You turned from me without a backward glance, moving away, forgetting I existed."

"That's bullshit." The first stirring of anger pierced the guilt he'd felt when she'd nailed the truth of what he'd done. But dammit, he wouldn't let her think he'd forgotten her. "You were correct up until you said I forgot you existed. I *never* forgot. You'd sneak into my thoughts at the most inopportune moments, right at a point in time when I needed to be thinking of anything *but* you."

"I'm not sorry you had to endure that," she tossed back, "seeing as it was your fault in the first place."

"You changed your number."

Dammit, *god dammit*, he hadn't meant to say that.

"How do you know that?"

Raking a hand through his hair, Owen kicked lightly at the base of the dishwasher. "I tried calling. From basic training. I needed to hear your voice, to tell you I was sorry, that I was wrong. Basic does something to a man. It makes you evaluate your life, your choices, your purpose. I knew I'd fucked up, knew long before I reported for duty, but I was too ripped up to admit it. I admitted it in training, but you'd changed your number, so I thought it was fate slapping me in the face for being such a wanker."

Keeley stared at him, mouth slightly open. "I'd tried calling you, to check in. I was worried about you, worried sick when you'd dropped out of school and off the face of the planet. It went to voicemail for a week straight, so I decided you were screening your calls and didn't want to talk to me."

"My phone was in my parents' basement while I was being put through my paces at basic."

"I didn't know that. Hell, I didn't even know you'd enlisted until I ran into Ty on campus right before finals. I was pissed and hurt, so I marched straight to the store and changed my number. A fresh start," she whispered.

Owen stared at her; at the woman he'd wasted too much precious time away from. It ate at him, as did the way she looked at him now, as if she wished they'd never reconnected. Regret and pain clouded her eyes, stabbed him in the heart.

"I know I hurt you—" he began, but she cut him off.

"Don't. Please. Spare both of us the tripe of an apology. You're not sorry you left, you're sorry you left the way you did. You needed to go, and I needed to let you. You were a total ass about how you went about it, but even if you'd stayed, there's no guarantee it would have worked out anyway. Even without the fire."

"You don't really believe that."

"Shit happens." Keeley shrugged those bare shoulders, causing the tip of her braid to slip under the thin material covering her breasts.

A different fire ignited in Owen's gut, hot and strong at a time he couldn't afford to start thinking with his *other* head. Blinking as if his eyelids opening and closing would rid his mind of the image a determined Keeley portrayed, he fought to maintain a modicum of control. She was a modern-day Viking, the armor replaced with a simple dress, an effectively wielded beer taking the place of a bulky shield. Owen wanted to throttle her, kiss her, and worship her all in the same breath. She'd always brought out the opposing savage and visceral sides of him, usually in tandem.

Whether he wanted her to or not.

However, standing across from her, he knew her well enough to know she needed space. As much as it pained him to do it, he set the full beer on the counter and whistled for Sura. "I need to get her home and check on Kore."

Surprise flitted over Keeley's face before she shut it down. "Kore?"

"The newest addition to my family."

"Another dog?"

"Crazy, I know." Owen backed away, his gaze never leaving Keeley's. "I'll call you."

"You named your school after your new dog?"

"No. I named both for a friend I lost."

"One of the three?'

"Yes, one of the three."

"I'm sorry you keep losing people close to you." Keeley set her own beer aside. "I'll see you out."

Her eyes portrayed the sincerity of her words. It eased some of the guilt, enough to allow the need to resurface. Shoving his hands in his pockets, Owen managed to cross to the door without tossing her over the back of any of the scattered pieces of furniture. Considering the night a success, he didn't push her when she knelt to say goodbye to Sura.

Which is why he was completely caught off guard when she stood abruptly, pushing him against the open door, her mouth hot and avid on his. His breath caught in his throat as she pinned him, her hips digging into him as her tongue warred with his. Every thought fled his brain as the outside world ceased to exist. There was only her, only Keeley, filling his senses to bursting.

Then, just as quickly as she'd started it, she finished it, pulling back out of arm's reach. "Don't call me."

Head still spinning from the unexpected assault on his glands, he stared at her. "What?"

"I hate talking on the phone. Just text me." With a little smile, she pushed him onto the porch and shut the door smartly behind him.

Glancing down at Sura, Owen was once again struck by the conflicting emotions Keeley evoked. Desire, exasperation, humor, and glee battled for dominance. Giving up fighting them, he let them run rampant as he led a whining Sura to the truck.

"I know, I don't want to leave, either." Opening the passenger door, he helped her onto the seat. He glanced back at the backlit windows and shook his head as he stroked a hand over Sura's soft fur. "Looks like we're both sunk, sweetheart."

CHAPTER 9

After a grueling twenty-four-hour shift, Keeley needed respite. She needed a moment to gather her thoughts, to sit in quiet and sort through the events of the past couple of weeks. Mostly, she needed to be alone, to remember who she'd become and who she swore she'd never be again.

Instead, she found herself in her car, driving to the only home she'd ever truly known. The apartment in college had been a temporary stop, her current house no more than a place to escape between shifts. But as she turned into the pretty little house lining the street of equally pretty houses, she felt the familiar tug of comfort and peace. Home.

Stepping out, she immediately noted where her dad had been hard at work in the flower beds. Flowers reigned supreme; weeds were eliminated like enemy combatants. Color exploded in the warm spring morning, a testament to sunny skies and precise plant food-to-water ratios.

Teddy Summers may have been forced into the role of a single dad, but he'd turned the role into his own, raising Keeley with equal parts tea parties and wood chopping. Studying the delicate blooms, Keeley let herself think of her mother, the woman she'd never known. Kimmy had died due to complications stemming from delivery. Apparently, she'd never even had the chance to hold the daughter she'd birthed.

Teddy made sure Keeley understood he never blamed her for her mom's death. She'd spent her teen years expecting to feel a hole left by her mom's absence, but she never had. Teddy had seen to that. While Keeley rarely thought of the fact she'd grown up without a mom, it was even more rare that she considered the reality of her dad going through life without his wife.

She considered it now, letting the questions flow through her mind. Would he have changed it if he could? Would he go back and tell her mom they would be fine without kids? Would he say the loss was worth the gain?

Keeley felt confident she could predict his answers but needed to ask them all the same.

Getting out, she headed inside, toeing off her shoes on the welcome mat as she entered. In her sock-clad feet, she headed back to her dad's office, where she figured he'd be up to his eyeballs with census records.

Turning the corner, she saw she was correct. Teddy squinted at the computer screen as he slid the mouse over the pad she'd given him for Father's Day two decades prior.

"Dad."

"You're not going to believe this, but I've found the ancestor who made the trip over from England." Shifting his gaze to her, Keeley couldn't help but smile at the light in his eyes. He'd been researching their family lineage for well over a year, attempting to piece together the history of their bloodline. He'd traced their ancestors to West Virginia, but had gotten stuck, unable to go back any further.

"I found him," Teddy repeated.

"Who was he?"

"Ludwig Winkle, born 1796 in Liverpool, England. He made the crossing with his aunt and uncle at the ripe old age of three months. They changed his name to Summers, which is what threw me off."

"But you found him."

"That I did." Sitting back in his cracked leather chair, he finally took a good look at her. Whatever he saw had his eyes narrowing. "You're tired. Rough shift last night?'

"I've had rougher."

Tapping his fingers on the wooden armrests, he studied her. "You know you can talk to me about it."

"I do know," she responded easily. "But that's not what I want to discuss."

"Sounds serious." Saving the notes he'd been typing, he stood, motioning her out. "I need coffee."

They sat at the breakfast nook, just as they had for more years than Keeley could remember. The normalcy settled her, as did the loud slurping from the World's Best Dad mug she'd made during middle school.

"What's up, honey?"

Keeping it brief, she filled him in on her run-in with Owen at his school, then the resulting baseball game and dinner date. Teddy took it all in, merely nodding for her to continue when she paused.

When she finished, he raised his brows. "Shouldn't you be talking to Chantel about this?"

"Chantel's never loved a man. Not like you loved Mom."

"Ah. There's truth to that. And perceptiveness." He reached across the small table to take her hand. "Do you love Owen?"

"I don't know Owen."

"Do you think the military changed him?"

"It would have to. I can't imagine anyone seeing what he's seen and coming through it as the same person they were when they went in."

"I hope not. We're touched by the horrors we experience. Soldiers and first responders see more than their fair share. You've changed since donning the uniform."

Surprised, Keeley leaned closer. "How?'

"You compartmentalize, minimize empathy, capitalize on logic. It's natural, even necessary, to survive twenty-five years on the job and make it to retirement in one piece. But it changes a person."

"But at the core of it I'm the same."

"Isn't he?"

"I don't know."

"Are you going to find out?"

And that was the crux of her debate. "I don't know if I should."

Teddy sighed, squeezing her hand. "There are so many times I wish your mom was here. She'd know what to say to you right now."

"I was thinking of her outside. Of the two of you."

"She'd be so proud of you."

"And you. I know it couldn't have been easy raising me alone."

"Eh, you were a good kid." Teddy waved his free hand. "Besides, I had a ton of help."

"But none of the helpers were Mom."

"True. But whenever I missed her, I only had to look at you and I saw her."

Tears pricked Keeley's eyes, but she batted them away. She'd let them fall later, but they had no place here. "How did you know she was the one?"

"I didn't."

Pulling back, Keeley rubbed her hands over her eyes. "What the hell, Dad?"

"Let me explain. Your mom wasn't just the light in a dark room, she was the *source* of the light. She was everything to me, and my love for her was so consuming I thought for sure it would burn out before long because that much emotion can't sustain over time. But it did. It shocked me every day to wake up and realize she was still beside me, that perfect light source."

"And she felt the same consuming love for you."

"Yes, she did."

"I don't know if it's like that for me and Owen. We had our chance and we blew it."

"Nah, just because it didn't work then, doesn't mean it was never meant to work."

Lifting a brow, Keeley stared at her dad, at the man who'd never found a guy he liked, who never approved of anyone she brought home. "Are you saying you actually forgive Owen for what he did?"

"I'm saying he'd just suffered an immeasurable loss and wasn't thinking clearly. He lashed out at the person closest to him. You," Teddy said with a squeeze. "While he was wrong, think of all the scenes you've worked. All the people you've watched suffer a blow like he did. How many of them were in their right minds at the time?"

Slowly seeing his point, Keeley squeezed his hand. "See, I knew there was a reason for coming here. You may not be Mom, but you do a damn good job at being Dad."

She spent another hour catching up on family news, skimming over his ancestral notes, and debating the Texans chances of having a decent season. More settled than she'd been in weeks, she rashly threw caution to the wind and drove to Kore K9. While she normally analyzed maneuvers with an abundance of caution and logic, she acted on her emotions and the need to see Owen. She'd either be rewarded with answers or she'd crash and burn. Painfully.

Pulling into the lot, she saw his truck parked beside a spiffy Mercedes convertible. If his clients could afford that sexy little machine, he shouldn't have to worry about paying someone to fix the kink in his alarm system.

Nerves jumping in her belly like a toddler in her crib, Keeley parked and walked into the school. The entryway was spartan, decorated only with photos taken while Owen was in the military. She ached to stop and study them, but she pressed on, following the high-pitched bark and Owen's cooler tone.

When she stepped into the training arena, she blinked in surprise. Unsure what she'd expected, the large room was chock full of equipment, gear, and toys. She didn't know the first thing about training dogs, but it appeared Owen had the best money could buy.

Her gaze settling on the woman seated on the bench in the corner, Keeley's lip curled. The bimbo had also indulged in the best money could buy. Her hair was perfectly curled, her molded breasts perky and massive beneath the skin-tight tee. Jeans tight enough to cause amputation encased thick legs that brought pinup images to mind.

Keeley wanted to snarl a warning but stopped herself just in time.

Thankfully Owen spotted her and waved her over. "Hey, babe, perfect timing. Do me a favor and come say hi to Quagmire."

Babe? Keeley opened her mouth with a smart retort, but the stress and silent pleas were pumping off Owen in hot waves. Biting her tongue, Keeley strode toward the exuberant pup. She couldn't be sure, but she thought it might be a poodle. Dogs had never been her thing.

Quagmire shook all over from excitement, but Owen's soft commands kept its furry butt planted on the training floor. When it started to rise, Owen gave a sharp tug on the leash followed by words in a language Keeley didn't understand.

When she stood in front of the quivering puppy, Owen smiled. "Reach out a fist, please."

She did so, impressed when Quagmire remained at Owen's feet, even though it was obvious he wanted nothing more than to jump up and lick her. Extending her fist near his pointy face, Keeley held her breath as Owen finally gave Quagmire permission to say hello.

Keeley rubbed his fur, which felt more like sheep's fur than dog fur, and shook her head at Owen. "Not too shabby."

"That's taken weeks of work," he murmured, anxiety interrupting the normally smooth cadence of his voice. Jerking his head, he gave Quagmire another command. The puppy trotted off to its owner who currently stared at Owen and Keeley with an unfriendly glare.

"Leesa, I'd like to introduce you to my girlfriend, Keeley. Keeley, Leesa is Quagmire's owner."

"He's a cute pup," Keeley said.

"Yes, he is. Same time next week?" Leesa asked Owen stiffly.

"I'll be here."

The woman didn't reply, all but marching out of the building in a huff.

Turning to Owen, Keeley raised a brow. "'Babe' *and* 'girlfriend'?"

"Punish me however you wish, but I'm ready to grovel at your feet for the unintentionally perfect interruption."

Rolling her eyes, Keeley crossed her arms. "This is quite the setup you have here."

Following her gaze, Owen nodded. "It's taken a while, but it's coming together."

"Why a K9 training school?"

Owen's smile dimmed. "That's a long story, but part of the reason is here, if you'd like to meet him."

"Kore?"

"He's in my office." Owen paused, uneasiness settling into his eyes. "He's doing better, but he's still antsy when meeting new people. My last attempt at socialization ended with four stitches and a very expensive bottle of bourbon to Ty as an apology."

"Kore bit Ty?"

"No, Kore grazed me trying to bite Ty. It was a goddamn circus."

Recognizing the tenseness in Owen's shoulders, Keeley softened. "Good thing I'm a trained first responder."

Owen's grin was a quick flash on his handsome face. "Lucky me." He led her back into the entryway, pausing when he placed a hand on the doorknob. "I'll go in alone first, take him out of his crate. He can already smell you, but he shouldn't go wild unless he sees you. Stay out here and I'll bring him to you."

Nerves prickled along her skin as Owen slipped into the office. Jesus, what kind of dog was this that he was afraid to even introduce it to people? Keeley knew Owen would do whatever he had to do to prevent her from being injured, but she'd faced enough pissed off dogs at work to give her a healthy appreciation for the strength of their jaws and the sharpness of their teeth.

Owen's voice was sharp, carrying a tone and edge Keeley had never heard. Intrigued, she stepped forward before stopping herself. The easy-going, light-hearted Owen sounded downright menacing as he gave whiplash commands.

Blinking, Keeley stumbled back a step as the office door opened. The dog at Owen's feet looked every bit the destructive killer she knew it could be. Ears slicked back in warning, it shook, but whereas Quagmire's had been in excitement, this dog exuded anger.

"Don't move."

Owen's order slapped her back to reality, and she watched, amazed, as he walked Kore around her in a slow circle. They stopped right in front of her, and Keeley knew enough about dogs not to stare into its eyes, challenging it. Instead, she marveled at the contrast of colors on its coat, from mud brown to pitch black.

His face echoed that dark hue, making him appear even more dangerous. Owen held the leash tight, his eyes never leaving Kore. Despite her fear, Keeley realized Owen was totally in control. Kore pressed into his leg, ready to spring but remaining still because Owen demanded it.

An unexpected surge of need cascaded through Keeley, shocking her to her toes. Dammit, now was *not* the time for her hormones to make their presence known. But she couldn't shake the desire that curled in her belly at the sight of Owen, dominant and sure, with the scary dog at his feet.

"Don't be scared. I won't let him hurt you."

Snapping back to reality, Keeley shook her head. "I won't lie, I'm afraid of him, but I trust you."

"He can smell your fear."

"Good for him."

Biting the inside of his cheek, Owen fought back a grin. "He's a good dog, he's just misunderstood."

"He looks like a mean bastard ready to rip out my throat."

"That's because he *is* a mean bastard ready to rip out your throat."

Keeley felt dizzy as the blood fled from her face. "Is that supposed to make me feel better?"

"No. You need to know who you're dealing with." Owen glanced down at Kore, then back up to Keeley. "Are you comfortable with me bringing him close enough to sniff you?'

"Nope, but you can do it anyway."

"Your courage floors me." Owen's voice may have been light but the intensity in his eyes was anything but carefree. "Don't move, and definitely don't reach toward him."

"Oh, no worries there. I have no desire to touch him."

But she couldn't stop the thrill of emotion that coursed through her as Owen and Kore moved closer. They moved as one, she realized, totally in-tune, a single unit made of two living, breathing entities. Impressed anew despite the fear mixing with desire, Keeley remained motionless.

When Kore growled deep in his throat, Keeley's heart skipped a beat. Owen merely snapped a command, gave the leash a sharp tug, and pulled Kore even closer. Keeley couldn't look away, mesmerized by the relationship between dog and master.

Then Kore's mouth dropped open and his tongue flopped out as he plopped his ass at Owen's feet and began to pant. Keeley wasn't sure who was more surprised at the abrupt change in the dog's demeanor, her or Owen. Turning bewildered eyes to hers, Owen maintained control of Kore, leading him away to the training room where he hooked the leash to a metal bar running the length of the wall and gave another command.

Kore gracefully lowered to the ground; head held high as he continued to study Keeley. Owen crossed back to Keeley, shaking his head the entire way.

"That was really weird."

"It felt more terrifying than anything."

"I'm sorry to put you through that, but it was better you meet him now."

"Why?"

"So you know what you're getting into."

Gaze returning to the Malinois, Keeley considered. "Why would you take on a dog like that?"

"I have my reasons." Pausing, Owen shrugged. "He's a great dog, he's just been mishandled and doesn't trust anyone. I can't say I blame him."

Keeley didn't respond, letting the new images of Owen play in her head. She couldn't make them fit, the soft-hearted Owen she'd known and the hard ass she'd just observed. It was another slap of reality that he'd changed over the years.

"I need to run him through his paces," Owen was saying. "Would you like to stay and watch?"

Instinct urged her to say no, but Keeley reckoned that was fear guiding her actions. Instead, she nodded, keeping a healthy distance from Owen as he unhooked the leash and led Kore to the center of the room.

"Stay on the carpet," he ordered her, then devoted his attention to Kore.

The next half hour gave Keeley a whole new appreciation for dog handlers. Off leash, it only took simple voice commands for Kore to heed Owen's every word. Owen placed a ball in the center of the floor then walked back to Kore. Keeping his voice low, he issued a sharp command which had Kore prowling toward the doomed piece of rubber, yet another command had him turning away, circling Owen's legs to rest at Owen's side once again. Over and over they practiced, exchanging the ball for other stimuli, other bait in Keeley's mind.

Her mouth dropped open in shock when Kore flopped onto his back and Owen knelt to run his hands vigorously on Kore's exposed belly. Looking over, he caught Keeley's eyes. The punch of heat no longer surprised her, no longer made her wary. Keeley accepted the blow, understanding she'd never escape its hold on her.

Snapping the leash back in place, Owen led Kore back to her. "I'm done for the day."

"It's barely noon."

"Perks of owning your own place."

"I'll say." Keeley resisted the urge to pet a now almost approachable Kore. "I'll get out of your hair."

"Come home with me."

Meeting his gaze, Keeley knew what would happen if she went back to his place. She could have hemmed and hawed, but the truth was she'd made up her mind long before stepping foot inside the school.

"Lead the way."

The drive was a blur as anticipation wracked her system. Memories she'd suppressed for years flooded her. Rough hands tugging down her shorts, his fingers working their way to her clit to rub and tug until she exploded. Strong arms pinning her down as he slammed into her, making her take every inch of his hard cock. Insistent lips on hers, tongue plunging into her mouth in time to the cock piercing her insides.

By the time she parked behind his truck, she was one touch away from imploding.

Instinct had her waiting as he led Kore inside, no doubt to put him in a crate somewhere. The house was a blob of color and shape, Keeley's eyes pulsing with the blood pounding in her head and preventing her from focusing on something as innocuous as Owen's shutters.

When he stepped back out and motioned her inside, Keeley's heart leapt. Not trusting her legs, she forced one foot in front of the other, stepping over the threshold only to be yanked inside. The door slammed behind her and she found herself shoved against it, Owen's hands racing over her, from her hips to her breasts and back down.

Moaning, she used her own hands, driving them under his shirt to the hard muscles beneath. Trembling, she fought to control her breathing, but he consumed her, controlled her. Keeley gave in, allowing her body to be plundered.

Cool air touched her bare skin as he pulled her shirt over her head. His hands were hot on her stomach, burning a trail down to her thighs as he pushed at her shorts. Within seconds she stood in her bra and a thong while he remained fully dressed. The realization aroused Keeley even more, as did Owen's growl of appreciation at the sight of her.

"Even better than I remembered."

"Stop living in the past," Keeley managed, her own hands busy unzipping his cargo pants. Tugging them down, she followed them, peeling his underwear down until his cock sprang free, already rock hard and throbbing.

Dropping to her knees, Keeley took his cock in her mouth with one long swallow. She heard Owen's curse, but ignored it as she worked him, sliding her lips over the taut skin as deep as she could manage, then easing back up to suck the very tip. Precum glazed her tongue, had her craving more, but before she could go deep again, he grabbed her head and forced her mouth off him.

He was on top of her in an instant, and she found herself on her back on the carpet, Owen's body pressing her down. "This wouldn't last long if you kept doing that."

"I don't want it to last long, not this time. For god's sake, stop talking and fuck me."

On another growl, Owen rolled her over, pulling her to her hands and knees. In one swift move, he pulled her thong to the side and mounted her. Stars exploded behind Keeley's eyes as his cock stretched her wide. Moaning, she didn't have time to adjust to the sudden onslaught before he was slamming into her, his hips smacking her ass hard enough to bruise.

She reveled in the scent of him, achingly familiar, yet somehow new. Enticing. Exciting.

The orgasm ripped through her without warning, leaving her so weak she couldn't support her own weight. Owen merely pushed her flush with the floor, burying himself in her so deep she swore she could taste him.

Slipping an arm between her bra-covered chest and the carpet, Owen held her tight as his cum shot out of his cock and filled her. Blast after blast coated her insides until Owen finally collapsed on top of her.

His harsh breaths against her ear made her smile. No, she hadn't wanted them to take their time. Now that their initial lust had been sated, maybe it wouldn't be such a damn distraction, rearing up to bite her throat at awkward times.

"I can literally hear your brain sprinting. It's exhausting."

"It is not," she retorted with a light chuckle. "Now get up, you're smothering me."

Pushing onto his hands, he looked down at her, a smug smile in place. "I smothered your insides for sure."

"Yeah, yeah, you were great, it was amazing, blah blah."

"Blah blah?" he repeated, eyes wide. "That was anything but blah."

"You're right. You were the best I've ever had. Stars collided, worlds shattered, the universe wept."

Laughing, he bent and nipped her jaw. "Stop, you'll ruin me for anyone else." He pushed to his feet, held out a hand. "Next time, lose the bra."

CHAPTER 10

Feeling loose and limber, Keeley stood at her window overlooking the bay and sipped her third cup of coffee. Sixteen hours down, eight to go. The station was quiet with Jillian and Juan crashed in the bunks for some shut eye. A rather uneventful shift, they'd even had time for a sit-down dinner of fried chicken, green beans, and cornbread, all prepared and delivered by Frank's wife of thirty years.

Patting her still-full belly, Keeley wandered out of the office and down the short flight of stairs to the main floor. Coffee in hand, she paused at the sight of the fire engines, cold and quiet. In a flash they could be hot and rumbling, carting people and supplies to an emergency. The timing of it, like partners in a complicated ballet, meant life or death for those who needed them.

Stroking a hand over the polished chrome front, Keeley continued toward the kitchen. Dark but for the stove light casting a low glare over the checkered floor, it had been scrubbed spotless after they'd devoured their last meal. Keeley rinsed her coffee mug, placed it in the dishwasher, and wandered back out.

The restlessness wasn't new for her, but it was unwelcome. At work, she needed to be at the top of her game. Distractions caused injury, or worse, death.

Owen was being damn distracting.

She couldn't lay the blame at his feet. At least, not completely. True, he'd been thrust back into her life by chance, but he'd made no bones about his intentions to stay wedged in it.

On a sigh, she turned into the main living area, with its low leather couches, recliners that sagged in the centers, and a flat screen TV large enough to make a grown man weep. Currently empty, she turned off ESPN, plunging the room into darkness.

Lowering to one of the couches, she could admit she didn't want Owen gone. It felt weak, she realized, and she couldn't stomach weakness. He'd left her, broken and aching, on the sidewalk. Turned and walked away, taking Sura with him.

Wasn't it pathetic of her to take him back? But her father's words echoed in her head and she knew it wasn't that simple. If Owen had been in his right mind when he'd walked away, yes, it would have been pathetic. But he hadn't been. He'd just lost his closest friend in a horrific manner, all while he stood by, helpless.

Keeley had matured enough and experienced her own first-hand accounts of how trauma could affect a soul. Shatter it. She couldn't judge him for an action taken while Owen's brain had effectively shut down his ability to think and act rationally.

Decided, she stood, intent on slipping into her own bunk, but the tone shattered the still night. Racing to the bay, Owen ceased to exist as Keeley listened to dispatch inform them of a residential fire in progress. By the time she'd fastened her jacket, the rest of her crew fell into step beside her.

Blood pumped in her veins as dispatch stated there were two victims trapped inside. Nothing needed to be said, no commands needed to be given as they loaded into the rigs and pushed the heavy trucks to their capacity.

Keeley's first impression of the fire sank her hopes. Hot and hungry, flames already leapt from the roof, fully engulfing the left side of the house. Gauging the wind, humidity, and her guys' temperaments, she began barking orders.

They moved as they always did, each independent of the other but very much in tandem. Masks in place, they unraveled the hoses and were carting them into place when their sister house arrived.

Marty jumped down from the passenger seat, issuing commands in his fluid, unhurried manner. His team quickly melding in to assist Keeley's, he joined her to study and assess the damage. As a unit, they quickly walked around the single-story craftsman style home, each lost in their own assessment. It didn't look good. In fact, it looked fucking terrible. Keeley estimated their chances at pulling anyone out alive at less than five percent.

"Thoughts?" Marty asked.

"We only have minutes before it spreads to the rest of the house." Worry built in her stomach, brick by greasy brick. "I'm giving my guys two minutes, max, to hunt for the vics."

"You don't think they can get them out."

"No, I don't." Bringing her radio to her lips, Keeley gave the all clear to enter from the west. Sensing more than feeling a change in the wind, Keeley decreased their chances even further. "You have approximately sixty seconds. Don't be stupid."

Frank used a crowbar to pry open the glass sliding door, his large arms making short work of the task. Juan and Jillian, the smallest of them, slipped inside first. Two suits followed on their heels, peeling off on the opposite wall. The seconds passed agonizingly slow as Keeley fought for a patience she didn't feel.

When the wind abruptly shifted direction once again, Keeley raised her radio. "Out, everyone out now."

"We're in the bedroom," Jillian's voice crackled. "We've got two on the floor in the far corner."

Fear joined the worry in Keeley's gut, turning her blood cold. Wielding the responsibility her rank demanded, she made the hard call. "Leave them. That's an order."

The radio went cold as neither Juan nor Jillian responded. The resulting silence fired Keeley's blood and kicked her into gear.

Knowing if she were in their place, she wouldn't back out either, she donned her own mask and started for the glass doors.

"Keeley, you can't." Marty grabbed her arm, surprisingly strong despite his small frame. "There's no time."

"My men are in there." Shaking him off, she managed another step before some unknown accelerant inside the structure ignited. The explosion was deafening, the blast powerful enough to knock several firemen off their feet. Far enough away to maintain her own stance, Keeley never heard her own scream as she watched the fire devour the roof, collapsing it atop Juan and Jillian.

Without thought, Keeley was sprinting, racing to get inside. Frank's face loomed in front of hers, and while she saw his mouth moving, she didn't hear the words spilling out. When she fought him, attempting to hook her leg behind his to move him out of her way, he simply slung her over his shoulder and carted her to the engines.

Raising her head from Frank's back, soundless tears slid down her cheeks as the remaining walls of the tiny house crumbled.

~

The knock at the door had Kore going ape shit. Cursing, Owen tossed back the bed sheets and grabbed the Glock off his nightstand. Ordering Kore to his side, the pair eased to the front door.

Passing the kitchen, Owen glanced at the readout on the microwave. Who the hell was paying a goddamn social visit at zero six hundred?

Peering out the living room window, Owen's irritation morphed to concern when he noticed Keeley huddled on the stoop, arms wrapped around her stomach as if holding in its contents. Setting the gun on the hall table, he grabbed Kore by the collar and opened the door.

She didn't speak, didn't have to. Owen had seen the grief and pain on his own face often enough to recognize it on hers. "Let me put him up really quick."

Nodding, she merely closed her eyes as tears began to fall.

Shit, shit, fuck.

Sensing something was wrong, Kore growled long and low. All but dragging him back to the bedroom, Owen ordered him into the crate and locked it. Hurrying, he rushed back to a quietly sobbing Keeley.

Without speaking, he pulled her inside, lifting her off her feet and carrying her to the couch. Rather than push him away, which he'd half expected, she curled into him, burying her face into his shoulder. The sobs broke his heart more effectively than a pissed off goodbye.

He didn't know what had happened, but he could guess. Knowing there was nothing he could say, even less he could do, he rocked her back and forth, using his presence and solidness to comfort as time passed unnoticed.

When the worst of it eased and her sobs morphed into sniffles, she finally leaned back. "Sorry."

"Don't. Whether you want to tell me or not is up to you, but don't apologize for being here."

Pushing her hair out of her eyes, Keeley turned her splotchy face up to the ceiling. "I lost two of my team today."

Though he'd been expecting those words, they still ripped at Owen's guts with sharp talons. "I'm sorry."

"Now it's my turn to tell you not to apologize." Keeley's watery sigh further shredded his insides. "I've been telling myself there's nothing I could have done differently, nothing I missed or overlooked. Maybe one day I'll believe it."

"It won't be any day soon."

"Will you tell me what happened to you?" Turning beseeching eyes to his, her lips trembled before she pressed them closed. After a moment, she spoke again. "I don't mean to dredge up your past, but I need to feel connected in a way few others understand. I need to know someone can empathize with what I'm feeling."

Owen sucked in a breath through his teeth, then exhaled on a gust. What the hell, she'd already laid him bare merely by bringing her grief to his door.

"My final deployment was the roughest. Everything about it – from the terrain to the weather, to the men and women we hunted – was on a different level than the first two. My dog Turbo and I were the working duo on a team of eight. Our platoon was larger than that, with dozens of guys, but the eight of us worked closely together."

He paused, remembering the heat of the sun beating down on his ballistic vest, Turbo panting at his feet. "We'd tracked our target to a compound, surrounded it. My team was slated for entry. We split up, four and four. I was in the group that stayed behind, just long enough for them to clear the innards of the courtyard."

The memory dragged at him, whispered intoxicating lies about those he'd lost. If only he disappeared into the memory, he'd see them again. Be able to change what happened. Save them.

It was all lies, every false glimmer of hope no more than his brain's fucked-up attempt to deceive him. All that waited for him in the midst of those memories was madness.

Taking his time, he kept his voice flat, his hands steady. "After the first four entered, Turbo and I followed behind. Our task was to find the IEDs we knew they'd strewn throughout the compound. This cell was smart, too goddamn smart. Turbo and I made the rounds, almost completing our designated area when I saw him. Our target. He poked his head out of a window, looked right at me. Later I'd find out it was a trap. A beautiful, deadly trap."

Everything fell into focus. The stench of the garbage Turbo had just sniffed, the sweat trickling down his chest beneath the vest. Turbo needed water but they couldn't spare the seconds it would take to give him a swallow. Pressing to the next pile of waste, Turbo suddenly turned, arrowing to the window closest to them. Boarded with ancient wood, it slammed open and a man in his early thirties stuck his head out far enough to gaze into Owen's eyes. Startled and more than a little pissed, Owen shouted commands in Farsi. Commands that went unheeded.

Moving to the window to hold their position, two of his team raced to his side. Only Korey remained, rounding the final corner. The area Owen and Turbo hadn't yet cleared. The radio traffic hummed in the background as Owen watched their target disappear down the corridor. Turbo barked incessantly and Owen felt that same drive, that need to capture and defeat, coursing through his veins. He shut out everything else, knowing their target was the goal. He was a bad motherfucker, a man who'd caused the death of hundreds. Who hoped to cause the deaths of thousands more.

"What happened?"

Snapped out of the images in his head, Owen stared at Keeley. "Huh?"

"What happened? When the man poked his head out the window?"

Clearing his suddenly raw throat, Owen picked a piece of lint off the couch cushion. "Turbo and I were given the clear to chase him down. We were closing in, so I released Turbo, knowing in a matter of seconds we'd make one of the most important captures of the entire operation. When I heard the explosion, I knew. I just knew."

Grief and an unstoppable aching pain wracked Owen's system; strangled around his heart. "Turbo caught the bastard, ripped a chunk of his thigh apart before I got to him. And as I was applying the flex cuffs, I heard the second explosion. Three men were dead," he continued flatly, "three men who should have walked out of that compound alive didn't. All because I pulled Turbo off our task."

Keeley pursed her lips, eyes searching his face. "Was it worth it?"

"The man we captured?"

"Yes."

"Fuck if I know."

Rather than the placating words so many others offered, even members of his own platoon, Keeley merely nodded. "It sucks, the not knowing. Tonight, Juan and Jillian tried to save two people. Only two, not the thousands you're talking about. What's eating me about what happened tonight is there's no one to blame. When the fire died out enough to enter the rubble, the arson investigator deemed it an accident. Faulty wiring. Four people are dead, and I can't hold anyone accountable except myself."

"With rank comes responsibility."

"I never thought I'd lose someone. I was too cautious, too careful, too goddamn smart. I'd yet to face a fire I couldn't read, couldn't predict. Until tonight." She paused, dragging in a ragged breath. "Except I did read it; just not in time."

"It's a rough road to walk. Some days will be easier, some days will drag you down until it feels like it's too much effort to even breathe."

"I was helpless. Useless. Standing there, safe on the outside, risking nothing. They went in, full of fire themselves, and now they're dead."

Understanding the emotions bombarding her, Owen nodded. "You're absolutely right, and nothing will change that. Not second-guessing, not blaming, not screaming and pounding and crying. They're dead today, and they'll be dead tomorrow. And every day after that."

"And I'm not."

"No. You're not. But part of you died today, Keeley, and it's important you realize that. You may not understand it, not for a long time, but just hear me when I tell you that you'll never be the same."

Rising to her knees to straddle him, Keeley cupped the sides of his face. The movement wasn't sexual, wasn't even sensual. It was a maneuver he'd seen countless children do when pleading with a parent. With their safe harbor. "How did you get through those first few days? After they died?"

"Honestly, I don't remember much about them. It was mechanical, ticking off the boxes until all the tasks were completed. That's when it got hard. When the action stopped, and the thinking started."

"I had to tell their families." Tears streamed down her cheeks again, hot and fierce. "I had to look them in the eyes and tell them their loved one would never come home again."

"I'm sorry, baby. So sorry."

"I'll see their faces in my dreams."

Owen didn't have the heart to tell her she'd see so much more than their faces when she slept. Instead, he ran a hand over her hair and pressed her cheek against his. "Some people will tell you to take it day by day, but that's too broad. Sometimes you'll have to go second by second, hanging on by your damn fingernails to get by." As Keeley drew in a deep breath, Owen caught the sheer exhaustion layered beneath the sorrow. "Let's go lay down."

"I don't want to sleep."

"You don't have to, but I want to hold you."

Pulling back, Keeley leaned her forehead against his. "I know it's a lot to ask but will you come with me to the funerals?"

"Of course I will. Whatever you need."

"I need *you*."

Carrying her to the bedroom, Owen knew her needs would change over the next days and weeks, but for now, he'd give her what comfort he could.

CHAPTER 11

With the funerals over, there was little Keeley could do but grieve. The services had been hard to stomach, but that was to be expected. Two fallen firefighters garnered support from all over the country, with departments small and large sending liaisons to offer condolences. The result was a room crammed with bodies; echoing with voices, both hushed and boisterous.

Several times throughout the eulogies, Keeley's knees threatened to buckle, but Frank stood on one side, her dad on the other, and held her upright. Surrounded by those under her command, they occupied a row of honor behind Jillian and Juan's families.

Every word uttered by the minister, every soft sob heard over the sniffles and whispered placations tore at Keeley's soul. Countless comrades had stopped by, telling Keeley it wasn't her fault, that she couldn't have made any choices other than those she'd made.

She didn't fucking believe them.

Owen had taken a seat in a pew a few rows back, and his mere presence settled Keeley like a warm bath amidst an ice storm. She had been cold, so goddamn cold, from her fingers to her toes. Everything ached, like she'd come down with the flu, but her eyes had remained dry even though her stomach cramped, and her heart pounded erratically.

Now, hours later, she stood and stared out her dad's back door. People inhabited every room in the small house, but Keeley tuned them all out. Thankfully most of them knew her well enough to keep their distance, but if they didn't, Teddy managed to strategically maneuver them to an opposite area of the house.

The grief was unspeakable, the regret consuming. Intellectually, she'd known this day could come. Hell, every firefighter on the line knew each call could be the last, but they did the job, day in and day out, because there was no alternative. You didn't think about the possibilities, not if you wanted to stay longer than five years. So they didn't. They didn't prepare for a line of duty death, didn't plan for the unthinkable.

Now that it had happened, all that remained was a shell-shocked void deep in Keeley's gut.

Merely the thought of donning her uniform made her want to vomit. She'd lost two of her team. Two. Though not deliberate, she'd directly caused their deaths. How could she expect anyone to follow her now?

Movement at her side had her snarling in the back of her throat.

"Easy, boss, I just wanted to say goodbye." Frank held up his hands, his creased face haggard. "Didn't want to duck out without telling you."

"I appreciate that." Shifting gears, Keeley focused on the few she could still affect. Could still save. "What can I do to help you?"

"Stop beating yourself up."

"That's the one thing I can't do."

"They knew what they were getting into, every man and woman who wears that jacket knows what it could cost." Frank's sad eyes turned fierce. "Yeah, you were in charge of that scene, but you weren't in charge of that fire. You may be the best LT I've ever worked under, but even you can't always predict what'll happen. Juan and Jillian knew the risks, and they accepted them, just like the rest of us. They died doing what they loved, with people they loved." The fierceness died, leaving his face hollow. Old. "Don't take their sacrifice onto your shoulders. It's not yours to bear."

With an awkward pat on her back, he walked to his wife, linking his fingers with his hers as they said their goodbyes. Tears clogged Keeley's throat, but she choked them back. She couldn't afford to shed them here, where those under her command still looked to her for strength.

Scanning the room, her gaze met Owen's. Standing with Teddy, he'd given her the space she'd needed while remaining within eyesight. Knowing he'd buried people he'd loved, people he'd felt responsible for, had her turning to him over others, even her dad. *Goddamn it!* She didn't know what to do, what to say. So many people here, so many lives forever altered, because she'd given the order to go in. How could she face them?

Sensing her distress, Owen eased toward her. His face full of compassion and worry, he took her hand, rubbing warmth into her cold fingers. "You're almost done."

"I know, just a couple more hours."

"That too, but I meant emotionally. You're closing in on the breaking point. You don't want to be here when that happens."

"I can't leave. Not yet."

"I know. That's one of the reasons every firefighter in here will continue to follow you."

Her calm facade dangerously close to cracking, Keeley pulled away. "Don't say the right things right now. I can't handle it."

Understanding, Owen nodded and tucked her into his side. Drawing from his hard form, Keeley managed to hold herself together during the lingering goodbyes and endless hugs. When only she, Owen, and Teddy remained, her dad took Keeley's face in his hands and studied his only child.

"You will get through this."

"I don't have a choice."

"They've scheduled your grief counseling?"

Nodding absently, Keeley grasped his forearms. "It's written down somewhere."

"Go, and be honest."

"I don't feel like dumping my feelings at the feet of someone I've never met."

"I agree, it's not a comfortable situation, but it helped me after your mom died. It made me a better father to you, a better commander to my team. Give it a chance."

Sighing, Keeley removed her hands. "I'll go and I'll talk, but I can't promise I'll spill my guts."

"Good enough." Stepping back, Teddy tilted his head to Owen. "Why don't you take her home? She's had enough for today."

Owen ushered her out to his truck, his movements hurried but smooth. A hard rain had started to fall, accented by spats of lightning and cracks of thunder. The raging weather matched the emotions cascading through Keeley's body, equal parts grief and anger.

Owen didn't speak on the short drive to her place, merely rested his hand on her thigh as he maneuvered the slick roads. The light pressure was somehow reassuring, and Keeley leaned her head back, closed her eyes, and allowed herself to drift.

In what felt like seconds, Owen parked, so the sound of the rain hitting the roof was the only sound in the small cab. Turning to her, he ran a hand along her hair. "Do you want me to go or stay?"

Keeley craved solitude but no longer trusted her gut. Unsure, she shrugged. "It's up to you."

"No, it's not." Getting out, Owen skirted around the truck, then opened her door, hunching against the slashing rain. "Let's get inside then you can decide."

Wet and irritable, Keeley dug her keys out of her clutch during the short race to the porch. Pushing open the door, they stood, dripping fresh rain all over her hardwoods. Keeley couldn't bring herself to care. She wanted to stop hurting, stop caring, stop *feeling* for five fucking minutes.

"You're staying." Shoving him back against the wall, Keeley pressed her lips to her. "I need to forget. Make me forget."

Rather than the fiery response she'd expected, Owen's lips were gentle on hers, his hands unhurried as they grabbed her hips. Craving urgency, she yanked him to her, lifting his shirt so her hands could roam his taut skin.

When she would've dropped to her knees, he scooped an arm under her legs and lifted her off her feet. "If you're going to use me, I get to say how I'm used."

Carrying her to the bedroom, he gently lowered her to the bed. Heart pounding, Keeley stared up at him. "What are you doing?"

"Loving you."

The tears that pricked her eyelids had nothing to do with the losses she'd suffered, and everything to do with the man in front of her. "I can't do the mushy stuff right now."

"I'm not asking you to." Dragging off his shirt, Owen lowered so they lay facing each other. "I'll do it."

Surprised to discover she could still laugh, Keeley reached for him. "So stop talking and do it."

Later, as she lay cradled on his chest, she realized even though the hurt from his actions all those years ago still lingered, a newly realized understanding was starting to weave its way through the hurt. Yes, he'd turned away from her, but wouldn't she have done the same? The only reason she lay here now was because he could relate to how she felt. That wouldn't have been possible a decade ago.

"Your thoughts are so loud they're deafening," Owen said softly as he stroked a hand over her bare back.

"Sorry."

"Care to share, or no?"

"I was thinking about us."

"Oh?" Owen's hand stilled. "What about us?"

"I'm starting to understand why you had to go."

Pushing up, Owen turned Keeley to meet his gaze. "You're thinking of leaving?"

The panic on his face made Keeley smile. "No, the opposite, actually. I'm thinking I know why you had to then, and why I have to stay now."

Relaxing a fraction, Owen resumed stroking her back. "Which is?"

"You get it. I didn't back then, not like you needed me to. Now we're finally on an even playing field." In a rare gesture of affection, Keeley touched his face. "It's not going to be easy, but I want to try to make this work."

"I'm a mess," he admitted as he took her hand. "And a package deal, with an even bigger mess with Kore."

"If you're trying to scare me away, it won't work. Since when have I ever taken the easy route?"

Grinning, Owen brushed his lips over hers. "I wouldn't love you if you did."

ABOUT RACHEL RIVERS

BURN FOR ME Series
Anchor Point
Burn Out
Flashover

THE SLEEPER TRILOGY
Embracing Betrayal
Conquering Fear
Forsaking Hope

Rachel Rivers lives in Knoxville, TN. Her first novel, Embracing Betrayal, finaled in the paranormal category of the Laurie, Montana Strong, and the Maggies. She lives with her smart, smoking hot husband in an historic home in a quaint neighborhood. Her day job consists of strapping on a bulletproof vest and Sig Sauer P220 as she protects and serves the citizens in her neck of the woods. During her down time she enjoys gardening, practicing yoga and spending time in nature, especially the Smoky Mountains. She'd love to hear from you so please contact her on Facebook, Twitter, or e-mail.

Find Rachel :
www.rachelriversauthor.com
rachel@rachelriversauthor.com

BAD BOY BLUES

JESSICA LEMMON

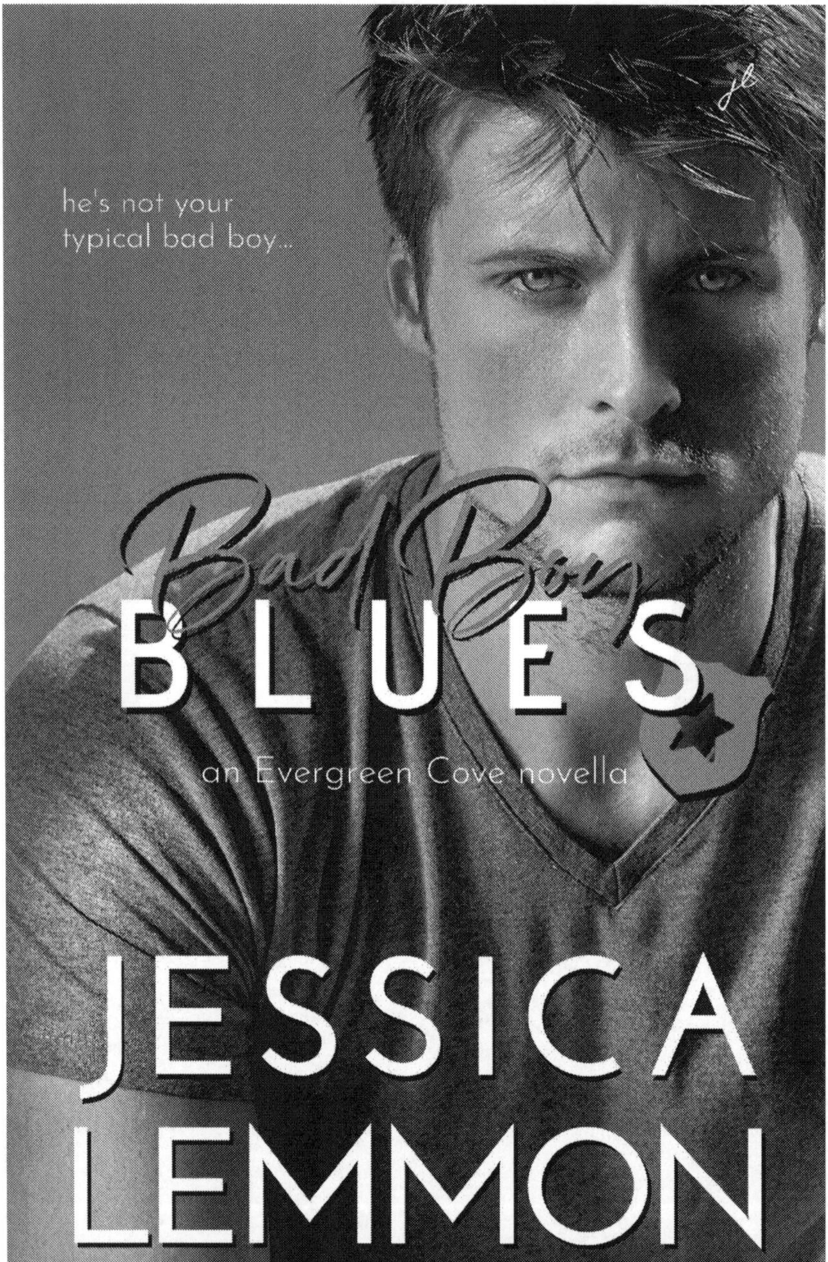
he's not your
typical bad boy...
Bad Boy
BLUES
an Evergreen Cove novella
JESSICA
LEMMON

CHAPTER 1

Brady Hutchins stepped out of the precinct into the perfect eighty-four-degree summer day and breathed in the fresh air. He felt like he'd been in there for an hour, but the meeting with the chief of police had only lasted about twenty minutes.

There hadn't been much to say. Brady's probationary time, or as Chief Clarence liked to call it, his "leave" was complete. They both knew that his "leave" was the epitome of bullshit, and that Brady had been made an example, there wasn't a hell of a lot he could do about it now.

Anyway, it was over. He was permitted to resume his duties beginning tomorrow morning and end two weeks of boredom and pacing. He understood he shouldn't have lost his temper even if the asshole had practically begged for an introduction to Brady's knuckles. But, as the chief had reminded him serve and protect included everyone, even the assholes.

The bright side to being off work was that he hadn't needed to leave Lila on her own. His girl was recovering from her own recent trauma. He'd offered his apartment as a safe haven away from the bad guys, but she'd cried the entire first night she'd stayed in his place anyway.

Honestly, he had no business with Lila given his insane hours. She hadn't trusted him enough to be consoled, curled into a ball, miserable. Thank God, that hadn't lasted longer than three nights. She'd kissed him goodbye this morning, which was a good sign she was feeling better.

His grandfather had agreed to keep Lila company while Brady worked. Not that Lila couldn't stay on her own or take care of herself. The company was good for both her and Gramps.

At the end of the day, Brady was a cop who'd hit a civilian. Even though said civilian was a *thrice*-offending criminal who manhandled his woman on the regular, it was up to Brady to be the professional. To deescalate the situation rather than ramp it up. He shook off the shadow that crawled over him whenever he thought of that night.

The run-down house outside of the nicer parts of town. The dilapidated porch. The dog tied to a post on a very short rope with no water or food in sight. The yellow light bulb over the porch, casting Mack Browning in a sickly sheen. Mack's wife June looked worse, her puffy eye growing more and more purple while Brady stood sentinel and vibrated with anger. She'd insisted she wasn't pressing charges, that Mack hadn't done anything. Then that abusive piece of shit took a swing at Brady and *pop!* Brady hit him square in the jaw before he thought better of it. At least he had the self-defense argument or else his "leave" could've been "no job."

Summer might be getting to him.

After Memorial Day, vacationers flocked to Evergreen Cove for lake activities and festivals. As recently as two years ago, Brady's hometown had felt lux and small, almost quaint by comparison. The tourists had doubled in the last two warm seasons, which meant he and his friends on the force had been running in circles in order to keep everyone safe.

He took his responsibilities seriously, and being off duty for two weeks had *seriously* fucked with his head. He'd be patrolling the street come tomorrow, thank Christ.

He'd right as many wrongs as the clock would allow.

Evan Downey crossed the street coming from the direction of the post office and gave Brady a chin-nod. Evan had come to the Cove five or six years ago now. He had a beautiful wife and son and had turned his love for tattoos into illustrating children's books instead. His paintings of superhero farm animals—Mad Cow and Swine Flu, among others—were some of the best artwork Brady'd ever seen.

"What's up, Hutch?" Evan asked, eyes hidden behind a pair of sunglasses.

"Finally back at it. How's the family?"

A genuine, happy grin lit Evan's face. "Lyon's a teenager. Making me crazy. Charlie's Charlie, so," he dipped his voice low, "making me *crazy*."

Brady grinned. He was happy for the guy. Evan had lost his wife when his kid was a toddler and moved here to start over. Brady understood starting over. He'd lost his own parents when he wasn't much older than Lyon.

"Hear you got a dog," Evan said.

"Evidently." Brady shrugged.

"Lyon's been begging for one." Evan shook his head. "What'd you name him?"

"Her. Lila," Brady answered. "Gramps calls her Pancake." He held up a hand. "Don't ask."

"I won't. See you around for the Fourth, yeah?"

"If I don't deck Mack Browning on the clock again, I'll be working, so you'll see me around."

"You did right by June, and Lila, sounds like. What an asshole," Evan said. Brady appreciated the support. He wasn't the only one in town who'd wanted to bloody Mack's lip.

Evergreen Cove might be a lux, wealthy, touristy lake town, but they were small enough to gossip. He nodded his goodbye as Evan ambled off.

Brady climbed in his truck to go home to his girl, Lila. He'd scratch her favorite spot behind her ears, eat dinner, and grab some time at the gym later tonight. He was glad to have his routine back and, even though it'd been a long time since he'd had a girl to go home *to*, he was looking forward to that part the most.

Elliott McKinley navigated the nighttime road blanketed by pines on either side. Every once in a while, the gap would give her a vantage of the ink-black lake, the cloudy night, and the barely there moon lighting its surface. She'd been on the road for hours and was dead tired, but her destination was nigh.

Since she'd spent all those hours alone, and the radio station had looped every song into a veritable ear worm, she'd had a lot of time to think. Her looping thought at the moment? A timeline.

Six years, two months, four days.

Over and over, she thought about that. Six years. Six YEARS. That was how much of her life she'd sacrificed to her narcissistic ex-boyfriend. Not *narcissistic* as a metaphor. He was a literal narcissist. She'd justified Neil's behavior at first. Sure, he'd seemed a touch infatuated with himself, but he'd also just landed partner at the most successful law firm in Northern Michigan. Yes, he was critical of her and intolerant of receiving criticism, but no one liked being judged. As each year rolled into the next, however, she'd noticed she missed working, missed being a part of a social network that wasn't Neil's. She'd missed having her own identity, which had been somehow lost behind his.

With spring, came rebirth. She'd left Neil and moved her few belongings to an empty part of her parents' garage. She'd then moved into the guest bedroom of her parents' gargantuan house in a gorgeous neighborhood north of Chicago.

But two months was way too long to live with her parents, much as she loved them, so she was embarking on an adventure. An independent one, though she didn't feel independent yet. The borrowed

BMW and the vacation house in Evergreen Cove were training wheels on a bike that was rickety from underuse. But her parents had insisted she lean on them. When Elliott's therapist had agreed it'd be a good transition, she'd packed up the car and left.

Elliott's father hadn't been happy about her making the drive from Chicago to northern Ohio alone, but she'd needed the reminder that she could do things on her own. It was her mother who'd insisted that Elliott could handle the trip solo, and Elli had needed that vote of confidence more than her next breath.

The BMW's trunk and backseat were stuffed with clothes, a cooler of food, plenty of beach reads in the form of physical paperback books, and an ancient laptop. The now-outdated computer had been ignored since Neil had outfitted their home with streamlined, cloud-based computers, tablets, and phones. He'd kept an eye on her that way, so those sleek, expensive electronics held zero lure now. As long as her clunkier version could connect to Wi-Fi, she'd be fine.

The map on the car's display announced she was twelve minutes from the beach house. A thrum of excitement raced through her. Almost there. Almost home. A temporary home, but it counted.

"Six years," she grumbled aloud, because no matter how much she felt like celebrating, six years was a horribly long time to have one's head buried in the sand.

She yawned behind her hand before cranking the air conditioning down to keep herself awake. She'd had a late start, and traffic leaving Chicago had been a bitch. Plus, she'd stopped for a leisurely dinner for no other reason than she *could*. A dinner alone, ordering whatever she wanted and without Neil's input. She'd actually heard his voice in her head as she ordered french fries to go with her steak. He'd criticized her for, among other things, eating unhealthy. Her therapist assured her this was normal, and that it'd take a while for that critical voice to be silenced.

Elli knew who she was with Neil. She knew who she was with

her parents. She was determined to find out who she could be on her own. It'd been a while.

Endless Avenue, and a long street of stores and restaurants, stretched out before her. Evergreen Cove had changed a lot since she'd last been here. The buildings were old, quaint, and somehow modern at the same time. There were pine trees everywhere, adorning the signs, painted on the windows, and physically standing guard in the distance. The cove itself was a dark splotch at the moment, but she remembered well what it looked like in dappled sunlight. How the water was cold in the deep spots, and how good it felt to touch the sandy bottom in the shallows.

Smiling to herself, and eager to reach the lake house just a few turns away, she was snapped from her thoughts when the car jerked to the left. She gripped the steering wheel tighter. The car pulling in that direction, paired with her having difficulty steering, hinted she was dealing with something more serious than a pothole.

The thumping sound that followed sealed her suspicion of a flat tire, or one that was well on its way. With a tired whine, she steered into the nearest parking lot, which happened to house a fitness center very near the library. As much as she lamented her bad luck, at least she'd broken down in a moderately safe place.

Once out of the car, she found the flat on the rear driver's side, and her options lined up before her. She could call Triple-A. She could call her father and ask how to change it.

Each of those solutions made her feel more like a little girl than an adult woman. She was capable. She was smart. No matter what Neil had told her during their time together, she could take care of herself. This was the age of female rebirth after all. She could change a damn tire.

"All I need," she said, closing her eyes and drawing on her own inner strength her therapist assured her was there, "is YouTube."

Then she pulled out her phone and did a search.

CHAPTER 2

The gym was dead at eleven at night, which was why Brady went at this time. He was a visible guy in the Cove, and the less hi-how-are-ya he could do during his off hours, the better. Touristy though she was, the Cove kept visitors in her clutches and near the water. Most vacationers were either lounging in front of a bonfire or laughing from the decks of their boats at this time of night.

He'd worked out hard tonight and had followed that workout with a long, hot shower. He'd fall into bed when he got home, after he took Lila outside first, of course. She'd been snuggled in her dog bed with her favorite stuffed monkey when he'd left. She was a good dog. He hadn't been looking for a dog, but it wasn't like he could've left her at Mack's.

"Is that your dog?" Brady gestured toward the matted dog hunching forlornly next to the post. The miserable mutt was filthy, wet from the rain, and had no water or food bowls.

"The mongrel's hers." Mack sneered at his wife. "Told her not to bring the bitch home, yet here she is. Planning on shooting it."

Shortly after, Mack threw a punch and missed. Brady's swing connected. Brady had been halfway to hitting Mack after seeing the state June was in, but managed to keep his cool. Mack coming for him had been the proverbial last straw.

Brady had reminded June to call him if she changed her mind about pressing charges, and then he'd untied Lila and informed the Brownings that the dog belonged to him now. Carrying the pup's shaking body in his arms, he'd murmured a promise into her ear that he'd find her a good home. That she'd never be tied to a porch post again.

The goal had been to keep her that first night and then re-home her. But after a vet visit assuring that she was more emotionally traumatized than physically ill, she'd forlornly watched him with intelligent, frightened brown eyes. They seemed to beg him to stay, and hell, he'd never fallen so hard so fast.

Out in the parking lot, he took in the situation around him in flashes. Habit, that. He always watched his twenty. His truck was parked off to the right, one other compact car probably belonging to the woman in pink who'd been monopolizing the stair-climber was on the left, and there was a vehicle at the back parked with the passenger's side facing the building. BMW. It was tipped, suggesting it was jacked up. The clang of metal on pavement further hinted that work was being done on the car—maybe a tire was being removed. Maybe hubcaps being stolen.

Staying alert, he tossed his gym bag into the bed of his truck as he passed by and walked to the car, calling in a low, authoritative voice, "Need some help?"

The delay made him wonder if they were hubcap thieves. He reached for his hip, only to remember he wasn't carrying a weapon. He wore nothing but a baggy tank top and shorts, and a pair of sneakers.

A head popped up over the trunk a second later and set him at ease. If she was a hubcap thief, she was a damn pretty one. Thanks to the overhead lights, he made out shadowed high cheekbones, big, doe-like dark eyes, and a rich, lush mouth.

"No, thanks!" she called out. "I've got it." And with that, she ducked down again.

Guard still up—because you never knew—he rounded the vehicle slowly. He found what he'd first suspected: a jacked-up car, one tire on the ground. The woman was crouched over her phone. A tinny voice coming from the device explained the ins and outs of replacing a tire.

"I can finish up for you. Without the video." He offered a smile when she jerked her head up at him. She was slight, her dark hair medium length, just brushing her shoulders. She wore leggings and an oversize gray T-shirt, one sleeve falling to the side and revealing a tanned shoulder.

"No." She stood and took a step away from him. "I've got it."

Definitely not from around here. She was safe in a well-lit parking lot, half a mile from the beach with the library behind her. Hell, the most crime he'd seen go down in Library Park was toilet papering done by local kids.

Her eyes narrowed, almost suspiciously, and her gaze roved over him. Of course, he wasn't in uniform. She probably thought he was out to take advantage of her.

"Okay, then." He nodded and backed away, giving her some breathing room. But when the jack gave, ratcheting the car down several inches, he moved into action on pure instinct. By the time her delicate shriek pierced the air, Brady had shoved her away from car, dropped knees-to-pavement, and reset the jack.

"You okay?" He held his hand out to let her know she shouldn't come closer while adrenaline zapped down both of his arms. Given his job, it didn't take much to put him on alert. So much for a good night's sleep. Any fatigue brought on by his workout was long gone.

"Yeah. I'm okay." Her hand was on her chest like she was checking her heartbeat. He stood to his full height, and her big eyes watched him the entire way. His cop instincts went berserk. The luggage in the back proved she was traveling, but something told him it was more than that. Something told him she was running.

"You're sure you're okay," he repeated, studying her closer.

"Well, I was." Her gaze trickled down to the jack.

"See ya tomorrow, Brady!" came a voice from the lot. He sent up a wave at the woman who'd been on the stair climber earlier. He hadn't recognized her, but she seemed to know who he was. That happened a lot. He was a small-town celebrity.

He turned back to the brunette. "It's not a problem to change it. Honest."

She folded her arms over her chest, checked the parking lot, and then gave him a jerky nod. He probably had the woman from the gym to thank for the yes. Most townsfolk didn't greet the local serial killer.

He pulled the donut out of the trunk and began the simple task of replacing the tire and tightening the lug nuts. "Meeting friends or family in the Cove?" he asked while he worked.

"Boyfriend. He's a, uh, he's a Navy SEAL." Her tone was both feisty and cautious, and Brady hid a smile.

Boyfriend, my ass.

"He's sleeping. I didn't want to bother him," she quickly explained.

"Uh-huh." He wasn't buying it. "You two renting a place, or is he local?"

"What are you, a cop?" she snapped.

He chuckled, but before he could say that yes, he *was* a cop, she talked over him.

"Look, I've been driving for over six hours. I have to pee. I'm tired. A little hungry. The ice in my cooler is probably water, and I need to put my food in the fridge and take a shower."

Finished with his task, he stood and brushed his hands on his shorts. "You're all set."

"What do I do with that?" She gestured at the flat tire.

"You mean your boyfriend doesn't know?" He cocked his head.

She pursed her lips.

"I know a guy who can patch it if you'll be in town for a while. His place is on my way home." Sort of.

"Wouldn't it be easier to buy a new one?"

"It's a perfectly good tire," he said. "Or will be once it's patched." He could let her go on her way, but he didn't want her disappearing when she was hands down the most interesting interruption he'd had in a while. Plus, that whole serve-and-protect thing didn't stop because he was off the clock.

She stifled a yawn. "How do I find him?"

"He's a craftsman. Makes furniture, but he's fixed up my truck a time or three. Kind of a jack of all trades. His name's Anthony Renaldo."

She bit her lip.

"Okay?"

She nodded. "Okay."

He hooked the tire with one forearm and stood. "Look him up online, or ask around. Most of the shop owners know him."

"Anthony Renaldo," she repeated, looking more tired than wary.

"Yep. Drive slow on the spare, okay? Ant can put your patched tire back on for you. He'll charge you a fair price."

She moved to put the jack and tools back into the trunk. Before he left, he needed to know one more thing.

"What's your name? To give to Ant for when you come to collect."

She hesitated for a second before answering. "Elliott."

"Elliott. I'm Brady."

"Yeah, I heard." Her eyes flickered to where the other woman's car had been parked.

"Okay, then. Remember—"

"Anthony Renaldo. Drive slow."

He smiled. He liked her. A lot more than he should since she didn't seem to like him at all. "About your Navy SEAL boyfriend…"

She paused with her driver's side door open.

"This fitness center is better than the commercial one on Elm."

"I'll let him know." A hint of a smile appeared, and that felt like a win.

"Welcome to the Cove, Elliott." He walked to his truck, tossed the tire into the bed and waited until she was on her way before leaving the lot.

CHAPTER 3

Elliott was pretty sure the good-looking stranger hadn't believed she had a boyfriend. She'd vacillated between trusting him and not trusting him. In the end, she'd landed somewhere in the middle.

She couldn't blame herself, and who would? She'd trusted Neil, and he'd been exactly the wrong person to trust with her heart or her person. His manipulations had been so subtle, and his control had increased so slowly, she was reminded of the metaphor of a frog in water. Drop the amphibian into boiling water, he'd leap out. But put him in warm water and slowly crank up the heat, he'd stay there until he died.

Wow. That's gross.

She shook off her musings about cooking harmless frogs and pulled out the cooler first. She'd parked in the garage of her parents' beautiful lake home. It was waterfront property, a grassy lawn leading to their sandy beach and dock. They'd sold the boat years ago, having rarely used it. According to her dad, he was too old to take care of it. But none of that mattered to her. She was looking forward to a new view, a break from the city, and she didn't need a giant house—even though she had one—or a boat.

She put her groceries away and dropped her suitcase in the master bedroom. Too tired to unpack, she instead pulled open the balcony door and admired the view. The water was dark, the sky choked with stars. She hadn't visited Evergreen Cove since she was a kid, and she hadn't realized until right now how much she'd missed it.

There was no pressing business, no one demanding she *sit here* or *stop doing that*. And while she hadn't walked on pins and needles at her parents' house, she still felt as if she should behave a certain way around them, whether they expected it or not.

She pulled in a deep, cleansing breath. Now she could just... relax. Which was a little unnerving, but she was trying to lean in. She'd been on guard for so long, she wasn't sure if she remembered how to relax anymore. Proving that point, she pulled her cell phone from her pocket and scrolled through her favorite social media app. The friends she'd had before Neil were still on her friend's list, and every so often, she'd see a party or a dinner or gathering they went to together. There was a time she would've been part of the mix, and there would be a time again. She'd vowed that after the break in Evergreen Cove, she'd go back to Chicago and reclaim those friendships. She just had to find herself first.

She closed the balcony door and went downstairs to put the kettle on for her nightly peppermint tea. She should've been tired enough to sleep without it, but the rush of a car nearly flattening her—and Brady—had left her alert.

She flipped on the burner under the teakettle, feeling relaxed in the homey atmosphere. Her parents had mentioned selling this place, or possibly renting it out. It was sad to think of them not keeping it, but it was equally sad to picture the house sitting empty, save a monthly cleaning to keep the shelves dust free.

Being here reminded her of scampering along the manmade beach and water's edge, lounging on the deck as a teenager, or sulking in the upstairs bedroom. This visit, she'd be inhabiting the master suite, the one with the balcony *and* the hot tub.

She was looking forward to reuniting with the woman she'd

been before she met Neil. The woman who knew what she wanted, had confidence to spare, and was generally happy and excited about life.

Neil hadn't wanted her to leave their shared house, insisting she had everything she needed in their corner of the world. And while the house had been home to her for years, it'd lacked a certain something she hadn't been able to put her finger on until today.

Love. It'd lacked love.

Love from Neil, love for her own life, and even self-love. She'd prioritized a man who purposefully kept her from her friends, her parents, a job, and her hobbies. He'd successfully isolated her from everyone she knew. He'd deemed it "wasteful" for her to visit a gym since there was a state-of-the-art in-home fitness center in the basement.

As a result, her girlfriends had grown distant. They were grainy, blurry images hovering in the background of what once was her life. There was no one in Chicago she was still in contact with—no yoga instructor, since she didn't visit the gym, no boss at work, since she didn't have a job. No one but Desmond and Rosella McKinley, otherwise known as Mom and Dad.

"That changes now," she decreed as she settled on the deck with her mug of tea. The moon, high and fat in the sky, winked its agreement. She'd once been social and savvy. She could be that again. Her eyes went to the darkened houses along the beach. Maybe she could introduce herself around while she was here. She might as well practice being social again.

She winced as she thought of the attractive guy who'd bailed her out tonight with the tire. She hadn't been that nice to him, and he'd seemed nice enough. His generous mouth and smile, his long, strong gait as he'd carried her tire off to the tire hospital. Against her will, her stomach fluttered with excitement, at the newness of a stray dart of attraction. At being in a position to react to a man like Brady.

But she wasn't in Evergreen Cove to be saved by a knight in

shining armor, or a hometown boy who was a helpful citizen. She was here to remember how to be her own person again. That didn't involve a guy with dark-blond hair and a warm smile.

No matter how nice he was.

CHAPTER 4

Seventy-five-year-old Emory Hutchins was Brady's dad's dad and quite possibly the best human being on the planet.

Though Brady was biased, given the man had raised him when his parents were killed at an intersection on their way back from an anniversary trip. Brady'd been five years old at the time, and what was meant to be a temporary stay with his grandparents had morphed into a permanent home and a truckload of grief too big for any kid to endure. In a blink, he'd been moved from his home in Cincinnati to the opposite end of the state to live with Gramps and Gram.

Brady didn't remember much from that time, save confusion. He hadn't had the tools to understand grief and its many nuances. Even now it had a way of walloping him out of the blue. He'd been a complacent kid and an angry teenager. Hell, his grandparents had assumed he would wind up on the opposite side of the law he now served.

The year his grandmother passed away of cancer had changed both Brady and Emory. His grandfather had been heartbroken, and while he'd lost that glimmer in his eye, his good-natured outlook on life rarely wavered. He'd loved and encouraged Brady more fiercely than before.

Gramps had never remarried or dated, which was why Brady insisted on dropping off Lila on the days he went to work. Leaving the dog alone at home for twelve hours was too long, and Gramps had leaped at the chance for canine company. Brady had thought they'd be good for each other, and he was right.

The old man was a playful, smiling burst of sunshine in Evergreen Cove, and since adding Lila to the mix, he'd become more of those things.

"Eat something," his grandfather demanded, sliding another pancake onto a plate of sloppily stacked flapjacks.

Lila, tail wagging, her eyes on the spatula in Emory's hand, gave an excited bark.

Gramps leaned down to the blond-and-white dog and patted her head with one hand. "You'll get one, Pancake. It's your namesake."

"You're spoiling her."

"Spoiled you," Gramps shot back, pouring batter into the pan. "You turned out fine."

Brady ate a plate of pancakes as instructed, even though carbing up wasn't a preferred morning activity. He would've liked to go for a run, stop by Cup of Jo's, and then head into work.

Instead, he skipped the run but made the stop at Jo's. An hour later, he was hunched over his desk, finishing reports he'd been putting off, his cup of coffee a memory.

"What are you up to tonight, Hutchins?" Fellow officer Darrin Strickland asked as he ambled by.

"Glorified bouncer. Patrolling Endless Avenue. You?"

"Night off. I'll be looking for a summer hottie to be the next contestant in *Who Wants to be Sexually Satisfied?*" Darrin grinned. "You spot me in one of those bars you're patrolling, brother, stay back and let me do my thing."

"Why? Afraid she'll like me better? I will be in uniform." Brady gave Darrin an exaggerated eyebrow waggle.

"Everyone knows I'm better looking than you." Darrin straightened his collar.

"I guess if I see you tonight, we'll find out." Brady stacked the report he'd just finished on top of the others. Thank God, that was done. His eyes were crossing. He was ready to be outside doing something useful.

"Be safe out there, man."

Brady liked Darrin, though his bragging about prowess was exaggerated. He'd bet Darrin struck out way more than he hit home runs in the dating department. As for Brady, he didn't date. He preferred mutually agreed-upon hookups that allowed him to resume his life as usual after. He'd had enough upsets in his life to try and put anything permanent in place. He was more comfortable knowing things would come to an end.

He refilled his cup of coffee with a less-than-desirable brand from the break room, his thoughts back on the woman he'd helped out Sunday night. Elliott, with her large eyes and larger chip on her shoulder had lingered in his periphery, even though he hadn't seen her around since.

"What are you smiling about?" Faye, one of their dispatchers, asked as she strode by.

Answering honestly—that he was smiling over a memory of dark hair and cautious eyes—would only get him into more trouble, so he called out, "Mind your business!"

Faye laughed.

Outside, Brady scanned the road as per his habit. He saw no Beemer with one spare tire. From a purely curious standpoint, he wondered what had put the shadow in Elli's eyes. It seemed different than the one that'd haunted him after his parents died, but no less poignant.

His cell rang. Anthony's name lit the screen. A kick to the chest that could be caution or excitement preceded his greeting. "Ant, what's up."

"Elliott's tire's still here."

"She hasn't picked it up yet?"

"Nope."

"She shows up, I'd appreciate a last name."

"It'll cost you," Ant said, a smile in his voice. "Pick out a piece from my stash. It's getting crowded in here."

Ant made unique, sturdy furniture and was an amazing chainsaw sculptor. But… "Not exactly a high-end-furniture kind of guy," Brady told his friend.

"You want a last name, Hutch, you're going to have to become one." Ant hung up.

Brady grunted a laugh. They'd been friends since they were both shithead teenagers. They might not be as infamous as the Penis Bandits—the nickname Evan and his friends earned for covering the library in spray-painted phalluses—but Brady and Ant had torn up this town in their own way.

They'd grown up, though. Now they were content to serve it.

Elliott's first week in Evergreen Cove had been uneventful. She hadn't left the house, having brought enough groceries for her meals for the week.

She did run out of beer, though, which was tragic. She was going to remedy that tonight, which meant taking the car out, and "driving slowly" as per her knight in shining armor's instruction. She realized she didn't know his last name, and then she reminded herself she didn't need his last name. She only needed her tire, which was an errand she intended on taking care of today, before this Anthony Renaldo guy was stuck with her patched tire and not being paid for his work.

Outside, she waded into the water up to her knees and waved—again—as a boat passed by. Her arm was tired from waving. Evergreen Cove had possibly the friendliest boaters she'd ever seen, and after spending quite a bit of time alone, it was almost jarring.

She heard a door open behind her and turned her head. A woman with sun-kissed brown hair stepped onto the porch of the house next door and put both hands on the railing, taking in the sunshine.

Elli had spotted the other woman throughout the week. She appeared to be around Elli's age, or a few years older, and had a cool, breezy vibe about her. Elliott wanted to introduce herself but had chickened out. She swallowed thickly. Guess today was the day. Turning, she strode up the sand.

The other woman smiled pleasantly as she came down her porch steps, her hands in the pockets of her shredded shorts, her thick bangs blowing over her forehead.

"Hi. I'm Elliott. I'm staying next door."

"Lourdes Daniels." She offered a hand, which Elliott shook. "Everyone calls me Lou. I didn't know the McKinleys were renting this place out until I saw you milling around." Lou glanced up at the house, one blue eye squinting against the bright afternoon sunshine.

"They're not. I'm their daughter."

"*Really*. Your mom skews young. I thought she was like, ten years older than me, and that you were sixteen."

"Thirty, actually."

"Me, too. Heard you live in Michigan. Your mom's the friendly, talkative type, and you'll find most Evergreeners are."

"Used to live in Michigan. I guess I'm an Ohioan. An *Evergreener*. Temporarily anyway," Elliott said, uncomfortable. Talking about herself was like an atrophied muscle since she'd done it so infrequently over recent years. "I was uh, wondering if you knew where a girl could get a drink around here?"

Ugh. That was even worse.

"Are you asking me out?" Lou grinned.

"No! Not that I wouldn't. I mean, you seem nice."

"Relax, I'm teasing you. If you'd like a girls' night while you're in the Cove, I'm up for it. What's your poison? Beer? Wine? Cocktail?"

Lou was easy to like, her confidence contagious. Elli could stand to catch a little of that for herself.

"I'm more a beer girl than anything. I'm out of stock, though, so

I thought I'd head to town later. If you'd like to come..." She was about to take her offer back for fear of being turned down—making new friends as an adult was harder than she'd thought—when Lou clapped her hands with excitement.

"Love to." Lou waved as another boat trolled by. "I was craving Salty Dog today. Best nachos on the planet. Have you been?"

"No. New place?"

"Ten years ago it was." Lou's smile was kind. "Don't visit much?"

Elliott shook her head.

"Well, then you must visit Salty Dog. My treat to welcome you to the neighborhood. It's the best place in town when you want fried food and great conversation. It lacks pretension, which is becoming a harder and harder thing to find around here. Assuming you're not one of them?"

"Pretentious?" Elli asked with a small laugh. "Far from it."

"That's a big, fancy house you live in." Lou hoisted an eyebrow.

"You're one to talk." Elli shot her chin out at Lou's behemoth.

"Divorce isn't always a bad thing."

"I thought I'd head out around six tonight. I have to pick up a tire for my Beemer from a guy named Anthony Renaldo."

Lou narrowed her eyelids in what might be recognition.

"Do you know him?" Elli ventured.

"Yeah. I know him." Lou gave nothing away in her tone, but Elli could feel there was a story there. "I can show you how to find his place."

"Sounds good," Elli said. "Thanks."

Maybe this making-friends thing wasn't so hard after all.

CHAPTER 5

Anthony Renaldo's "shop" was actually a huge garage-slash-warehouse next to a beautiful log-cabin-style house. The crazy-tall doors hinted that he stored a boat there on the off-season, and the rest of it looked like an ode to sawdust.

The man himself was an attractive, wide-bodied guy with a big grin and fantastically long eyelashes. He flashed her one of those grins when she introduced herself.

"Elliott McKinley." She extended her hand, and he shook it.

"McKinley. Got it. I'm Ant." He released Elli's hand and lifted his chin. "Lou."

"Ant." Lou, arms folded, turned and walked among the tables, chairs, and shelves.

"Did you make all this?" Elli asked.

"Every bit of it," Lou answered for him. "He's also a chainsaw artist. Ever seen anyone do that?" She pointed out a tall log in one corner, its top and sides had been carved into an intricate owl on a nest.

"You did that with a chainsaw?" Elli walked over to the piece.

The detail was stunning. The owl's toenails and the twigs making up the nest were carved with amazing precision and detail.

"Yeah." Ant joined her and Lou. "I've done garden benches and wedding arches, too. Some brides believe it's lucky to have one of my pieces in their wedding."

Lou harrumphed.

"I said *some*." Ant smirked.

There was definitely something going on between these two, but Elli wouldn't find out more here. She'd fare better at Salty Dog after Lou had a pint in her.

He addressed Elli next. "You're here for your tire, not a dining set, I assume."

"Yes. Your work is lovely, though."

"Appreciate you saying so." His eyebrows jumped. "Tire's patched and ready to go. Did you bring the Beemer? I can put it on for you."

"Yes, but, no. Thanks. I'm going to do it myself." Elli felt Lou's interested gaze on the side of her head.

"Hutch said you'd say that." Ant chuckled.

"Hutch?"

"Hutchins. Brady. Have a look around, and I'll replace your tire." He held out his hand. "Keys."

"No, like I said—"

"I respect that you *can*, Elli, but it ain't happening. I took in a tire with a hole in it. I patched it. I'm not sending a lady out to hunch down and replace the tire I just patched. Even if Brady wouldn't castrate me for doing a half-ass job, I'd insist on putting it on myself before you drive it. Yeah?"

Elli looked from Ant to her brand-new friend and found Lou's expression had softened.

"You can trust him," Lou told Elli.

Elliott fished her keychain out of her purse and offered it to Ant. Before he took the keys from her, she pulled them away slightly and insisted, "But I'm paying you."

"Sorry again, Beemer" he said with a smile. "Your bill's settled. You don't like it, take it up with Hutch."

~

With a tall, frosty glass of beer in front of her, Elli settled onto the barstool at Salty Dog. The large U-shaped bar took up most of the right side of the restaurant, the warm woods and shining bar top welcoming any thirsty patron. The restaurant beyond was lined with booths and tables, the chatter offering up the right amount of background noise. The atmosphere was at once comfortable and lively.

"What did Ant mean about a wedding arch?" Elli asked Lou, dying for a hint at what was behind the silent drama that'd unfolded earlier.

"He made the arch I stood under with my ex to say our vows. I was the one wearing white who took monogamy seriously, my ex was the asshole in the suit standing next to me."

Elli winced. "I'm sorry."

"Ancient history." Lou waved a hand. "We're here to have fun, and stories about my ex-husband is a surefire way to guarantee we won't have any." She poked Elli's arm playfully. "What's your story with Brady Hutchins? And why did he pay your tab? And how did he come across you when you haven't left the house?"

Elli took a hearty gulp of her own beer. Apparently, Lou had her own curiosities. "He was leaving the gym, and I was trying to change my tire. The jack gave, and he swept in to save the day."

Lou laughed. "Sounds like him."

"I can't let him pay for my tire. That's too much." It bothered her to take advantage of a stranger almost as much as it bothered her to feel like a charity case. She'd been doing too much of that since she left Neil. "I have money."

"It's not about money," Lou said. "Brady's good friends with Ant. Probably agreed to buy one of Ant's tables or something. I wouldn't sweat it too much. Ant wouldn't have charged you anyway since you were with me."

"How fascinating." Elli leaned on her hand and waited for more.

Lou wagged her finger in the air. "Uh-huh. You owe me a story first. You're visiting alone. What's the deal? Need a quiet place to write your novel?"

"Not exactly." For the last several years, Elli had repeated a scripted, *"We're doing well. Keeping busy. Everything's going great."* to anyone who would ask of her and Neil. Now was her chance to be honest, to say what she wanted instead of what was expected. "I lived with my boyfriend in Michigan. We split, and I moved home to Illinois a few months ago. I love my parents, but I needed a break to figure out who I am without them. They're great, don't get me wrong, but they can be..."

"Parents," Lou finished. "I know what you mean. After my divorce, I opted to keep the lake house. My ex moved to Virginia with his new girlfriend. My parents were visiting and checking up on me every two minutes at first. I felt like I couldn't *breathe*. I wanted to rely on myself for a change, you know?"

"Yes." Elli pointed at Lou in confirmation. "That's exactly it. Here I am trying to be independent and two, admittedly decent, guys swoop in to save me. I don't want to be saved."

"Aw, hon, sure you do." Lou smiled, her cheeks lifting. She was pretty with her wavy hair and her tanned skin, and mostly with her generous, open personality. *Hashtag goals*. "We say we don't want to be saved, but what we mean is we want to be respected. It's rare to find chivalry."

"Chivalry can also be code for a guy poking around for a weak spot," Elli mumbled against the rim of your glass.

"Did a number on you, your ex, didn't he?" Lou asked gently.

Elliott set her glass down and pulled in a deep breath. "Nothing I can't come back from, but since we've been apart, I keep uncovering layers upon layers of crap I have to deal with."

"Relate." Lou raised her glass, and they both drank to that.

From that topic, they moved to lighter talk of great places to eat and shop in Evergreen Cove. Lou pointed out some of the locals in the restaurant and gave Elli the rundown on who they were and where they worked.

They ordered a second beer apiece and a huge plate of nachos to soak up the beer, and then Lou was off to the restroom, leaving Elli at the bar by herself.

Typically, she'd be tempted to bury her attention in her phone, but she was too intrigued by the cast of characters in Salty Dog. Including the guy two stools down, who'd been drinking steadily since she and Lou arrived. He looked utterly miserable hovering over a glass of beer and a shot of whiskey. Elli felt for him. He ordered a refill, but the bartender shook his head.

"Sorry, Patrick," the bartender answered, leaning on the bar top and showing off impressive tattoos tracking up his left arm. His trimmed beard was neat, his voice gruff and firm. "I'm not serving you anything else. For your sake, man. You won't want to be you in the morning if you drink another."

"Gimme a break, Xavier," Patrick slurred. He finished his glass of beer and slammed it down. "Refill that, too."

Xavier shook his head. "Not happening, man. I'll buy you a cheeseburger and a coffee, though."

"Fuck you," Patrick snapped. Voices quieted in the bar. Next, he iced Elli with a glare, and she decided to check her phone after all. The drama between this guy and the bartender was none of her business. She'd come here to fix her problems, not invite new ones.

She was digging through her purse when she sensed another presence and looked up.

A navy blue policeman's uniform blocked her view of Patrick. The cop's shirt stretched over a muscular back and his hair was neatly combed back. His arms were at his sides, thumbs hooked into his belt. She admired his muscular forearms and the pale hair covering them.

Hot-cop alert.

The cop told Patrick he didn't want trouble, which was so cliché that Elli had to smile. Then he asked if Patrick's brother was around, and Patrick's arm appeared from behind the cop to point across the room.

Out of curiosity, she looked that direction, too. She spotted Lou at a far-off table laughing with a few friends. At the table next to that one, a guy regarded the bar unhappily. Patrick's brother, she assumed.

In a blink, the man rose from his chair and collected his brother. Some terse words preceded Patrick and his brother exiting the bar, but after the door shut behind them, everyone went back to business as usual.

Xavier pulled Patrick's glasses from the bar top. "Good timing as usual, Hutch. Coffee?"

Hutch? Elli's cheeks warmed. Ant had referred to Brady as Hutch.

"Yeah. Thanks, Xav." The cop turned, giving her a view of his profile and her world lurched into slow-motion.

"*You.*"

Brady Hutchins—*Officer* Brady Hutchins—faced her and smiled the same way he had in the parking lot the night she arrived. "Elliott?"

He was ripped like she'd reluctantly noticed that first night. Sinewy forearms, strong shoulders, that long, lean build with plenty of long, lean muscle to go with it… He was too hot to be a civil servant.

"Are you a stripper or something?" she asked.

Lou guffawed as she retook her seat next to Elliott. "Oh my God, did you seriously just say that?"

"Yeah, I guess I did." Elli's cheeks grew warmer. She hadn't had enough practice in society for this level of surprise.

"Not a stripper. And the gun is real," he answered with a cheesy wink. "But I'll take that as a compliment."

He should. His dark-blond hair was offset by even darker eyebrows, eyes that were an alarming shade of green, full lips and a firm jaw. In that uniform, Brady could easily pass for a stripper.

"How's the tire?" he asked, those paralyzingly gorgeous eyes locked on Elli.

"Fine. Great. But I owe you—" She stuck her hand into her purse and felt his warm touch on her arm.

"Ant and I worked it out." He pulled his hand away, thanked Xavier for the coffee, and threw a five-dollar bill on the bar.

"Brady. Uh, Officer, I can't let you pay my way."

He faced her again, his handsome mug stunning her stupid. "No? Why not?"

Why not, indeed. When an answer eluded her, she shook her head and admitted, "I can't remember."

He grinned one last time and dipped his chin. "All right then. You think of a reason, you let me know."

With that, he was off, stopping to chat with a couple and their children lounging in a booth. She watched until he walked out, staring in his wake.

"You're drooling." Lou offered up a napkin.

Elliott faced front in her barstool in time to catch a hint of a bemused smile from Xavier.

"Are you a stripper." Lou laughed.

"Shut up." Elli snatched the napkin from Lou's hand, but laughed, too. It felt good to laugh. And maybe Lou had a point. It did feel nice to be treated well. By anyone.

But especially by Officer Brady Hutchins.

CHAPTER 6

Nearly a week had passed since the *Bar Incident*.

Elli was fairly certain Brady couldn't care less about her accusing him of taking his clothes off for money, but she felt as if she owed him an apology anyway. And a thank-you for covering the tire repair.

It was like she'd lost all semblance of how to be a polite human over the years of solitude with Neil.

After debating how to appropriately show her gratitude to Brady, she settled on buying him coffee. She knew he liked it, since he'd ordered some from Xavier. Though she had no idea if Brady's coffee had been black or creamed or sugared, or both.

While Salty Dog was a great place for beer, she doubted it was the *best* place to buy coffee. Instead, she drove down Endless Avenue before spotting Cup of Jo's and stopping there.

The coffee shop was cozy with its rich mahogany tables and upholstered chairs. A long, tall table was the centerpiece of the room, complete with metal stools lining both sides. Cup of Jo's was charming, smelled amazing, and she had no problem spending money while she was there. In addition to a branded mug, a bag of freshly ground beans, and a medium caramel latte all purchased for herself, she bought coffee for Brady.

Correction: she bought *four* coffees for Brady in a variety of ways he might take it.

Drink carrier on the passenger seat of her car, she drove to the police station. She had no idea if he was here, but she figured someone here could tell her how to find him. By the time she arrived, though, she lost her nerve and circled the block once. Then one *more* time. By her fourth loop, she was beginning to feel foolish and was slightly worried someone was watching her and growing suspicious.

She parked and stepped into the warm June sunshine, a speech prepared for whomever she encountered inside, when the man in blue himself walked out of the building and saved her the trouble.

She was once again struck by how capable and safe Brady looked in his uniform. Shiny shoes, dark pants, belt, gun, badge, all the way up to the full-lipped smile that spread his generous mouth the second he recognized her.

Hot cops weren't common in Grand Rapids, but the Cove seemed to grow the men nice around here if Ant, Xavier, and Brady were anything to judge by. Before she could objectify him further, she stepped forward with the tray of coffee cups.

Might as well get this over with.

"Brady. Hi. Um, should I call you officer?"

He ambled down the steps to the sidewalk, thumbs hooked in his belt. "Do you want to call me officer?"

Her heart skipped a beat, no doubt due to the extra shot of espresso she'd already enjoyed in her Cup of Jo's latte.

"Making a delivery?" He nodded at the drink carrier in her hand.

"I wanted to thank you, so I brought you a bunch of coffee." She pointed at the one in the ten o'clock position on the tray and went clockwise around it as she described them. "This one is an Americano. This one is a plain, black coffee. This one is decaf, and then I panicked and ordered you what I ordered myself: a caramel latte with an extra shot of espresso, which I'm now regretting, because I can feel how fast I'm talking."

His grin endured, but she didn't give him a chance to speak.

"I have cream and sugar in the car if you need them. And a stir stick, because I hate when you put in the cream, and then it sits in the middle of the coffee instead of turning it a lovely pecan color. I'm still talking, aren't I?"

He laughed, a deep, throaty sound as warm as the sun on her shoulders. "Yeah, but I like it."

"Coffee?" she asked, a blush warming her cheeks.

"I was referring to you talking, but I like coffee, too." He stepped forward, pointed at a cup and asked, "Black?"

"Yes."

"Thank you." He took a sip and licked those very full lips while she stared. "It's not necessary to pay me back, Elliott, but I appreciate the coffee. You meet Jo yet?"

"The barista's name was Zack. I didn't know there was an actual *Jo*."

"She's great. A staple in the Cove." He took the tray and gestured across the street. "Want to sit in Library Park and enjoy one of these with me?"

"Um..." Did she?

"I'd hate for the caramel... What was it?"

"Caramel latte with an extra shot of espresso."

"I'd hate for the caramel latte with an extra shot of espresso to go to waste." He gestured for her to go ahead of him, and she did, trekking to a bench at the edge of the park facing the police station.

"I also wanted to apologize for accusing you of being a stripper," she said as she sat down. "I hope I didn't offend you." Or flatter him to death, which she suspected was more likely.

"Again, I appreciate the gesture, but you don't have to pay me back in coffee beans. I saw a woman in need and wanted to help. Comes with the job," he said dismissively.

She suspected there'd been more to him helping than that. He seemed like a guy who was duty bound in every aspect of his life.

"Not all men are so magnanimous," she mumbled.

Quietly, he assessed her with electric green eyes, his smile gone. He was more attractive when he was serious. "Talking about your Navy-SEAL boyfriend?"

"There is no Navy-SEAL boyfriend. Only an ex not worth mentioning." Only now she sort of had. Dammit. She took a sip of her coffee to keep from saying more.

"Now you have my curiosity piqued. First you arrive alone in the Cove in middle of the night with a flat tire you refuse to let me help you replace—"

"But you did anyway," she interjected.

"—then you lie to me about a boyfriend—"

"I was being cautious."

"—and then you show up with Lou at a bar and tell me I'm a stripper."

"I *asked*."

"And now you're trying to pay me in coffee for the tire I told you was taken care of, plus casually mention an unmentionable ex." His jaw hardened suddenly, his eyes alert and snapping around their immediate environment. "He's not in the Cove, is he? He didn't follow you here?"

"No. He's not here."

"You're safe?"

"Yes. Very." More so in Brady's presence. She almost couldn't process how kind it was that he was concerned.

"And you're staying at the McKinley place?"

"How do you know?"

"I don't." He shrugged. "Ant told me your last name. I checked on the houses in town. It's my job to know what's going on."

That made sense.

"Plus, I have to keep the riffraff down to a minimum." He took another drink of his coffee, the shadow of seriousness on his face receding. "I think I'll let you stay anyway, though."

"Ha ha." She couldn't help smiling back at him.

"How long are you in our fair city?"

"Not sure yet. I thought about staying the summer, but..." She lifted and dropped a shoulder, unsure how to admit that she needed to find herself as quickly as possible so she could go back to Chicago and make something of that person.

"But...you don't like it here?"

"It's not that. At all. It's—" she gestured to the pine trees, the gorgeous houses, and the water beyond both, "—utopic. How could anyone not like it here?"

"Glad to hear you say that."

They smiled at each other for a beat before she looked back down at her coffee and took another sip she absolutely didn't need.

"I should get to work," he said, turning his head to look over his shoulder.

"Right. Sorry to keep you." She moved to stand, and he offered a hand. Chivalry, indeed.

"No sorry necessary. I invited you to sit." She noted the pleasant warmth of his palm in hers. "One more question."

"Okay." She pulled her hand from his and missed the contact instantly. Interesting.

"Have you seen the lake yet?"

"Of course. My parents' house is on the water."

"I mean the *entire* lake. From a watercraft."

"Not since I was a teenager. My parents sold their boat."

"I'll show it to you, Coffee Bean." He tipped his cup to his lips and then gestured to the drink carrier. "Want me to take those extra coffees to the library? I know Mrs. Anderson, the librarian, drinks decaf."

"Oh, sure. Good idea. Did you...did you just call me Coffee Bean?"

"Do you prefer just Bean?"

He was so oddly charming, and so not what she was used to. "I prefer Elli."

"Very well." He took the drink carrier. "Elli Bean."

He walked in the direction of the library entrance with a long-legged, confident stride, and she watched, her hand wrapped around her coffee cup and her mind lit up like a marquee. From the caffeine, or from his presence, she wasn't sure which.

"Saturday afternoon," he called back to her. "Meet me at Mariner Dock at two. Yeah?"

She wanted to say yes but felt awkward about it.

He stopped walking and faced her, either because he'd noticed her hesitation or because he seemed to notice *everything*. "It's just a tour, Elli Bean. You in?"

Time to stop being so hermit-like. If she was here for the summer, she might as well get comfortable. "Sure." She lifted and dropped an arm. "Why not?"

But after he walked away and she climbed into her parents' BMW, she thought of a few reasons *why not*. A few really good reasons.

At the top was that she shouldn't be hanging out with a guy when she was trying to reestablish her independence. And she definitely shouldn't be hanging out with a guy who intrigued her as much as Brady Hutchins.

CHAPTER 7

By the next afternoon, Elli was exhausted.

She'd spent the morning cleaning the house and doing laundry. Halfway through cleaning the keyboard on her laptop, she realized she had too much time on her hands.

Since she'd arrived in the Cove, she'd organized and reorganized the photos on her phone, gone to the grocery store twice, alphabetized the spice rack, and had watched countless videos of cats on the internet.

If she was staying here even a moment longer, she needed to find a job. For one, she'd been putting off using her father's credit card—which he'd insisted she take for emergencies—and she was nearly out of money of her own. For another, she needed to keep her idle hands busy.

She hadn't worked in almost six years, but she had a business degree and had organized many a dinner and cocktail party for Neil's firm. Plus, she was damn smart. Surely someone would want temporary help with the tourist traffic around here.

But after spending two hours visiting shops in town, she'd learned that most people weren't looking for temporary help. She'd popped into the shoe store, the bakery, a furniture store, and even the grocery she'd frequented this week. No luck.

She'd worried she would find herself uncomfortable around people, but she'd made those inquiries without embarrassing herself. And even though no one she'd talked to was hiring, they'd each asked her how long she was staying, and if she was enjoying herself. The people in this town were easy to like, that was for sure.

Elli made a beeline for Cup of Joe's, having craved coffee since before starting her job hunt. She'd naively thought she'd come here to celebrate her success, but now the visit would instead fuel her to continue.

Inside the coffee shop, a woman in her early forties was straightening mugs on a shelf. She wore stylishly torn jeans, high-heeled wedge sandals, and her shirt was Cup-of-Jo's maroon with her name stitched in marigold yellow over one breast. It read *Jo*.

"Morning, sweetheart," the raspy-voiced blonde greeted, her painted pink lips offsetting the bold blond streaks in her hair. "That's a gorgeous dress."

"Oh. Thank you." Elli swept her hands over the navy-blue dress she'd pulled on and paired with sandals. She was on her way to the counter when it occurred to her... Why not work here? She liked coffee. She loved this atmosphere. "I was wondering if you're looking for summer help?"

Jo's eyebrows rose. Her expression wasn't unfriendly, but it held an authority that almost made Elli eat her words.

You can do this.

Elli smiled. "I need a temporary job while I'm in the Cove, or else I might lose my mind. I've checked with some of the local retail stores, but I haven't had any luck."

The other woman wordlessly examined Elli with her head cocked to one side. "You like coffee?"

"She loves it," answered the barista behind the counter. "She spent forty bucks here yesterday."

"I do love it," Elli agreed.

"Ever work in a service-based establishment?" Jo propped a fist on her hip.

"Um." Elli thought back to her work experience. "No, but I used to serve dinner to a dozen people my ex-boyfriend worked with. Entertaining is in my blood."

"Perfect." Jo broke into a smile. "Just so happens, I'm looking for a barista to fill in when Zack isn't here. He could use some advice on being more entertaining."

"Hey!" Zack, tying on his apron, called in mock protest.

"How soon can you start?" Jo asked.

"Tomorrow." Elli grinned. Yes, she could picture herself here. Wearing an apron. Making coffee. Wiping down tables. The place smelled like heaven. And it was close to home.

"How about Monday?" Jo said with a laugh. "Grab an application from Zack, and we'll expedite it. Unless you're hiding a criminal record, you're in."

Now why did that joke make her think of Brady arresting her? Blushing, Elli extended a hand. "Thank you, Jo."

"You're welcome..." Jo raised her eyebrows, waiting.

"Elliott McKinley."

"You're welcome, Elliott." Jo released Elli's hand and turned to greet another patron. Jo gave the tattooed guy with earrings a big hug paired with a hearty laugh.

"Asher, as I live and breathe," she said to the man as Elli stepped out of the way.

Wait... Is that...

Elli blinked. Asher as in *Asher Knight* from the band Knight Time. He was hands down the biggest celebrity she'd ever seen in person. She stared for another few seconds before remembering her manners and turning to Zack.

"Is that..." She shot a thumb over her shoulder.

"The one and only," Zack answered. "He lives in the Cove with his wife and kids."

"Wow." She shook her head to reset her brain. Totally not who she'd expected to bump into while she was here, that was for sure.

"So what'll it be?" Zack asked, clearly far less star struck than Elli. "Another five coffees today?"

"Just the one. A caramel latte—"

"Extra shot," Zack said, tapping the screen.

"You know, why don't I add on a donut?"

"Freshly baked by Sugar Hi." Zack approached the glass case. "Chocolate, glazed, or Devil Dog?"

Elli's eyes locked on the Devil Dog, and her mouth watered. It wasn't a donut, but a rectangular chocolate-dipped cake topped with whipped cream and a cherry.

"Devil Dogs are their specialty," Zack encouraged.

"I'll take it." Looked like she was celebrating her job hunt after all. "On second thought, make it two."

Live a little, part of her whispered, thrilled at the rare experience of no one around to stop her from eating one or both of the tasty desserts.

CHAPTER 8

Elli arrived home from Cup of Jo's fully intending on a dessert binge, but once she was standing in the empty kitchen and spotted Lou, she changed her mind. She crossed the narrow patch of grass to Lou's deck and held up the treasured cakes. "Devil Dog?"

"Heck yes, girl. Bring 'em over." Lou opened a second lawn chair and set it next to the one she'd been lounging in.

"Cute dress," she said as Elli served them each a Devil Dog with napkin.

"Thanks. I start my new job at Cup of Jo's Monday."

"Well, look at you. In town for two weeks, and you're already employed." Lou tapped her Devil Dog with Elli's in a "cheers."

Elli took a bite of the sinfully delicious cake and watched the boats on the water in the distance before turning to her new friend. "What do you know about Brady?"

After Lou finished chewing her bite and swiping her mouth with a napkin, she shrugged. "Good looking. Great cop. Never seen him with anyone long-term."

Elli chewed on that statement and her Devil Dog.

Lou's eyelids narrowed. "Why do you ask?"

"He offered to show me the lake today."

"Oh, really?" Her neighbor grinned. "Considering a fling with a hot cop while you're here?"

"No! No. Of course not." Elli shook her head. That had "bad idea" written all over it in giant letters. No matter how good it sounded out loud. "He was being friendly. I'm not looking. Trust me."

"I hear you on that." Lou nodded in solidarity.

A fling was exactly what Elli *didn't* need. A job? Yes. A temporary stay on the lake in order to recover her independence? Sure thing. But a great cop who was good looking—although Elli thought Lou had those two adjectives reversed—no, Elli didn't need that in her life.

"Plus, if you end up staying long-term, having a fling could end up being awkward," Lou added.

"Yeah." That was wise. Elli needed some wisdom in her life. "Although, I won't be here too much longer. Just until… I have to go home to Chicago. My mom keeps calling me and reminding me that Dad put in a good word for me at his office. No way could I see my Dad at work every day, but I do need to find a responsible job, you know?"

Lou snorted. "I used to have one of those. I left it to follow a passion, which I highly recommend doing at least once."

It occurred to Elli she didn't know what Lou did for a living. "What do you do?"

"Travel vlogger."

"Really?"

"Yep. I share video diaries of my trips. Though I do some blogging as well. I love to write."

"Wow. That's the coolest job I've ever heard of." Elli had no idea anyone could make a living vlogging.

Lou grunted. "It's cooler when you travel. Haven't done that in too long. But I have a lot of video and blogs banked from when I did. I've featured Evergreen Cove plenty. It's a pretty cool place to live or visit."

"It really is," Elli said wistfully.

"I hear you on the responsibility thing. I've been thinking about returning to the world of finance, which is not a passion, but it does pay the bills."

Lou's voice dipped into an almost remorseful tone. Elli hoped Lou didn't have to give up what she clearly loved—travel—for finance. But who was she to give advice? She was just now figuring out her own stuff.

On her walk home from Lou's, Elli thought about all they'd talked about. Specifically, about Brady's invitation to see the lake. She didn't want to give him the wrong impression, especially since she'd likely bump into him a time or three after she started working at Jo's.

The smartest decision was to sit this one out and keep her distance. If she had no intention of finishing anything with Brady, there was no reason to start.

Brady hadn't stopped thinking about Elli since she brought him coffee a few days ago. She'd been sweet and trying damn hard. And she liked him. He could tell by the furtive glances she gave him whenever he'd smiled at her. He could read people, and he'd read Elliott McKinley like oversize words on a billboard.

She was cautious, thanks to an ex-boyfriend who sounded like he needed his ass kicked, but she was also interested.

Brady had never intended to be a summer-fling kind of guy, but that was where he'd ended up. He'd had a long-*ish*-term girlfriend a few years back, but after three months of dating, Meghan had bailed on him and the Cove in one fell swoop. Before she'd left, she'd told him she couldn't handle his wacky schedule. Part of him thought that might be true, but he also knew Meghan couldn't stand that he was never fully off the clock. He was always watching his back, hers, or someone else's. He had never successfully turned that off, and she hadn't liked sharing his attention with others.

Sometimes, he wondered if he cared too much. Not that he blamed her. He didn't even resent her for leaving. It'd reinforced what he'd always suspected. Relationships were hard, and for cops, ten times harder.

After Meghan, he'd dated on and off. Most of the women he knew in the Cove were either married or on their way, so he dated the ones who weren't living here year-round. Whether it was for dating, sex, or casual hangouts—or a combo of the three—the women he saw didn't much care about the hours he kept or the dangers on the job. It made for an easy, if unsatisfying, way to be a part of a relationship. He'd gotten used it, though. Some nights that was sad, and others, it was just what he needed.

Anyway, he had a girl in his life now. *Lila*. His pup was a long-term commitment for him. She'd never experience another harsh word or touch as long as she lived.

His date with Elli Bean tonight was another matter altogether. He was just being friendly.

Bullshit.

Okay, he was being friendly with a *very open mind*. Long term might not be in the cards, but he couldn't deny his instincts that had twanged to life when he'd first met her. They twanged again now as he sped across the lake on the Jet Ski. Wind slapped his face, water splashed his legs, and the sun warmed his arms sticking out of the life jacket.

Whenever he thought of Elli, he wondered what she'd been through with the ex that had sent her fleeing for the Cove. Brady had a protective streak a mile wide. Hell, he'd become a cop because he wanted to help people. He'd be the first to admit he had a hero complex, which could be why he was preoccupied with Elli's situation.

No one, especially a woman, should have to put up with a guy who wasn't treating her like gold. He was determined to treat the women in his life well, even if he wasn't going to be around permanently.

Similarly, if he could help Elli through a rough patch in her life, why not? His life was full enough without another attachment. He had Gramps and Lila to look after. He had the *entire town* to look after.

He powered down the Jet Ski and floated near Mariner's Dock. He'd chosen it because it was close to the marina, and he figured Elli would enjoy seeing that as well as grabbing some dinner at one of the gourmet food trucks that parked here on weekends.

He waited. Watched. Waited some more. Then he parked and climbed off to poke around. He ran into people he knew, which was pretty much everyone, before deciding that something must've come up for Elli. She wasn't here. Even in the crowd, he'd spot a petite brunette looking for him.

He climbed back onto the Jet Ski and zipped across the lake to her house. If something had happened between there and the dock, Lou might know. He tried not to imagine a disaster as he drove over the water, but he did anyway. Thinking the worst was another side effect of being a cop.

Since Lou had once owned a Jet Ski, but her dick of an ex-husband had taken it, there was an empty spot for Brady to dock.

He climbed off and dropped the life vest, pulling on a shirt and a pair of flip flops next. The second he moved to the side yard, he caught sight of Elli in her kitchen window. She caught sight of him, too, her brown eyes widening with guilt.

She pointed to the back door and he met her there as she was sliding it open. Her blue dress hugged her small curves, and the sandals boosted her ass and her calves in a way that sent his mind to the gutter.

"Didn't see you at the dock," he said.

"I stood you up."

Well. That's honest.

"I didn't know how to get a hold of you," she blurted as she shut the door behind her.

"Lou knows."

"I didn't want to tell Lou I was being a jerk." She squinted one eye as she studied the lake behind him. She was damned adorable. "Where's the boat?"

"I came on a Jet Ski." He pointed at Lou's dock. "Any reason in particular you stood me up, Elli Bean?"

"I didn't think it was a good idea."

"To take a tour of the lake?" He was officially confused.

"To start something with you I couldn't finish." Before he could ask what she considered starting and finishing, she added, "My ex wasn't great to me. He didn't hit me or anything, but he controlled me with guilt, and sometimes that's just as bad."

"Sometimes it can be," Brady said gently.

"I'm not in Evergreen Cove to date. I'm here to learn how to be independent. To remember who I am."

"How very *Lion King* of you." He winked to show her he was teasing, and she smiled and covered her face with one hand.

"I overreacted, didn't I?" She let out a muted *ugh*. "You were being neighborly by offering to show me around."

"In your defense, I was being more than neighborly," he admitted.

"So the bolt of attraction I noticed between us didn't escape your attention."

He had to laugh. She had a way of surprising him at every turn, which was not common. "Yeah, okay. I noticed that, too."

She bit her lip and looked past him at the water.

"Look, Elli. Our lake tour isn't going to end up being more than that unless you want it to. But if it works out that way," he added with a grin, "that'd be the best news I've heard all summer."

CHAPTER 9

Elli turned over what Brady said while running her eyes along his exposed arms. Biceps *bulged*. He had attractive forearms, nice hands. Great knees. She'd never seen him in shorts before. It wasn't a bad sight.

"You're thinking about it," he accused.

She was. She'd surprised herself by admitting her attraction to him, but she was even more surprised to hear that he was willing to act on it. There was only one problem...

"I'm trouble," she blurted. "I've been in therapy."

"Okay." He nodded.

"My ex was a narcissist," she continued explaining. "I went along with his wishes, which was completely out-of-character for me."

"And you're worried if we go out that I'll take over your life given this daunting and immediate attraction?" He wasn't laughing, so he must not be kidding.

Chewing her lip, she turned the question over in her head. No, she wasn't worried about him "taking over" her life. For whatever reason, she trusted him. Maybe it was the uniform, or maybe it was her gut, but to her, Brady was a tantalizing combination of safe and exciting. A rare mix.

"Once I stole a magazine from a library," she told him. "Tucked it into my backpack and walked out with it."

"Elli—"

"And another time, I didn't pay a parking ticket for *three entire years.*"

"Is this supposed to dissuade me?" His eyelids lowered to half-mast as if he were bored. He rested a hand on the railing of her deck like he could stand there all afternoon while she ogled him. Sounded great to her.

Wait, no. Resist.

"You don't have to build a case for not going out with me," he said. "Tell me no, and I'll leave. I won't make you do anything. I don't think I could."

He might not know it, but that was the most flattering thing he could've said. That he respected her answer. That he couldn't sway her once her mind was made up. And he was right. She *was* strong.

She was just out of practice.

"What if my answer is not yet?" She took one step toward him and then another. Now that he might leave, she wasn't sure she wanted him to. On the second step, eye to eye with him, she felt the attraction to him tenfold. He must've felt it, too. His gaze snapped to her mouth and then back to her eyes.

"Like I said. I can't make you," he repeated, "but that doesn't mean I'm done trying." His mouth flinched into the barest smile before he touched her, a gentle tip of her chin with his knuckles. "See ya, Bean."

He turned and strode that long, lean body to the Jet Ski. She watched as he stowed his shoes, lost the shirt and, way too soon, covered his golden chest with a life jacket and climbed aboard. He took off like a shot over the waves. She watched him until the red blur of the Jet Ski was not but a memory. Sweat clung to her skin, either from the hot day or the interaction with Brady.

She wished she would have said yes, climbed on behind him, and wrapped her arms around that marvelous torso...

Good Lord.

She was an indecisive head case. Fresh out of a relationship and on her own for the first time in six years was no time to joyride on the water with Brady Hutchins.

Or kiss him. Which she also wanted to do very badly.

"Earth to Elliott." Lou's voice was outlined with laughter. "What was that about? Did he bail on you?"

Elli faced her neighbor. "Other way around. I turned him down."

"If only every guy I'd stood up came over to beg."

"He didn't beg."

"He didn't kiss you, either, but you looked like you wanted him to," Lou sang. "I wasn't leering out the window like a weirdo. I saw a mysterious Jet Ski on my dock and came out to investigate. Then I saw you lean toward him like you were made of metal, and he had a magnetic mouth."

"Ugh." Elliott palmed her face. "Was I?"

"I don't think he noticed, if that's any consolation." Lou crossed the lawn and stood where Brady had a moment ago.

"I don't know what to do." Elli turned her attention to the water.

"Poor thing." Lou patted Elli's hand. "A gorgeous guy with a sexy smile is hot for you. I feel for ya, honey."

Elli laughed. "He's not hot for me. Although he did say he wasn't done trying."

"That sounds promising. I mean, it would if you were open to having a little one-on-one fun this summer."

At the insinuation of being one-on-one with Brady, Elli's cheeks grew warm. She didn't *need* sex. She certainly hadn't come here looking for someone to have sex with, either. But if her body's reactions were anything to go by, one-on-one fun with Brady was a pleasant thought, indeed.

CHAPTER 10

Lila's toenails scraped the floor while Brady attempted to remove her leash. Once free, she bounded into the kitchen and nearly knocked Gramps over. He paused in his pancake making and bent to give her a nuzzle. The dog's tail swept back and forth so fast she created a breeze.

After the two lovebirds greeted each other, Brady leaned on the kitchen counter and watched his grandfather flip pancakes. Gramps making pancakes always reminded Brady of his grandmother when he was a kid living in this house. There were good memories from those days, but they'd taken a while to manifest.

Growing up, Brady had talked to Gramps about everything from homework to sports to girls. And since he didn't relish the reaction his buddies at work would give him when they learned he'd been stood up *and* shut down, Brady decided to run the situation past the old man in search of any takeaway wisdom.

"I helped a girl change her tire a few weeks back," Brady offered.

"Uh-huh," Gramps said distractedly while he watched over his pan.

"Then I paid Ant to patch her tire."

Gramps looked up, interest in his deep-set eyes.

"She brought me coffee as a thank-you. Four kinds, since she didn't know what I liked." He smiled, remembering how sweet that gesture had been. "I invited her out to tour the lake, she accepted. But when I showed up on the Jet Ski, she was nowhere to be found. Well, that's not entirely true. I eventually found her. At her house. When I asked her why she was home, she admitted she stood me up."

Gramps barked a laugh, and in response, Lila *literally* barked. "Almost done, Pancake," he told her before turning back to Brady. "Win some, lose some."

"She confessed to stealing a magazine and not paying a parking ticket. She told me she's trouble." Brady smiled to himself as he recalled the confession. Like he was a priest who could absolve her of her law-breaking sins. God, she was cute. "I told her I wasn't done trying."

"The best ones are always worth it, kiddo." Gramps plated the pancakes before pouring more batter in the pan.

"Have a story about Gram for me?" Brady knew the story of his grandparents meeting, and he never tired of hearing it. It was as charming as a Norman Rockwell painting.

"Naw, but I have one about your dad and your mom." Gramps smiled a sad smile Brady couldn't quite return.

His parents had been gone for decades, but Brady still missed them with a fierceness he assumed would never end.

"They met here. In Evergreen Cove. Your dad was with a group of friends, and your mom was on vacation with family. He came to visit your Gram and me the day after he met your mom. He was so smitten he could hardly string a sentence together." Gramps chuckled.

Brady smiled as he tried to imagine his strong, self-assured father falling over himself for a woman. At first, he couldn't fathom it, then he pictured his beautiful blond mother, and he totally could. "They were meant for each other."

"Yes, sir," Gramps said. "Pancake!" Lila danced at his feet, and Gramps tossed a pancake into the air like a Frisbee. She caught it.

"New trick," Gramps said proudly.

After turning down the offer of pancakes, Brady headed to Cup of Jo's. On his drive to Endless Avenue, he admired the water. The lake was sparkling like someone had thrown diamonds onto the surface, and after spending most of Saturday on the back of a Jet Ski and Sunday boating with friends, he wanted to play hooky. He was as susceptible to summer fever as everyone else in this town.

He brushed a blond dog hair from his dark-blue uniform and entered the coffee shop, waving at a few regulars as he walked to the counter. Chin up, he perused the board, even though he always ordered the same thing. He was a simple guy, but curious about the new concoctions Jo invented. The iced peanut butter chocolate latte sounded...interesting.

"Let me guess. Coffee. Black."

He jerked his attention to the barista. Elliott, as it turned out. She was standing behind the counter wearing a maroon T-shirt, a green apron tied at her waist. Her dark hair was pulled back in a ponytail, and her big eyes hadn't yet left his.

"Elli Bean. You're living up to your nickname."

She grinned, which made his whole damn morning.

"When'd you start working here?"

"This morning. I only know how to make a few drinks though, which is why Zack's here to babysit me."

The other barista waved from where he stood stocking bags of coffee on a shelf behind the counter. "Hey, Brady."

"Hey." Brady reached for his wallet.

"It's on me. I'm paying you back for the tire, remember?"

"I don't want paid back, *remember*?"

Defiantly, she punched a button and stuffed money from her pocket into the cash drawer before closing it again.

"Maybe you're right. You are trouble."

A feisty glint lit her eye. "Does that mean you're not going to *try*, Officer?"

Something in her had shifted. He could sense the tension simmering between them. She turned her back to pour his cup of coffee and snapped on a lid. When she handed him the cup, his fingers lingered on hers.

She didn't pull away. And her smile endured.

"I haven't yet begun to try, Elli Bean. When I do," he dipped his chin, "you'll know it."

"Or maybe," she said, her voice low and flirty, "I'll beat you to it."

Oh, she wants to play? It is on.

"Thanks for the coffee." He held up the cup. "I'll get out of your way since you have customers."

"But there's no one else—" The door dinged as a couple entered. She glanced at them and then back to Brady. "You notice everything, don't you?"

"Especially what people don't want me to notice," he added with a tip of his imaginary hat. "Ma'am. Have a good day."

It wasn't until he was outside of Jo's and halfway down the block that he realized he didn't notice everything. He'd totally missed that Elli had written her phone number on his coffee cup.

CHAPTER 11

Turned out that Brady "trying" looked a lot like him arriving at her house in a white T-shirt and board shorts. He looked as good as he had the other day when he'd brought the Jet Ski by. Or almost as good. Lost in the vision of the glimpse she'd had of his naked chest that day, she forgot her manners.

"Morning," he greeted. Likely because she hadn't said a word yet.

"Hi." She'd had a brief, daring moment of insanity when she'd written her number on his cup. When he didn't call or text that day, she convinced herself she'd made a grave error in her assumptions. After a phone call with her therapist, though, she felt a lot better. Elliott had needed the reminder to trust herself. She'd been through a trauma with Neil, but she'd come a long way, and quickly.

Brady had finally texted her this morning. A simple *"You home, Bean?"* and chills had skated up her arms.

Her response had been, *"Just made coffee if you want a cup."*

"I came to collect," he said now, gesturing to her coffee mug.

"Lucky you," she told him as he stepped into her parents' house. "I made a freshly ground, slow-dripped pot of Cup of Jo's."

His eyes warmed to a distracting degree. "You know what I like, Elli Bean."

In the wide kitchen, he somehow filled the room. He exuded both competence and comfort, and both of those were distracting to the nth degree. An infectious smile, a wide chest—those were nice features on anyone. But a man who'd never mistreat her just to feel better about himself? *Yes, please.*

She poured a mug of coffee for him. When he took it, his fingers lingered on hers the way they had at the coffee shop.

"Is this you trying?" she whispered, unable to break the intense eye contact.

"Yeah. Is it working?"

She'd been nervous he might pressure or overwhelm her. Turned out his version of trying was earnestness and a whole lot of sexy.

"It's working."

He leaned a hip on the countertop next to her. "In that case, Jet Ski or boat?"

"Pardon?"

"I owe you a tour. It's a cloudless, sunny day, and your chariot awaits."

"And by chariot, you mean..."

"Jet Ski or boat," he repeated.

It'd been so long since a guy had asked for and respected her preference she nearly hesitated. But once again, Brady had left her charmed and flummoxed at once.

"Jet Ski."

He took a sip of his coffee, but not before he smiled down at her and said, "That's a good choice."

She wasn't *particularly* fond of the idea of zipping across the lake at warp speed, but she'd been uncovering her braver side since she'd arrived in Evergreen Cove. Brady was part of that discovery.

Even if she *hadn't* called her therapist, she could admit she was drawn to Brady's confidence—something Neil never had. Neil had been manipulative and mean, both signs of a lack of confidence.

On the Jet Ski, she was as shaky as a newly born foal. But when she clutched her thighs tightly around Brady's, smelled the coconut scent of suntan lotion on his warm skin, well, she was shaky for another reason entirely.

She clamped her inner thighs against his legs, and he made sure she was snug in place by flattening his palm on her leg. When she rested her hands on each side of his waist, he reached back and hugged her arms tightly around his middle instead.

"You gotta hang on, Bean." He patted her arm when she tightened her grip. The touch was respectful and quick, but tingles spread through her veins like wildfire.

He started the engine and she felt more than heard the rumble of laughter in his chest. Arms around his solid body, she held on as instructed. He gunned the watercraft and took off over the waves.

After several minutes of wind in her hair and laughter when he went faster—the Jet Ski really was fun—he slowed down long enough to let her catch her breath. She swept a few loose strands of hair back into her ponytail as Brady began his tour.

He pointed out huge mansions and other more reasonably sized houses and then puttered past the marina and the beach, where residents of the Cove flocked on hot days like this one. When they passed by a white house with a sprawling deck and in-ground pool, he floated and took a long look at the house. It overlooked the lake and the entire front—or was this side the back?—was a wall of shining glass windows.

"This one's my favorite," he told her, longing evident in his voice.

"It's beautiful. I had no idea there were such opulent houses here. Granted, it's been a while, but I remember the Cove differently."

"It's changed over the last few years. Not a bad thing. There is a lot more tourist money than before. We strive to keep an everyone-knows-everyone feel. People are friendly around here, and since the Cove is home to most of us, we try and get to know everyone." He reached back and squeezed her leg. "Some more than others."

"You've lived here your whole life?" she asked.

"Pretty much." Slowly, he began puttering along the water again. "My parents passed away when I was five. I'm from Cincinnati, but grew up in the Cove with my grandparents."

Wanting to soothe the hurt she heard in his voice, she touched his arm. "I'm sorry."

"Thanks, Bean." He patted her leg, and she held his hand on her bare skin for a moment, wanting to comfort him further, and not quite ready to end what was happening between them.

"Are you hungry?" she asked.

"Are you kidding? I'm always hungry." His smile returned, and her heart throbbed in response. Making him smile made her feel good, and feeling good had been in short supply over the last several years.

"Do you like tacos?" She was taking the innocent lake tour to a next level, which she'd sworn earlier she didn't want. But hey, a girl could change her mind.

"Everyone likes tacos."

"Take us to my place. Tacos are my specialty."

~

Half an hour later, she'd warmed the cooked ground beef she'd prepped yesterday, opened a can of seasoned black beans and nuked them, and pulled out every taco topping from the fridge.

They ate, every once in a while pausing to talk about the boats or houses they'd seen today. She couldn't help thinking about Neil and comparing him to Brady. Other than the looks department—where Neil fared the worst—her ex was rigid and took himself too seriously. Neil had a lot rules. They'd started out merely insulting —*don't eat on the new sofa*—and had graduated to troubling—*check with me before you schedule a hair appointment.*

Brady definitely wasn't rigid, and while he took his job seriously, he didn't seem to take himself that way. He was both laidback and protective—perfect for his profession. He could comfort and look out for someone while remaining alert. He was likable and able to deescalate a situation. Like at the bar with that guy Patrick. Brady had taken the other man from belligerent to willingly leaving in a matter of minutes.

"This is good. Thank you," he said after he polished off his last taco.

"You're welcome. Can I ask you something?"

"Shoot."

She fiddled with the spoon sticking out of the sour cream, suddenly shy about her curiosity. "When did you know you wanted to be a cop—uh, a police officer?"

"When Ant and I were wrangled up at age sixteen for skipping school to smoke pot at Library Park."

"Yikes," she said on a laugh.

"It was the only time we were caught." His smile was reminiscent. "Officer Dickens. He retired a few years ago. You'd think most kids would be resentful of being busted, but he was cool. He told Ant's parents and my grandparents what we did."

"He ratted you out, and you liked him?"

"I did. Ant and I ended up doing community service, and I watched how people interacted with Dickens. They loved and admired the guy. I'd been content to bad-boy my way through my teens, but at that moment I knew what I wanted."

"To be loved and admired?"

"Sounds cheesy when you say it. But, yeah."

"And now the town adores you." He was so darn likable. How could anyone help themselves?

He lifted one eyebrow in argument. "I'm less revered than you might think."

"Give me an example."

He chuffed. "No way. I'm trying to win you over, not scare you off."

"I told you about my thievery and my law-breaking."

"Right. The scandalous magazine heist and you ducking the law for three years for a lethal parking ticket." He grinned, and she grinned back. So. Damn. Likable. "I was an angry kid. I stole money from my grandfather when I was a teenager, ran around with a rougher crowd. That's how I met Ant, actually. He was a lot like me and didn't have the stomach to be a true delinquent. But we could have been if we weren't caught young. That entire summer, we picked up trash together and talked about what we wanted to do with our lives."

"And he said chainsaw artist, and you said a cop?"

"Hell, no. At the time, I wanted to be a rock star, and he wanted to be a firefighter. Things change. What about you? Did you want to be an Elli Bean when you grew up?"

"I never knew." She pulled in a deep breath. "I attained a degree in business...after several changes of my major. I think I just wanted to be...important. Seen. You know?" She felt foolish admitting that, until he nodded.

"Yeah. I know." He watched her mouth for a second before those deep-green eyes trickled up to hers. Then he cupped her jaw lightly, swiped her bottom lip with his thumb once, and pressed his lips to hers.

Heat engulfed her.

When he started to pull away, it was Elliott who lingered, holding his wrist and deepening the kiss. Their tongues touched, and she was *lost*. He gripped the stool she was sitting on and jerked her closer, his full mouth gently sipping at hers.

Her skin sizzled. Her nipples peaked. Thankfully, she'd pulled a T-shirt over her bikini top, or else he'd see exactly what he did to her. Just how crazy he made her. They'd connected on a deeper level today. She refused to let opportunity pass her by.

He sifted his fingers into her hair, and familiar warmth pooled in her belly before trickling lower. When he paused, she regained enough common sense to pull away, her chest heaving. Meanwhile, her hormones were throwing a Welcome Home party in her honor.

It'd been a long while since she'd been kissed by someone who wanted her as much as she wanted him. And oh, did she want him. Despite her thin arguments to the contrary. This close to him, she mused she could drown in his sea-green irises and not regret a thing...

"Elliott." His voice was husky and low, his hand still cupping her face. "Is your answer still *not yet*?"

"My answer..." Her heart thrummed with excitement as she considered a host of possibilities. In the end, she went with the one she wanted most. "My answer is *right now*."

A ping of certainty registered in her belly. She was sure, so sure. Feeling sure was a newer sensation. One that made her feel powerful and strong. She wanted to satisfy her own needs and his. A slow summer day's worth of lazy kisses and sex so hot it'd scorch the earth sounded *divine*.

He took her hand as he stood and backed from the kitchen, his eyes on her. She followed.

"Point me to the nearest bedroom," he told her as he lifted her into his arms and climbed the stairs.

"There," she obliged with a rolling laugh.

Brady was safe. He was sexy. He was impermanent.

That made him *perfect*.

"I don't usually do this." She felt the need to explain as he set her on her feet in the guest bedroom.

"Then I'll have to show you what you've been missing," he said. Then he lit her afire with a kiss.

CHAPTER 12

She broke the kiss to sit on the bed, and a second later, all six-foot-something of Brady was over top of her. Tanned skin. Sun-kissed dark-blond hair. Trance-inducing green eyes. She caught his face in her hands and his lips with hers, pulling in a breath through her nose as he kissed her hard.

Her head was swimming with ideas—there were too many things she wanted to do, and all at once. A faint warning rang in the back of her head, reminding her to be smart. Not to get taken advantage of, and to maintain control before they spiraled out of it...

"Brady, wait," she breathed.

He froze, his body taut, his arms locked straight as he held himself away from her. The desire was alive in his eyes and heavy in the erection resting against one of her legs. Just like that, he'd heeded her command. Having power after years of powerlessness was intoxicating. Her finger on his face, she traced the faint blond whiskers along his jaw.

"Second thoughts?" he asked.

She reconsidered before shaking her head. "None."

She wasn't going to be in the Cove forever. She would eventually go home to Chicago and find a job and an apartment. She was here to remember who she'd been before Neil had eroded her self-confidence. Since her stay in the Cove was going to be brief, this chance with Brady was once in a lifetime.

"What about you?" It seemed only fair to ask.

Brady chuckled, the deep sound encouraging. "Elli Bean, I am *not* having second thoughts." He blew out a breath. "Can barely think about anything except what's hiding under your bikini. He lifted the edge of her shirt and tickled his fingers along her bare belly.

"Good." She pressed a fast kiss to his lips.

"Good." He pulled her shirt over her head, and her ponytail canted to one side. She yanked the elastic from her hair as he whipped his own shirt off with one hand in a sexy, fisted, over-the-head grab. Even the way he took his shirt off was sexy.

She unclasped her bikini top, and he tossed the scrap of fabric over his shoulder, his smile feral. Again, her heart rate ratcheted up. She was crazy excited to take what she wanted. She wanted him.

Their mouths mated, his lips tugging at hers while his fingers mimicked the motion with first one of her nipples, then the other.

She shut her eyes, and sparks burst on the inside of her eyelids. She was lost in the sensations his seeking mouth and the rough pads of his fingers created. When his lips left hers and he suckled a nipple into his mouth, her mind blanked. When he kissed his way down her stomach, she thought her head might explode.

He rolled the bottoms of her swimsuit down her legs, his eyes dark and locked onto what he'd revealed. Standing at his full height, he stripped himself the rest of the way. She took a long look.

Long was a good word for him.

"I like the way you look at me, Elli Bean," he murmured, lying over her, nothing but hot, suntan-lotioned skin between them. "Like you want to take a bite."

He kissed her before sliding down her stomach. He stopped between her thighs, tossing her legs over his shoulders, and ducking his head. His fingers skimmed up her torso, lazily plucking her nipples while he laid the flat of his tongue on her clit and gave her a stroke.

"*Oh God.*" Her words were more prayer than expletive. She needed this—but she hadn't known how badly.

"Let me know what you like." He grabbed her hand and put it on his head.

She gripped his hair, guiding him, her hips matching the rhythm as she rode his tongue. So close.

So, *so* close...

Elliott tasted like heaven. Like honey and sunshine.

On the Jet Ski, she'd clung to his back, her strong thighs locked around his. All he'd been able to think about was her legs wrapped around his waist. Or his neck. Hell, he didn't care. He'd just wanted more of her.

When she'd stopped him a few minutes ago, he'd been sure it was so that she could tell him she'd changed her mind. They barely knew each other, and beyond flirting, they hadn't done anything physical until today.

He'd worried that whatever'd happened between her and her ex had leaked into what was between them now. He would have understood if that was the case.

Thank Christ, it hadn't come to that. And now, with her fingers in his hair, his face buried between her legs, he'd make sure she wouldn't regret the yes she'd given him.

He wedged his hands under her ass and lifted her, swirling his tongue over her clit. She grabbed his hair with both hands and tugged. That, she liked.

"Brady," she moaned, her voice breaking.

Fuck, he liked hearing her say his name like that.

She came on a cry, her back arching, her nails digging into his scalp, her voice going scratchy at the end when she ran out of steam. He lapped up what she gave him, waiting until she pushed him away to stop.

Climbing her body, he laid kisses on her tan lines, the one under her flat belly, the triangle ones that whited out each breast. He suckled her nipple as aftershocks rocked her petite form. She let out a soft hum, her long lashes hiding her eyes. Then he moved to her neck and kissed his way up to her ear, where he gently bit down on her lobe.

"Your golden skin tastes as good as the pale parts," he rumbled in her ear. "Every inch of you is delicious."

She opened her eyes, those deep browns more caramel in color in the sunlight. Wrapping her arms around his neck, she smiled. "You're very good at that."

His grin couldn't be stopped. Or so he thought. When her hand found his cock, that grin fell off his face. He liked her small hand on his favorite body part way too much.

"I want this," she said. "Every *inch.*" Her strength regained, she kissed him, working him into a white-hot lather. He let her. He wanted what she wanted, to ease into her creamy channel and move inside her until she was boneless and shouting his name.

She guided the tip of his dick to her entrance, and before he could slide in and make both their dreams come true, he remembered one crucial detail. "Condom, sweetheart."

Her eyes flew open and landed on his. "Oh. Shit."

It was so cute, her disappointment so pronounced, he nearly smiled.

"I don't have any," she told him. "I wasn't planning… *Shit.*"

She was even more adorable when she swore.

"How mad at me would you be if I told you I have some in my bag?"

"The bag you brought in after our ride?" she asked, hope in her voice. "I wouldn't be mad at all. Well, I might be mad if you only brought one."

"I'm an optimist. There's more than one, Bean." He kissed the tip of her nose and reluctantly left the cradle of her thighs. He jogged downstairs bare-assed naked, open curtains be damned.

He returned in record time and rolled on the condom. She held out both arms to invite him in and he liked that as much as he liked everything else about her. He eased forward into her warmth. He could already tell that one time with this woman wasn't going to be enough. Her back arched, her nipples brushing his chest as he glided in to the hilt. He sucked air through his teeth. She was a tight fit, which he liked a whole hell of a lot.

"So good," she praised on her own slow exhalation.

He stroked out and back in, earning a, "Damn, Brady," for his efforts.

"Flattery," he told her, repeating the motion, "Works on me."

"And here I thought you were playing hard to get," she teased with a chuckle. She laced her fingers together at the back of his head. Her eyelids were at half-mast, her hold on him loose. She was sated thanks to him, which was more flattering than any compliment she could've given him.

"You have another one for me?" he asked as he stroked into her again.

"Another...orgasm?" Her eyes grew wide. "Who do you think I am?"

"Not accustomed to multiple orgasms?"

Her cheeks tinged a deep shade of pink, confirming his suspicions.

"Hang on, honey." He kissed her quickly. "You're in for a treat."

A gasp eked from her throat as he doubled his efforts. She took every inch he gave, opening her legs wider to accommodate him. He bent to kiss her, but had to retreat when her high, tight moans started up again. Her eyebrows bent and her cries grew louder. The cries that'd been muffled by her thighs while he'd been eating her out earlier were now echoing off the chambers of his skull.

He fucking *loved* it.

He kept up the frantic pace until she trembled against him, until he was forced to slow down and catch his own breath. She let go on a shout. One he followed with an unrestrained release of his own. A hard, teeth-rattling orgasm that shook his spine and blurred his vision.

Who-knew-how-many minutes later, he opened his eyes and emerged from the blissful blackness. Her lust-blown pupils were hidden behind dropped eyelids—exactly the look he'd been going for. Triumphant, his ego punched the air.

Elli stroked his jaw the way she had earlier, her fingernails raking against his whiskers and sending a chill down his back.

He was accustomed to satisfying a woman and being able to walk away. But as he studied her relaxed smile, he realized he wasn't ready to walk away from her.

Not just yet.

CHAPTER 13

Brady had to work the next two days, and so did Elli.

He'd texted her this morning and invited her over for dinner after his shift tonight. She hesitated over her response, typing out that she was busy and then erasing it. Then she typed that she'd love to but was tired and erased that, too. Finally, she'd pecked in a quick "sounds good!" and sent it before she could overthink—some more—about saying yes. He'd replied with his address, and she'd offered to bring drinks.

She'd told herself that she'd only have sex with him once, but...damn.

Damn.

A girl could get used to sex that good. And "getting used" to anything with Brady wasn't on her agenda. She hadn't expected to want more, given her past experiences. Sex was typically *okay,* and if it was better than okay the first time, she could bank on the second time being *less* okay. So she'd assumed sex with Brady would be a one-time thing, a checkbox she could tick before moving on. Instead, she'd been side-eyeing her vibrator and wondering how she'd ever thought of it as a suitable substitute for the real thing.

She'd never had a man like Brady in her bed.

Damn.

She shook off her thoughts as she strolled the aisles of Abundance Market, hunting for a bottle of wine to take to his place tonight. She didn't know what was for dinner but figured it didn't matter. Any food or drink combo would pale in comparison to the amazing sex they'd have after.

Or before. She wasn't picky.

She lapsed into a memory of him between her legs, those lamplight-green eyes on her while she ruffled his hair with her fingers... *Mmm.*

"Can I help you find anything?" a tall red-haired woman, wearing a nametag that read Julia, interrupted.

Elliott jerked out of her daydream. *Sexdream.*

"What's a good middle-of-the-road?" Elli gestured to rows upon rows of wine bottles. The selection was overwhelming.

"Red or white?" Julia asked.

"One of each?" As with the coffee, she wasn't sure what Brady liked. She already had two varieties of beer in her cart in case he didn't drink wine. That seemed like something she should know about a guy she was sleeping with, but she wasn't going to over-examine that right now.

Elli chose two bottles and made her way to the cashier. She arrived at Brady's apartment early, but after a brief debate, she decided not to sit in her car for twenty minutes while the beer grew warm.

At the top of the stairs on the third-floor landing, she rapped her knuckles on apartment 3C. The building was surrounded by trees so the lake was less visible. Definitely he wasn't in his dream home yet, she thought, remembering the house he'd pointed out during her lake tour.

"You're early," she heard behind her. She swung around to say hello to her chef for the evening, but the sight of Brady Hutchins nearly naked glued her tongue to the roof of her mouth.

He stood in the doorway, a bath towel slung low on his waist, hiding the part of him she'd enjoyed so much a few nights ago. Screw dinner, she wanted to *screw him*.

"Keep looking at me like that, Elli Bean, and you'll get more than a kiss hello." He raised one eyebrow, which made him sexier. "You look amazing."

"Thanks." She swept her hand over her simple white dress and stepped inside.

He shut the door behind her and moved the towel to dry his damp hair. Her eyes traveled along the planes of his abs and down to his heavy cock, hanging temptingly to one side. By the time she'd forced her gaze back to his mouthwatering chest and then up to his talented mouth, she'd forgotten how to breathe.

"You want to put those in the fridge while I get dressed?" A smile spread his mouth. "Or we can eat naked. Your call."

"Yes, of course." She shut her eyes, but the outline of his nude body was burned on the inside of her eyelids.

She felt his palm at the back of her neck, and when she opened her eyes, he was close enough to kiss.

"At least let me feed you first," he rumbled, sounding amused. He took the bags from her hand, set them on the counter, and then laid kiss on her mouth. She touched his damp chest. His skin was warm from his shower, tempting her to lean in and taste his soap-scented skin.

"Sorry," she said, not sorry at all.

"Be right back. Try and pull yourself together." He winked before turning for the hallway. She admired his bare ass until he vanished into a back bedroom.

"Pull yourself together," she reminded herself as she stashed the beer and white wine into the fridge. She set the red wine on the counter next to the stove and bent to see what was in the oven.

"Frozen pizza." Brady appeared around the corner, pulling a blue shirt over his head. He wore shorts and no shoes, and his damp hair was everywhere. "It was supposed to be lasagna, but I was called in early and ran out of time this morning. I didn't even have time to pick up Pancake."

"Pancake?"

"My dog. She's at my grandfather's house. Her name's Lila, but Gramps calls her Pancake. Don't ask."

"I didn't know you had a dog." It suited him though. A hot bachelor with a dog.

"Yeah. Wasn't supposed to have one." He knelt to check on the pizza and then stood again, closer to her than before. "I came across Lila on a call. She was tied to a porch. Underfed and terrified. I intended to give her to someone else, or drop her at a shelter, but she apparently deems me a suitable guardian."

Elli's heart ached for the poor pup. Dogs deserved better than chains. "Poor thing. Sounds like you saved her."

"What can I say? I'm a sucker for cute females." He touched her elbow, and she lifted her chin to take him in. He was a lot taller than her, which could be intimidating, but like everything else about him, his height only made her feel safe. "Kiss me again, Bean, I'm dying."

She wrapped her arms around his neck and climbed to her toes. Kissing him was like enjoying a cup of coffee. He relaxed and revved her up at the same time. He was an illustration of tantalizing opposites.

"I brought beer and wine. I wasn't sure what you liked," she said as she lowered to her heels. She hadn't managed to take her arms from his neck yet.

"I like you."

Unable to reply as boldly, she continued, "White wine, red, an IPA, and a summer shandy."

His grin was slow and made her recall vividly how amazing his mouth felt whenever it was on her. "So careful."

No, she wasn't. If she were careful, she wouldn't be here. She let go of his neck, and he moved to the oven to check on their dinner. He pulled out the hot pizza and set it on the stovetop.

"While our dinner cools, how about a drink?" He powered off the oven and dropped the oven mitt. "Which of those options did you buy for yourself?"

"Salty Dog's summer shandy."

"Wise choice." He grabbed two bottles from the fridge, popped the tops, and poured them into glasses. After they'd each taken a long draw, he grasped her hand and they walked into the living room. The decor was manly yet warm and inviting, like Brady himself. His deep-brown leather couch sat in front of a large, round ottoman stacked with a few books. A TV dominated one wall of the room, and a gas fireplace served as the focal point for another.

He eased into the corner of the couch, fatigue outlining his features.

"You had a long day," she said, picking up one of the novels. "We could've rescheduled."

"Hell, no. How are you? Tough day slinging coffee beans?"

"Oh, *brutal.*" She set aside the novel. "Your job's hard."

"Sometimes." He didn't elaborate, and she guessed he didn't want to discuss whatever—or whomever—he'd encountered on his shift.

"Were you a barista before you came to the Cove?" he asked, smoothly changing the subject.

"Nope. Jo took a chance on me. I have that business degree I mentioned, but…ah, I haven't worked outside the home for the last five years or so." She offered a tight smile. "Neil, my ex, didn't want me to work. It took me too long to realize he was manipulative. He had a way of making his ideas seem like mine."

"What a fucking dick." Brady's good humor was gone. His attractive face hardened.

"Pretty much."

He reached for her hand, giving it a gentle squeeze. "Sorry you had to go through that, Bean. You shook him off completely? He doesn't have any contact with you?"

"No. I moved out one day while he was at work. My parents came to help just in case… Well, I wasn't sure how he'd react. Turned out he didn't react much. He told me he was sorry things didn't work out, and then he shook my hand. Six years, and he shook my hand like I was a business acquaintance." That part made her nauseous. "That was, I don't know, maybe ten weeks ago? I haven't heard from him since. I saw a photo of him online with a woman on his arm, so I don't think my leaving shattered him. I don't want him back, but it hurts to know I meant so little to him."

She paused when she realized that Brady had asked a simple question about where she used to work and she'd spilled her guts.

"Ignore me. I didn't mean to say all that." She moved to pull her hand from his, but he kept hold of her.

"Don't be embarrassed. What you told me makes him look bad, not you. He didn't know how to treat a woman so that she blooms in his presence instead of withers. You—look at you—" Brady studied her earnestly. "Elliott, you've already bloomed. You came to the Cove and *exploded*."

Flattered, she ducked her head. "Lou said something similar. I remember when I was strong."

Silence invaded the room. She let it for a moment before turning the tables on him.

"What's your story? Nice guy, skills in the bedroom, handsome cop in a wealthy tourist town. Where's your wife and kids?"

"You think I'm nice?" He winced.

"Well, you're no Neil," she teased.

"No, honey. I'm definitely not Neil. You summed up a few of the reasons why I don't have a wife and kids. Cop. Wealthy tourist town."

"Lou hinted that you're not a long-term guy."

"Is that why you're here?" He didn't break eye contact. And like she was being interrogated, she answered honestly.

"It didn't hurt your chances."

He took her beer glass, set it next to his, and slapped his thighs. "Come here."

"On your lap?"

"Yeah." That grin would be the death of her, but oh, what a way to go. "Make out with me."

"You're crazy." She shook her head with zero conviction.

"Come on." He slapped his thighs again.

She straddled his lap, settling over him. They fit together. Her open thighs against his strong ones, her breasts brushing his chest. Even their mouths lined up perfectly, without their noses getting in the way.

He wrapped his palms around her hips. "Whatever shit you went through in Michigan is in the past, Elliott. He swept her hair away from her face. "You're here now. Evergreen Cove is a fresh start for a lot of us."

A fresh start.

She'd considered Evergreen Cove more of a temporary stop on her journey. She still did. But a miniature fresh start during the weeks she was here didn't sound so bad, especially if it started, and ended, with Officer Brady Hutchins.

CHAPTER 14

After some *spectacular* couch sex, Elli and Brady ate pizza at the kitchen table. He'd talked about his friends in the Cove, his grandfather, and what he remembered of his parents. She told him about her own parents, admitting she felt ungrateful saying they sometimes drove her crazy.

He took the conversation in stride, the way he took everything. He listened and asked questions and listened some more. And then he took her down the hall and they had more spectacular sex, with her having three orgasms right in a row.

Right in a *row*.

Later as they lay in bed, he said, "You smile a lot more than you used to, Elli Bean. Like to think I have something to do with that."

She was so unaccustomed to a guy being the reason she smiled she wasn't sure what to say. But he wasn't wrong. She smiled a lot more in Evergreen Cove, and he had a lot to do with the reason why.

The next week was a busy workweek for both of them. Cup of Jo's kept her busy, and since there were a lot of summer events that required traffic and crowd control, Brady was scheduled at various venues.

Zack had unexpectedly asked her to trade shifts so she was free for the weekend, and debating texting Brady. He'd popped into Cup of Jo's a few times during the week, but left quickly.

She vacillated over contacting him like life or death hung in the balance, her hesitation fueled by her own temporary status in the Cove. Just when was she supposed to break things off with him? Should she cut her losses now? Continue until the day she left? She had no idea what protocol was for a fling, though he probably did. Maybe she should ask him for advice.

After her shower, she dressed and wandered into the kitchen. She watched raindrops slide down the window over the sink and debated some more. To see him or not to see him, that was the question.

When she reached into a cabinet for the bag of Jo's coffee beans, a knock sounded from the front door. It was too early for the mailman. Could be Lou, though she was more likely to come to the back patio.

Elli opened the front door and found Brady standing in the threshold, his hair styled neatly, raindrops darkening his shirt and dotting his arms.

"You weren't at Jo's." He held up a tray with two coffee cups. "I'm delivering."

"I traded shifts." Her smile was back like he'd brought it with him. It was so easy to forget everything except how he made her feel when he was in front of her.

"Zack told me." Brady caught her by the waist and kissed her. She melted into him. "You taste better than you look, and that's saying something."

"I'm wearing a sundress, no makeup, and my hair is wet," she argued.

His eyes flared with heat. "Yeah. I see that."

He kicked the door closed behind him, continuing to kiss her. She couldn't resist him. Well, she *could*. She just didn't want to.

"Coffee can wait," she murmured against his mouth.

"Agree." He set the tray on the breakfast bar in the kitchen before lifting her dress over her head. "No bra. I approve."

He rewarded her choice by kissing her breasts, taking his time on her nipples. Quite possibly, this was better than drinking coffee, and she really, *really* liked her morning coffee. She was fuzzy without it. But she was fuzzy with him, too, only in that lovely, gauzy, orgasmic way.

Her pulse moved from her chest to pound between her legs. It was an ache that needed soothing, and Brady was just the man to do it.

"I didn't like sex this much before you," she said as she wrestled with his shirt. "What are you doing to me?"

"Flattery, Bean." He whipped his shirt over his head and dropped it on the floor. Then he dipped his fingers into her panties. His touch had her bracing against the counter to hold herself up. He'd literally weakened her knees.

She shut out thoughts of the future. When she left town and no longer had a man show up to deliver coffee and an orgasm. Right now was about right now. She'd lived too many years reining herself in. This was her opportunity to be free.

He peeled her panties down her legs, kissing a trail along her thighs. When he snaked his tongue along her center, she let out a sharp breath, clutching his hair and holding him close. Her head swam as she recited his name like a prayer. When she was close, *oh so close*, he stood abruptly and unbuttoned his shorts. He rolled on a condom in record time.

"Countertop, Elli Bean," he said as he lifted her and deposited her on top of said countertop. He spread her legs and wedged his body between them. "Unless you have a better idea."

"Nope," she answered. Everything he did was perfect.

He flashed a cocky grin, angled his hips, and slipped past her wet folds.

Being filled by him, each powerful thrust in clumsy sync with their out-of-control breaths, was absolute heaven. He was completely in control of her pleasure, and he knew it. He pulled her down roughly on his cock, driving her absolutely wild.

"Yes!" she cried into his ear, gripping his shoulders and hanging on for dear life. They were perfect together, the glide of him and the give of her. She both never wanted it to end and greedily chased his release. He'd gifted her with more than her fair share, but as he'd confessed the night they had sex on his couch, he wouldn't have it any other way.

"Come for me, Elliott."

Her stomach coiled in delicious anticipation. "Close. I'm close."

"Now, honey. I can't hold off much longer." His voice was a low growl in her ear. "I've been thinking about this all week, and it's been damn distracting."

That did it for her. Knowing he'd thought of them together all week was the highest compliment. Her orgasm was no less intense than the previous ones with him. He came with her, his eyes squeezing closed as he bared his teeth. His arms locked around her back, and he drew her into a tight hug, dropping his face into the space between her neck and shoulder.

They stayed there, connected, his weight heavy against her. Eventually, she shivered, suddenly chilly from in the air-conditioning.

His arms loosened. He lifted his head and gave her a lazy smile. "Good morning."

There was something under his smile that scared her. It tempted her to stay and made her want to run and hide. Dirty, quick, countertop sex shouldn't feel intimate.

And yet...

"Elliott." His heavy-lidded gaze drew her in.

A breath away from kissing him, another knock sounded from the front door, followed by a bone-chilling, "Yoo-hoo! Elliott!"

"Oh my God." Through the frosted glass, she made out the blurry outline of her mother. When the doorknob twisted Elli shoved Brady away and hissed, "My parents!"

"Seriously?"

"Yes!"

He didn't appear alarmed enough for her taste.

She scrambled off the counter, grabbing her clothes and his hand. "Bathroom. Go." If they ran for the bedroom, her mother, and probably her father, too, since they rarely went anywhere without each other, would witness both Elli's and Brady's bare asses jogging up the stairs.

She grabbed his discarded clothes and hers, and he thankfully followed her into the bathroom. She was fuzzy and unsteady from her orgasm, and she'd really, *really* like to avoid her parents seeing her like this.

"Hey, it's okay." Brady pulled on his shorts. The nightlight plugged into the wall lit his chest in a warm honey-colored glow.

"It's not okay." She gestured to her reflection in the mirror and hissed, "I look like I just had the best sex of my life."

She'd meant to underline the severity of the situation, but he took it as a compliment. "The best?"

"Now is not the time," she warned, fighting with her sundress.

He fisted the dress and pressed her back against the door, lighting her up with a kiss that made her temporarily forget her predicament.

"Elliott! It's Mom and Dad! Elliott?" Her mother's voice was closer than before.

"In the bathroom! One second!" Elli shouted back. She slipped away from Brady, who was clearly amused, and pulled her dress over her head. "I'll distract them. You can sneak out the patio door."

"Yeah?" He pulled his shirt on and stuffed his feet into his shoes. "How you going to explain the truck in your driveway?"

Crap. She forgot about that.

"Relax, Elli Bean. I won't tell them we just had sex in the kitchen." He chuckled lightly before opening the bathroom door. "Can't wait to meet them."

CHAPTER 15

She left the bathroom first, rushing to the front door before her mother walked into the kitchen. That would give Brady a second to come out of hiding. Her father was wiggling the door back and forth and muttering about oiling the hinges.

This entire situation, from hiding a boy in the bathroom to her mother mentioning that the blinds needed dusting, made Elli feel sixteen years old again.

"There's a strange car in the driveway," her mother said.

"That, uh, that belongs to Brady. My friend. Brady." Elli hazarded a glance at her father, who stopped wiggling the door and frowned. He looked decidedly unhappy about *her friend Brady*.

"Who?" her mother asked, but then her eyes went past Elliott and focused on the tall, fit, drop-dead-gorgeous man strolling out of the kitchen.

"Brady Hutchins, ma'am." He extended a hand in greeting to each of her parents. "Elli and I have been friends since she moved here."

"Visiting. I'm visiting," Elli rephrased. She turned to her mother. "I wasn't expecting you. At all."

"Your father wanted to surprise you."

Or check in on me, Elli thought. That was one of the reasons why she'd been eager to move in with Neil. Her dad had hawk eyes when it came to her. While his version of smothering was nothing like Neil's control, neither were ideal.

"We didn't expect you to have company." Her dad's frown deepened when his gaze landed on her houseguest. "What'd you say your name was?"

"Brady Hutchins."

"He's a police officer here in the Cove," Elli added, not sure if that would ease her father's concern, but it couldn't hurt.

"I knew your face rang a bell," her mother said, all smile. "Hope you're not in trouble, Elliott. Did he put you in handcuffs yet?"

Aaaand Elli's mind went just where it shouldn't while her parents were in the room. Brady's laugh told her that his was in the same place.

"She hasn't required restraining yet," Brady said. Elli's mom giggled, and her dad grumbled something about grabbing the bags from the car before he vanished outside.

"I'll get out of here and let you visit." Brady dipped his chin at her mom. "Good to meet you."

"But your coffee," Elli said, not wanting him to leave now that her parents knew about him. Uncomfortable questions were sure to follow once he left.

"Do you like coffee, Mrs. McKinley?"

"Are you kidding? Coffee's my blood type."

"Well, you're welcome to mine. I have to pick up Lila. My dog," he explained.

"We didn't mean to run you off," Elli's mom told him.

"It's all right. I was here long enough to deliver. Wasn't I, Elli Bean?"

"Yes." Elli's cheeks flamed red. "You were."

"I'll help myself to the coffee." Her mom bustled into the kitchen.

"Don't look now, beautiful," Brady murmured into Elli's ear, "but the condom wrapper's on the floor by the sink. I don't think she's seen it yet."

"Oh, great."

"Elli Bean. *Breathe.*" His low tone drew her in. He pressed a kiss onto her lips. A long, lingering kiss. The sort of kiss she didn't want her dad to witness. But of course, he witnessed it.

"Sir, good to meet you," Brady said smoothly. All confidence, this one. Where had he acquired so much of it?

"One of the reasons we came to see you," her father said, ignoring Brady completely, "was to help lighten the load around the house so you could focus on job hunting."

"I have a job, Dad." Her smile was shaky.

"A real job." Her father faced Brady. "I put in a good word for her where I work. There's no guarantee, but she's more than qualified."

"If that's what she wants." Brady glanced at her meaningfully. He might've thought the gesture small—reminding her that she had a choice—but to her, it was huge.

Her father, unimpressed, grunted as he shuffled up the stairs with the bags.

"Hang in there, Bean," Brady told her.

"Easy for you to say," she joked. She shut the front door behind him and then dashed into the kitchen to retrieve the condom wrapper she prayed her mother hadn't spotted yet.

~

"He's terribly good-looking," her mom was saying as she poured creamer into what was meant to be Brady's cup of coffee. "And a police officer."

"In our house. Acting awfully familiar with our daughter," her father growled. He was making his own pot of coffee while Elli drank the latte Brady brought for her.

"I think it's great that Elli's met a nice man," her mom said in her defense.

She doubted by "nice man" her mom meant a guy who'd stripped Elli down and sexed her up in the middle of her parents' vacation home, but whatever.

"Look how happy she is." Her mom said to her dad.

Elli hid her smile against the edge of the cup. "Why don't I make breakfast?"

"Do you have bacon?" Her dad's mood brightened.

"With your cholesterol, Desmond? No," her mother said.

"I have vegetarian sausage, and I promise it's really good." Elli laid a consoling palm on her father's shoulder.

He muttered a surly, "We'll see," as she moved to the fridge for eggs and pig-free sausage.

"How long are you visiting?"

"We thought a week or maybe two." Her mom stood to help with breakfast prep. "We didn't want you to be lonely, but we didn't mean to intrude."

Elliott nearly laughed. Her parents had totally meant to intrude.

"It's your house, Mom. You're paying the bills." Even though their arrival felt like an intrusion, she couldn't ask them to leave. "Remember, I have a summer job here, so I might not be home much." Even less if her parents were staying.

"That's not a real job. You can't live on what you make at a coffee shop," her father argued.

"Jo pays really well, actually," Elli defended. "I like making my own money. I didn't want to rely on your credit card the whole time I was here, even though it was a nice gesture," she added graciously.

"Tom at the office said—"

"Dear," her mother warned, "we have all week for that."

Elli sighed. She knew her dad meant well. He wanted her to be successful and happy. But she hadn't expected to enjoy her job at

Jo's so much. Hell, she hadn't expected to enjoy Evergreen Cove so much.

That, like everything else going right, had a lot to do with Brady Hutchins. He seemed to be a big part of her happiness lately.

CHAPTER 16

Lou invited Elliott to girls' night on the same Saturday Elli's parents packed up to leave for home.

Just one week later, their departure hadn't come a day too soon. Elli was running out of excuses not to be in the house. There was no way she was inviting Brady over with her parents hovering. She had managed to slip out and spend a few hours at his place one evening. He'd baked lasagna, which was delicious. The sex, as usual, had been even more delicious.

She'd settled in easily over the last month. Waking up to a view of the lake and enjoying her morning coffee on the deck had become a habit she wasn't looking forward to leaving behind.

Brady was another element she wasn't looking forward to leaving behind.

On Lou's deck, a glass of white wine warming in her hand, Elli thought about leaving Evergreen Cove, her new friends, her job at Jo's, and her amazing view. She loved Chicago. Loved the city vibes and the energy. But there was a different energy here—almost dreamlike. Sometimes she felt like she was on vacation, other times in suspended reality...

"Earth to Elliott." Lou waggled a half-full wine bottle in front of

Elli's face. "Are you going to drink that wine or cradle it to your bosom all night?"

Elli swallowed the end of her wine and handed over the glass.

Lou, her friends May and Lisa, and Elli were seated on Lou's upstairs deck enjoying the sunset. They'd already enjoyed cheese and crackers, and Devil Dogs from Sugar Hi Bakery. They'd also discussed Lou's ex-husband, Liam. He'd cheated on Lou, which made Elli's heart break for her new friend. May mentioned Ant, Liam's former best friend, with a curl of her lip. According to Lou, Ant knew about the betrayal before Lou. That explained the bad blood between those two.

True to form, Lou had quickly diverted the subject and refilled her wineglass. Since then, they'd been chatting about fashion and the shoes Lisa purchased at Cobbler's Cove. Elli hadn't had a girls' night in so long she was almost overwhelmed. Which might be why she'd zoned out, lost in her own thoughts.

"Is it new?" May asked as she topped off her own wineglass. From her ruby-red painted lips and puff of black curly hair, her bright patterned dress, and thick black eyelashes, May was positively beautiful.

"Is what new?" Elli looked down at her sandals, assuming they were still talking about shoes.

"Not your wardrobe." May gave Elliott a playful nudge. "The man on your mind."

"How did you—"

"Please, honey." May clucked her tongue. "Only one thing will make you gaze wistfully off into the sunset. Must be new. When they've been around a while, we bitch about them."

Elliott laughed at the truth in that statement. Both May and Lisa had offered up tales of their exes in camaraderie when Lou had mentioned Liam. Elli had remained silent, not wanting talk of Neil to ruin her evening.

"You know her guy," Lou told May. "We all do. It's Brady."

"*Hutchins*? Oh, girl!" May elbowed Lisa. "Did you hear that? Her and the hot cop. Good for you, Elliott." May tapped her glass against Elliott's.

Lisa swept a lock of glossy brown hair behind her ear. Blue eyes wide with interest, she asked Elliott, "How long?"

"Are you inquiring about his package or the amount of time they've been seeing each other?" Lou asked with a raucous laugh.

"Both." Lisa dissolved next to her.

"Mercy, I can tell they're a glass ahead of us." May's bronze skin was practically aglow in the pink and purple sunset behind her. "So things are good?"

"I guess so. We're seeing each other while I'm in town, which probably won't be much longer." Her parents' visit had been a wake-up call. Elli needed to get her shit together. She couldn't stay in limbo and pretend *Vacationland* was her life. She needed her own place. An office job—not where her dad worked. She needed to rebuild the life Neil had stolen from her.

"That sucks." Lisa was suddenly serious. "I was hoping we could have girls' night a few more times while you're here." She pouted at Lou, "I like her."

Lou gave Elli a sad smile. "I like her, too."

"I like you all," Elli said honestly. "But like May said, Brady and I are new. It's bound to go south." Good things didn't last, if they ever showed up. Elli was in the honeymoon phase of Evergreen Cove. "Besides, Chicago awaits. I have a business degree gathering dust. I need to find somewhere to live that isn't my parents' vacation house where they can come over whenever they like."

"Oof. Say no more." Lisa held up a hand in solidarity.

It was probably past time to end things with Brady. They'd had a good run, one that seemed to be getting better and better. But why wait for the demise of the relationship when she could end it on a high note? It was time to stop pretending he was a permanent fixture.

"I haven't had a girls' night in forever, and I don't want to waste it." Elli was here to have fun, not sing her own swan song. She drained her second glass of wine and offered her empty glass to Lou. "Fill 'er up."

"That's my girl," Lou said approvingly before topping off the glass.

~

By the time Brady picked up Lila and drove to Elliott's house, it was well past midnight. He knocked on her front door. No answer. Then he heard the hoots of laughter coming from the direction of Lou's house. Sounded like girls' night had gone longer than Elli had anticipated. That made him smile.

He led his dog through the side yard, happy for Elliott. She'd been in a bad situation and had made friends in the short time she'd been here. He counted himself on that list. Their friendship came with perks he would miss when she was gone.

He had plenty to do in her absence, though, he argued to himself. His grandfather was a handful. He had Lila to look after. Plus, he'd been considering pursuing a detective position at work. That left little time for the "wife and kids" Elliott had once asked him about. If he wanted career advancement beyond being a beat cop, he had to have his head in the game.

"The countertop!" He heard as he rounded the backyard. He craned his head to the upper deck and spotted Lou's friends, May and Lisa. Lou was out of sight, but he heard her comment that kitchen sex was difficult.

What came next made his night.

"Not with Brady," Elli said. The girls applauded before offering their congratulations, and he pulled his shoulders back with pride.

Lila, enthusiastic about the excitement above her, broke through the girls' laughter with a sharp bark. Elliott's face peeked over the railing a second later.

"Sorry to interrupt!" He waved.

"You are not," May accused with a headshake.

"Hi, May. Lisa." He grinned cockily. Hard not to be cocky when he was the subject of Elli's praise. "You're right. I'm not. I can listen in some more if Elliott would like to continue bragging about me."

Lou's head appeared next. "You're so full of shit."

"Love you, too, Lou."

"I was about to leave anyway." Elli's smile was mischievous, if a little wonky. She'd probably enjoyed her fair share of wine tonight. He was glad she'd allowed herself to unwind. "Be right down."

Hand on the railing, Elli trotted down the steps as May, Lisa, and Lou leaned over the railing to watch. Each of them offered some version of, "Take care of our girl, Hutch!"

"They're drunk," Elli said with a wave of her hand. "I mean, I am, too, but only a little. Sorry you had to hear that."

"Don't be," Brady said.

Elliott bent to nuzzle Lila. "Aren't you so cute! I love dogs. I couldn't have one before. Neil didn't like pet hair. But you're probably too good of a girl to shed, aren't you?"

Lila wagged her tail, pushing against Elli and almost knocking her over. Elli scratched Lila's flank and murmured to the dog some more.

Despite the adorable scene of his girls getting along, he gritted his teeth the way he did whenever Elli mentioned her ex. In his line of work, he came across men who abused their power in relationships. It never failed to piss him off. Hell, Lila's former owner had been one of them.

"Come on, Lila." Elli's tone turned somber as she walked to the patio and let herself in to the house. No kiss for him, evidently.

Inside the house, he unhooked the leash. Lila glued her nose to the floor and began blazing a trail.

"She's house-trained," he said when Lila disappeared around the corner. "Just nosy."

"She's a great dog."

Again, he thought how Elli sounded sad. "You okay?"

"I'm going to miss girls' night." At the sink, she filled a glass with water. "Want anything? I have water. Beer. Wine?"

"I'm good, thanks. What do you mean, you'll miss girls' night? You're not gone yet." Lila wandered by, her nose still on the ground.

"Yeah, but..." Elli ran a fingernail along the edge of the countertop, not meeting his eyes, "I'm leaving soon."

"Soon?" News to him. "I thought you were staying another month."

"Well, I need somewhere to go when I leave, don't I?" she asked a tad defensively. "I've been job hunting this week. Once I find a job, I can find an apartment close to work. I like the idea of living in the city. I love Chicago."

He'd known from the beginning she would be leaving, but he hadn't expected her to leave this soon. Or maybe what he hadn't expected was for six weeks to zip by so quickly. And he definitely hadn't expected to like her as much as he did.

Elli bent and addressed the dog, "Can you sit?"

Lila put her butt on the floor, tail wagging.

"Good girl!" Elli looked at Brady. "What else can she do?"

"Tell her to put 'em up." He pointed his finger like a gun.

Elliott mimicked the gesture and repeated the command. Lila pushed to her back legs and stuck both front paws in the air. Elli's laugh carved into his chest like a knife.

He wasn't ready for her to leave. Now wasn't a good time for that conversation, but hell, when *would* be a good time? "Were you planning on telling me you were job hunting?"

She blinked at him, looking scarily sober. "Why's it matter? I'm sure there are plenty of women who'll gladly fill my shoes."

Anger spiked his adrenaline, which shot down his arms in twin lightning streaks. "What the hell is that supposed to mean?"

She busied herself by filling a teakettle with water. "May and Lisa think you're hot. I'm sure finding a woman to warm your bed won't take long after I'm gone."

"You think that's what you are to me, Elliott?" Still pissed, his voice was louder than he intended. "A bed-warmer?"

Her shrug was weak, her eyes tired. "I don't know."

"Let me enlighten you." He stalked over and gently gripped her biceps. He needed her to hear him. She tilted her head back to look up at him, and he was floored by the vulnerability evident in her wide, brown eyes. She'd seen pain in her recent past. She'd been kept down, marginalized. *Controlled.* She believed she meant nothing to the asshole that had trapped her in a relationship before. Brady would be damned if he let her believe he could shrug her off as easily.

"You weren't supposed to mean as much as you do, Elli Bean," he said softly. Her eyelashes fluttered, but her gaze held his. "I'd never stop you from pursuing the life you want. Never. You deserve to run down your dreams the way I ran down mine. But you're not walking away from the Cove—or me—without me giving you a few reasons to stay."

CHAPTER 17

Fear trickled into Elliott's stomach as she looked up at Brady. Big, strong, handsome, safe, fun, sexy Brady. She wasn't scared of the way he stood over her, but she was terrified of what he was implying.

He wanted more. She could feel it.

Neil had wanted more, too. She hadn't been ready for more but had agreed anyway. And now? How could she be ready for more with Brady when she'd only been apart from Neil for a handful of months? It was too soon. Made no sense.

Plus, she wasn't staying here and Brady was a Cove fixture. He wouldn't give up his life to be a city cop. He loved Evergreen Cove.

"I'm flattered," she said, trying to sound as neutral as possible. "But great sex isn't a foundation on which to build a future."

His jaw hardened, his eyes with it. "Why not?"

She laughed. When he didn't, she compressed her lips. Maybe she could blame the wine for her lack of clarity. She was tired. It was late. She hadn't prepared for an argument, if that's what this was. She'd assumed when she told Brady he'd react like Neil and just... let her go. But Brady wasn't Neil. She should've expected more.

"We don't have to end things tonight," she clarified as she pulled a mug and tea from the cabinet. "I was giving you a heads-up."

And giving myself an out.

"What's the rush?" he asked. "You have a job here. You have friends you like. You have me."

Her heart ka-thumped. Her head swam. Brady was supposed to be a fun, temporary fling. What he was saying...

You have me.

She didn't think he meant for a few days or weeks. He meant... She couldn't fathom what he meant. Her hand resting on her stomach, she tried to calm herself by taking a deep breath.

"I know you were mistreated by someone who should've cared about you," he said, his voice as hard as his expression. "I know you'd like to lump me into a pile with that piece of shit, but I am *not* him, Elli Bean."

That was true. Brady was more of a man than Neil could ever aspire to be. Still...

"I'm not ready for anything serious."

He drew away from her, stung.

"I don't need rescuing like Lila." Hearing her name, the dog padded into the room, her tail wagging. The teakettle screeched. "I can rescue myself."

"Do I make you feel trapped? Smothered? Do I demand you do things you don't want to do?" He folded his arms over his substantial chest and glared at her.

He hadn't made her feel anything but safe, happy. Sexy. But...

"You're making me feel trapped now," she admitted.

"By telling you I don't want you to leave? How's that trapping you, Elli? I didn't say you *couldn't* leave. I'm not manipulating you into a decision. I'm telling you—and this isn't easy for me, by the way—that I don't want you to live in Chicago, because I don't want you to forget about Evergreen Cove." He swept his tongue over his bottom lip before he added, "Or me."

She stared. Speechless. Shocked. He didn't let up.

"I lost my parents when I was a kid. Lost my gram when I was a teenager. I've experienced some deep, dark hurts over the years."

"Join the club," she said, her defenses sky-high. She did that when she was afraid, and his confessions were scaring her. Shakily, she poured hot water into her mug.

"I'm not saying I cornered the market." He was calm. And kind. So kind. "Losing people I loved wasn't in vain. Because of the bad, I recognize the good. You and me? We're the good. I know this isn't on your timeline." He paused to let out a short laugh. "It's not on *my* timeline. I had a plan before you got here, you know. You messed it up."

He stood close, hip leaning against the counter, her steaming mug of tea between them. Him in front of her, real and live and in the flesh, she had an even harder time thinking of leaving. Leaving him and the life she'd begun here.

It was easy to believe in happily ever after when there was nothing but the soft sound of a dog snoring in the background. She opened her mouth to say… God, she didn't even know what, but he spoke first.

"It's late. I'm exhausted. I shouldn't have said anything. I actually came here with Lila to make a request."

"Oh?" Resetting her brain would take a minute. He'd turned her world upside down tonight.

"Gramps wants to meet you." He held up a hand to stay any argument she might have. "I know. Bad timing after what we've been talking about. But he won't stop asking about the woman who's been taking up my free time. His words."

"Brady…" Meeting his family was a level up, especially after she suggested they end things between them. But she had been the one to say they didn't have to end it right away.

"Make an old man's day," he said with a half-smile.

"That's a cheap shot." She sighed. She liked him way too much to say no. "I'll think about it."

"Thank you." He sounded sincere. "You okay on your own? I can stay. Lila might try and crawl into bed with you, though."

"You don't have to stay. I'm going to drink my tea and crash when my head hits the pillow. I'll be fine."

"How you ever believed you lost your independence is beyond me." He kissed her forehead. "I can sleep on the couch. Wake you in the morning in a creative way."

"Stop being irresistible."

He watched her, his smile soft. He looked tired. The dog was already asleep. Elliott was about to drop. But her defenses were low when he was near, and she desperately needed clarity. That would only come if she was alone.

"Goodnight. Drive safe."

"Hear that, Lila? Classic blow off." He grabbed the leash. The dog stood up and stretched, tail swishing back and forth.

Elliott walked them to the door and waved when Brady backed down the driveway. It hurt her heart to see him go, but she let him.

She'd made the right decision.

CHAPTER 18

Elliott spent the next morning hunched over her laptop, a cup of coffee next to her elbow. She'd sent her resume off to three more companies and had spent the last hour browsing apartments online. Since she didn't know where she would work yet, the housing search was going absolutely nowhere.

True to her word, she'd fallen asleep almost immediately after Brady left. She'd woken up at 4 a.m., tossing and turning. She thought about what he'd said. What he hadn't said. What he *could've* said.

She thought about how she could feel about him if she stayed in Evergreen Cove. The town bordered on utopia. She was half-surprised residents didn't randomly burst into song.

Amused by the image, she smiled to herself and admitted that life wasn't perfect in the Cove. There were plenty of examples of struggle. Brady's family. Lila's situation. Lou's divorce. They just happened to live in a beautiful place.

Elliott had been picturing a life in Chicago for months. She couldn't give it up to take a chance on a relationship that likely wouldn't work out. Brady had bad timing, which wasn't his fault.

Besides, her parents, therapist, and friends from college lived in Illinois. Visiting the Cove was one thing, but living here? She would have to start from scratch. She'd already culled her life down to the bare minimum once this year.

With a sigh, she carried her empty coffee mug to the sink. She loaded the dishwasher and changed her clothes, taking the time to straighten her hair and smooth it back into a ponytail. At the balcony off her bedroom, she watched out the window as a lone seagull flew by. She'd always pictured gulls as ocean birds, not lake birds. A seagull had no business living in Ohio.

"Neither do I," she reminded herself.

Worse, she'd been considering honoring Brady's request to visit his grandfather when she should be cutting ties, not making more. But Brady was her friend. She was curious about the man who'd raised him.

A text chimed on her phone, and she shut her eyes. She knew who it was without looking. When she reopened them, sure enough, the text was from Brady.

"Talk to me, Elli Bean."

Damn him. She wished he would have made it easier for her to say no. But then, where Brady was concerned, her ability to push him away had the shortest shelf life ever.

She keyed in her response. *"Alive and well. Ready when you are."*

His reply came quickly. *"Glad to hear it. Pick you up at 1."*

An hour later she exited her front door and climbed into Brady's truck to sit next to Lila. The dog licked Elli's cheek, her tail thumping the seat when Elli used both hands to hold her scruffy face.

"She's the cutest."

"Careful. Making me jealous," Brady warned with a smile.

"You're cute, too."

"What every guy dreams of, Elli Bean," he said as he reversed out of her driveway. "Being *cute.*"

Well, he was.

A short while later, she had the same thought about his grandfather, though she kept that to herself.

"Emory Hutchins," he introduced himself. "You're a pretty thing."

"Gramps." Brady shook his head in warning.

"Oh, right." Emory cleared his throat. "What I meant to say is that you're an intelligent, capable woman who I respect mightily." He grinned. "Do you like pancakes?"

Elli laughed. She saw where Brady had inherited his charm. "I appreciate both compliments, Emory, thank you."

"You can call me Gramps. That's what this knucklehead calls me." He shot a thumb at his grandson.

Lila let out a bark to protest being left out of the conversation. Gramps promptly bent down to stroke the dog's blond fur.

"I didn't forget you, Pancake," he said in a soothing voice. He turned to Brady. "Well, whether you're eating them or not, she obviously has to have a pancake." He pointed to the dog.

"Obviously," Brady said drolly as Gramps and Lila walked into the kitchen.

"I can't control him." Brady lifted a hand and dropped it to his side. Seeing him here, in a cozy familial setting made her heart squeeze.

"You're a good dog dad."

He didn't blush, but there was something shy about the way he shoved his hands deep into his pockets. There was nothing shy, however, about the way he leaned forward and muttered, "You forgot to kiss me last night, Bean. And today."

"I didn't forget." Creating distance was hard. Especially while in the same room with him. "I was deciding if I should."

He gripped her neck and lowered his lips just over hers. "You should. You definitely should."

So, she did. Despite the arguments about why she shouldn't. She lifted to her toes and pressed her mouth to his. He moved his lips on hers in a long, open-mouthed, carefully quiet kiss.

Or at least, she thought it was careful.

"Mercy's sakes," came Emory's reply from the threshold of the kitchen. "I was going to ask you two if you needed pancakes, but apparently, you need a fire hose." He threw a hand and then disappeared into the kitchen again.

"He doesn't know the half of it." Brady took her hand and sat with her on the sofa. "Any news on the job search?"

She swiped her palms down her shorts, suddenly nervous. "Not yet. I've narrowed down my number-one companies. But the apartments, *oy*. There are a lot of options in every price range. And without knowing my salary or where I'll be working, it's hard to commit."

"A theme with you." He smiled and quickly added, "I'm kidding."

But he was wrong. She'd committed to Neil. As a result, she hadn't done anything she wanted to do for the last half-decade.

"I've spent the last six years with my life on pause," she said. "I'm not waiting for life to happen to me anymore. I have to be proactive."

"I understand that." His eyebrows closed in over his nose.

She assumed there was more he wanted to say. "But?"

"No but. As long as you've thought about what you want."

"Of course I have." She knew what she wanted. Chicago, a job, an apartment.

"When life changes, Bean, we have to change with it. Chicago sounds like an old dream you're resurrecting. Not a new one. Better make sure it's not decomposed before you dig it up."

The noise that came from her throat was between a laugh and a grunt.

He leaned forward, elbows on his knees. "What do you want, Elli? What do you *really* want?"

It'd been a long time since anyone had asked her that and

listened for an answer. Most people who asked that question already had an answer in mind. Neil had told her on countless occasions what she should want, and why she should want it. Even her well-meaning parents had planted the seeds in her mind about her returning to Chicago and working with her father. They had their own reasons for feeling that way. They lived outside of Chicago and wanted her close by. Neil had had his reasons for pushing her, too.

What *did* she want?

It was frightening to think about. The world was vast, the possibilities endless. And who among them did what they wanted anyway? Who was able to live exactly the way they wanted on their own terms? Didn't being a responsible adult mean doing what she had to, not what she *wanted*?

"Chicago's a good fit for me," she said rather than voice any of the confusion swirling in her head.

Brady remained silent, which frustrated her further. She'd already put herself on the path back to Illinois. Forward momentum was crucial. If she stopped now, she'd have to start over. *Completely* over.

"Staying here longer than necessary is a waste of time," she continued defending. "I could be earning a living and moving on with my life." She rewound what she'd said and closed her eyes. "I didn't mean I'm wasting time with you. I meant—"

"Pancakes!" Gramps called. "Get in here before Lila and I eat them all!"

When she opened her eyes, Brady's expression was carefully neutral.

"You don't have to explain why you're doing what you're doing, Elli Bean. I just wanted to make sure the choices you're making are for *you* for this time around. That you live the life you want and not the one someone is trying to create for you." He bit down on his bottom lip, chagrined. "Guess that goes for me, too. Hell, I'd love it if you stick around. But you know that already. I respect your decision."

He stood and helped her to her feet. Her heart raced as she took his hand. He'd said what she thought she wanted to hear. That the decision was hers. That he wouldn't interfere. But at the same time, she felt like he was letting her go.

And like watching him leave last night, being let go felt awful.

CHAPTER 19

Brady hated to acknowledge it, but part of him was rooting against Elliott.

On Sunday, they'd eaten pancakes and laughed at Gramps's colorful sense of humor. Brady had witnessed firsthand the chink his grandfather put in her armor. Seemed only fair. She'd battered Brady's suit of armor half to hell.

But another part of him, the part that understood she was on her own journey and needed to make choices for herself, was betting on her to win. Her journey was just that: *hers*. He'd started up with her because he wanted her, not because he'd intended on *forever and ever amen* with her.

At least that's what he kept telling himself.

"No charge, officer." Elli pressed a button, shoved some cash from her pocket into the cash drawer and closed it before he could pay for his coffee. Jo chuckled, one hand on the bakery case, the other hand on her hip.

"Do you train your baristas to be this stubborn?" he asked.

"This one came with that feature. Didn't need training," Jo said. "I'll miss her when she goes. Haven't you talked her into staying yet?"

Elli's playful smile tightened at the corners. Jo didn't know she was dancing around a landmine, so he let her off the hook.

"You know me, Jo. Can't tie me down. I'm a loner." He slid his sunglasses onto his nose and his radio crackled in his ear. He recognized the address of the call. Mack and June Browning's house.

Adrenaline shot down his arms as he recalled their last heated exchanged. When he'd punched Mack. Took Lila. Left June crying.

He pressed a button on the radio and replied he was on his way.

"Is everything okay?" Elliott's concern for him was written all over her face.

The truth was no, everything *wasn't* okay. A call to Mack's likely meant he was hitting his wife again, and this time, if June didn't press charges, Brady might kidnap her and relocate her to an undisclosed location. Protocol or not.

"If Brady's answerin' the call, everything will be okay. Won't it, Officer?" Jo knew plenty. Including Mack's address. She'd employed June for a short while until Mack had refused to let her work. That reminded Brady of what Elli had been through, and the thought of her bending to her ex's will made him want to chew nails.

"Perfectly fine." He gave Elliott a cocky smile to communicate that she didn't have to worry about him. "I'm a professional."

He turned to leave, coffee in hand, when she called out, "Dinner at my house tonight? Seven o'clock?"

Slowly, he turned. She was standing at the counter, her face filled with a desperate sort of hope. He hadn't expected the invitation. She'd blown him off since the visit with Gramps. He'd seen her here at the shop, and they'd had a few short text exchanges, but she hadn't been eager to invite him over.

Until now, evidently.

The smart move would be to turn her down. She was leaving soon, and there was no sense in dragging this out longer than necessary. Except the look on her face was killing him. Her concern combined with ample longing was his weakness.

"Everything goes the way it should, I can be there at eight." He had a full day ahead, but he wouldn't miss the chance to spend time with her. Maybe she'd changed her mind about the Cove after all. And about him.

"Eight o'clock." Her smile was nervous when she added, "Be careful, okay?"

That sank into his skin.

He hadn't had a woman worry about him in a long time. Probably since his grandmother. She'd had her rosary beads out daily, praying for his safety.

He thought about Elliott worrying about him as he drove to Mack's residence. He thought about what it'd cost her to stay in the Cove, to stay with him. What it'd mean to have her home waiting for him each night, concerned over whether he'd come home or not.

He parked in front of the Browning home and climbed out. He'd always been safe, but there was a chance that one time, he wouldn't be. And if Elliott wasn't willing to risk her future in a new place while dating a cop she barely knew... Well, hell.

Could he blame her?

~

When Brady left Cup of Jo's, his jaw had been welded steel. He'd spoken in code into his walkie, and Elliott had watched his posture change. His spine had gone ramrod straight. One fist had balled at his side. He'd looked ready to rumble, despite his easy response of "I'm a professional."

She considered what he faced day in and day out. He could snap from laidback Brady to superhero in a blink. That made her feel two things simultaneously—impressed and worried.

She'd never worried about him before. Back when they'd been fun and light and temporary. That seemed to have altered without her permission.

She'd blurted out a dinner invitation, figuring she'd see him in person after the call he took and could rest knowing that he was safe. But she'd spent the rest of her shift fighting off one unreasonable thought after another. What if he'd run into trouble? What if he'd been hurt? Or worse.

At home, she busied herself preparing Dijon-herb-crusted salmon and roasted red potatoes. The meal came together quickly and finished in the oven, which gave her time away from the stove.

She pulled on a striped sundress and slipped her feet into a pair of hemp sandals. The wedge heels gave her some height, and the dress made her feel pretty. She even took the time to barrel roll her hair into large, wavy curls. She kept her makeup simple: mascara and a touch of blush. She brushed her teeth and swiped on lip gloss, and now there was only one thing left to do.

Decide how to tell Brady the news.

The knock at her front door came as she was sliding a large serving fork beneath the skin-on piece of salmon on a white platter. The potatoes were steaming away in a bowl between their two place settings—plates, silverware, and a pair of pilsner glasses.

When she opened the door to find Brady standing there safe and whole, she was overwhelmed with relief. It would make what she had to say harder, but she was strong. Her mind was made up. She could do this.

"Hi." The word came out a little breathless. Couldn't be helped. He wore trousers and a short-sleeved polo shirt that hugged his impressive physique. He seemed to get better looking every day she stayed, and that, too, was problematic.

"Hi." His green gaze moved over her body like a touch. "You look incredible."

She wasn't sure if he stepped forward first or if she did. Next, he was kissing her, his palms heating her waist, and his tongue sliding into her mouth. She shut her eyes and savored the moment—and him. The smell of his piney aftershave, the feel of his strong arms around her.

"I made salmon," she said when he pulled away. "I lit a few candles in the hopes the house wouldn't smell like I made salmon."

"It smells like dinner, and I'm not going to complain after the day I had." He linked their fingers. "Can I pour the drinks?"

"Sure."

Once they were seated across from each other at the dining room table, each of them having sampled the food and agreeing it was delicious, she asked him about his day. "How'd it go?"

"With?" He appeared genuinely confused as he forked a potato cube into his mouth.

She remembered the moment when he answered the call in the coffee shop vividly. Were emergencies that commonplace? "The call that came in when I gave you your coffee this morning seemed intense."

"Oh, that." His posture eased some, and she assumed it hadn't gone as badly as she'd imagined. And, boy, had she imagined some scary scenarios. "I can't say too much about it, but remember how I found Lila?"

"Tied to the porch in the rain. A guy who abused his wife."

"Yeah," he said softly, his eyes lingering on her. "His wife pressed charges this time. I was able to arrest and hold him for a while."

"And she's safe?"

"She's safe." His smile was proud.

"That's good news."

"There's not always a happy ending," he said, sounding tired. "But sometimes there's a happy for right now, and that's almost as good."

Happy for right now. Fleeting, but precious. She picked at her salmon and announced to her plate, "I have a job interview."

"Oh, yeah?"

She glanced up. "In Chicago. It's next Thursday, but I thought I'd go ahead and pack up now. Head back to my parents' house since they live close to the city."

His nod was slow. "Convenient since you'll be searching for an apartment nearby."

"Exactly." She offered a shaky smile.

"Need help with anything?"

She shook her head. "I don't have to pack much, other than my clothes and whatever groceries are in the cabinets. Everything else stays here."

Everything including him, she thought with a stabbing sense of dread.

"Congratulations," he said, again with a slow nod.

"I didn't think I'd have an interview already. Everyone I've talked to says it's a tough job market, and that I should be prepared to wait."

"They must've seen what I see," he murmured, his eyes warm on hers. "A strong, capable woman who would make a damn good… What position did you apply for?"

She laughed and then told him more about the position and the company. How she was worried she'd get it and worried she wouldn't. He listened as they finished their dinner, and then they loaded the dishwasher.

When she took his hand to lead him upstairs, he followed. He stripped her down slowly, and she undressed him just as slowly, each savoring the moment. He kissed her body, and she kissed his.

They made love slowly, too, as if neither of them wanted the night to end. Neither of them admitted this was the last night they'd be together, but both of them knew.

It seemed *happy right now* didn't last long at all.

CHAPTER 20

Brady was exhausted.

He'd fully intended on stopping by to see Elli off the day after their final steamy night between the sheets, but he never had the chance.

An early morning call across town turned into an all-day stakeout. He ended up sitting in a patrol car with Darrin for hours on end and sending Elli a goodbye text.

Not ideal.

He supposed the official goodbye was the last time he made love to her, but he still would've liked to tell her goodbye in person. Life had other plans.

The day of Elliott's interview was his day off. He texted her good luck, but he didn't hear back. He wasn't sure if she was cutting ties with him completely or just busy.

Restless, he paid Ant a visit, figuring he could make good on his outstanding debt and purchase a piece of furniture. That, too, was a link to Elliott, he thought as he parked his truck outside of Ant's studio.

Brady followed the sound of a chainsaw to the side yard. Ant was buzzing away at a tree trunk, safety glasses on. Ant saw him and shut off the blubbering engine.

"Afternoon," Brady greeted.

"You look like shit," his friend told him.

"Thanks a lot." Brady ran a hand through his hair. He hadn't slept well last night. Or any night since Elli left. He was trying really hard not to be irrational. Not to call her parents or show up in Chicago unannounced. She'd become a big part of his life while she was here, but it was over. She'd made that clear.

God, that sucked.

"Came to peruse your furniture store," Brady said, changing the subject.

"Uh-huh." Ant set the chainsaw aside and pulled off his sawdust-covered fedora, then his safety glasses. He tossed his gloves and glasses on top of a stump before setting the hat back on his head.

"What are you making?" Brady studied the textured dents in the wood, impressed with the detail even though it didn't resemble anything yet.

"Money." Ant squinted up at the sculpture. "It's a wolf howling at the moon. Or it will be. Special order."

"Nice."

"You want a beer?"

"Why not?"

They headed into the garage-slash-studio, and Ant handed over a bottle of beer but opened a water bottle for himself, explaining that chainsaws and alcohol didn't mix.

Brady drank down half the beer in one swallow. Tasted good on a hot day.

"You are misery personified, man." Ant shook his head. "What happened? She leave?"

"Who?"

"Beemer. Chick with the flat. What do you mean *who*?"

"She left the Cove last week. Job interview. Her life is in Chicago."

"And you let her?" Ant looked almost pissed off.

"You expect me to tie her up or something?"

"She didn't go back to him, did she? The guy who was a dick?"

"You know plenty."

Ant shrugged, not offering up how he'd learned about Elliott's past. Brady assumed Lou had something to do with it.

"No. Nothing like that. He's out of her life." *And she's out of mine.*

Somber, Ant nodded. "Sorry, man. You two were good together."

Just what Brady didn't need to hear. He set the beer aside. Good as it tasted, he didn't want it. "She was only here six weeks."

"Love hits you when you least expect it." Ant strode along the rows of furniture. "I have a new rocking chair. A butcher's block on wheels. Been making cutting boards, too."

Alarmed by what Ant had said, Brady froze in place. Brady hadn't said anything about love. "What are you talking about?"

"Cutting boards?" Ant asked, holding one up.

"No, you asshole. The other thing. I never said I was in love with her."

Ant had the audacity to laugh. "You didn't have to, man. It's all over your sad face." He stepped forward, slapped Brady's cheek in a challenge, and put up his fists.

"You'll pay for that." Brady lifted his own fists, and they danced around each other.

Brady rushed his friend and was able to pin him. But when Ant swiveled and shot his knee out, Brady lost his hold. Before he knew what happened, Ant had reversed their positions.

"Her being gone," Ant grunted, his arm over Brady's throat, "has made you rusty. What are you going to do about that?"

"She's trying to move on." Brady gritted from between his teeth as he twisted his buddy's arm. Ant scrambled to keep his hold, but Brady won out, pinning Ant again. "I'm letting her."

"That's dumb," Ant said as his hat fell off his head.

Brady released his friend and swiped the sweat from his upper lip. He hadn't come here to autopsy his relationship with Elliot.

He'd come to tie up the final loose end so he could *stop fucking thinking about her.*

"I'll take that one." Brady pointed at the rocker. "Do you gift wrap?"

Ant, lying on his back on the shop floor, laughed.

"I love you, kid, but you're a dumbass," Gramps said as Brady hauled in the custom-made rocker.

Brady had endured a similar you-look-like-shit conversation when he'd arrived here after leaving Ant's shop.

"I bring you a custom-made rocking chair, and this is how you thank me?" Brady grunted as he carried the heavy chair through the living room. Lila danced around his feet, having no idea how difficult it was for him not to step on her paws.

Once the rocker was in the corner, Brady swiped his sweaty forehead with the bottom of his T-shirt. "You're welcome."

He glanced at the clock on the wall. It was a little after six. Elli's interview had been at four o'clock.

"Good-looking chair."

"Enjoy it." Brady grabbed Lila's leash, and her tail whapped him in the leg.

"So about you being a dumbass," Gramps continued. "Why'd you let her leave?"

"Well, Gramps," he said as he clipped the leash to Lila, "she's her own woman and makes her own decisions."

"Hell, I know that." Gramps followed him to the door. A hand landed on Brady's shoulder. "Son, listen to me."

Brady turned, despite wanting to flee the scene. Gramps stood on his front porch, squinting at the setting sun.

"Life is short. You know it. I know it, too."

"I know." Between them, they'd shared many losses. Brady's grandmother, aka, Gramps's wife. Brady's mother and father, aka, Gramps's son and daughter-in-law.

"Did you tell her everything she needed to hear before she made her decision?"

"What the hell is that supposed to mean?"

"You love her. Did you tell her that?"

Had he been talking to Ant? Had everyone lost their damn minds?

"She wants to be in Chicago."

"That was the answer she gave you the night she was here, but you didn't tell her how you felt. She didn't have all the information to make that decision." Gramps tapped his ear and explained, "Turned up my hearing aid. I heard everything."

"Stubborn, old—"

"Runs in the family. To honor Elliott is to let her know how you feel when you feel it." Gramps tagged Brady in the chest. "If you didn't tell her you love her, either you've had your head in your pants, or you've been protecting yourself. I thought your job was to protect others."

"I *am* protecting her," Brady growled.

His patience wasn't what it once was. He didn't want to give an ounce of thought to Gramps and Ant's claim that he was *in love* for one very good—and, yes, self-preserving—reason. It didn't matter how he felt if Elliott didn't feel the same way.

"I appreciate the advice, but with all due respect—"

"Here we go." Gramps rolled his eyes.

"You don't know her. I do. She loves Chicago." *Not me.*

"Hi, Emory!" one of his grandfather's neighbors called out.

"Hey, Mabel!" He waved and smiled but when he turned to Brady his frown returned.

It made Brady aware of how exposed he was on the front porch. The neighborhood was alive with commotion. People were returning home from work, and Gramps's neighbors were watering their grass and tending to their flowers now that the midday heat had died down.

"Can we not do this outside?" Brady was tired. Tired of hoping and trying for something that wasn't going to happen.

A car door shut. Another neighbor called out that she had someone else's mail.

"Brady," Gramps started.

"Now's not the time."

His grandfather's gaze flickered off to the side. He set his jaw stubbornly, his green-brown eyes burning a hole through Brady's head.

"You love her. Admit it." He thrust out his whiskered chin. The old man was in need of a shave as much as he apparently needed to have this damn conversation. Lila tugged on the leash and whined again, and Brady tightened his fist.

"Yes. I love her. I'm in love with her, and she left. Are you happy? Is that what you wanted to hear?"

Gramps's mouth pulled into a smug smile. "Yeah. That oughta do it."

His gaze went over Brady's shoulder, and this time, Brady followed it. A familiar BMW was parked in the driveway. Elliott stood in front of it.

CHAPTER 21

Brady Hutchins was in love with her. She'd heard him say it himself.

She'd known how he felt about her leaving. Knew that he'd wanted to continue and possibly build on what they had. But she had no idea how she felt about him until it was too late.

It'd taken all of twenty-four hours after she left the Cove to figure out she'd made a mistake. She'd arrived at her parents' house and sat down to a dinner she didn't touch. After, her mother had poured them each a glass of wine, and they'd moved to the terrace. That was when Elliott voiced aloud for the first time that she'd screwed up everything.

"I fell in love with him, Mom. He asked me to stay, and I bailed because he wasn't part of the plan."

Her mother had argued that plans change. That Elli should trust her gut. "We raised a smart, beautiful, talented woman," she'd said. "And if the setback with Neil taught you anything, it should have taught you what you don't want. Now you have to decide what you *do* want."

It had reminded Elli so much of what Brady said to her that she'd only cried harder. She'd intended on going to the interview, stubbornly committed to the path she'd chosen for herself. But by this morning, she'd realized she didn't want to be in Chicago another moment. She'd packed and left for Evergreen Cove.

"Hi," she said now, twisting her fingers nervously.

"Hey." Brady was clearly surprised to see her. Gramps had spotted her. He'd led Brady to the rocks with that admit-you-love-her bit. She could kiss the old man for that.

She'd had no idea what to expect when she returned. No way was she calling or texting—she needed to see Brady in person. She needed to look into his eyes and see if she was too late. After going to the police station and Brady's house, she hadn't known where else to look. She'd driven to Emory's house hoping he could help.

Success.

"Can we talk?" she asked after giving an excited Lila a pat on the head.

"Give her here. I'll make us some pancakes." Gramps took the leash. "Nice to see you, Elliott."

"You, too." She meant it. It was nice to see him. It'd also been nice to drive by Cup of Jo's and walk past the bench in Library Park where she and Brady had shared coffee.

It was nice to be *home*.

Evergreen Cove shouldn't feel like home any more than Brady should feel like a necessary part of her existence, but it did and he was. She'd missed him so much.

After Gramps took Lila inside, Brady stepped closer to her. "This is a surprise."

She'd recited a speech all the way here. She knew what she wanted to say. Now that she was looking up at him, though, she was nervous.

Now or never.

"I didn't really know what I wanted the day you asked me," she told him. "It hit me when I arrived in Chicago. I was driving through lanes and lanes of traffic, gazing up at the tall city buildings. I imagined living there and having a tiny apartment to myself. Walking to work. Buying a fancy cup of coffee every morning.

Sliding onto a bar stool at my favorite club and ordering a martini. Then something strange happened." She shook her head, remembering her epiphany. "That seemed like another woman's life. Not mine. I want to walk past the pine trees in town. I want Cup of Jo's coffee in the morning. The only barstool worth sliding onto is the one at Salty Dog. And then I thought of the people. Lou. May. Lisa. Gramps. Jo." She ticked off the names on her fingers. "Even Xavier, the bartender." She fisted Brady's shirt. "And you. You most of all."

Brady's smile made her feel instantly better about everything. Coming back—to the Cove and him—was the right choice.

"Staying here didn't make sense before. Now I'm looking at you, and it still doesn't make sense, but I want it so badly I can't deny myself any longer."

"What is it you want so badly, Elli Bean?" He pulled her into the circle of his arms.

"You. Of course."

His lips shifted into a cocky tilt. "I like the sound of that."

"I want to work with Jo. I want to be Lou's neighbor. I want a house on the lake. My parents are selling, by the way. They offered me a very fair price."

"That's a nice house."

"It's a very nice house." She pictured him in that house. She could easily imagine waking in the morning to coffee or kisses. Or both.

"But—" he loosened his hold on her, "—I come with my job. I can't ask you to accept a life that isn't what you bargained for."

"I'll worry sometimes. But only because I love you so much."

He gaze intensified. "Say that again."

"The worry part?"

"*No*."

She smiled. "I love you *because* of your job. You're a good man, and I was stupid to consider a life without you."

"We all make mistakes, Bean. I never should've let you go." He bent his head and kissed her. She loved being held by him. Being a part of him.

When they parted, Brady shook his head as if he was still in disbelief. "You're sure you want to be in Evergreen Cove for good?"

"One hundred percent. I'll have you any way I can get you. *Every* way I can get you. For as long as we can make *right now* last." She hadn't been going home to Chicago. She'd been running *away* from her home in Evergreen Cove. "I love you."

He touched her nose with his. "I love you, too, Bean."

"That's a relief, or else this would've been really embarrassing."

"Let's spend the rest of the day making up for lost time." He lowered his lips to hers, and she wrapped her arms around his neck. "We can try out handcuffs for the first—"

"Pancakes!" came a yell from the front door. Gramps stood in the doorway, spatula in hand. "The dog and I can't eat them all. Get your lovebird butts in here!"

Brady looked down at her. "The truck's right there. We can sneak off without him noticing."

"I heard that," Emory called from inside.

"One pancake won't hurt." She took Brady's hand, but he stopped her on the second step.

"All the *right now* we can stand, huh?"

"Was that cheesy?" She wrinkled her nose.

"The cheesiest." The next kiss he gave her was slow and satisfying and almost made her change her mind about the pancakes.

They were still kissing when Gramps came back to check on them. This time, though, he didn't interrupt.

ABOUT JESSICA LEMMON

Second Chance (Connected Series)
Bringing Home the Bad Boy
Rescuing the Bad Boy
A Bad Boy for Christmas
Return of the Bad Boy

Billionaire Bad Boys
The Billionaire Bachelor*
The Billionaire Next Door*
The Bastard Billionaire*
A Crane Family Christmas (novella)

Real Love
Eye Candy*
Arm Candy*
Man Candy
Rumor Has It
America's Sweetheart*

Standalone Title
Forgotten Promises

**Also available as playable stories on the Chapters Interactive App*

For a complete book list, click here.

A former job-hopper, Jessica Lemmon resides in Ohio with her husband and rescue dog. She holds a degree in graphic design currently gathering dust in an impressive frame. When she's not writing super-sexy heroes, she can be found cooking, drawing, drinking coffee (okay, wine), and eating potato chips. She firmly believes God gifts us with talents for a purpose, and with His help, you can create the life you want.

Jessica loves to hear from readers. You can learn more at: www.jessicalemmon.com.

Thank you for reading!

Sign up for book release news via the Lemmon Insider newsletter and download fun freebies while you're at it. Click here to sign up with your best email.

EPILOGUE

Thank you for reading our stories. It is our hope you have enjoyed each one. Without you we wouldn't get to do what we love.

Don't forget to visit us on social media or on our websites to find out more about us, our books, or where you might see us in person.

Patti Fiala - www.PJFiala.com
Stacey Joy Netzel - www.StaceyJoyNetzel.com
Donna Marie Rogers - www.DonnaMarieRogers.com
Rachel Rivers - www.RachelRiversAuthor.com
Jessica Lemmon - www.JessicaLemmon.com

Made in the USA
Monee, IL
17 June 2020

33022987R00337